To Mum and Dad
for everything.

MIKE GAYLE

ALL THE LONELY PEOPLE

HODDER &
STOUGHTON

First published in Great Britain in 2020 by Hodder & Stoughton
An Hachette UK company

2

Copyright © Mike Gayle 2020

A CIP catalogue record for this title is available from the British Library

Hardback ISBN 978 1 473 68738 7
Trade Paperback ISBN 978 1 473 68739 4
eBook ISBN 978 1 473 68740 0
Audio ISBN 978 1 473 68742 4

Typeset in Plantin Light by Palimpsest Book Production Ltd, Falkirk, Stirlingshire

Printed and bound in Great Britain by Clays Ltd, Elcograf S.p.A.

Hodder & Stoughton policy is to use papers that are natural, renewable
and recyclable products and made from wood grown in sustainable forests.
The logging and manufacturing processes are expected to conform
to the environmental regulations of the country of origin.

Hodder & Stoughton Ltd
Carmelite House
50 Victoria Embankment
London EC4Y 0DZ

www.hodder.co.uk

The loneliest moment in someone's life is when they are watching their whole world fall apart, and all they can do is stare blankly.

– F. Scott Fitzgerald, *The Great Gatsby*

I

Now

Moments before Hubert met Ashleigh for the first time, he had been settled in his favourite armchair, Puss curled up on his lap, waiting for Rose to call. When the doorbell rang he gave a tut of annoyance, wagering it was one of those damn courier people who were always trying to make him take in parcels for his neighbours.

'Would you mind accepting this for number sixty-three?' they would ask.

'Yes, me mind a great deal!' he would snap. 'Now clear off!' and then he would slam the door shut in their faces.

As he shifted Puss from his lap and stood up to answer the door, Hubert muttered angrily to himself.

'Parcels, parcels, parcels! All day, every day, for people who are never in to receive the damn things! If people want them things so much why them no just buy it from the shops like everybody else?'

With words of scathing condemnation loaded and ready to fire, Hubert unlocked the front door and flung it open only to discover that the person before him wasn't anything like he'd been expecting.

Instead of a uniformed parcel courier, there stood a young woman with short dyed blond hair. In a nod towards the recent spell of unseasonably warm April weather she was wearing a pink vest top, cut-off jeans and pink flip-flops. Holding her hand was a small child, a girl, with blond hair, also wearing a pink top, shorts and pink flip-flops.

The young woman smiled.

'Hi, there. I'm not disturbing you, am I?'

Hubert said nothing but made a mental note that should he need to contact the police he could tell them that the woman spoke with a funny accent. To his untrained ear it sounded Welsh or possibly Irish, though he couldn't be entirely sure it was either.

She held up her hand as if in surrender.

'It's okay. I'm not trying to sell you anything or nothing. I just came round to say hello really. We've just moved in next door.'

She pointed in the direction of the block of low-rise flats adjacent to Hubert's property.

'We're new to the area and don't know a single soul. Anyway, this morning I was saying to myself, "Ash, you're never going to get to know anyone around here unless, you know, you start talking to people." So I called round to see the couple in the flat below but I think they must be out at work. Then I tried the family across the hallway but they didn't open the door, even though I could hear the TV blaring away. So then I tried all the other flats and got nothing – all out or busy, I suppose – so I got Layla ready and took her to try the mother and toddler group at the library but it's just closed due to funding problems apparently so . . .'

She paused, looking at him expectantly, perhaps hoping for a smile or a nod of comprehension, but Hubert remained impassive.

The young woman cleared her throat self-consciously but then continued.

'My name's Ash, well it's Ashleigh really but everyone calls me Ash. And this little madam here . . .' She glanced down at the small child. '. . . is my daughter, Layla.'

The little girl covered her eyes with both hands but peeked up at Hubert through the cracks between her fingers.

'Layla,' said Ash, her voice warm with encouragement, 'say hello to our lovely new neighbour Mr . . .'

Ashleigh looked at him expectantly but Hubert continued to say nothing.

'I think she's a bit shy,' said Ash, returning her attention to Layla. 'You won't believe it to look at me but I used to be dead shy too when I was a kid. Wouldn't say boo to a goose, me. My mam was always saying, "Ashleigh Jones, you won't get far in life being shy now, will you?" and my nan would be like, "Oh, leave the poor child alone, Jen, you'll give her a complex." Then Mam would say, "I just don't want her to get set in her ways, like," and then Nan would say, "She's only a babby, she's too young to get set in her ways." Then Mam would roll her eyes like this . . .'

Ashleigh paused to illustrate. She did it so well that for a moment Hubert thought her pupils might have disappeared for good.

'. . . and say, "Like she isn't set her ways . . . she already hates vegetables," and then Nan would shrug and say nothing. The thing is, though, Mam was right, I hated vegetables then and I can't stand them now. Hate the things.'

She smiled hopefully at Hubert.

'I'm going on, aren't I? I do that. I think it's nerves. In new situations I just start talking and I can't stop. Anyway, I suppose what I'm trying to say is that it's nice to be neighbourly, isn't it? And this . . . well, this is me being exactly that.'

She thrust out a hand for him to shake and Hubert noted that her nails were painted in bright glittery purple nail polish that was chipped at the edges. Then from inside the house Hubert heard his phone ringing.

'Me got to go,' he said urgently, and without waiting for her response, he shut the door and hurried back to his front sitting room to answer the call.

'Rose?'

'Yes, it's me, Dad. Are you okay? You sound a bit out of breath.'

Breathing a sigh of relief, he settled back down in his chair.

'Me fine. Just someone at the door, that's all. But you know me, me dealt with them quickly. No one comes between me and my daughter! So tell me, Professor Bird, what have you been up to this week and don't leave anything out, me want to hear it all!'

It had been almost twenty years since Hubert's daughter Rose had relocated to Australia and rarely a day went by when he didn't wish that she lived closer. He'd never say this to her, of course; the last thing he wanted was to prevent her from living her dreams. But there were moments, usually when he least expected, when he felt her absence so intensely he could barely draw breath.

Still, she was a good girl, calling every week without fail, and while it wasn't the same as having her with him, it was the next best thing. Anyway, international calls had moved on from when Hubert used to ring his mother back home in Jamaica. Gone were the days of hissing static, crossed lines and eye-watering phone bills. With today's modern technology, the cost was minimal and the lines so crystal clear it was almost like being in the same room.

Without need for further prompting, Rose told him about the faculty meetings she'd chaired, the conferences in faraway places she'd agreed to speak at and the fancy meals out she'd enjoyed with friends. Hubert always loved hearing about the exciting and glamorous things she'd been up to. It made him profoundly happy to know that she was living such a full and contented life.

After a short while, Rose drew her news to a close.

'Right then, that's more than enough about me. How about you, Pops? What have you been up to?'

Hubert chuckled.

'Now tell me, girl, why does a fancy, la-di-dah academic like you want to know what a boring old man like me has been doing with his days? You a glutton for punishment?'

Rose heaved a heavy but good-natured sigh.

'Honestly, Dad, you're like a broken record! Every single time I call you say: "Why you want to know what me up to?" and I say, "Because I'm interested in your life, Dad," and you say something like, "Well, on Tuesday me climbed Mount Everest, and on Wednesday me tap-danced with that nice lady from *Strictly* and then I say, "Really, Dad?" and then finally you laugh that big laugh of yours and tell me the truth. It's so frustrating! For once, can you please just tell me what you've been up to without making a whole song and dance about it?'

Hubert chuckled again. His daughter's impression of him had

been note perfect, managing to replicate both the richness of his voice and the intricacies of the diction of a Jamaican man who has called England his home for the best part of sixty years.

'Me not sure me like your tone, young lady,' he scolded play-fully.

'Good,' retorted Rose. 'You're not meant to. And if you don't want to hear more of it, you'll stop teasing me and tell me what you've really been up to this week!'

'Me was only having a little fun, Rose, you know that,' relented Hubert. 'But me consider myself told off, okay? So, what have I been up to?'

He slipped on his reading glasses and reached for the open notepad on the table next to him.

'Well, on Tuesday me take a trip out to the garden centre, the big one on Oakley Road, you know it? Me buy a few bedding plants for the front garden – make the most of this mild spring we're having – and then me stayed on there for lunch.'

'Sounds lovely. Did Dotty, Dennis and Harvey go too?'

'Of course! We had a whale of a time. Dotty was teasing Dennis about him gardening skills, Dennis was play fighting with Harvey in the bedding plants section, and all the while me trying to keep that rowdy bunch in line!'

Rose laughed.

'Sounds like a good time. I wish I'd been there. How's Dotty's sciatica by the way? Still playing her up?'

Hubert referred to his notepad again.

'Oh, you know how these things are when you're old. They come and they go.'

'Poor Dotty. Give her my love, won't you? And how about Dennis's great-grandson? How did he get on with his trials for . . . who was it again . . .?'

Once again Hubert referred to his notepad, only this time he couldn't see the entry he was looking for.

'Me think . . . me think it was Watford,' he said panicking.

'Are you sure? I would've remembered if you'd said Watford because that's where Robin's mother's family are from. No, last time we spoke you definitely said . . . West Ham . . . that's it! You said it was West Ham.'

Hubert frantically flicked through his notebook and sure enough there were the words 'WEST HAM' underlined next to 'Dennis's great-grandson'.

'Actually you might be right about that,' he said eventually. 'But really Watford or West Ham, what does it matter? Him not my great-grandson!'

Rose chuckled heartily, clearly amused by her father's charming indifference to details.

'No, Pops, I suppose he isn't. But how did he get on anyway?'

'Do you know what?' said Hubert abruptly. 'Me didn't ask Dennis and him didn't bring it up.'

'Oh, Dad,' chided Rose, 'what are you like? You really should take an interest in your friends, you know. They're good for your health. I came across a very interesting study the other day that said people with a small group of good friends are more likely to live longer.'

'Well, with friends like Dotty, Dennis and Harvey, even if me don't live for eternity it will certainly feel like it!' Hubert laughed and then cleared his throat. 'Now, darling, that's more than enough about me. Tell me more about this conference you're going to in Mexico. You're giving a big speech, you say?'

They talked for a good while longer, covering not just her trip to Mexico but also the new book proposal she was working on and the plans she had to finally landscape the garden so that she could make the most of her pool. Hubert relished every last detail she shared with him and could have listened to her talk all day. And so, as always, it was with a heavy heart that he realised their time was coming to an end.

'Right then, Pops, I'd better be going. I've got to be up early in the morning as I'm picking up a visiting professor flying in from Canada. What are your plans for the rest of the week?'

'Oh, you know. This and that.'

'Now come on, Pops, remember what we agreed? No messing about. Just tell me what you're up to.'

Hubert flicked to the most recent page of his notebook.

'Well, tomorrow night Dotty wants to try bingo down at the new place that's just opened up in town. Saturday, Dennis and me have talked about going to a country pub for lunch. Sunday, Harvey is having everyone round for a big roast. And Monday me having the day to meself to work on the garden. As for the rest of the week, me have no idea, but me sure Dotty's cooking up some plans.'

'That certainly sounds like a packed schedule!' said Rose. 'I don't know how you do it.'

'Neither do I, darling. Neither do I. Anyway, you take care, me speak to you soon.'

Ending the call, Hubert sat for a moment contemplating his conversation with Rose. He'd nearly put his foot in it once or twice. He really was going to either have a brain transplant or at the very least get himself a better system for making notes. Picking up the pen from the table beside him, he wrote down, 'MAKE BETTER NOTES' in his pad, then tossed it to one side with such force that Puss, who had curled up in his lap again, woke up and stared at him accusingly.

'Don't start with me,' said Hubert, trying to avoid her gaze.

Puss continued to stare.

'You know it's not like me enjoy doing this.'

Still Puss stared.

'It's not like me got a choice in the matter, is it?'

Puss gave Hubert one last disdainful glower before jumping down to the floor and stalking out of the room as if to say she didn't tolerate liars. Because the truth was Hubert Bird was a liar. And a practised one at that. Not a single word he'd said to his daughter was true. It was lies, all lies. And he felt absolutely wretched about it.

2

Then: Hubert, June 1957

It was early evening and Hubert Hezekiah Bird was enjoying a glass of rum with his friend Gus at Karl's, a ramshackle shebeen that was the closest thing their village had to a bar. Karl's consisted of a shack made entirely of sheets of corrugated metal painted in a patchwork of bright colours, with a few mismatched tables and chairs outside. A stray dog lay on the ground nearby, soaking up the last rays of the setting sun.

Draining his glass, Hubert asked Gus if he wanted another and his oldest friend gestured for him to wait.

'Let me tell you my news first,' he said.

Gus reached into the inner pocket of his suit jacket and produced a piece of paper which he waved in the air with an exaggerated flourish.

Hubert's eyes widened.

'Is that what me think it is?'

Grinning, Gus handed the one-way ticket from Kingston to Southampton to his friend. Hubert couldn't quite believe what he was looking at.

'You're going to England?'

Gus laughed that deep laugh of his.

'Yes, man! I've been saving like crazy these past few months. Didn't you wonder why I haven't been able to stand you any drinks lately?'

Hubert laughed. 'Me just thought you were being tight with your dough!'

'I been wanting this really badly, Smiler,' said Gus. 'There's nothing for me here. You know Cousin Charlie left just last month and he wrote to Auntie that he's already got a job and he's even managing to send a bit of money home too. He must be rolling in it!'

Gus sighed and gazed over Hubert's head dreamily.

'I can't wait to have some money, get myself some nice clothes and maybe even an English girl too!'

He picked up the glass of rum he'd been drinking, downed it in one and put his arm around his friend's shoulder.

'Come with me, Smiler. You and me in England! We'll have a wild time! What do you say?'

For the rest of the evening and long into the night the two friends spoke of nothing but life in England: all the things they'd heard about and all the things Gus would see and do. It seemed unreal, like they were talking about a fantasy, but within just a few short weeks Hubert found himself standing at Kingston docks, waving his old friend off on the journey of a lifetime. As he watched the boat disappear over the horizon Hubert made the decision that he too would make this same journey.

Over the weeks that followed Hubert took on all the extra work he could handle to supplement his income, and within a few months he'd scraped together the money for his passage. The day he bought his ticket, the very first thing he did was tuck it safely in the back pocket of his trousers and the second was head home and break the news to his mother.

Hubert was dreading telling his mother about his plans. The year before, when his sister Vivian had moved to Kingston to train as a teacher, his mother had been inconsolable for weeks, so he dreaded to think how she'd feel losing her eldest son. This was why he had picked a date to leave that was a little way off in the future. It would give her time to get used to the idea, for his siblings to learn the ropes around the house and, if needs be, for them to find someone to employ to help around the farm.

As he approached the home that he shared with his mother and younger siblings, Fulton and Cora, he sniffed the air. Wood smoke and the unmistakable aroma of one of his favourite meals: pork, stewed peas and rice. He tracked his mother down to the cooking shack at the rear of their one-storey wooden house that had been built by his grandfather. She was wearing a clean white apron over an old faded blue floral dress with a yellow silk head-scarf tied over her hair.

Stepping out of the shack, its walls and roof made of sheets of corrugated iron, she greeted him with a kiss on the cheek. Before speaking, Hubert studied her for a moment, suddenly keenly aware that there were now a finite number of times he would see her before he left.

Lillian was tall and elegant but at the same time formidable, a force to be reckoned with. She had no time for fools or small talk but would show the greatest kindness to anyone in need. People often told him that he was the spitting image of his mother, with her high cheekbones and almond-shaped eyes, but Lillian always claimed that he had a greater likeness to his late father than any of his siblings.

'How are you, son?'

'Me good thanks, Mother. And me have some good news. Me . . . me . . . going to England.'

His mother raised an eyebrow but he could see that she wasn't angry or upset.

'Are you now?' she said. 'And there was me thinking all this extra work you've been taking on was to buy me a fancy birthday present!'

She took his hand and held it tightly.

'It's the greatest shame your country has nothing to offer you. But that's the thing about Jamaica at the present time: there are more dogs than bones, but in England all the bones a dog could eat.'

She took his face in her hands and kissed his cheek fiercely.

'You go full your belly up, Hubert Bird! Go full your belly and make me proud!'

The journey to England in the January of 1958 had been rough, not least because an hour into his three-week voyage Hubert discovered that despite several uneventful trips on his Uncle

Leonard's fishing boat in his youth, it turned out that he was somewhat susceptible to seasickness. By the time the ship arrived in Southampton, however, not only had he learned the best way to combat it, which was to eat as little as possible, but he had also vowed that he was never getting on another boat again. When the time came, he decided, his return journey home would have to be by plane.

From Southampton Hubert caught the train to Waterloo and was met by Gus straight from a long shift at a telephone factory on the outskirts of the city. It had been good to see Gus after so long apart, but Hubert couldn't help but be taken aback by the change in his friend's appearance. The Gus Hubert remembered was tall, broad-shouldered and brimming with confidence, but the man standing in front of him looked thin, drawn, and tired, all of which made him seem smaller somehow. He wanted to ask what was wrong but thought better of it. Instead, as they made their way back to Gus's rented room in Brixton, he allowed his friend to grill him on the news from back home, or as Gus put it: 'Smiler, man, tell me who dead, who born and which of the girls back home miss me most?'

After a night spent in Gus's digs, sleeping top to tail in a tiny lumpy bed in a sparsely furnished freezing-cold room, Hubert made his first visit to the Labour Exchange. It was a daunting prospect made all the more uncomfortable when, despite informing the clerk that he had experience in bookkeeping and carpentry, he was instead handed a piece of paper marked 'General labourer' and told he would be starting work that very afternoon at a building site in Stockwell.

Hubert hadn't liked the work at all – it was hard, dirty and cold – but he was so determined to stick it out that it took a week and a half before Gus finally persuaded him to return to the Labour Exchange in search of something better. 'That's the beauty of this country, Smiler,' his friend had explained that evening as they sat smoking cigarettes on the steps in front of the boarding house. 'You can walk out of one job at midday and have another by two!'

This time Hubert was firm with the clerk at the Labour Exchange, a portly middle-aged man who spoke with a trace of a lisp. He was open to any work as long as it wasn't on a building site.

'Here you go,' the man had said after a short while looking through his file. 'How does warehouseman at Hamilton's department store sound?'

Hubert had never worked in a warehouse before but he liked the idea of a department store. At least it would be indoors, he reasoned, which in this country was a definite plus point.

'Very suitable,' Hubert replied gratefully.

The clerk wrote out some details on a scrap of paper and handed them to Hubert. 'Go to this address at 6.30 a.m. – you can't miss it, it's just off Oxford Circus – and at the service entrance ask for the foreman, Mr Coulthard. And whatever you do,' he added ominously, 'don't be late. It's not unheard of for Mr Coulthard to sack people on the spot just for being a minute behind.'

And so it was, clutching the piece of paper tightly, Hubert had returned to Gus's digs and after a meal of tinned soup heated up on the tiny range and some sad-looking ham sandwiches, he went to bed early, rising and dressing in darkness on the rainiest day of the year to board the 56 from Brixton Hill to Oxford Circus.

Taking a seat on the sparsely populated top deck, Hubert paid the conductor his fare and then slipped his ticket into his wallet. Determined to make the most of this respite from the rain, he turned up the collar on his now sodden overcoat, adjusted his trilby, its felt so saturated that he doubted it would ever return to its original shape, and rested his head against the cold hard glass of the window next to him. Closing his eyes, he allowed himself the luxury of a half-doze for the duration of his journey but within seconds, despite the savage beating of the rain against the side of the bus, Hubert was fast asleep and snoring loudly as he dreamed of the Jamaican sunshine he had left far, far behind.

Waking with a start at the sound of the bus's bell, Hubert wiped at the condensation on the window to discover that he had missed his stop. Leaping to his feet, he raced downstairs and jumped off the bus at the first opportunity. It was now raining even harder than it had been before. Such was the extent of the downpour that even those with umbrellas were sheltering in doorways for protection, but it only took one glance at the watch his mother had given him on his eighteenth birthday for Hubert to realise that he could afford no such luxury.

With one hand holding his hat in place, he ran full pelt through the pouring rain, dodging past men and women scurrying through the deluge to work, and didn't stop until he reached the service entrance of Hamilton's. He was sure he looked a mess. He was so drenched that even the suit he wore under his overcoat was clinging to his every contour and in spite of the biting February chill he was pouring with sweat, thanks to his dash across London.

Reaching up, he pressed the bell next to a door marked 'Deliveries: ring for attention' and took off his hat in preparation to greet Mr Coulthard, only to funnel rivulets of freezing-cold water from its brim down his back.

Hubert rang the bell several times more but could hear nothing in the way of response on the other side of the door. He pressed again even harder, wondering if the bell was working, and then stepped back several feet to examine the side of the building to make sure he was in the right location. Just as he was about to try walking further up the street to see if there was another entrance, he jumped with surprise at the sound of a bolt snapping back, followed by the rattle of keys. The door swung open to reveal a tall, thin man with grey hair cut short at the sides, the longer hair on top neatly combed and Brylcreemed into place. Aside from a studiously maintained pencil-thin moustache, the man was clean-shaven. Under a navy-blue warehouse coat he wore a crisp white shirt and dark brown tie. His black Oxford shoes were so polished that even in this dim light they seemed to shine.

The man stood for a moment, back held straight, unsmiling,

eyes fixed on Hubert, regarding him with a mixture of curiosity and disdain.

'Can I help you?'

'Me looking for Mr Coulthard.'

The man grimaced. This was clearly the wrong answer.

'You are, are you? And who might you be then?'

Hubert reached into his pocket and took out the sodden, barely hanging-together piece of paper the clerk at the Labour Exchange had given him and handed it over. The man's lips, already pursed, narrowed grimly as he alternated between studying the note and Hubert. Finally he squeezed the drenched missive into a tight ball and said, partly to Hubert, but mostly to himself: 'That lot are bloody useless.'

Hubert didn't know how to react to this. He assumed he was talking about the Labour Exchange but couldn't be sure. The one thing he was positive about, however, was that if the man didn't let him inside soon he was sure to die of hypothermia.

The man stroked his moustache pensively.

'The lads are not going to like this. They are not going to like this at all.'

He regarded Hubert carefully.

'You done this line of work before?'

Hubert nodded, even though he wasn't entirely sure what the job entailed.

'And anything new me can pick up real quick. Me is a fast learner.'

The man pulled a face. 'I think I'll be the judge of that. You're West Indian, I take it?'

'Yes, sir, from Jamaica.'

'And you're a hard worker?'

'Yes, sir, my mother brought me up to always give my best.'

There was a long pause and then finally the man sighed heavily, shrugged, removed a packet of cigarettes from his coat pocket and pulled one out. Once again more to himself than to Hubert, he said: 'What do I care? We're already three men down as it is and I'm sick and tired of management breathing down my neck.'

He lit his cigarette, inhaled deeply, then shrugged and stepped aside.

'Come on then, you can't be standing around here all day. You're late enough as it is. Come in, get yourself a warehouse coat and we'll get you started.'

3

Now

It had been six days since Hubert's call with Rose and in that time he had spoken to precisely one other person: the receptionist at the vet's in whose waiting room he was currently sitting. Regardless of his lack of interaction with other people, however, it occurred to Hubert, as Puss padded about in the cardboard box on his lap, that a good use of his waiting time might be to prepare for his upcoming call with his daughter. What sort of things might he, Dotty, Dennis and Harvey have been up to this week? Could they have been to watch a play or see a musical? Perhaps something in the West End that he could claim to have fallen asleep in, lest Rose ask him what it had been about? Or perhaps it had been more of a quiet week, the kind that might see the four friends take in a pub lunch before enjoying a game of dominoes.

It had never been Hubert's intention to lie to Rose. And certainly not for so long or so elaborately. It was, Hubert thought, one of those things that just sort of happened while you weren't looking. Much like catching sight of a long hair sprouting out of your own nostril and wondering, 'How could I have missed that?' Hubert felt as if one moment he'd been going about his life as honest as the day was long and the next he'd concocted a trio of fictional friends with extensive back-stories for the sole purpose of convincing his daughter that she didn't need to worry about him.

It all began because one day five years ago something happened. It was the sort of thing that meant Hubert didn't want to go out any more. The sort of thing that meant he stopped returning friends' phone calls or even answering the door if he could help it. In fact, it was the sort of thing that meant all Hubert wanted was to be left alone.

Gradually his once-full life had emptied. One by one his friends, even Gus, who he'd known since they were children, stopped calling and soon Hubert Bird was alone, without a single friend in the world.

Rose had been furious when she'd found out how things were.

'So you're telling me you don't see anyone at all any more?'

'No.'

'Not even that lot from the Red Lion?'

'Me not see them in ages.'

'Even Uncle Gus?'

'Same for him too.'

'But you always used to love going out and being around people.'

Hubert sighed. 'Look, sweetie, me just lost touch with them, okay? It happens when you get old like me. You go your way, they go theirs – it's just how it is.'

Proving to Hubert, if he had been in any doubt, that she was her mother's daughter, Rose called the following week with a solution.

'I've been doing some research on the Internet,' she said, 'and I think I've got an answer to your problem: it's called the O-60 Club. It's for people just like you, Dad. People over sixty looking for a spot of company or to make new friends. They meet every Wednesday at the community centre next to the library. It costs one pound per session and for that you get unlimited tea and coffee and even biscuits too! Now doesn't that sound amazing?'

Hubert didn't think it sounded amazing. He thought it sounded about as enjoyable as a prostate examination.

'So what do you think?' Rose prompted. 'Will you give it a try?'

Hubert had his reservations but Rose was someone he simply couldn't say no to. So when Wednesday came around he got up early, put on his best clothes and even trimmed his moustache, but as he'd checked his reflection in the mirror he'd got cold feet.

He told himself that no one would talk to him. He told himself that even if they did, he probably wouldn't like them anyway. He told himself that he would be better off staying at home. And so that's exactly what he did.

But when Rose called to find out how he'd got on he'd felt so guilty, so mortified by his failure, so eager not to disappoint her that the first words that sprang to his lips were: 'Me had the best time ever! The people them were chatty, me enjoyed a nice cup of tea and even made a couple of friends.'

While it was a lie, Hubert reasoned it was a small one, not said purely to deceive but rather to prevent his lovely daughter from wasting energy worrying about him. It was harmless.

'That's fantastic news,' said Rose. 'Tell me all about them.'

'Well,' said Hubert without missing a beat. 'Them called Dotty, Dennis and Harvey and them all a real hoot!'

In retrospect this should have been the first and last mention of Dotty, Dennis and Harvey. After all, Hubert had brought up both his children not to lie, but Rose had been so pleased that he had some new friends, and sounded so relieved that she no longer had to worry about him, that he felt he had no choice but to keep the lie going. And before he knew it, he was creating long and involved histories for his fictional friends, giving them sons and daughters, grandchildren and great-grandchildren, and the whole thing became so complicated that he had to make a record in a notepad to help him keep track.

'Puss Bird?'

Hubert lifted his gaze to acknowledge the receptionist and noted once again with annoyance how the vet's policy of calling out a pet's name rather than that of their owner caused its usual flurry of sniggers. Ignoring them, Hubert rose to his feet and, clutching the box with Puss inside, made his way into the consulting room.

'So what exactly is the problem today?' asked the vet Mr Andrews, a tall, grey-haired man, with a bushy beard and a lilting Irish accent.

Hubert opened the box and gently placed Puss on the examination table.

'She not eating.'

'When was the last time she ate?'

'Three days ago,' replied Hubert. 'She had breakfast on Sunday morning but nothing since.'

As Mr Andrews began to scrutinise Puss, placing a hand on either side of her body, carefully feeling with his fingertips, paying special attention to her stomach, Hubert thought about how the animal had come into his life.

Hubert was by no means a fan of cat-kind and would chase any feline intruder from his garden with whatever weapon happened to be closest to hand. But one day three summers ago he had been cleaning his kitchen floor when he'd heard a mewling at his back door and had discovered a plump black and white cat sitting on his doorstep. Enraged, Hubert had made a swing for the cat with the dripping mop in his hand, shooing it all the way down to the bottom of the garden. The following day at the same time, however, the cat returned while Hubert was doing the washing up and mewled even louder. This time armed with a soapy fish slice, Hubert had chased it until it disappeared over the fence and into his neighbour's property.

This pattern continued every day for an entire fortnight until finally Hubert decided enough was enough. Determined to rid himself of this menace once and for all, he purchased a water spray from Poundland, filled it with dirty dishwater and then sat waiting at the kitchen table for the cat to appear. The moment he heard it Hubert leaped to his feet, threw open the door and pointed the spray directly at his target like a Jamaican Dirty Harry. But this time, instead of running away it remained where it was, staring up at him with its big copper-coloured eyes and mewling louder than ever before. Confused, Hubert stood with the spray gun poised ready to dispatch the cat, but as he went to pull the trigger he realised he just couldn't do it. Lowering his weapon, he let out a deep heartfelt sigh, stood to one side and, addressing the cat directly, said wearily, 'Well then, Puss, if you're so determined, me suppose you'd better come in.'

Concluding his examination, Mr Andrews' diagnosis was that Puss was likely getting over some sort of virus. 'I think we should try one of those convalescing cat food brands. I could prescribe one for her but to be honest it would be cheaper if you just popped to a pet store and got some yourself. I'll give her an antibiotic just to be on the safe side and if she's still not eating by tomorrow morning bring her back in and I'll take another look at her.'

Hubert exchanged glances with the vet and sighed. Seventy pounds plus VAT for one measly injection and a quick examination. What was the world coming to?

Returning Puss to the cardboard box, Hubert left the consulting room muttering about 'Rip-off Britain' under his breath. Back in reception he rested Puss's box on the counter and as he slipped on his reading glasses to deal with the bill he heard someone say, 'Oh, hello, again.'

He turned to see a young woman with short dyed-blond hair. She was looking at him as if she knew him, but while she seemed sort of familiar he just couldn't place her.

'Ashleigh,' she prompted.

Hubert said nothing.

'Layla and I knocked on your door the other day to introduce ourselves. We live at the flats next door to you.'

The strange next-door neighbour! That was it. Hubert cast his gaze down towards the ground and sure enough there was the same little girl standing next to her. Once again she'd covered her eyes with her hands and was peeking back at him through her fingers.

'I'm just here dropping in my CV and seeing if there's any work going,' continued Ashleigh. 'I love animals, me, I love all the different sorts. Cats, dogs, rabbits, guinea pigs, hamsters, rats, gerbils, cockatoos, snakes, tropical fish . . . even tortoises!'

Hubert blinked several times but said nothing.

'Is that your pet in there?' she asked, considering Puss's cardboard box. 'What is it? No, don't tell me, I'll guess. A rabbit?'

Hubert said nothing.

'A hamster?'

Hubert remained silent.

Ashleigh laughed. 'A small dog maybe . . . no, what am I thinking, it's got to be a cat, hasn't it?'

Hubert didn't respond but instead turned his attention to the receptionist, who he paid in cash.

'Thank you,' he said, taking the receipt, which he tucked inside his wallet. He picked up the box with Puss inside. 'Good day to you,' he said in a manner so general it was impossible to tell if he was addressing the receptionist, his neighbours or indeed all three, and without another word he left.

Following Mr Andrews' advice, Hubert went in search of the special cat food Puss needed and found exactly what he was looking for in the rear aisle of the large pet store in the centre of Bromley. He gave Puss a pouch of it as soon as he reached home but all she did was sniff it disdainfully. Disgruntled by his lack of success, annoyed by Puss's seeming ingratitude and exhausted by the day's activities, Hubert made himself lunch, after which he took an unscheduled nap in front of the TV. An hour later when he woke up, he discovered that not only had Puss polished off the whole dish of food but she was now mewling loudly for more.

That evening, in the back room, with a full-bellied Puss lying contentedly on the sofa beside him and a fresh mug of tea cooling on the table next to him, Hubert settled down in front of the eleven o'clock film on cable. He watched films most evenings, his favourites being Westerns, Hollywood gangster films from the Forties and war films, preferably ones starring Robert Mitchum or Anthony Quinn. That said, he would watch almost anything, which explained why in recent weeks he had not only seen classics like *The Maltese Falcon, The Sons of Katie Elder* and *The French Connection* but also *Mamma Mia!, Bridesmaids* and *Brokeback Mountain*, which although a cowboy film hadn't been exactly the kind he had been expecting.

Tonight's offering was a horror film called *Saw 3* that he didn't hold out much hope for. Hubert didn't really enjoy horror films as he found all the blood, guts and gore too ridiculous to entertain seriously. Still, he was here now, and having checked to see if there was anything good on the other channels, he told himself he would give it half an hour to prove itself.

As the film began Hubert, for reasons he couldn't quite fathom, found his mind drifting to the young woman with the small child from next door. He'd never met anyone quite like her in his life. Talk the hind legs off a donkey? That one could do the same to a whole herd! And that accent too – Welsh, Scottish, whatever it was – it was the funniest thing he'd ever heard! And the way she'd chatted to him at the vet's as if they were old friends, when he didn't know her from Adam – strange behaviour indeed!

Of course it wouldn't have been strange back in the good old days, he reasoned. Back in the Eighties when the kids were young and Joyce was alive, neighbours would talk to each other all the time. He used to know everyone in the road and they knew him too. There would be parties and get-togethers, people minding your property whenever you went on holiday – it was a proper community. Not like now. These days people kept themselves to themselves and so did Hubert. He didn't know the names of his neighbours, and what's more he didn't want to. So quite why this young woman was being so friendly towards him he had no idea.

Returning to the film, Hubert attempted to get back into the action, but he couldn't make any sense of it and after a few minutes reached across for the remote to switch it off. And that's when something odd happened.

The phone rang.

Hubert checked the clock on the wall above the fireplace. It was twenty minutes past eleven. Who would call him at this time of night? As he reached for the phone his gut told him the most likely culprit was that damn Virgin Media, if only because they hadn't replied to his last angry missive about unsolicited sales calls. Well, if it really was them calling at this hour he would give them the telling off of a lifetime!

'Hi, Dad, it's me.'

At the sound of Rose's voice Hubert's anger immediately turned from annoyance to delight before ending up in fear.

'Rose! Is everything okay? Why you call so late?'

'Everything's fine, Pop,' said Rose. 'In fact, it's better than fine. I know it's late in the UK and everything but I honestly couldn't wait to tell you my good news: I'm coming home, Pops! After all this time, I'm finally coming home!'

4

Then: 22 March 1958

As soon as the bell rang for dinner Hubert left the lorry he was unloading and made his way to the locker room. It had been a long and difficult morning. After one too many nights scrunched up on the edge of Gus's uncomfortable bed his back was aching. He was coming down with a cold, no doubt due to the constant rain of the past few weeks, and right now in the gloom of the draughty delivery bay at Hamilton's he was missing the warmth of the Jamaican sun against his skin so much that his heart ached. The only thing that had kept him going through the hard slog of unloading the morning's deliveries – boxes of clothing, pallets of cooking oil, bolts of expensive fabric from the Far East – was the thought of the meal that was waiting for him.

The food – a rich and spicy pork and pea soup – was a gift from the Antiguan family downstairs. He and Gus had helped them move in at the weekend and as a thankyou the wife had left them with a tray of wonderfully fragrant food. Hubert and Gus had guzzled down half the delicious soup and all the dumplings that accompanied it and both agreed it was the best they had tasted since leaving home.

English food had been something Hubert had particularly struggled with. While he accepted that beggars couldn't be choosers, he'd found the offerings in Hamilton's staff canteen so bland as to be almost inedible. Some days it was so awful he preferred to go hungry, rather than wrestle with another piece of tasteless gristle that back home his mother would've been ashamed to feed to the dog. So when Gus suggested that rather than polishing off the soup for breakfast they should save what was left for dinner at their respective places of work, Hubert readily agreed. Even though it would be cold and a day old, he didn't doubt for a moment that it would still be tastier than the canteen alternative.

The moment Hubert opened the locker-room door he sensed that something wasn't quite right. Although normally buzzing with the chitchat of his fellow workers at this time of day, the place was deserted. Stranger still, there was a faint but unpleasant smell in the air as if someone had brought something in on their shoe.

As Hubert walked towards his locker the odour grew in intensity and alarm bells began to ring in his head, getting louder and louder with each step. He spied his locker, the door ajar and the lock he'd placed on it lying broken on the floor. Flinging it wide open, Hubert was hit by an overpowering stench. His dinner flask was open, the lid resting by its side.

While the work at Hamilton's had proved strenuous, it was straightforward. Hubert's colleagues, however, were anything but. They consisted of half a dozen or so young English men, and their unofficial leader, Vince, had taken an instant dislike to Hubert. This was a fact he had made plain to all around when he'd protested to Mr Coulthard about the perils of letting 'monkeys' loose in the warehouse. 'I don't see why we need to be hiring coloureds,' he'd opined. 'Not when there are plenty of decent Englishmen in need of work.'

Hubert had ignored these comments, reasoning this was simply the way people were with strangers: wary and suspicious to begin with, relaxing once they got to know you. There were, after all, Hubert considered, very few people in the world who he didn't get along with, and in spite of their initial reaction he didn't see why Vince and his friends should be any different.

Despite his best efforts, however, all of Hubert's friendly overtures were rebuffed. His attempts to make conversation were met initially with silence then later with mocking mimicry of his accent. On his second week Hubert discovered that he'd spent half the day with the words 'Jungle monkey' chalked on the back of his warehouse jacket.

On his third, his clocking-in card mysteriously vanished, turning up at the end of the day with the words 'Go home Darkie!' scrawled across it in red ink. Then a few days later while on his morning break Hubert took a sip of his tea, only to discover that someone had heaped salt in it while his back was turned. These were all childish pranks that he might have overlooked had indeed the perpetrators been children. But they were men his own age and there was a level of malevolence behind the tricks that spoke of something much more sinister.

Throughout these trials Hubert tried to remain stoically optimistic. After all, he thought, he'd heard of much worse treatment than this. A workmate of Gus's had stones thrown at him by a gang of children while on his way to work. A Barbadian neighbour had been spat at and refused service by a local greengrocer just because of the colour of his skin. And recently Hubert had read in the papers of a West Indian man who had been beaten unconscious by a group of Teddy boys late one Saturday night. The mischief Hubert's fellow workers had been up to, while annoying, hadn't harmed him physically and until now he had hoped that they would either tire of their games or come to their senses. But as he stood staring at his flask he felt a rage of an intensity he had never felt before.

They had gone too far this time. Too far by a very long way.

Hubert found Vince and his cronies chatting and smoking on the crates in the loading bay, and as he approached them, Vince rose to his feet to face Hubert.

'You look like someone who's lost his appetite.'

Hubert squared up to Vince, an action that caused his opponent's friends to rise to their feet too.

'You lot are filthy pigs! Putting dog dirt in my dinner flask! How could you do something so disgusting?'

Vince pushed his face so close to Hubert's that he could smell the tobacco on his breath.

'You accusing me of something, Gorilla man?'

'You know damn well what you did. Don't you dare try and deny it!'

Vince laughed and his friends chimed in.

'I don't explain myself to the likes of you,' he said, without breaking eye contact with Hubert. 'Last time I checked, this was still England.' He dipped his head towards the floor and spat on the ground, only narrowly missing Hubert's shoes. 'You're not even a proper human, are you? You're just a monkey! A monkey from the jungle.'

As if he hadn't made his point clear, he started making monkey noises, and was quickly joined by his friends. Soon the whole of the loading bay echoed with their hatefulness. Without thinking, Hubert threw a punch so fast that it was impossible for Vince to intercept and it connected squarely with his nose, sending him sprawling backwards into his friends.

Within seconds the men were all over him, punching, scratching, kicking and biting. Hubert was determined to give as good as he got but he was just one man against half a dozen and in no time at all he was overpowered. As he lay on the ground enduring his beating, he couldn't help wondering if this was it, the moment his short life would come to an end, here on the cold, oily floor of a warehouse thousands of miles away from his country of birth.

A commanding shout that could only have come from Mr Coulthard brought both Hubert and those attacking him to their senses. His aggressors stood back, allowing Hubert to uncurl, and he attempted to open his eyes, only to discover that the right one was swollen shut. With his one good eye he could see that Mr Coulthard was now standing over him. Next to him there was a young woman wearing a look of horror and concern on her face.

Mr Coulthard jabbed a finger in the direction of two of Vince's cronies.

'You pair get him to his feet now!'

He turned to the young woman.

'Take him to the break room and get him cleaned up! The last thing I want is to have to explain to them upstairs why there's a dead West Indian on my warehouse floor.'

Finally he turned and addressed Vince and his remaining associates.

'You lot, my office, now!'

As instructed, the young woman attended to Hubert's wounds in the break room while Hubert seethed with fury, desperate to return to the loading bay for a second round.

'The only thing . . . stopping me is that me . . . me . . . need the work,' he railed between winces as the young woman dabbed iodine-soaked cotton wool on to his cuts. 'Otherwise . . . me would dash them right into next week . . . you see if me wouldn't.'

'They're not worth it,' said the young woman. 'Like you said, you'll end up losing your job and why should you have to suffer when it's them at fault?'

'It no matter anyhow,' said Hubert. 'It'll be their word against mine and who's Mr Coulthard going to believe, eh? Them who he's worked with day in day out for years or me who just arrived here on a boat?'

The young woman stifled a laugh and Hubert looked at her quizzically.

'I'm sorry,' she said quickly, 'I know it's silly. It's just that when you said that, a picture popped up in my head of you sailing down Oxford Street in an ocean liner!'

Getting the joke, Hubert smiled but then immediately regretted it as his bruised upper lip began to throb.

'I know what they've been doing,' said the young woman, meeting his gaze briefly. 'Everybody does. It's not as if they've been keeping it a secret. Bragging about it as if it was something to be proud of. They did it to the last Caribbean gentleman we had down here. Drove him out within a fortnight with their tormenting they did, poor soul. I don't think it's right myself but what can I do? I just work on the shop floor.' She threw away the blood-soaked cotton wool in her hands and tore off a fresh strip. 'Anyway, that's enough talking for now. I've got to concentrate on this next bit. You've got quite a nasty cut on your forehead and I need to get you cleaned up.'

Closing his eyes, Hubert allowed himself to be tended to by

the young woman. Her fingers felt soft against his skin and every time he breathed through his nose he caught a hint of her perfume. It was something sweet and floral that he imagined was exactly how the English countryside he had heard so much about must smell in the height of summer.

As the young woman rustled about in the first-aid tin, she filled the silence between them with good-natured chat about life on the haberdashery counter. It was fun for the most part, getting to see and touch all the latest designs from Paris and beyond, and the girls she worked with were good company and sometimes they all went out together to the pictures of a weekend. The only fly in the ointment was her manageress, Miss Critchlow. She was a hawk of a woman, a stickler for presentation and punctuality, never overlooking an opportunity to tell the girls off for even the slightest infringement.

'Mark my words,' she said as she finished attending to the cut above Hubert's eye, 'she'll be sending a search party out for me in a minute and talking about how much to dock my pay for wasting company time. Mr Coulthard will put a good word in for me, though. Despite all his noise and bluster he's a good sort, and for all her airs and graces, I reckon Miss Critchlow's actually a bit sweet on him!'

As if summoned by the mere mention of his name, Hubert's boss stormed into the break room and Hubert got to his feet straight away.

'Mr Coulthard, me can—'

'Save it, lad, it's all been dealt with. I've sacked that lazy so-and-so Vince and I can't say he'll be missed. As for the others, well, right now they're cleaning your locker. And take it from me, there won't be any more trouble.'

He sighed heavily, then checked his watch.

'Dinner break is over in five minutes. Don't be late clocking back on or there'll be trouble.'

Without another word he swept out of the room, leaving Hubert and the young woman alone. The young woman raised an eyebrow.

'Vince Smith, sacked! Who'd have thought it? Good riddance, that's what I say.'

She closed the first-aid tin and returned it to the shelf.

'You're all fixed.'

Hubert gingerly traced a finger over the cut above his eye.

'Thank you, thank you very much.'

The young woman smiled.

'You're welcome Mr . . . in all that kerfuffle I don't think you actually told me your name.'

'Hubert, Hubert Bird. And yours?'

A faint smile played on her lips as they shook hands.

'Joyce,' she replied, 'Joyce Pierce.'

5

Now

Hubert didn't often leave Bromley; in fact he couldn't think of a single occasion over the past five years when he had left its confines and yet here he was, Freedom Pass at the ready, boarding the 10.42 to London Victoria. Relieved to find the train relatively empty, Hubert congratulated himself on having avoided the rush hour and with the pick of seats to choose from, selected a window seat with a table and surveyed his fellow passengers. Across the aisle there was a young man wearing a black baseball cap, reading a thick paperback, and opposite him two young women, both with brightly coloured backpacks, were chatting animatedly to each other in a foreign language.

As the train pulled away Hubert settled back into his seat and with a heavy heart recalled the details of last night's unscheduled call from Rose and the delightful and yet daunting news she had delivered.

'You're . . . you're . . . you're . . . coming home?'

'Yes, I've finally done it! I'm taking a sabbatical, albeit a short one! I've booked the tickets and I land at Heathrow just after midday on the first of August.'

'But that's . . .' He did a quick calculation in his head. '. . . that's just four months away!'

'And it'll fly by in no time!'

Overcome with emotion, Hubert had bitten his lip in an effort to hold back tears. After so long away, his darling daughter was finally coming home. In a short time she wouldn't just be a voice at the end of a phone line, she'd be someone he could touch, hold and see face to face. It's what he'd dreamed of, hoped for, for the longest time and at last it was happening.

'Dad . . . I know I've been a terrible daughter, leaving it so long to visit. I didn't mean to but with one thing and another I just haven't been able to make it over until now. But you've never once moaned, you've always been so patient, so encouraging of my career. That's why I'm coming home for a good stretch of time. Six whole weeks! I want to make it up to you. I want to spend some proper time with my wonderful dad. I want us to visit all the places we always said we'd go. Take a tour of Buckingham Palace, go shopping in Harrods and have tea at the Ritz . . . how amazing would that be, Pops? Me and you taking a fancy la-di-da tea at the Ritz! We could even invite your whole pensioner gang to join us!'

She let out a little squeal of delight, but at the mention of his fictional friends Hubert's stomach had lurched violently.

'Rose, come now. There's . . . there's no need for that kind of extravagance. It will be fine just the two of us.'

Rose had laughed as if Hubert had been making a joke.

'Oh, Dad!' she'd chided. 'What are you like? Tea at the Ritz is the least I owe Dotty, Dennis and Harvey after all they've done for you. I mean, how about the time Harvey took you to the hospital for your cataract operation and stayed with you while you recovered? Or the time you had that terrible cold and Dotty made you the pea soup with the gammon bits in it, just how you like it? And don't even get me started on the time Dennis surprised you with tickets to Lord's to see the West Indies play. It was all you could talk about for weeks!'

It was more lies of course. With no friends to help him, Hubert had no choice but to attend his cataract operation alone, even though he'd been terrified that it might leave him blind. The time when he'd had the terrible cold, the nearest he'd come to pea soup with gammon bits was a tomato flavour cup-a-soup he'd found languishing at the back of the cupboard. And as for watching the West Indies play at Lord's, Hubert had as always listened to the match on the radio while sitting alone at the kitchen table.

'Dotty, Dennis and Harvey have been there for you, Dad,'

Rose had continued. 'There for you in ways I haven't been able to be myself, so of course I want to thank them! To be honest I want to kiss and hug the lot of them and treat them to a good night out too. It's the least I can do. They've taken care of you, Dad. And anyone who looks after my dad when I can't be there myself is certainly a friend of mine.'

Hubert had felt sick.

'Rose, this is lovely of you but there's no need to be making this kind of fuss about me friends them. Truth be told, my dear, them are all old and stuck in their ways. Me tell you, them sooner stay in and listen to *Gardeners' Question Time* than take high tea at a fancy West End hotel.'

Rose had laughed.

'Surely they can't be more stuck in their ways than you, Pops! You get twitchy if you're forced to eat tea any later than five o'clock.'

Hubert had tried not to sound frantic.

'Look, darling, just come as you are and leave my friends out of it. Then just the two of us can have a nice time together.'

'Oh Dad, I know what this is all about. And I want you to know that you don't have to worry. You're worried about me spending money, aren't you? But there's absolutely no need, Dad. I'm not poor. I've got a great job, no dependants and plenty of savings. Plus, I got a good deal on the plane ticket and this trip is long overdue—'

Hubert interrupted.

'But you're forgetting . . . August is holiday season here in England. There's a good chance Dotty, Dennis and Harvey will be away.'

'For six whole weeks?' scoffed Rose. 'I didn't know you'd all been doing the lottery together. Where are they going? Monte Carlo? And anyway didn't you tell me that Dotty didn't like to go away from home for too long because her cat stops eating whenever she puts him in a cattery?'

Hubert had never wanted to box his own ears more than he did right at that moment. Why had he lied to Rose all these years?

And more importantly, why had he gone into so much detail?
All that nonsense about Harvey and the hospital trip, Dotty and
the soup, and Dennis taking him to the cricket! He'd made a rod
for his own back with those lies and now they were taking the
opportunity to beat him black and blue.

'The cat's dead.'

'Dead? When?'

'Yesterday. It was sudden. She just woke up and the cat was
gone.'

'Oh poor Juju! And poor Dotty too! She practically worshipped
that cat, didn't she? And didn't she have him from when he was
a kitten? I think I remember you telling me she bought him after
her husband died. Oh, how sad. Give me her address and I'll
pop a sympathy card over to her.'

Hubert had shaken his head in disbelief. Every time he'd tried
to dig himself out of the hole all he'd done was sink deeper.

He tried again.

'She's . . . she's . . . moving house and me haven't got her new
address yet.'

'Oh. Is she moving far?'

'Not really . . . she's . . . she's what you call it . . .'

'Downsizing?'

'That's the one. Anyway when me get her new address me
give it to you but in the meantime me need to go because . . .'

Hubert's mind went blank. What excuse could he give to cut
this conversation short?

'Me need the loo something desperate. It's not easy being an
old man.'

That night he'd barely slept a wink for tossing and turning with
worry. Why hadn't he just come clean? Why hadn't he simply
told her the truth? How could he have been so stupid? How was
she going to react when she turned up in August only to find
out he'd been lying all this time?

But on waking, Hubert suddenly remembered something his
mother always used to say when he was a little boy and troubled

by a situation. 'Hubert,' she would say, 'you need to spend less time fixing on the problem and more time working out what you're going to do about it!' And as he lay there in bed it occurred to him that she was right. Lying around feeling sorry for himself wasn't going to sort anything out. What he needed was a solution to his current predicament. A way forward. A plan.

And then it hit him. His daughter was undoubtedly going to be angry once she discovered that he'd been lying to her about Dotty, Dennis and Harvey. So what if in their place he presented his old friends? Gus and the Red Lion crowd. Surely she wouldn't be quite so angry once he had explained that he'd gone to the effort of reconnecting with them just to please her?

With this in mind, Hubert decided that the best place to start would be with his old friend Gus. But when he tried calling all he got was a message saying that the number was no longer in use. Refusing to fall at the first hurdle, Hubert made up his mind to get the train over to Brixton and visit Gus in person.

Despite having made the journey from Bromley South to Brixton countless times over the years, it felt strange being back after such a protracted absence. Looking around, he wondered what might have changed, but the truth was everything – from the modern-looking benches on the platform, to the signs pointing in the direction of the exit – seemed new and unfamiliar.

Following the crowds, Hubert made his way out of the station, only to struggle to get his bearings. On the one hand it seemed a lot like the Brixton High Street he had always known, but on the other it was very different. Shops had closed down and reopened as something else, road markings had changed, even the people passing by seemed unfamiliar. He saw people of races that weren't immediately recognisable, languages and accents that he couldn't quite identify. It almost seemed like another country.

As he stood wondering which way to go, Hubert heard people tut at him for blocking the way and one young man even swore and told him to move. Finally, he realised that he needed to be on the other side of the main road and so, heading to the traffic lights a little further on, he pressed the button and crossed over.

Ignoring the overtures of a young man staffing a bright yellow gazebo with the letters AA emblazoned across it, Hubert carried on walking until he reached the first of a series of drab-looking low-rise flats. Coming to a halt in front of the third block along, Hubert slipped on his reading glasses and consulted his address book several times to make sure he had the right number, because the ground-floor flat that was supposed to belong to Gus didn't look at all the way he remembered it.

The place seemed to have been abandoned. The paint on the woodwork was peeling, the once bright white net curtains at the windows were dirty grey and torn in places and one of the panes of glass at the front was cracked and boarded over from the inside with a piece of plywood. In a small area to the left of the front door that corresponded with the balconies of the flats above, someone had abandoned a small yellowing fridge-freezer, two broken garden chairs, some dead plants in pots and at least half a dozen full-to-bursting black bin bags.

Hubert could think of only one explanation as to why Gus's home had fallen into such disrepair: his old friend had moved and the people who had taken over the property clearly couldn't care for themselves. The Gus he knew had always been so house-proud. Hubert recalled with a smile the day he first got this place, his first council home, at the age of thirty, having waited seven years for one to become available. 'Smiler, man,' he'd said as they had carefully navigated a dining table through the front door on the day Gus moved in, 'I'm going to turn this place into a palace!'

The building had been brand new back then, smart and modern-looking, fresh and clean, the perfect starter home for single people or those with young families. Hubert and Joyce had been delighted for their friend and Joyce had secretly confessed that she thought this might be the beginning of Gus finally settling down. 'You'll see,' she'd said. 'Now he's got a home of his own the next step will be to find a nice girl to share it with.'

Considering Gus's track record with women, Hubert hadn't been at all convinced but this hadn't stopped him from chiming in with her opinion. 'Well,' he'd said, 'me certainly hope you're right because me don't like the idea of him living the bachelor life all his days.' He'd paused and smiled at Joyce. 'He's been such a good friend to me and me hate the idea of him ending up alone.'

Hubert considered the flat in front of him again. It was now in such a sorry state that you wouldn't credit it with being the same building he'd helped his friend move into all those years ago. He recalled seeing a programme on ITV about people who didn't look after their homes and filled them up with rubbish. What were they called again? He thought long and hard but it was a good few minutes before the word finally came to him. Hoarders. That was what they called them. Hoarders. It was sad really. These people would fill their homes – living rooms, kitchens, bedrooms, the lot – with all manner of junk because they weren't right in the head. And now clearly a hoarder had moved into his old friend's home and turned this once smart place into a rubbish tip.

Hubert wondered what to do next.

On the one hand, if Gus had left a forwarding address and there was indeed a hoarder living here, then for once Hubert might be in luck. If anyone were to have kept Gus's new address then it would be a hoarder, surely! One knock on the door and perhaps the offer of a bit of help rummaging through the mountains of rubbish and Gus's new address would be his. But on the other hand, if this person was a hoarder then there stood a chance they might have all manner of mental illnesses and might, even worse, be violent too. It was a real dilemma.

Hubert reasoned that he had come too far to give up this easily and so, steeling himself, made his way up the path to the front door. Shifting a few of the bin bags out of the way, Hubert pushed the bell, only for it to fall off in his hands. Through the cracked frosted windowpane of the front door Hubert could hear the sound of a TV but could see no other signs of life. He knocked on the doorframe, fearing that a rap on the glass might cause it to shatter, but there was no response from inside. He knocked several more times, getting louder and louder with each one, but still nothing. Finally he decided to try the letterbox but the flap was missing. Instead he peered through the gap to see what he could see. There were huge piles of newspapers in the hallway and yet more bulging rubbish bags but no signs of life. Hubert continued knocking on the door for a good few minutes before reluctantly concluding that he had done all he could. Whoever was living there now was either out or not interested in talking to him.

Hubert allowed himself to think about his old friend and where in the world he might be. Had he met a woman and moved in with her somewhere new? Had he simply decided on a change of scenery and moved to another part of London, or indeed England? Maybe he'd even won the lottery and returned home to Jamaica to live out the rest of his days in the sun.

These, of course, were the best-case scenarios, the ones Hubert preferred to imagine. But there were others, less favourable ones that, given their age, were just as likely (if not more so) to be true. Had Gus succumbed to illness or frailty and moved into a care home? Even worse, had he died without Hubert having any idea that he had long since been buried? Hubert shuddered at the thought. When you don't see someone regularly you imagine them carrying on their lives as they'd always done from one year to the next but the truth was things changed. People grew old and got sick, they sold up and moved on; they weren't stuck in aspic waiting for the day that you knocked on their door looking for them.

6

Then: April 1958

It was Saturday afternoon and Hubert was draped in an old bed sheet and perched on a rickety dining chair. The dingy Stockwell bedsit belonged to Elwood, a Trinidadian friend of Gus's who, though he worked in a bakery near King's Cross, styled West Indian hair in his spare time. While only self-taught, Elwood was good at what he did and was able to recreate all the latest styles coming from America and back home, which was why Hubert had sought him out.

'So,' said Elwood, 'what you want from me today?'

Fumbling under the bed sheet, Hubert reached into his jacket, pulled out a picture torn from the pages of a movie magazine and handed it to Elwood.

'Me want to look like this.'

Examining the image of a smiling Nat King Cole, Elwood frowned.

'You do know that to get this look you're going to have to straighten your hair?'

Hubert nodded.

'It's not a problem.'

'Are you sure?' asked Elwood. He reached under his bed and took out a jar of Kongolene from a box and showed it to Hubert. 'You know this is mighty powerful stuff. I've seen fellows lose chunks of their hair from this after only using it once.'

Hubert swallowed hard. Was the benefit of looking like Nat King Cole worth the risks of losing some of his hair? He decided it was.

'Do what you've got to do.'

'Fine,' replied Elwood, and he glanced from the picture of Nat King Cole to the comb in his hand.

'Well, friend, this isn't a magic wand and I'm no magician but if you want to look like Mr Smooth right here, then I'll give it my best shot!'

Hubert had never relaxed his hair before, preferring to wear it greased and combed back like most young West Indian men. But this coming week was important, perhaps the most vital of his life, and he needed to make a good impression. Because this was going to be the week that he asked out Joyce Pierce.

Until the day of his fight with Vince, all of Hubert's encounters with the English had been a mixed bag of hostility, curiosity and fear. But then he'd met Joyce and she had treated him as though he was just another person and it had been an oddly refreshing experience. Ever since, much to Hubert's surprise, he had found himself doing a lot of thinking about Joyce Pierce.

Soon thinking about Joyce became a pastime so agreeable that he became oblivious to the cold stares and murmurings of Vince's now leaderless crew. In fact, soon Hubert began to quantify how good or bad a day was simply by the quality and quantity of interactions he had with Joyce. A glimpse of her in the service lift was wonderful, but a chat as he delivered a bolt of imported Chinese silk to the third floor could make his entire day. In spite of the hideous food it served, Hubert had begun frequenting the staff canteen again, in the hope of standing in line next to Joyce or sitting at a table opposite the one she shared with the girls from haberdashery.

Quite when exactly Hubert's thoughts shifted from distant admiration to drawing up a plan of action was a mystery even he couldn't fathom. But in a short space of time he went from believing that there was no way a girl like Joyce would go out with him to becoming convinced that if he just said the right thing in the right way and looked handsome and debonair while doing it, he might be in with a chance. And it was with this end in mind that Hubert had sought out Elwood.

The Kongolene had burned his scalp like hell while he was

waiting for it to take effect, but when he saw the finished result Hubert forgot all about the pain in an instant. Okay, so he didn't exactly resemble Nat King Cole, or even Nat King Cole's slightly less attractive brother, but he was in no doubt that with his freshly straightened hair sculpted into a low quiff, there was an air of sophistication about him. His new hairstyle showed off the sharpness of his cheekbones to best effect and his freshly trimmed moustache perfectly complemented the fullness of his lips. Joyce Pierce wouldn't be able to resist him.

Arriving at work on Monday morning, the first thing Hubert did after donning his warehouse coat was to check his reflection in the cracked mirror above the sink in the staff toilets. Still pleased with his new look, he doused himself liberally in his favourite cologne before clocking on.

Making his way to the loading bay, Hubert discovered Mr Coulthard talking to three much-needed new recruits to the warehouse staff. Of the three, two were English and Mr Coulthard assigned Hubert the task of showing the third, a young West Indian lad, the ropes. The boy was called Kenneth – a spindly, clueless-looking fellow who was so fresh off the boat, Hubert could practically smell the sea on him. He was eighteen but seemed more like eight and, much to Hubert's frustration, could barely hold one instruction in his head without it being pushed straight out by another.

The other two didn't seem much better, so much so that when the deliveries arrived, the old hands like Hubert had to work twice as hard to undo all the mistakes they were making. By midday Hubert was exhausted, dripping with sweat, his new hair awry and the smell of his cologne long since faded. This was of course the exact moment an exasperated Mr Coulthard sent him up to the haberdashery department to sort out a problem with an order. All the way up in the service lift Hubert hoped and prayed that it wouldn't be Joyce waiting for him on the other side of the doors.

Hubert stepped out of the lift.

'Hello, you,' said Joyce. 'Long time no see. The cut's healed nicely.'

'Yes, it has, thank you.'

He ran a hand casually through his hair in a desperate bid to subtly tidy it up and immediately regretted it, covered as it now was in a thin greasy sheen of hair pomade. Hubert thought briefly of Nat King Cole and wondered whether this sort of thing ever happened to him.

'I like your hair,' said Joyce. 'Very dashing.'

Hubert was overjoyed. Maybe this was the right moment to ask her out after all.

'Me glad you like it.'

'Anyway,' said Joyce after a long pause, 'much as I'd like to, I can't spend all day gabbing with you. Critchlow's in a foul enough mood as it is and if she clocks that I'm not on the shop floor there'll be hell to pay.'

She held out an order form for Hubert to see.

'I don't know what's been going on down there this morning but what we've had delivered up here twice today bears no resemblance to what's on this form.'

Hubert examined the piece of paper but such was his focus on what he was about to say next that he couldn't see a single word. This was it. This was his moment. It was now or never.

He cleared his throat. His mouth was suddenly dry.

'Joyce . . . Joyce . . . well . . . me need to . . . me need to ask you something.'

'About the order?'

'About . . . about . . .' For a moment he thought he might pass out with the anxiety of it all. '. . . about whether you might be free to go out on Saturday night?'

There was a long silence. Hubert couldn't read Joyce's expression. He cleared his throat again and decided to clarify his intentions in case she was confused.

'Me mean with me. Would you like to go to the pictures with me on Saturday night?'

'Oh,' said Joyce.

Hubert felt his heart sink.

'I'm really flattered, Hubert . . . really I am but—'

Hubert tried his best to salvage what remained of his dignity. 'You don't have to say anything. Me understand completely.'

'No, Hubert, you don't. It's not like that, it's—'

The door behind them creaked open and a short plump girl in a Hamilton's uniform poked her head around it.

'Whatever you're doing, you'd best do it quick. Critchlow's on the warpath!'

Hubert folded the order in half then, without waiting, stepped back into the lift and pulled the door closed. This was the end for him and Hamilton's, Hubert decided. He would have to find himself a job elsewhere.

Later that day, Hubert returned to the bedsit in Brixton Gus had helped him find a few weeks ago. Despite its damp walls, peeling wallpaper and draughty windows it wasn't the worst lodgings he'd seen. And in addition, it had all the essentials: a battered armchair next to a tiny coal fire, a gas ring to cook on, a single bed with a lumpy horsehair mattress. It was, however, miles away from the comforts of the home he missed so terribly.

Taking out a sheet of light blue airmail paper and a stub of pencil from a battered suitcase under the bed, Hubert grabbed the Bible his mother had packed for him. Using it to rest his paper on, he sat down in the armchair and began to write.

Before leaving Jamaica Hubert had promised his mother that he would try to write at least once a week. To start with, his letters had been full of energy and optimism, describing in vivid detail the sights and sounds of London, the place they'd all imagined for so long. He told her about the smoke coming from all the chimneys, a sight you'd never see back home. And of his delight in seeing snow for the first time, which he and Gus had played in for hours like children, throwing snowballs and making snowmen. He wrote about all the grand buildings with their history and beautiful architecture and how on his first free day in London he had walked all the way from Brixton to Buckingham

Palace to silently pay respect to the queen, on his own behalf and also that of his family in Jamaica.

His mother had received all his news with delight and her replies had been full of questions, about the weather, London fashions, and of course, about whether he was looking after himself. She would sign off each letter always in the same way, 'I'm so proud of you, my son, may the Lord bless and keep you.' Because of this, Hubert hadn't had the heart to tell her the truth that had gradually dawned on him: he was miserable, lonely and homesick.

He hadn't told her about the English families that would cross the road just to avoid walking past him. The signs in the windows of boarding houses making it clear that neither he, nor the Irish nor people with dogs were welcome. He hadn't told her how cold it got, how in bed he struggled to get warm even when fully clothed. He hadn't told her about the dreadful food, the filthy streets, and how hard he had to work just to keep a roof over his head. Instead he'd kept his letters brief and cheerful, but as he sat shivering, pencil poised and thinking about how much his heart hurt knowing that his feelings for Joyce were unrequited, for the first time ever he felt like telling his mother the truth.

In the end Hubert didn't bother going to the Labour Exchange, reasoning it was a case of better the devil you know. Who knew what sort of job he might be offered next and the horrors that lay in store? No, he would stick with Hamilton's with its long hours and hard graft for the time being. He would avoid Joyce at all costs, keep his head down, steer clear of the canteen and designate all calls to the third floor to his reluctant protégé Kenneth.

When a week and a half went by without any sight of Joyce, Hubert began to relax. While he wasn't over Joyce, he could at least imagine a time when he might be. In the meantime Gus had recently started dating an English girl he'd met at a dance and this girl had told Gus she had a friend who would be perfect for Hubert.

'You always look too serious these days, Smiler,' he'd said. 'Come out with us and have a little fun.'

This was an offer that Hubert had so far declined, but with the weekend looming he started to question the wisdom of his position.

Early on Wednesday morning a call came down from the third floor for an order of several bolts of Lancashire tweed. Hubert searched for Kenneth but he was nowhere to be seen and when he asked after him, he discovered that he'd gone up to the furniture department on the fourth floor with an order some time ago and hadn't been seen since. Cursing the boy under his breath, Hubert made up the order and took the lift to the third floor himself. If it was Joyce waiting for him he would be polite but brief, keeping conversation to a minimum, and then later, once he'd recovered from being in her presence, he would find Kenneth and box his ears.

As he opened the lift doors Hubert poked his head out, only to discover that the delivery bay was empty. Breathing a sigh of relief, he began to unload the fabric but then, just as he hoisted the last bolt on to his shoulder, the door to the shop floor opened. It was Joyce. Looking more beautiful than ever. Even from a distance Hubert could see that she had done something different with her hair, winding it up into an elegant chignon that made her appear older and more sophisticated somehow.

She gave him a smile.

'I was beginning to worry that you'd left us. Whenever I pick up an order these days it's always the young boy who gets sent up.'

Hubert resisted the urge to kiss his teeth as he put down the material in front of her.

'You mean Kenneth? That damned boy is hopeless. He got sent up to a job on the fourth floor and no one has seen him since.'

'I expect it's quite busy up there,' said Joyce. 'I've heard the new floor manager has been having a sales promotion and things are all at sixes and sevens. I'm sure your man will reappear soon.'

Hubert held out the order form. She scribbled down her name with a flourish and handed it back to him.

'It's been lovely to see you,' said Joyce. 'And now you've broken the streak hopefully you won't be such a stranger. I was beginning to think you were avoiding me.'

Hubert said nothing and instead, feeling like his face was on fire with embarrassment, he quickly turned back to the lift, but then she called out after him. He turned around, expecting her to produce a forgotten order form, but instead she was smiling.

'I've got a question for you . . . What are you doing Saturday night?'

Hubert stared at her confused.

'Me . . . me . . . got no plans.'

'Good,' she replied. 'In that case you're taking me to the five o'clock showing of *South Pacific* at the Regal in Blackfriars.'

Hubert stood frozen to the spot, speechless.

A wry smile played on Joyce's lips.

'What? You haven't seen it already, have you?'

Even if he had, twenty times, he would gladly see it twenty times more if it meant going with her.

'No, me haven't seen it.'

'Good,' said Joyce. 'Then I'll meet you outside the Regal at four thirty so we can chat before the film.'

For the rest of the day Hubert couldn't stop grinning. He grinned in the lift on the way back down to the warehouse. He grinned as he passed Mr Coulthard yelling at the new lads. And he grinned all the more later when Kenneth told him a very odd story about being sent on a wild-goose chase to the fourth floor by a girl from haberdashery.

7

Now

Hubert approached the middle-aged woman with preternaturally bright red hair who was staffing the reception desk at the community centre.

'I wonder if you could help me?' he asked using his extra-formal voice, the one he usually reserved for talking to the professional classes. 'I'm looking for . . .'

He reached into his jacket pocket, took out the flyer he'd picked up from his GP's waiting room, slipped on his reading glasses and read aloud from it.

'. . .the O-60 Club: meeting and mixing for the over-sixties.'

The woman pointed vaguely towards the café.

'Take a left down the side of the caff, go through the double doors and you're there.'

It was official: the number of friends Hubert had in the entire world was zero. He knew this because after his failure with Gus he had spent the past week making various enquiries and trying to track down his friends from the Red Lion, and the news hadn't been good.

Septicaemia following a heart by-pass had put paid to Biggie a year and a half ago. The end of his marriage had sent Mister Taylor back home to St Kitts. Alzheimer's had left Teetus in a care home near his daughters in Bristol. And romance had transported Oney to Switzerland to live with some rich German lady he'd met on a cruise.

As for the friends Hubert had once shared with Joyce, the news was equally dismal. Following a stroke Joan Reid was in a care home and her husband Peter had passed away from throat cancer. Carlo Stewart had returned to Jamaica after divorcing

Pamela and she in turn had moved to Edinburgh to be near their children. Leonard Walker had died suddenly following a heart attack while on holiday and his wife Rita was now living with her sister-in-law in a bungalow in Bourton-on-the-Water.

Death, disease, divorce and relocation: these, it appeared, were the four fates consuming all that remained of Hubert's generation. It was a sorry state of affairs, made all the more poignant by receiving this news in one go. It was as if he'd been asleep for the past five years only to wake up in another world, in another reality where an entire generation had been wiped out and he alone was the sole survivor.

A whole week had gone by since Rose's announcement and now, because of his lack of friends, Hubert was faced with an almost impossible choice: disappoint his darling daughter or force himself back out into the world from which he had retreated. As terrifying as he had found both propositions, there was no doubt in his mind which of the two he feared most. And so here he was attempting to do the one thing he had failed to do all those years earlier and which, it could be argued, was in part respon-sible for the creation of Dotty, Dennis and Harvey.

Within a matter of a few short moments Hubert found himself standing at the entrance to the community centre's main hall. Through the small square of glass in the door he observed half a dozen tables set out at one end of the room with groups of mostly women sitting at them.

At the opposite end a small group of women and a solitary man were practising a line dance routine to a country song playing from a paint-splattered CD player in the corner. Their thumbs were curled around their belt loops like cowboys as they hopped, stepped and twirled in time to the music. In the centre of the room was a table-tennis table that two couples were using to rest their coffee cups on while they chatted animatedly.

Hubert did not want to go into this room. He was scared and he felt vulnerable and the last thing on earth he wanted was to try to make friends with these strangers. He wished with all his heart that Joyce were here with him. After all, it was always easier to meet new people if there were two of you. It gave you confidence and made you feel at ease. Look, it said to the world, I already have one friend so I can't be all that bad. And Joyce always made him feel like his best self anyway, so there would be no resisting him.

From his vantage point Hubert couldn't help noting that compared to the few men present, who were wearing short-sleeved shirts and jeans, he was somewhat overdressed. He had wanted to make an impression but they would all probably think he was trying too hard in his sports jacket, tie and pressed beige summer trousers. It also dawned on Hubert that aside from an Indian woman playing cards, everyone in the room was white.

While Hubert couldn't easily recall the last time he'd been the victim of racism, that didn't mean it hadn't happened. These days, like smoking in public, racism was less socially acceptable than it used to be and therefore more subtle. Yes, people were less likely to abuse Hubert in the street, refuse to serve him in a shop or physically attack him than they were in the Fifties but that didn't necessarily mean he was welcome everywhere. And while he was more than happy to be rejected by strangers for being ill-tempered, awkward or stubborn, it hurt more than he cared to admit that he might be rejected simply because of the colour of his skin.

The woman on reception lifted her head up from a magazine as Hubert passed her desk on the way out.

'Couldn't you find it? I can show you where it is, if you like.'

Hubert adopted his formal voice again.

'No, thank you. Your directions were perfect but I don't think it's for me.'

That afternoon, following a ham sandwich washed down with a cup of tea, Hubert settled on the sofa with Puss. Scanning up and down the TV channels, he went in search of an old black and white film to distract him from the morning's failure. While there were game show repeats and cheap daytime soap operas galore, black and white films were thin on the ground. Then he found a station playing *The Adventures of Robin Hood,* and best of all it had only just started. Joyce had always had a thing for Errol Flynn, ever since she'd seen *The Modern Adventures of Casanova.* Whenever one of his films came on the TV she would drop everything to watch it and Hubert would always tease, 'Oh, your fancy man is back on the scene!' and she would reply, 'I don't need a fancy man, Hubert Bird, I've got you,' and then she'd give him a peck on the cheek. It was a little routine they had, one of many that never failed to make him smile to remember.

Hubert quite enjoyed the film to begin with, but for some reason it wasn't enough to lift the dark mood that had descended on him. He couldn't help it. He felt like a failure and a fraud. He'd wasted his one and only opportunity to do right by his daughter and to make friends. Now he would have no choice but to tell her the truth. Rose would be absolutely livid when she found out and so worried about him that he didn't doubt for a moment that she'd pack up her life in Australia and come home to care for him. He couldn't have that on his conscience. He couldn't have her giving up on the career she'd worked so hard to establish, just to spend her days looking after a foolish old man.

Filled with despondency, he picked up the remote control and switched off the TV, plunging the room into a silence that was broken a moment later by the sound of the doorbell.

Whether it was a parcel courier hoping to leave something with him for a neighbour or a police officer coming to take him away for being such a terrible father, Hubert cared not. All he wanted was a distraction from his current thoughts and so, gathering his wits about him, he answered the door. It was the young woman from next door who he'd last seen in the vet's. She was dressed differently to how she'd been when he'd seen her before: smarter, in a navy-blue jacket, matching skirt and heels. She looked as if she might be going to work or possibly a funeral. Her young daughter was with her too, but this time she was strapped into a pushchair and was too busy playing with a book attached to the frame to take any notice of Hubert.

Hubert considered the young woman more carefully this time and much to his dismay observed that she was struggling not to cry.

'Sorry to disturb you . . . I know you don't know me from Adam . . . and I know it's a massive favour I'm about to ask but I've completely run out of options. I literally don't know what else to do. I'm not trying to sound dramatic but the thing is you really are my last hope. Would you . . . could you . . . find it in your heart to look after my Layla for a bit?'

'You . . . you . . . want me to do what?'

'Just mind my daughter for twenty minutes . . . half an hour tops.'

A tense desperation inched its way into her voice.

'I wouldn't ask if there was any way round this. Really I wouldn't. But I'd booked a babysitting service and they've liter-ally just let me down at the last minute – something to do with a double booking – and now I don't know what to do. I said to them, "There's no good saying, 'I can only apologise,' when I've got a job interview in ten minutes. What am I supposed to do, just rock up there with my daughter and tell the vet, 'Don't mind my little girl, she'll be fine there with her colouring book and crayons.'?" She wouldn't mind – she loves colouring, but that's not really the point is it? It's just not professional.' Her pale green eyes searched Hubert's face, hoping to discover if he was following her line of argument. 'That's why I need your help,' she continued, more slowly this time. 'I've got an interview you see. Remember the other day when I saw you at the vet's when I was dropping in my CV? Well, they got back to me this week and asked me to come in today to meet them, so that's got to be a good sign, hasn't it? I know it's only for a receptionist's job, and of course it wouldn't be the end of the world if I didn't get it, but I really think this is a great opportunity. You see, I don't just want to be a single mum all my life, I want to be somebody one day, maybe even a veterinary nurse. So my Layla can be really proud of me and grow up with a good role model.'

Her words came out so quickly and so tightly wrapped in that strange accent of hers. Hubert had to strain the entire time he was listening and although he didn't quite follow all of it, he grasped more than enough to get the gist of what she was asking. He concluded it was madness.

'Look, me see you in a pickle. Really, me see that. But have you lost your mind? You can't just ask a complete stranger to look after your child. Don't you watch the news?'

'Of course I do,' said Ashleigh. 'And yes, I know sometimes the world's a horrible place but not always. Sometimes it's a lovely place where nice things happen for no reason and I'd much rather . . .' She began to get upset. '. . . I'd much rather live in that world than the other one!'

She burst into tears, leaving Hubert feeling very uncomfortable indeed. He never had been able to bear the sight of a woman crying. Whether it was his mother upset because she was worried about how they were going to afford to feed themselves, Joyce fretting about one of the children, or a young Rose sobbing over a grazed knee. Women in peril always brought out the chivalrous side of him. And now here he was with a strange woman weeping on his doorstep.

Surely this wasn't his problem to solve. He didn't know this person. He didn't know how to look after a child – at least not any more. And anyway, last time he checked he was an eighty-four-year-old man. Who asked eighty-four-year-old men anything other than whether they took their tea with one lump of sugar or two?

Hubert reached into his trouser pocket and withdrew a hand-kerchief.

'It's clean,' he explained, handing it to her. 'Me like to put a fresh one in my pocket every day.'

Ashleigh gratefully received the handkerchief but just as she was about to dry her eyes, she stopped suddenly and sniffed.

'It's cologne,' explained Hubert. 'Me like to spray a little on to make it smell nice.'

'It smells well lush,' said Ashleigh.

She dabbed her eyes with it, then used it to blow her nose

several times. Finally she attempted to return the sodden hand-kerchief to Hubert but he refused.

'Keep it, me have plenty more where that come from.'

Ashleigh stuffed the handkerchief in her bag, glanced at her watch, bit her lip and then fixed her eyes on Hubert imploringly. Hubert felt his resolve crumbling. He couldn't bear to watch this woman cry any more. He couldn't bear another second.

'Fine,' he said. 'Me will help you out, okay?'

He offered Ashleigh his hand and she shook it.

'The name is Hubert . . . Hubert Bird. Just tell me what it is you want me to do and me do it.'

8

Then: April 1958

The sense of relief Hubert felt when he saw Joyce walking towards him as he waited outside the entrance to the Regal was enormous. Her desire to go to the pictures with him hadn't been an elaborate dream, a figment of his imagination or a practical joke. She was here, she was really here and the sight of her made him grin from ear to ear. She was, he thought, even more beautiful freed from the confines of her Hamilton's uniform of demure black dress with dainty white bow and lacy collar. Sporting a navy-blue duster coat over a flowery lemon dress with green heels, she was a vision of spring and Hubert told her so.

'Thank you,' she replied. 'The dress is new. I made it myself from a pattern in *Vogue*. Mum wasn't sure about the colour but I think it's cheerful, don't you?'

Hubert smiled.

'It's like a piece of sunshine on a dull grey day.'

Joyce gave him an admiring glance.

'You look very smart by the way. Very dapper. I love your tie. It almost matches my dress.'

'Great minds think alike!' said Hubert, pleased by the connection, and he handed her the flowers he'd bought for her. 'I didn't know what kind you like so I just bought carnations.'

Joyce admired them fondly.

'Oh Hubert, they're lovely. Absolutely beautiful. Thank you.'

Following Hubert's lead, they joined the line for the cinema, made up almost exclusively of courting couples, already snaking out of the door. They chatted about the little they knew about the film, and then talked about other pictures they had seen recently. Hubert tried his best to sound knowledgeable but the truth was the sign on the wall next to them detailing the various ticket options was distracting him. The cheapest seats were at the front and the most expensive on the back row. Gus had given Hubert strict instructions to get back row tickets. 'Them the best seats in the picture house,' he explained, 'because no one can see what you're getting up to!'

This information had left Hubert with a dilemma. If he asked the cashier for back row tickets there was a good chance Joyce might think he was only after one thing, but then if he got the cheaper tickets it might look like he wasn't willing to spend money on her, which he absolutely was. With all this in mind, Hubert reasoned that the best way forward was to buy tickets for seats slap bang in the middle of the picture house even though in his heart of hearts he actually wouldn't have minded sitting at the back, even if all they did was hold hands.

As it was, however, by the time they reached the front of the queue the decision had been made for him.

'The only tickets we've got left are two singles towards the back or these two,' the cashier said. He pointed at the plan of the auditorium inlaid on the counter to two seats on the front row.

Hubert searched Joyce's expression for guidance.

'We'll take the two at the front,' she told the cashier, then turned to Hubert. 'At least we'll be sitting together then. And anyway, if it's any good we can always see it again and sit at the back.'

As they waited for the doors to open, Hubert noticed for the first time that he and Joyce were attracting the attention of a number of couples and not in a good way. One woman, a tall bottle blond standing next to an equally tall man dressed in a dark suit and knitted waistcoat, had thrown a look of disgust in Joyce's direction, but Joyce had been so busy chatting to Hubert about her favourite film stars that she hadn't noticed.

Hubert didn't care about the looks for himself, as after nearly four months in this country he was used to it and had almost stopped noticing, but he did mind when it came to Joyce. He stared so hard at the woman that in the end she had no choice but to look away and mutter something in the ear of her date that made them both collapse into a fit of mean-spirited giggles. Hubert, however, carried on looking right at them and once they realised this, they stopped laughing and kept their eyes fixed ahead until the usherette opened the doors and everybody filtered slowly into the auditorium and took their seats.

Not being a fan of musicals, Hubert thought the film only mediocre, but the fact that he got to sit in such close proximity to Joyce in a darkened room more than made up for the songs, the story (which Hubert found perplexing to say the least) and the strange artificial colour of the film. Because he didn't want Joyce to feel bad for suggesting it, Hubert told her that he'd enjoyed it, to which she'd replied that she had too, but even though Hubert didn't know her very well, he couldn't help feeling that perhaps this might not be entirely true.

As they made their way out of the cinema, Hubert's mind turned to thoughts of what might happen next. The last thing he wanted was for the night to be over, but with his budget and already down the cost of two cinema tickets his options were limited. Thankfully, not only was Joyce in no hurry to get home but she also had an idea of what they might do, which to Hubert's relief would cost nothing.

'Why don't we go for a walk?' she suggested. 'It's lovely down by the river and it'll give us a chance to talk a bit more.'

Hubert agreed that this would be good and added that he'd never seen that part of the city. 'In that case,' she said, taking his arm, 'I think you might be in for a treat.'

As they walked and talked, Hubert, keen to know everything there was to know about her, peppered Joyce with question after question about her life. She was twenty-one years old and had been working at Hamilton's ever since she left school at fourteen, starting out as a general dogsbody in the staff canteen before being promoted, first to waitress and finally to assistant in the haberdashery department.

She lived at home with her parents, John and Rose Pierce, in

Bromley. John worked for the post office, while mum Rose was a housewife. She had three siblings, an older sister Peggy, who used to work at Hamilton's until she got married last summer, a younger brother Eric, who worked with her dad, and a big brother George, who worked as a bus mechanic and was married with three children.

'They're an all right bunch, my family,' she concluded, 'especially when you catch them in a good mood. Dad can be a real joker at times and when him and George get going it's like a proper double act!' She paused, as they finally reached the river and began walking along the bank. 'Anyway,' she said, 'that's enough rabbiting from me. Tell me about you and your family, and life in the West Indies. I want to know everything, don't leave anything out. Tell me all about the sights and sounds and smells. I'm not very well travelled I'm afraid. The only trip I've ever taken out of England was a coach tour to Edinburgh a few summers ago and I was sick the whole way there and back.'

As they strolled along arm in arm Hubert told her all about his family and the farm back in Jamaica. He told her about the cockerel that used to wake them up every morning, about the old dog that slept in the yard and was meant to be a guard dog but which his mother fussed over so much he had grown fat and lazy. He told her about the fruit trees lining the path they used to take to school and how for breakfast they would help themselves to guava, oranges and soursop, arriving at their classroom fingers sticky with juice. He told her about his mother, who was a terrific cook and could transform the most meagre of ingredients into a feast fit for a king. He told her about his brothers and sisters and their funny ways. How, as the eldest, Vivian would still try to mother them all long after they had stopped being children, how his little brother Fulton was easily the best mimic on the island and his impression of the local pastor would make them all cry with laughter. How the baby of the family Cora, dear sweet Cora, would as a child always insist that Hubert piggyback her to bed every night.

'And what about your dad?'

'He's not around,' said Hubert quietly. Joyce didn't press him any further. Instead she said: 'You must miss them all something rotten being so far away from them, not to mention Jamaica, it sounds wonderful.'

Hubert smiled.

'It is and I do. But me come here because this is where the work is. There just isn't enough to go round back home right now. And a man can't sit twiddling his thumbs all day.'

'Well, if it helps, I for one am glad you came.'

Hubert smiled again.

'Yes, that does help. It helps a lot.'

They reached Westminster Bridge and halfway across came to a halt looking out across the inky black Thames, its surface dotted with patches of light reflected from streetlamps and passing boats. It was, thought Hubert as they shifted their gaze from the water towards the Houses of Parliament and Big Ben silhouetted against the evening sky, a romantic moment, one that would be the perfect backdrop for a first kiss.

Joyce gave Hubert's arm a tender squeeze.

'It's no Jamaica,' she said. 'But London's not half bad when you see it like this.'

Hubert glanced down at Joyce to find that her eyes were already fixed on him. This was it, he thought, this was the moment. But before he could lean in for a kiss, Big Ben sounded and Joyce glanced up at the world-famous landmark suddenly worried.

'I hadn't realised it was so late. I told Mum I'd be back by ten at the latest and if I don't get a shift on I'll have no chance of making it.'

Hubert was unable to hide his disappointment.

'Oh, of course, I'll walk you to your bus.'

'Would you? That's so kind. I'm sorry to have to dash off like this, especially as we were having such a nice evening.'

As they made their way across the bridge Hubert wondered where Joyce had told her parents she was going tonight and with whom. Would she have told them about him or not? Were they the sort of people who would mind if they knew about the colour of his skin? Perhaps this was why she had suggested a picture house in Blackfriars, so far away from where she lived, to reduce the chance of seeing anyone she knew, to keep their time together a secret. Even if this was true, Hubert didn't care. The only thing that mattered was that she had wanted to be here with him tonight.

The closer they got to the bus stop the quieter they both became, and Hubert wondered if this was because she, like him, was sad that the night would soon be over. He wished they could start the evening all over again; he would manage his time more carefully so that their perfect moment on the bridge might not have been ruined by the tolling of Big Ben. In his cinematic remake of the evening Hubert would take her in his arms just like the hero of a film, tell her that time didn't matter and then give her a kiss so passionate and full of feeling that she would never forget it.

Joyce unlinked arms with Hubert, bringing him crashing back to reality, and pointed up the road to the oncoming bus.

'This one's mine. I've had a really lovely time, Hubert Bird, thank you so much.'

Hubert wondered if now was the right time to ask if he could see her again. As he opened his mouth to say the words Joyce took a step towards him, and looked up into his eyes in a manner that only ever means one thing. To Hubert's elation, their kiss was everything that he had hoped for in his Technicolor remake and more, full of passion, hope and longing. It was a kiss that more than answered the question he'd been preparing to utter. It was a kiss that didn't so much say goodbye as hello.

9

Now

Hubert and Ashleigh were standing at the entrance to the vet's.

'Right then,' said Ashleigh. 'She's got all the snacks she'll need in the basket under her stroller. She went for a wee before we came out so she should be fine until I'm back. And like I said, she'll be happy enough if you take her for a walk around the park. If she starts making a fuss and tells you that she wants to get out of the pushchair and walk just ignore her, she'll be okay in there for a little while longer.'

Keen to show Ashleigh he had listened to her every word, Hubert repeated the key details.

'Snacks in basket, doesn't need bathroom, don't let her out of pram. Got it.'

Ashleigh knelt down on the ground next to the pushchair, pressed her lips urgently against her daughter's cheek, then glanced earnestly up at Hubert.

'You will look after her, won't you?'

'Of course, me is a man of my word.'

Ashleigh let out a little sigh, grateful for the reassurance.

'My nan always said I was a good judge of character and I am. Obviously maybe not so much when it comes to boyfriends, but people, regular people, I'm like that.' She pointed a finger directly at Hubert's heart. 'Like a laser. You're a good man, Hubert Bird, I can just tell. You remind me of my granddad a bit, he was always smartly turned out just like you. And just like I know my granddad would do everything in his power to keep my baby safe if he was here, I know you will too.'

As he watched Ashleigh disappear inside the vet's, Hubert felt strangely calm. It was a good thing he was doing. The sort of thing Joyce would've done had she been around. And he was sure there would be no problems.

But then he peered down at the girl in the pushchair and his stomach gave a sudden almighty lurch. He was in charge of a child! An actual human being in miniature! And not just any child – which would be bad enough – but one that belonged to a next-door neighbour he didn't know at all.

What if someone snatched the girl while he wasn't looking? What if she fell ill and needed to be rushed to hospital? What if she started screaming for her mother and people thought he had kidnapped her? Hubert shuddered at the very thought of all these catastrophic scenarios. He was sorely tempted to rush into the vet's and hand Layla to her mother.

Assuming that the safest thing he could do was to remain exactly where he was, Hubert positioned himself just to the side of the entrance to the vet's and waited. Seconds later, however, a passing lorry belched out a huge cloud of black diesel fumes so noxious that he feared for the child's heath.

He peered over the edge of the pushchair and addressed Layla.

'Change of plan. Me can't just stand by and watch you choke on car fumes so we're going to the park for some fresh air.'

As Hubert turned the pushchair around it occurred to him that he probably hadn't pushed such a contraption since the late Sixties when David would have been two or three. This thought alone was enough to make Hubert's heart ache, but then tiny snippets of memories he'd thought long lost resurfaced. David kicking his sandalled feet in the air as he sat in the stroller. Rose singing nursery rhymes softly to herself as she ambled along by his side. The smoothness of the pushchair's hard plastic handle under his fingertips. The warmth and softness of Joyce's hand resting on his own.

Hubert hadn't been to this park since he and Joyce stopped taking their daily strolls. Every day when his wife suggested it he'd say something like, 'There's nothing in the park for me,' or, 'Why go to the park when we've got a perfectly good garden sitting empty at home?' But secretly he had enjoyed these walks with his wife. He loved the fact that she knew the Latin names of flowers and trees. He adored the depth and breadth of the conversations they would have about subjects like religion and politics, music and film, that rarely got an airing whenever they were sat on the sofa at home. But most of all Hubert liked to walk in the park with Joyce because it made his heart swell with pride that everyone would know he belonged to her and she belonged to him, and in marrying her he had won the jackpot of life.

As a tribute to those days, Hubert decided he and Layla would follow exactly the same route around the park he and Joyce used to enjoy. That way, as long as they didn't dawdle too much, they could take in all the vibrant colours of the flowerbeds, enjoy the antics of the ducks and geese on the pond, and still make it back to the vet's long before Ashleigh's interview was over. Hubert relayed his plans to Layla as best he could but her only response was to point intently at a nearby pigeon and laugh and so, reasoning that she had no objections, he began to walk.

He'd barely managed to take more than a few steps, however, when a woman passing by in the opposite direction stopped him. Although Hubert wasn't very good at judging this sort of thing, he guessed she was probably in her mid-seventies. She had short, softly waved white hair, a lovely smile and was wearing perhaps a touch too much make-up. She wore a long, floaty beige skirt and cream floral blouse. Her feet were clad in white open-toed sandals and her hand rested on a pink floral-patterned canvas shopping trolley.

'What a gorgeous child!'

Hubert shifted his gaze from the woman to Layla and pondered his charge. She was, he conceded, fairly cute for a small child.

'Thank you,' he replied.

The woman continued to gaze adoringly at Layla.

'You must be so proud! Is this your . . . your grandchild?'

Hubert considered the question. Would anything good come from going into the details of what was undoubtedly an odd situation with a complete stranger? He decided it wouldn't.

'Great-granddaughter,' he said succinctly.

'Oh, how wonderful! And how old is she?'

Hubert regarded Layla carefully and had to resist the temptation to shrug. He had no idea what the correct answer to this question was.

'Five,' he said tentatively.

The woman's eyebrows shot up in surprise. Hubert immediately corrected himself.

'Me mean *fiveteen months* . . . she's *fifteen* months old.'

The woman's eyebrows shot up again.

'My, she's very big for a fifteen-month-old, if you don't mind me saying.'

'That's Caribbean genes for you,' countered Hubert. 'Our children, you see, grow up that much faster.'

There was an awkward moment as he watched the woman carefully taking in Layla's blond hair and blue eyes, but thankfully she said nothing more on the matter.

'Well,' said the woman, 'she certainly is a sweetie.' She bent down until she was level with Layla's eye-line. 'Absolutely gorgeous, aren't you?'

Layla pointed at another pigeon and giggled impishly while the woman prepared to continue on her way.

'Anyway, I suppose I'd better leave you two to get on with your stroll. Enjoy your time in the fresh air!'

As Hubert continued walking, he couldn't help smiling to himself.

'What a difference sixty years makes,' he thought, reflecting briefly on the countless acts of prejudice he'd suffered across his lifetime. 'Me, an eighty-four-year-old West Indian man walk round with a blond-haired, blue-eyed child in a pushchair and not a one blinks an eye.'

The moment Ashleigh spotted Hubert and Layla she let out a scream of delight so loud that people walking across the street turned to stare. Unaccustomed to such displays of emotion, Hubert saw that she was crying again. Before he could ask what was wrong, she bent down, undid the buckle on the stroller and, whisking her daughter out of the chair, smothered her in kisses.

'Is everything . . . all right?'

'I'm fine,' she replied. 'Honestly I am. It's just that . . .' She became tearful again. 'It's just that when I came out and saw you and Layla waiting for me, happy as anything . . . well . . . I don't know . . . I'm just so grateful, that's all.'

'So you're not crying because the interview went badly?'

'Badly? It literally couldn't have gone any better! They absolutely loved me, they did! I know that sounds big-headed but like I said, I'm good at reading people. They said they had a couple more applicants to see, so you never know, but I'm hopeful. Really hopeful!'

'Good,' said Hubert. 'Me glad it went well.'

Ashleigh smiled at Layla.

'Did you have a good time with Granddad Hubert?'

Choosing to ignore Ashleigh's reference to him as Granddad, Hubert said, 'We had a lovely stroll around the park. No swings though, she stayed in the pram the whole time.'

'Layla loves that park. It's her favourite place in the whole world at the moment.'

As they walked and talked, Ashleigh told Hubert all about a park her granddad used to take her to back home in Wales. As she spoke, he tuned out her chatter and reflected on just how truly odd this past hour of his life had been. While it was Hubert's constant wish that Joyce was still around, more than ever he wanted to open his front door, give her a kiss and a cuddle and tell her all about his morning of madness.

At Hubert's front gate they came to a halt. Ashleigh lowered Layla to the ground and smiled at Hubert.

'I had a good feeling about you. From the moment I saw you I thought to myself, 'Me and him are going to be mates.''

Hubert didn't like to remind her that up until that afternoon he'd only said a handful of words to her, most of which had been offered in a bid to get rid of her. So instead he raised his hat in a farewell gesture and turned to leave, but as he opened the gate he felt something brush past his legs. Looking down, he saw that it was Layla toddling up the garden path towards his front door.

'Come on, Missy!' chided Ashleigh. 'Let's leave Granddad Hubert in peace now. He's done more than enough for us today.'

Ignoring her mother's request, Layla sat down on Hubert's doorstep, folding her arms in a gesture of defiance.

Ashleigh called after her, more sternly this time.

'Layla! Back in your buggy now, please. Let's leave Granddad Hubert alone.'

Perplexed, Hubert continued to his front door and, much to his bewilderment, as he opened the door Layla stood up, stepped confidently inside the house and without looking back began waddling down the hallway.

'I'm so sorry,' said Ashleigh, coming down the path. 'I don't know what gets into her sometimes.'

In turn, Hubert carefully considered the child inside his house, its mother and the situation as a whole, and found himself coming to an unexpected conclusion. In fact, it was so unexpected that for a moment he wondered if all the excitement of the day was making him somewhat delirious.

'Well,' he said, 'it looks like she wants to come in . . . so me suppose you'd better come in too.'

10

Then: May 1958

'So, where your parents think you are this time?'

'Seeing a show with some girls from work,' replied Joyce. 'But Mum gave me a funny look before I left the house, like she knew I was seeing a boy but was just keeping quiet because of Dad.'

They were hiding from prying eyes in the shop doorway of a tobacconist round the corner from Victoria Station.

'It could've just been your new outfit,' said Hubert, who had himself noted over the past few weeks how Joyce had gradually been changing her look, moving away from conservative floral dresses and skirts to the more fashionable cropped trousers and fitted tops. Tonight she was wearing a houndstooth checked coat over a fluffy cream jumper with black cigarette pants and flat patent leather shoes. Her hair was different too; instead of being tied up in her usual ponytail or bun it was swept back from her face with a cream-coloured bandeau. She was cool and fashionable, more swinging Soho than suburban London.

Joyce checked her reflection in the shop window.

'Do you like it? I saw a girl wearing something similar in the store the other day and I thought it would be perfect for tonight because I want to make a good impression.'

Emboldened by the privacy the shop doorway offered, Hubert encircled her in an embrace and pulled her towards him. 'The only person you need to make a good impression on is me,' he said, grinning, 'and you did that the moment me laid eyes on you!'

Joyce gave him a peck on the lips and surveyed him adoringly.

'I just want your friends to like me.'

'Don't worry about them. They'll love you, you'll see. Now

let's tidy ourselves up and get going, otherwise we'll be late.'

It had been six weeks since Hubert and Joyce had shared their first kiss and since that day the relationship had gone from strength to strength. While careful to keep their distance at work, the two made the most of every opportunity they had to spend time alone together during the working week, whether it was forgoing lunch in the works canteen in exchange for a shared sandwich on a park bench, or a quick after-work cup of tea in an anonymous café in the back end of nowhere. At the weekends they went to what was fast becoming 'their' picture house to see whatever was playing, followed by coffee and cake in a tearoom or if the weather was half decent, a walk in St James's Park. To them it didn't really matter what they did, because as long as they were in each other's company they were happy.

Of all the dark clouds that loomed on their horizon, however, the darkest and most significant was the matter of Joyce's parents. 'I think my dad would have a heart attack if he ever found out about us,' she said to him one day as they sat eating lunch in a tiny neglected square a few streets behind Hamilton's. 'And if he didn't, Mum certainly would. They're always going on about "darkies this" and "darkies that" as if West Indians are to blame for everything that's wrong in the world. It drives me up the wall so much, I almost want to scream at them: 'I'm seeing one of those "darkies" you keep talking about and let me tell you he's the sweetest, kindest bloke you'll ever meet and more of a gentleman than any of the English boys I've ever stepped out with!'

Walking side by side past groups of young couples heading out for a night of dancing, older wealthier types making their way to dinner at one of the swanky hotels or restaurants, tooth-less old men singing with their hats held out, hoping for a penny for a cup of tea, and families loaded down with shopping bags, waiting for buses to take them home, Hubert and Joyce picked their way through the bustling streets to the underground. Here they bought two tickets from the seller at the booth, before they descended to their chosen platform on the Victoria Line. Boarding the first south-bound train that came along, they got off at Brixton, and it was here and only here that they finally relaxed enough to hold hands as they made their way to their destination for the evening, the Princess Club on Acre Lane.

The Princess Club was a former private members club that had struggled to stay open after the war. Desperate to make ends meet, the owners had become one of the first in the area to not only forgo operating a colour bar but also employ West Indian staff, and because of this, it had quickly become a mainstay for the immigrant community. Gus had been going to the club ever since his arrival in London and had been on at Hubert to join him for months, but Hubert had always been either too busy or too broke to go. So when Hubert told Gus he would like his friend to meet Joyce, it had seemed like the perfect opportunity to kill two birds with one stone.

Although it was only a little after seven o'clock as Hubert and Joyce descended the steps into the club, once inside it seemed more like midnight. The place was packed full of young people, dancing shoulder to shoulder to the band playing on the stage. Most of the crowd were black, with a few white faces here and there, but here race didn't seem to matter, you just were. The music the band was playing – covers of all the latest rhythm and blues hits – was so infectious that Hubert immediately started dancing and Joyce, although a little unsure at first, joined in too.

As they swayed in time to the music, she mirrored his actions, swinging her arms and bending at the waist. Within a few songs however, she was so confident that she was improvising moves of her own, a side step here, a little knee-bend there. He closed his eyes, imagining for a moment that he was back home in Jamaica enjoying a night out with friends. Here he wasn't an oddity or an exception, here he was just one of the crowd, a young person just like any other out for a good time.

They remained on the dance floor for a good hour, enjoying themselves so much that they didn't even bother getting a drink, and they only stopped when Hubert felt a tap on his shoulder and turned around to see Gus's grinning face looking back at him.

'Smiler, man!' exclaimed Gus loudly over the music. He wrapped his friend in a massive bear hug. 'You're looking sharp!'

Hubert glowed with pride. He'd made an even greater effort with his appearance than usual and was not only wearing his Sunday best suit and freshly polished shoes but also a brand new trilby hat, a dove-grey number with a wide black grosgrain ribbon, that he'd purchased from a gentlemen's outfitters that very afternoon.

'Thanks, man!' Hubert bellowed. 'You're not looking so bad yourself! Let me introduce you to my girl, Joyce.' He turned and grabbed Joyce's hand and led her forwards.

'So lovely to meet you, Gus!' she called over the music. 'Hubert has told me all about you!'

She held out her hand for Gus to shake, but instead he flashed her one of his hundred-watt smiles and before she knew what was happening he had whisked her up into his arms in a hug that quite took her breath away. 'This is how we say hello to friends in the West Indies!' he joked, before returning her to the ground. He planted a kiss on Joyce's cheek. 'Any friend of Smiler's is a friend of mine!'

Imagining they were done with introductions, Hubert began moving towards the bar so that he could get them all drinks but Gus stopped him. 'Where you going?' he said, placing one of his huge hands on Hubert's shoulder. 'There's somebody I want you to meet.'

Hubert followed his friend's gaze to a young woman standing behind him. She was tall and well dressed in a cream short-sleeved blouse and navy swing skirt, a frothy white petticoat just showing beneath. She had beautiful flawless brown skin and eyes that seemed to smile even when she wasn't. She looked like a fashion model, or a film star, and Hubert instinctively felt that he ought to bow before speaking to her and only just stopped himself.

'Smiler.' Gus beamed at his friend. 'This is Lois. Lois, this is Smiler, my best friend in the whole wide world, and his girl, Joyce.'

They tried to talk for a little while but it soon became clear that a decent conversation was going to be difficult over the music and so instead they moved away from the dance floor, found an empty table to sit at, and then the men took drinks orders and headed to the bar.

'Well, Smiler,' said Gus as they stood waiting to be served, 'what do you think of her? She sure is something, isn't she? I know it's early days but I think she might be the one, you know?'

Hubert was used to hearing Gus eulogising over women. He'd been exactly the same back home. Every week it was one girl or another who was the object of Gus's affections, only for him to move on when the next 'prettiest girl ever' came along. But Gus had been talking about Lois for a long time now, and the fact that she had appeared impervious to his charms had only stoked the fires of his desire.

'So when did this happen? I thought she wasn't interested.'

'She wasn't. But you know,' Gus added slyly, 'I always gets what I want in the end.' He laughed that deep laugh of his again. 'I was here last weekend with some of the guys from work and who should walk in but Lois. We got talking, I gave her a bit of the old Gus magic, added in a few lines of Shakespeare, showed her my moves on the dance floor and well . . .' He paused and gave a little flourish. '. . . she couldn't resist!'

As they both burst out laughing the barmaid came to take their order and while she prepared their drinks, the two friends continued their conversation.

'And what about you, Smiler?' Gus slapped his friend on the back in a congratulatory manner. 'You've done well there friend, your Joyce is a cracker.'

'Me know,' said Hubert. He couldn't help but smile to himself. 'Me the luckiest man in the world.'

Gus glanced in the direction of Lois.

'Second luckiest!'

Hubert put a hand on his old friend's shoulder.

'Gus, man, me pleased for you, really pleased, but can me give you some advice?'

'If I say no will it make any difference?'

Hubert smiled. 'Don't let this one get away. Don't mess things up the way you always do, chasing all the girls around town, okay?'

With mock seriousness Gus placed a hand across his heart. 'Smiler, man, you have my word!'

The next hour was a blur of drinking, chatting and dancing. Hubert discovered that once she'd relaxed, Joyce was something of a natural when it came to dancing, quickly picking up moves that he himself had yet to master, just by watching the other girls around them on the dance floor and doing what they did. It felt good to see her so carefree and happy, not always looking over her shoulder, able to be who she wanted to be with him, and do what she wanted to do. During fast songs they danced with exuberance and energy, barely a hair's breadth between them, and during the slower songs the distance between them all but disappeared as she draped her arms about his neck as they danced, hip to hip, swaying in time with the music.

Having danced non-stop for over an hour, Joyce gestured to Hubert that she needed some air and leaving their friends behind, the two of them climbed the stairs and made their way outside the club and, leaning against the window of the launderette next door, they both caught their breath and cooled down in the chill of the late spring evening.

'Gus is so funny,' said Joyce, fanning her face with her hand, 'and Lois is pretty and lovely with it. Have they been an item long?'

Hubert shook his head.

'Gus has been crazy about her for a while but me think she's been wary until now.'

'Because he's such a charmer?'

'Me love him like a brother, but that boy doesn't know what's good for him. Him always have one eye on the next thing.'

'Well, he certainly seems happy right now,' she said, and then smiled and added, 'Nowhere near as happy as us, though.' Putting her arms around Hubert's neck, Joyce leaned in and they kissed, one long slow passionate kiss after another, as they both revelled in this opportunity to let themselves go. It was like nothing else existed, nothing except the two of them and the feelings they had for one another.

Afterwards they held each other close and as Hubert wondered if this might be the right time to tell Joyce that he loved her he felt her tense, an expression of horror on her face as she turned his body towards her and hid behind him. Scanning the area, all Hubert could see was an excited group of university students, two men and two women emerging from a taxi. At first nothing about the scene seemed out of the ordinary, but then Hubert noticed that the cab driver was looking over in their direction intently, shaking his head, his eyes narrowed in disgust. After a few moments, he wound down his window and spat on to the road and then, casting one last loathing glance at Hubert, drove off.

'Has he gone?' asked Joyce, ashen faced and shaking as she clung to him.

'Who was it?'

'Do you think he saw us?'

'Who?'

'The cabbie.'

Hubert shrugged. 'He was giving me filthy looks, but what's new about an Englishman doing that? Who was it?'

Joyce leaned forwards, her hands on her knees. She seemed as if she were about to pass out or be sick.

'Who was it, Joyce? Just tell me.'

She took a deep breath.

'One of my dad's friends from the Connie club. His name's Al, he and my dad go back a long way, they were in the same regiment together during the war. He's got a mouth like the Mersey Tunnel so if he did see me, that'll be me pretty much done for.'

It was Hubert's turn to feel sick, not on his behalf, but on Joyce's.

'Me pretty sure he didn't see you. It's dark, he was across the road and anyway you look so different tonight me doubt he would have recognised you.'

Joyce looked up at Hubert, eyes full of tears.

'Do you really think so?'

'Absolutely certain.'

'I suppose you might be right,' said Joyce, her voice taking on a note of relief. 'Al's not exactly backwards in coming forwards, if you know what I mean. If he'd been sure it was me he wouldn't have been able to stop himself from charging over, giving you a good hiding and dragging me all the way back home to tell Dad what he'd seen.' Hubert put his arms around Joyce to comfort her but it seemed to make things worse. She started to cry. 'I hate this,' she said between sobs, 'I hate this so much. Why should anyone care what colour your skin is, when underneath it all you're the same as me?'

As he held her Hubert thought about a Charles Dickens book he had to read at school, *A Tale of Two Cities*. The tale of a man who gave up his own life for the woman he loved just so that she could be happy. At the time he had thought the idea nonsense – how could the man ever be happy knowing that he'd never be with his girl again? – but in this moment Hubert finally understood the character's motivation. In this moment he knew that he too would do anything, absolutely anything to prevent his girl from enduring pain no matter what the cost to himself.

'Joyce,' he began as a group of jovial young men congregated at the entrance to the club, their laughter at odds with the gravity of the situation. 'It's not what me want at all, and it won't be easy but me can't stand seeing you like this. Me can't stand that you're the one who is having to bear the load. So . . . if you want to stop seeing me, you can.'

Joyce looked up at him with eyes full of love. She placed a finger on his lips and smiled. 'Never,' she said. 'Never.'

With Ashleigh sitting at his kitchen table and Layla playing at her feet with a bemused Puss, Hubert took the opportunity to leave his guests, hang up his hat and coat in the hallway and think about this new situation. Other than the man who came to read his gas and electric meters back in February, no one had crossed his threshold all year. It felt odd having someone else in his own private space, as if they had entered his mind too, free to open cupboards and riffle through drawers both real and metaphorical.

Returning to the room, Hubert made two mugs of tea, and poured pineapple juice into a third mug that he handed to Layla. The child took the heavy vessel from him solemnly and would've attempted to drink from it had Ashleigh not immediately plucked it from her grasp.

'I think she probably needs something smaller,' she explained. After a few moments digging around in the basket underneath Layla's buggy, she finally withdrew a pink plastic two-handled cup with a lid on, poured a tiny bit of the juice into the water within, gave it a swirl and handed it to her daughter. 'Toddlers can't have too much juice. It's bad for their teeth.'

Shrugging, as he recalled happily giving bright orange cordial to both of his children without there being any adverse effects, Hubert reached into the cupboard above the toaster, took out a biscuit barrel, shook half a dozen biscuits carefully on to a plate and then handed Ashleigh her mug of tea.

'Right then,' he said, 'my Joyce always used to insist that guests were entertained in the front room so let's go in there.'

Feeling as though he was having an out-of-body experience,

Hubert led Ashleigh and Layla out of the kitchen, back along the hallway and into the front room. Much like the rest of the house, the front room, though clean and tidy, was somewhat dated. The ceiling was artexed with a swirling circular pattern painted magnolia, the wallpaper was pale green with an embossed motif of dark green fern leaves, the overstuffed sofa and two armchairs were covered in a beige velour fabric the like of which hadn't been manufactured in at least thirty years.

In one corner of the room stood a small bookcase and in another a china cabinet that was crammed full of delicate cups, saucers and plates that Hubert could only remember using a handful of times. The walls and mantelpiece were decorated with a series of family photographs, framed prints of country scenes and decorative plates.

Placing his mug and the biscuits on the tiled coffee table in the centre of the room, Hubert took a seat in the armchair nearest the fireplace and gestured to Ashleigh and Layla to take the sofa opposite.

'It's a lovely home you've got here,' remarked Ashleigh, pulling some tiny plastic ponies with rainbow-coloured hair out of her handbag and handing them to Layla. 'Have you lived here long?'

Hubert smiled. Although dates and times were hard to recall these days, the day he and Joyce moved to Park Avenue wasn't one he would ever forget. 'Since August 27th 1964,' said Hubert proudly. 'It was a proper old wreck but though it took a lot of time and effort, my Joyce soon made it a lovely home.'

'Is that you and Joyce there?' asked Ashleigh, gesturing towards a silver framed wedding photo on the mantel featuring a handsome suited black man standing next to a young white woman in a beautifully simple dress.

'That's us all right. One of the best days of my life.'

'Aww! That's lovely. She looks well lush. A right catch.'

Hubert smiled fondly. 'That she was.'

'Oh, I'm sorry. How long has it been since you lost her?'

'Coming up to thirteen years now.'

'I bet you still miss her, don't you?'

Hubert smiled sadly at the picture on the mantelpiece. 'Every day. Every single day.'

There was a moment of silence that threatened to turn towards the melancholy, then Hubert said, 'Me tell you now if you'd visited when Joyce was alive you wouldn't have to be putting up with supermarket own-brand biscuits! My Joyce was a fantastic cook! She could make anything from a Victoria sponge to a beef Wellington. And she was a quick learner too. After West Indian friends of mine showed her how, she could rustle up some of the best Caribbean dishes me ever tasted! Rice and peas, ackee and saltfish, you name it, my Joyce could do the lot!'

'She sounds amazing,' said Ashleigh. Her gaze shifted to a framed portrait on the wall above the fireplace of a young woman wearing a graduation cap and gown.

Hubert was unable to hide the pride in his voice. 'That's my daughter Rose. She's a professor at the University of Melbourne in Australia.' Getting to his feet, he edged around Layla playing on the floor with her toys and made his way to the bookcase next to the fireplace. Sliding back one of the glass doors, he plucked three books from the top shelf and handed them to Ashleigh.

'My Rose wrote these. Them what they call . . . *academic* books.'

'*Political Ideology in the New Millennium*,' said Ashleigh, stumbling over the word 'millennium' so many times that in the end she gave up. 'She must be a right brainbox to write books like these, I can't even read the titles!'

'Me tried to read one once,' confessed Hubert, 'but me didn't get very far. Couldn't make head nor tail of it!' As Ashleigh flicked through one of the books, Hubert pointed out the dedication inside, which read, 'To Mum and Dad, who taught me how to think.' Hubert laughed. 'That's the one part of this book me never get tired of reading!'

Ashleigh returned the books to Hubert.

'You must be so proud.'

'Couldn't be prouder,' said Hubert. 'And me tell her so all the time.'

'Do you FaceTime?'

Hubert grimaced.

'You know, on the mobile or the computer?'

Hubert shook his head.

'Rose is always trying to talk me into getting one of them mobile phones or computers but me can't be bothered with all that stuff. It doesn't interest me. Anyway, she's coming home to visit in August. First time in a long while. She'd have come before now but she's very busy. Still, she always calls me every week without fail. She's a good girl, my Rose. Always looking out for her old dad.'

'Aww, she sounds lovely. Any grandkids? Great-grandkids?'

Hubert shrugged.

'She never find the right man at the right time. It's just one of those things, me suppose. You can't win them all.'

'Well,' said Ashleigh brightly, 'I can't wait to meet her and get some tips on how to inspire Layla. Who knows, if I play my cards right she might grow up to become a professor too!'

Hubert considered the little girl carefully. Never mind how long it had been since he'd had visitors in the house, how long had it been since there'd been a child here?

'Me think your daughter will be whatever she wants to be,' said Hubert as he returned the books carefully to the bookcase. 'That's the thing about kids . . .' He paused for a moment, remembering David. '. . . in the end they're going to go their own way. All you can really do is hope that whichever way they choose, it's in the right direction.'

Much to Hubert's surprise Ashleigh and Layla spent the whole of the afternoon sitting in his front room. He learned about Ashleigh's start in life growing up in a small mining village in Wales and how at the age of seventeen, using something called Facebook, she'd become friendly with a young man from London. 'He was dead funny to begin with,' she said, 'and so charming with it that I pretty much just fell for him. And living in London and DJing and stuff, he seemed really glamorous compared to all the boys in my little village. We did the long-distance thing for a bit but then one day I just thought, "Enough's enough!" and I jacked in my job and caught the train down here and that was that.'

'Leaving home is always difficult,' said Hubert. He thought not only of his own journey from Jamaica but also of Joyce's from the comfort of her family home in Bromley to a dingy boarding house in Brixton. Then of course there was Rose flying halfway around the world to start a new life in Australia.

'It was,' said Ashleigh, 'I missed home something dreadful at first. I missed my family and my friends, and you know, the closeness of it all. But I was in love, and I thought he loved me too, so I just got on with it. And when this one came along two years ago,' she leaned down and stroked the top of Layla's head tenderly, 'things were great, and I thought to myself, "This is it, Ashleigh Elizabeth Jones, this is your happy ending."'

'So what happened?'

Ashleigh sighed.

'I won't go into the details but it turns out he'd been having it away the whole time I'd been in London with – get this – the only girl down here that I felt close enough to call my best friend! I was proper devastated I was, and then he dropped the bomb that he'd got her pregnant too and I was like, "That's it, I've had enough. I'm out of here."

'I packed my bags and everything and I even bought a train ticket back home, but then as I was waiting for the taxi to take me and Layla to the station I thought to myself, "No, you are not going to just run back to south Wales with your tail between your legs! And you're not just going to sit here in Enfield feeling sorry for yourself either! You're going to make a fresh start, in a new area, make new friends and you're going to make a new life for you and your daughter."

'So that's exactly what I did. I kicked him out, applied for a flat swap through the housing association and three months later I was here, and now look at me! I've got a new flat, the chance of a job at the vet's, and to top it all, I've got you, Hubert Bird, my new friend! How's that for hitting the ground running?'

Hubert was not at all sure how to reply to her comment about them being friends. Granted, due to his lies about Dotty, Dennis and Harvey, and Rose's upcoming visit, he was in the market for new companions, but a young Welsh single mother certainly wasn't what he had in mind. He needed friends of his own age, friends who his daughter would think appropriate company for a man of his advanced years, not someone young enough to be his own granddaughter.

'Me think you're doing very well,' he said in the end, as it seemed the kindest thing to say under the circumstances. 'Me think you're doing very well indeed.'

They talked for a good while longer, mostly about the neighbourhood and how it had changed. 'These days the neighbours are mostly all them . . . what you call them again? Yippies, or what have you . . . with them fancy suits and big cars,' Hubert had noted. Eventually, however, the conversation had drawn to a natural conclusion, Ashleigh had collected together the dirty plates and cups and insisted on washing them up, and then once they'd been dried and put away by Hubert, it was clear that their time together was over.

'Thanks again for everything.' Ashleigh leaned down to strap Layla back into her buggy. 'You really have been amazing.'

Hubert shrugged.

'It was nothing.'

Ashleigh regarded him intently.

'It was *not* nothing, Hubert Bird. At least not to me. London's a really big and scary place and as a single parent with no friends or family nearby it's easy to get lost and feel lonely.' Without fanfare she stepped towards him, threw her arms around him and hugged him with a ferocity that almost took his breath away.

Other than his GP, Dr Aziz, and the nurses who checked his blood pressure, Hubert hadn't felt the touch of another human being, let alone been hugged by one, in so long that he'd almost forgotten what it felt like. Moments later as he stood on the doorstep waving goodbye to his new neighbours, the embrace was all he could think about, and once he'd closed the door firmly behind him, he felt his legs buckling as tear after tear rolled down his cheeks. And in that moment, as he attempted to stem his tears, Hubert realised something he hadn't quite understood before now: he was lonely, really lonely and most likely had been for a very long time.

12

Then: August 1958

'Third floor needs these special deliveries going up, pronto,' shouted Mr Coulthard over the usual Monday morning hubbub, boxes being opened, cages loaded with stock, the telephone ringing non-stop.

'I'll take it,' said Kenneth, raising his hand.

'No, you won't,' replied Hubert. 'You've got enough to do. Me sort it out, Mr Coulthard.'

'Do I look like I care which one of you bleeders sorts it out?' snapped Mr Coulthard, exasperation heavy in his voice. 'Just stop dithering and get it done.'

Glaring at Kenneth, as it was likely to cause less trouble than glaring at Mr Coulthard, Hubert loaded the special deliveries into a cage and then made his way to the lift. Pushing the button for the third floor, he took a moment to smooth down his hair and straighten his tie. It felt like for ever since he'd seen Joyce, even though it had only been Friday. They'd met up for lunch in their favourite square and it had been on the way back to work that Joyce had told him she wouldn't be able to come out on Saturday night. 'I've got family coming over for my niece's christening,' she'd explained. 'A whole load of aunties and uncles and they're staying for the weekend.' Though disappointed, Hubert had tried his best to hide it, not wanting her to feel guilty for not seeing him, and told her that they would make up for lost time in the coming week. So when Monday came around, he had been so desperate for a glimpse of her that he had jumped at every opportunity to visit the third floor, but he had yet to catch sight of her.

As the lift came to a halt, Hubert pulled back the door and

pushed out the cage, scanning the stockroom for Joyce, and this time was rewarded as she and Sue, another girl from her department, came through from the shop floor.

'Your delivery, ladies.' Hubert gave a comical bow. 'All present and correct.'

Sue giggled and playfully told Hubert off for flirting on work time but Joyce didn't even crack a smile.

Hubert began unloading the cage. 'Did you have a good weekend, girls? Get up to anything interesting?'

'I went to the pictures and saw that new one with Max Bygraves in it,' said Sue. 'It was ever so good.'

Hubert looked expectantly at Joyce but she said nothing.

'How about you, Hubert?' asked Sue. 'Did you do anything fun?'

'No, my girl was busy so me stayed in and saved my pennies so me can give her a real treat next weekend.'

'Lucky girl,' said Sue wistfully. 'I wish someone was saving their pennies to take me out at the weekend.' She smiled and added, 'Put in a good word with the boys downstairs for me, will you?'

Hubert took his time unloading the boxes, desperately hoping that Joyce might come up with a reason to send Sue on an errand, leaving the two of them alone, but she didn't. And now all that was left for him to do was leave.

'Right then,' said Hubert. He closed the door on the cage. 'That's me done.' He eyed Joyce carefully, hoping for a smile, a flicker of affection in her eyes, but there was nothing. Hubert was worried. Although it was an unspoken agreement that they would keep their distance at work, this coldness was new and strange and made him uneasy. He flashed her a look, one that desperately begged for some small recognition of who they were to each other, but none came.

'See you later,' called Sue over her shoulder. Hubert watched her and Joyce turn and walk away. 'And don't forget what I said about putting in a good word for me in the warehouse!'

As they left, Hubert told himself that everything was fine. She would come back in a minute. Explain that she had to act that way because some of the girls suspected something was going on between them. Or perhaps she was just tired after being with her family all weekend. Or maybe she'd just missed him so much that a casual smile or friendly wink would've seemed like too inadequate an expression of her true feelings. He stood there for five whole minutes in the silent stockroom, ears straining for the sound of her return, but she didn't come and as he entered the lift and closed the door behind him, a cold, slow fear began to take hold. Something was wrong. Something was very wrong. And it took until after work that evening for Hubert to find out what it was.

'I think . . . I think . . . I'm pregnant,' stammered Joyce.

They were sitting on what had become their bench in their square. It overlooked a small rose garden, the flowers of which were in full bloom in the summer heat. They had the square to themselves with the exception of an elderly man across from them who had fallen asleep and a young, smartly dressed woman wearing sunglasses walking a tiny dog.

'You're . . .' Hubert struggled to find the words to finish his response. '. . . you're absolutely sure?'

Joyce nodded, keeping her eyes fixed to the ground. 'I missed my monthlies for the third time in a row, and I've already started putting on weight.'

Hubert's temples began to throb and he could feel his blood rushing through his veins.

'But me thought we'd been careful.'

Joyce shrugged. 'Well, not careful enough it seems.'

There was a long pause. Hubert couldn't think through the implications of what he was hearing because the roaring sound in his ears was making it difficult to think of anything at all. The man across the way woke suddenly as a mischievous young boy broke free from his mother's grasp and ran into the square towards a flock of feeding pigeons, sending them into the air with a loud beating of wings.

'How long have you known?'

'I've been worried about it for a while. I've just been praying that it wasn't true. It wasn't until last week I was really sure. That's why I didn't come out on Saturday.' She started to get upset. 'I've tried everything, Hubert, hot baths, gin, every old wives' tale in the book.'

Hubert put an arm around Joyce's shoulders and pulled her towards him. 'Come now, don't you worry. Everything's going to be all right.'

Joyce wiped her eyes on the sleeve of her jacket. 'You don't know that. You can't possibly know that. What am I going to do, Hubert? My parents will throw me out on my ear the second they find out and I won't be able to keep it a secret for ever. Tell me, what am I going to do?'

Taking a few deep breaths to calm himself down, Hubert considered the question as best he could but he drew a blank.

'Me don't know.' Hubert drew her even closer to him. 'Me really don't know. The only thing me do know is we'll get through this together.'

They stayed in the square watching the world go by, barely saying a word for a good half-hour, before Joyce checked her watch and told Hubert she had to get home before her parents started to worry.

'At least let me walk you to your bus. Me hate seeing you upset like this.'

Joyce shook her head.

'There are too many people who could see us. And you know how they like to gossip. They'll see me upset and you with me, and put two and two together just like that. And before you know it, the whole world will know.' She stood up. 'No, let's say our goodbye here. It's for the best.'

Hubert couldn't help feeling that this wasn't any ordinary goodbye, but rather a final one, and it broke his heart that she might be thinking like this.

He put his arms around her and held her so tightly he could feel her heart beating against his chest.

'Me promise we'll be fine, Joyce,' whispered Hubert. 'We'll be fine.'

That night, Hubert turned up at Gus's lodgings and was relieved to find that his friend was not only home but also alone.

'Smiler, man! To what do I owe the honour?'

'Me need advice,' said Hubert shakily, 'and me need it fast. Joyce is . . . well she is in the family way, if you know what me mean.'

After standing in the doorway for a second in stunned silence, Gus ushered Hubert inside his room. Sitting him down on a chair next to the fireplace, he reached under his bed and fetched out a half-drunk bottle of rum and grabbed two chipped enamel mugs from the shelf over the sink. He poured them both a generous measure and then sat down heavily on the chair oppos-ite. Once they'd both taken a fortifying sip, Gus asked Hubert to tell him what had happened from beginning to end.

'Well, Smiler,' he said as Hubert finished, 'the good news is that you aren't the first man this kind of thing happen to, and I doubt you'll be the last. But if it's advice you want, the way I see it you have three options: one, see if Joyce can get rid of the baby somehow.'

'Me can't ask her to do that and anyway me wouldn't want to, it's not right.'

'Cha man! It doesn't have to be in the way you're thinking. You could have the child adopted.'

'And have my own flesh and blood brought up by a stranger or even worse stuck in a children's home?' Hubert shook his head in disgust. 'Me couldn't live with myself if me did that.'

Gus sighed. 'Then just run for your life! If not back to Jamaica then maybe Birmingham or Manchester? I hear there's plenty of work there, just like London.'

Hubert reached for the rum and topped up his mug. 'Me can't abandon Joyce like that. That girl is my life. Me love her more than anything. Me can't just leave her when she need me most.'

Gus snorted, took the rum from Hubert and refilled his own mug. 'Right then, all that's left is for you to marry her! But mark my words, love will be no use to no one when the two of you are living in a tiny room with a screaming pickney and not two pennies to rub together because only one of you is working!' He shook his head. 'Smiler, man, the deed is done. There's nothing you can do now to change things, so what good is both your lives being ruined? Take it from me, Joyce's parents might be vex with her when they find out but you know what these English people them like, they look after their own. They'll come round and she'll be fine, just you wait and see.'

Hubert gulped back his rum in one go, causing his throat to burst into flames. The pain felt right, exactly what he deserved under the circumstances. How could he have been such a damn fool not to think something like this might happen? Gus had painted such a bleak picture of the future. Under these circumstances Hubert couldn't imagine how either of them could ever be happy, even if they were to stay together. Surely their love would turn into resentment when faced with the realities of raising a child with no money and no family to help. Hubert couldn't bear the thought of it, but equally the prospect of life without Joyce seemed just as impossible to contemplate. It was a no-win situation. He was damned if he did and damned if he didn't.

Gus refilled their mugs again, then lifted his as if about to make a toast. 'Drink up, we're not going to fix this problem today.'

It was late when Hubert finally left, having helped Gus not only finish off the half bottle of rum but also make a sizeable dent in a second. Waving goodbye to his friend, Hubert staggered out of the road, briefly enjoying the sweet relief the alcohol offered from his problems. At the same time, however, he was keenly aware that when the rum wore off, not only would his problems be there, but he would have a king-sized hangover to deal with too.

In a bid to lift his spirits, Hubert began singing calypso tunes one after the other, songs that spoke of love gone wrong, of hearts broken and joyous reunions. As he turned into his road, singing loudly enough to wake the neighbours, he saw Joyce. She was standing outside his lodgings, a suitcase at her feet.

'I . . . I . . . told my parents.'

Shocked, Hubert walked towards her and took her hand.

'My mum guessed and so I told them about the baby and about you. My dad was so angry he packed my bag and threw me out. I've got nowhere else to go.'

'That's not true, you've got me.' Letting go of her hand, Hubert reached into his jacket pocket, took out a small velvet box and then unsteadily got down on one knee. 'Me been carrying this round for weeks waiting for the right moment, but me wanted to do things properly, to ask your father for your hand first, but it wasn't to be.' He took the ring, the ring he had bought back in June that cost every last bit of his savings, and slipped it on to her finger.

'Joyce Anne Pierce, would you do me the honour of being my wife? And not because of the baby, and not because you have nowhere else to go, but because me don't want to waste another single minute without you.'

13

Now

When Hubert had woken up that morning he'd been well aware that with Rose's visit now just over three months away he really should be doing something, anything, to make some new friends. But at a loss as to what to do, all the odd jobs he had been putting off for months suddenly became pressingly urgent. And so it was that he found himself clearing out the drawers in the sideboard in the front sitting room.

It had taken him a good hour to go through the contents, file what needed to be filed and shred what needed to be shredded. And now here he was, faced with a large pile of items that didn't belong in the drawers but which he didn't feel right about getting rid of either. For instance, there were a couple of David's old school reports, a receipt from the undertaker for Joyce's funeral and several years' worth of Father's Day cards from Rose. And that was only the items on top of the pile.

He picked up one of the school reports and flicked it open to the first page, which read: 'David is a pleasant, intelligent and engaged member of the class and has settled in well to senior school life. He has excelled both academically and on the sporting field and I have no doubt that he will continue to build on this early success and go far! Well done, David!'

Hubert tried to read the name of the teacher but struggled to decipher the signature. Did it say Harris or Hughes? He wasn't sure, but before he could decide for certain the doorbell rang.

Heading to the bay window, Hubert carefully edged aside the net curtains just enough to determine who was at the door. Much to his surprise, he saw that it was Ashleigh and Layla.

It had been a week since that day when he'd helped them out.

A week since they had brought light and laughter into a home that had been without either for a very long time. Moreover, it had been just seven days since that moment when it had struck him, as if by a lightning bolt, that despite his unspoken conviction he was self-sufficient, he was in fact undeniably lonely.

'I got the job!' screamed Ashleigh excitedly. 'Can you believe it? I got the job and it's all because of you!' Without fanfare she thrust the large Tupperware box she was holding towards him. 'Layla and I spent all morning making this to celebrate!'

Hubert peered down through the semi-transparent lid and discerned some sort of cake.

'You look after that.' She tapped the top of the box. 'And I'll pop the kettle on, shall I?'

Hubert glanced at the cake, then at Ashleigh, then Layla, who beamed a smile at him. His gut instinct was to shoo them out of the house and close the door behind them but then he recalled that moment again. The moment it had dawned on him that he wasn't an island. That, in spite of himself, he missed the company of other human beings. No, he wasn't really in the mood for cake, company or conversation but he had to acknowledge that this was something he needed, even if it wasn't necessarily what he wanted.

He stood aside to let them both in.

'Tea with two sugars please,' he said, 'and not too much milk.'

While Ashleigh put the kettle on, Layla stroked Puss, who had just come in from the garden. Hubert busied himself fetching plates and napkins out from the cupboard and arranging them on the kitchen table. Despite his initial reluctance, he had to admit that it felt good to have company again. He didn't even mind that Ashleigh talked non-stop. In the time it took her to make a pot of tea and pour it into two mugs, Hubert had learned about the beverage preferences of her entire extended family and their favourite biscuits too.

Hubert gestured to the alarmingly yellow, slightly lopsided Victoria sponge cake on the table between them.

'Well, this looks lovely. You want me to cut it?'

'Go on, then,' said Ashleigh. 'Then we can all taste it together at the same time.'

Hubert cut three slices, shared them around and then on Ashleigh's count took a bite. He had never tasted anything quite so foul in his life but politeness prevented him from spitting it out. He glanced at Ashleigh.

'This is horrible, isn't it?' she said, her mouth full of cake. 'Spit it out before it kills you!'

Relieved to have her permission, Hubert did as instructed while she quickly snatched away Layla's slice before her daughter could take a bite.

'I must have made a mistake with the recipe,' she said sadly. 'Put in too much baking powder or left out some ingredient or other. It was meant to be a thankyou not a death threat. I bet your Joyce could make a Victoria sponge that didn't taste like . . . you know . . . an actual sponge.'

'Not everybody can be good at everything,' said Hubert diplomatically. 'When me was a child my mother would always say to me, "Hubert, the good Lord gave us all different talents," and she was right. You just have to find your thing.'

Ashleigh shrugged, unconvinced.

'I just wanted to do something nice for you, that's all.'

'And you have. What is it them always say? It's the thought that counts.'

Layla began to cry, only now mourning the loss of the cake that she had been saved from eating.

'I think she's hungry, poor thing.'

Ashleigh glanced at the clock on the wall, picked Layla up from the chair and put her on her lap.

'It's nearly lunchtime, but I left the kitchen in such a state that I can't face going back and tidying up on an empty stomach.'

Hubert went to the cupboard and took out his biscuit barrel, which he hadn't yet got around to replenishing after their last visit.

'There's a couple of Rich Teas and half a bourbon, if she's interested.'

Ashleigh fished out a biscuit and, handed it to Layla but then suddenly her eyes widened as if she'd had an idea.

'Hubert . . . grab your coat,' she said. 'We're going to McDonald's.'

Hubert hesitated. His immediate reaction to Ashleigh's suggestion was to politely decline. After all, what was the point? She'd already thanked him more than enough for helping her out. And anyway, he had never been a fan of fast food. He had a faint recollection of Rose and David asking to be taken to a Wimpy bar back in the Seventies but he and Joyce hadn't liked the idea of it. She and Hubert preferred their food slow, unprocessed and tasty, which was why the fast-food revolution of the past thirty years had passed him by.

'Fine,' he said, reasoning that if he didn't let his neighbour pay him back this way, she might very well attempt to bake another cake. 'Just give me a minute to get ready.'

The journey into Bromley flew by with Ashleigh talking non-stop: about her new job, about the perils of baking and how the day before yesterday she'd got lost for three hours after taking the wrong bus home from town.

'Still,' she concluded as they finally reached their destination, 'like my nan used to say, "Sometimes the best way to get to know a new place is to get lost in it."'

Hubert followed Ashleigh into the busy restaurant and the three of them squeezed into what looked like the last empty booth and made themselves comfortable. He looked around him. It was too busy, too noisy and worse still the seats were hard.

'So, what do you fancy?'

Hubert shrugged.

'Me don't mind.'

Ashleigh rolled her eyes. This was clearly the wrong answer.

'What do you mean you don't mind, Hubert? You can literally have anything you want!'

Although Hubert doubted he could *literally* have whatever he wanted, it was difficult to make any sort of choice given that he didn't know exactly what they served.

'Do they have a menu?'

Ashleigh laughed.

'Have you never been to a McDonald's before? They don't really do menus as such. Not like ones you'd get at a restaurant.'

'Then how you know what to have?'

'It's all on boards at the front above the checkout and those big computer things over there,' she said, pointing to the tall touch screens on the other side of the restaurant.

'Me see,' said Hubert, wishing that he'd stuck with Rich Tea biscuits. 'Can't me just have what you're having?'

'No, I want you to have something *you* like. I told you this is my treat, my way of saying thank you. Now, I know this is difficult for you because you've never been here before so let's start with the basics: beef, chicken or fish?'

'Beef,' said Hubert.

'Good, now we're getting somewhere. That means you'll be having a burger. Now what sort of burger do you think you'd like? They do plain burgers, burgers with cheese, burgers with an extra burger, and burgers with cheese *and* bacon. If you're feeling really hungry they do bigger burgers, double bigger burgers or bigger burgers on a brioche bun, which I won't lie to you aren't my favourite.'

The range of options made Hubert's head swim.

'The one with cheese and bacon. Me like the sound of that.'

'Brilliant. And to drink? They do lattes, flat whites, hot chocolates, espressos, ice coolers, frappés, tea, milkshakes, fruit smoothies, Coke, Sprite, Fanta, fruit juice, still water or sparkling.'

'Just a cuppa, please.'

'Are you sure? Their vanilla milkshakes are proper lush like, I promise. Imagine drinking half a tub of nearly melted ice cream. It's a bit like that.'

Hubert didn't really like the sound of drinking half-melted ice cream but he reasoned he didn't have to drink it if he didn't like it and could always have a brew when he got home.

'Okay,' he said. 'Me try one of them.'

'Great, so that's a Chicken Legend, fries and a banana milkshake for me, a chicken nugget Happy Meal and an orange Fruit Shoot for Layla, and a bacon double cheeseburger with fries and a vanilla milkshake for you.'

While Ashleigh queued for the food, Hubert and Layla amused themselves playing an extended game of peek-a-boo, which, it turned out, Hubert was rather good at. Every time he hid his face and then revealed it Layla was in fits of giggles, which attracted the attention of some children stationed at a bank of iPads across from them. Soon these children were laughing at Hubert's antics too and only stopped when a harassed-looking Ashleigh returned with their food.

'It's absolutely rammed in here,' she said, setting down the tray and sharing out the various containers and boxes on it.

Hubert opened his cardboard container and stared at the burger within. He was unsure of what exactly to make of it, and even less certain when he asked Ashleigh where his knife and fork were, only for her to laugh.

She indicated towards the food.

'You use your hands, Hubert. Like a sandwich.'

Gripping it carefully in two hands, he lifted it to his lips and took a tentative bite. Given that his expectations were low he was pleasantly surprised, as he was with the meal as a whole. The meat was tasty, the things she insisted on calling fries even though they were clearly chips were hot and salty, and just as she'd described, the milkshake was like drinking half-melted ice cream, only better.

He contemplated his burger.

'What you call this thing again?'

'A bacon double cheeseburger. Why, don't you like it?'

'Like it?' Hubert grinned. 'Me love it! Tastiest food me have in a long while.'

As he finished off his fries and pretended to listen to Ashleigh tell a long and involved story that was either about an overweight German shepherd or possibly a dog and its overweight German owner, Hubert's thoughts turned to his last conversation with Rose. It pained him that he was still having to lie to her, but with no friends to speak of and his failed attempt to visit the O-60 still fresh in his mind, he was at a loss what to do next. August was now just over three months away, which was really no time at all.

As he considered the young woman sitting opposite, an idea struck him. Here was Ashleigh miles away from home, having plucked herself out of trouble and now busily making a fresh start. Unlike Hubert, Ashleigh was willing to try new things, talk to new people and go to new places. In short, she was open to life and all its possibilities in a way he himself hadn't been in a very long time. If he was to have any hope of making new friends, he was going to have to take a leaf out of his neighbour's book. He was going to have to be more open. He was going to have to be more Ashleigh.

14

Then: September 1958

Since arriving in England back in February, Hubert had felt out of place in a whole host of locations in the mother country, everywhere from the streets around Mayfair through to the pubs of east London and beyond. But as he stepped off the 09.20 from London Victoria that Saturday morning, all previous experiences paled in comparison to how he felt standing on platform two of Bromley South Station.

He felt like a character from one of the Westerns he enjoyed seeing at the pictures, not the hero, cowboy or sheriff, but rather the stranger in town. The man who walks into a bar full of life, music and chatter, only for the whole room to fall into a complete and uneasy silence the moment they notice his presence. As he made his way to the exit, he could feel eyes on him from every direction. Hubert didn't let the stares and whispers put him off. He was a man with a mission, a very clear mission, and he didn't have time to mess around or allow himself to be diverted. He was here to talk Joyce's family round, to get them to see sense before it was too late, because if they didn't, in a few short hours they would miss their one and only opportunity to see her getting married to the man she loved.

It had been a tough few weeks since Joyce had arrived on his doorstep with her suitcase. That first night she had spent cradled in his arms sobbing, neither of them sure what to do next. But then as a second night followed and a third and Hubert's Polish landlady began to make grumbling noises about her lodgings not being 'that kind of establishment', new plans had to be made. The following day, having persuaded the landlady to let Joyce stay, Hubert moved back in with Gus, sleeping top-to-tail in his lumpy old bed again.

As the days wore on, Hubert and Joyce tried their best to carry on as normal, going to work and pretending that they barely knew each other, even though they were both keenly aware that Joyce's pregnancy couldn't be kept a secret for ever. An unmarried pregnant woman working in the haberdashery department of a prestigious store like Hamilton's would be outrageous enough, but the fact that the father was Hubert, a black man fresh from the West Indies, would be unconscionable.

In the meantime, they made plans to make good on Hubert's proposal as soon as they could, making an appointment at the register office, and having their banns published. The only good news was that as Joyce was twenty-one and therefore of age, she didn't require her parents' permission to get married, which was, as she said, just as well. There had been no mistaking the sadness in her eyes as she said it, and it was then that Hubert made up his mind that he would make every effort to convince her family to see sense and change their minds. That night he tried to write a letter to her parents but gave up after several attempts, plagued as he was by the memory of the vile things Joyce had told him they had said about her. In the end he decided that of all Joyce's family, the one most likely to come around was her sister Peggy, who had at least responded to letters his fiancée had sent. He hadn't said a word to anyone about it, but this was why he was here in Bromley on his wedding day instead of getting ready for the celebrations with Gus, his best man. He was here because he loved Joyce and knew just how much family meant to her, and he couldn't bear the thought of this, her special day, being ruined by their absence.

Outside the station, Hubert got his bearings, checked his A–Z and started walking in the direction of Peggy's address that he'd secretly copied from one of the letters he had posted for Joyce.

It was a glorious day, a perfect day for a wedding, and aside from the constant stares of strangers and abuse yelled from the open window of a passing car, Hubert's journey was pleasant enough and in less than fifteen minutes he had arrived at his destination, 16 St Peter's Avenue.

As he knocked on the door it occurred to Hubert that he hadn't really thought his plan through. While Peggy herself might have been the most amenable member of Joyce's family, that didn't mean she would be pleased to see him on her doorstep, or indeed that her husband wouldn't take it upon himself to administer a beating on behalf of the wider family. As he heard the sound of footsteps in the hallway, he braced himself for whatever was to come and whispered a prayer of thanks for the fact that he had had the foresight not to wear his wedding suit.

The door opened to reveal a woman who was unmistakably Joyce's sister, albeit older and thicker-set. She stood blinking at him for a moment, not speaking, and in that instant Hubert knew that she was aware of exactly who he was.

'Come in, before the neighbours see you.' She quickly scanned the street in both directions. 'The last thing I need is tongues wagging about you on my doorstep.'

Hubert did as he was instructed and, taking off his trilby, followed her into the sparsely furnished back room where a toddler was playing with some wooden blocks on the floor, while a baby lay fast asleep in a pram.

She sat down in an armchair next to the range over which hung a wooden rack of drying washing.

'Whatever it is you want, you'll have to be quick. My Bill will be back home soon and let me tell you now he won't take very kindly to you being in his house.'

Hubert took a seat in the armchair opposite her, even though he hadn't been invited to do so.

'It's about . . . it's about Joyce—'

She snorted scornfully.

'You don't say.'

'Look, me know—' He stopped and made an effort to modify his grammar, hoping it might persuade Peggy that they had more in common than she believed. '*I* know you don't approve of me but I've come all the way here today to appeal to your better nature and I'm begging you . . . pleading with you, please come and see your sister get married. You mean the world to Joyce, she told me so, and I know it would break her heart not to have you there.'

'Break her heart?' Her voice was raised. 'What about mine? What about our mum and dad's? What about our brothers'? Do you think our hearts aren't breaking too?'

The baby stirred and, getting to her feet, Peggy took hold of the handle and gently pushed the pram back and forth until the child settled again.

'We love each other,' said Hubert as Peggy returned to her seat. 'Doesn't that count for anything?'

'Well, let's see how far that love gets you when people are spitting at Joyce and her baby in the street.'

'There will always be ignorant people in this world but I will protect Joyce and our child 'til my dying breath.'

'And what about when you're at work? What about those early days when a young mother needs her family? She's got no one now because of you. She's on her own. Did you think about that?' She started to cry then, quietly at first, but increasing with intensity with each passing moment.

Hubert sat forward in his chair, desperate to comfort this poor woman, who was clearly suffering, but aware all the same that to touch her would only inflame matters. The toddler, seeing his mother upset, began to cry too, which was enough to break the spell, to bring her to her senses, and as she soothed her child she too calmed down.

'Look, I'm sorry you've had a wasted journey but you're going to have to go now.'

She rose to her feet, balancing the child on her hip.

'Thank you for your time,' said Hubert, getting to his feet, 'but please promise me you'll at least think about coming today.'

'I can't. My family would never forgive me. They've already been betrayed by one daughter, it would kill them to have it happen a second time.'

'So you're going to wash your hands of Joyce, your own flesh and blood, just because me got a different colour skin to you? Me made of flesh and blood just like you!'

'I don't make the rules.'

'No, you don't,' Hubert retorted, 'but you go along with them just fine, which in my eyes makes you just as bad.'

Blinking back the hurt and anger that threatened to overwhelm him, Hubert left Peggy's house, returned to the station and jumped on the first train to central London. The more distance he put between himself and Bromley, the lighter his mood became, and by the time he reached Brixton he had succeeded in pushing his encounter with Joyce's sister to the very back of his thoughts. Making his way through the streets of his neighbourhood, past English people at the bus queue, West Indians picking through goods on market stalls, Guyanans chatting on street corners and Jews returning from synagogue, a strange sensation settled on Hubert. In a way he'd never felt until this moment he realised that this place, with its strange mix of people, its problems and all its faults, was starting to feel a lot like home.

Heading to Gus's lodgings, Hubert opened the door to see his friend pacing up and down the hallway.

'Smiler, man! Where you been? When I got up this morning and saw you gone, I thought you'd got cold feet and run away on them!'

He decided that he would leave explanations for another day.

'Me just had a few errands to run but they're done now. Let's get me looking spick and span so me can marry that beautiful girl of my dreams.'

It was just after two thirty when Hubert and Gus arrived at Lambeth register office, both dressed in their finest suits, slim bow ties and formal gloves that Joyce had managed to get a discount on from Hamilton's. Hubert had barely had a chance to sit down in the waiting room before the doors swung open to reveal Lois and his bride-to-be.

Hubert was rendered momentarily speechless. Joyce looked stunning, in a knee-length cream dress that she had made for herself and which was cut in such a way as to disguise her growing baby bump. Her hair had been elaborately arranged and studded with pearls by Lois and the outfit was finished off with a small bouquet of pink carnations, a tribute to their first date, just four short months ago.

'You look . . . you look beautiful,' said Hubert, finding his voice. 'Absolutely beautiful.'

Grinning from ear to ear, Joyce plucked two carnations from the bunch and placed one carefully in the buttonhole of Hubert's jacket and then handed one to Lois so that she could do the same for Gus.

She stood back, taking in both the men.

'There,' she said finally, 'now you look perfect.'

The photographer, a Hungarian Jew called Mr Darvas, arrived minutes later from his studios just around the corner. Hiring a photographer had been a large expense, one that Hubert and Joyce could ill afford, but neither had wanted to forgo it. 'It'll be something to show our baby,' said Joyce. 'And something to show my family back home,' Hubert had added, hoping that it might go some way towards making up for the fact that there was no way they could have afforded to travel to England to attend the wedding, no matter how much they'd wanted to be there.

Mr Darvas led them all back outside for some formal photos before the ceremony began. Once they were done, they filed back inside just as the dozens of guests from the preceding ceremony were leaving. Hubert found it impossible not to compare the two events, the wedding of the previous couple attended by so many family and friends and his own, which only featured him, his bride-to-be, his best friend and best friend's girlfriend. They hadn't got the money to invite any more people and as it was, none of Joyce's friends or extended family would've come even if they had. As for Hubert, in his short time in England he had only come to know a handful of people, and they were more acquaintances than people you'd invite to a wedding, and so here it was, just the four of them.

He caught Joyce's eye and wondered whether she was disappointed but she smiled, and as if reading his thoughts, held out her hand and whispered, 'The only thing that matters is that you're here.'

With so few people in it, the room in which they were married seemed cavernous and impersonal, and without the hymns, prayers and solemn traditions of a church wedding, the ceremony was over all too quickly, and before they knew it, they were heading outside as man and wife.

Mr Darvas took several more photographs, formal portraits of the bride and groom, of the best man and bridesmaid, and of every conceivable combination of the quartet. He took so long over it and took so much care with each photograph that Hubert suspected he felt a little sorry for them and their poor show of a wedding party.

When he finished, Hubert thanked the photographer profusely and even invited him to join them at the Italian restaurant they had booked for dinner but he politely declined. 'You children go and enjoy yourselves,' he said, 'and I'll make sure that you have something to remember this special day with.'

At the restaurant, a tiny traditional establishment with red-and-white checked tablecloths and wax-encrusted wine bottles as candle holders, they filled their bellies with creamy pasta, fresh seafood and red wine. Afterwards Gus stood up, removed an envelope from his jacket and read out a letter from Hubert's mother that had arrived that very morning. She expressed her regret at not being able to be there in person but wished her son and his new bride all the very best for their future lives together.

'That was the most wonderful surprise,' Joyce said, wiping tears from her eyes. 'I can't wait until I get to meet her.'

Later that evening, as Gus and Lois flirted with each other by candlelight, Hubert and Joyce took the opportunity to enjoy a first dance as husband and wife when a small band consisting of an accordion and violin player began playing old Italian folk songs. They were the only people dancing, but they didn't seem to care, having, as they did, eyes only for each other.

Halfway through the song, Joyce lifted her head and smiled.

'It's been such a wonderful day, hasn't it?'

Hubert kissed her gently on the forehead.

'I just wish you could have had your family here with you.'

Joyce tilted her gaze to the small bump just visible under her dress and patted it fondly.

'It doesn't matter any more.' She paused a moment, then her eyes met Hubert's. 'You're my family now.'

15

Now

'Nice weather we're having, isn't it?'

The elderly Indian man standing in the bus queue in front of Hubert turned and faced him.

'I'm sorry, did you say something?'

Hubert wanted the earth to open up and swallow him. Why was the man speaking so loudly? Hubert had only wanted a polite conversation about how warm it was and how they'd said on the radio that morning that it could be the hottest summer for thirty years. Now everyone in the queue behind him would be listening in to every word.

'He was talking about the weather being nice!' shouted the man's wife into her husband's ear.

'Yes!' said the man a little too loudly, 'it *is* lovely weather we're having!'

The man's wife raised an eyebrow wearily at Hubert and followed up with an apologetic smile.

'I'm afraid my husband's hearing isn't quite what it used to be.'

'What did you say?' bellowed the man. 'I didn't quite hear what you said?'

The woman sighed heavily.

'I told the gentleman that your hearing isn't what it used to be!'

Her voice was as loud as, if not louder, than before and to make matters worse she had gestured several times in Hubert's direction for her husband's benefit while she was speaking.

'Oh yes!' said the man loudly. 'I'm afraid my hearing is *not* at all what it used to be!'

Hubert smiled politely but couldn't think of what else to say that wouldn't result in further embarrassment. Instead he let a silence fall between them but while he was certain the conversation was over, the Indian couple seemed less convinced and stood looking at him expectantly. With each passing moment the situation became increasingly awkward and when Hubert heard the hydraulic screech of bus brakes he let out an audible sigh of relief.

'Me thought it was never going to come!' he said jovially, in an attempt to explain away the exuberance of his sigh.

The man pulled a face in Hubert's direction as the bus doors opened.

'I'm sorry. I didn't quite catch that!'

'He said he thought—'

The woman stopped mid-sentence, then sighed dramatically.

'Oh, forget it, Ragesh!' She smiled apologetically at Hubert as she tugged at her husband's arm to get him on the bus. 'I'm so sorry but at this rate we'll be here all day! It was lovely talking to you anyway, have a nice day!'

It had been over a fortnight since Hubert had decided that the way to win new friends was to be more open. Still scarred by his failure at the O-60 Club, he had decided that rather than looking for new companions at a club or a society he would instead try to find some in the real world.

So far he had engaged in conversation a woman staffing the express checkout lane at Marks & Spencer, a man in his GP's waiting room who was there to get his blood pressure checked, a couple looking for directions to the Glades shopping centre, and at least half a dozen people at bus stops (not counting the elderly Indian couple).

All of the people Hubert approached so far were approximately his age and while, without exception, they had all been more than happy to engage in conversation, converting a few moments of idle chitchat into something more substantial had proved impossible. It seemed to Hubert's mind that no matter how open he tried to be, nothing he did seemed to be making any difference.

People, it seemed, were either too busy, too closed off, too suspicious, or too deaf to make friends.

As Hubert watched the bus he had been pretending to wait for depart, he imagined he was observing his own future happiness disappear along with it. How could he possibly find friends of his own age in the time required, when making new acquaintances was so difficult? He was all out of both ideas and energy but, even so, he knew he couldn't give up. He had to keep on going, if not for his own sake then for Rose at least.

To cheer himself up as he walked home, Hubert wondered whether Ashleigh and Layla might pop by today. Their impromptu visits had become something of a feature of Hubert's week ever since their trip to McDonald's. Sometimes they would pop in on their way to the shops to ask if there was anything they could get for him. Or they'd simply turn up on the doorstep, perhaps with a packet of biscuits for them all to enjoy with a cup of tea at the kitchen table, or if the weather was fine outside, in the garden.

Hubert liked the fact that even if he wasn't in a particularly chatty mood, Ashleigh would simply fill the air with talk of her own. He liked the sound of Layla laughing whenever he pulled a funny face or made a rude noise on the back of his hand, but more than anything he liked that in a very short space of time his new neighbours had made life less humdrum. Now instead of huge swathes of his day being predictable down to the last minute, there was an element of surprise. Would the two of them drop by in the morning or in the afternoon? Would Ashleigh inflict more of her baking on him or bring round some of those nice chocolate cakes from Asda she'd brought with her last time?

Hubert noticed that she would often refer to him as her 'friend', to which he would say nothing because he was certain that they weren't. Yes, they were 'friendly', and enjoyed one another's company, but even with the best will in the world Hubert couldn't imagine introducing Ashleigh, a woman sixty years his junior, to Rose as anything more than a neighbour.

Reaching home, Hubert filled the kettle to make a cup of tea but no sooner had he taken out his mug than the doorbell rang. Smiling, Hubert took out an extra mug and a plastic cup in preparation for his guests. However, when he opened the front door he was surprised to find a courier holding a large cardboard box.

'Er . . . please . . . Could you . . . take in package for neighbours at . . . number fifty-six?'

Hubert didn't much like the people at number fifty-six. Despite the fact there were only two of them, they had three cars and were always leaving at least one parked outside his home. Even so, he decided he would take in the package for them anyway because it seemed like the kind of thing a person might do if they were trying to be more open.

As the courier fiddled with the electronic pad he needed signing, Hubert carefully considered the man before him. He appeared to be eastern European, or something like that. He was young too, early twenties at most, with olive skin and dark brown eyes. He looked tired, Hubert noted, really tired, and wore several days' worth of stubble on his chin. The hair sticking out from underneath his baseball cap was plastered to his skin with sweat.

Hubert signed the pad and then glanced past the man to gauge the weather. It had been warm when he'd been out earlier but in a short space of time all traces of cloud had disappeared and now it was like a furnace.

'Hot out there today, isn't it?'

'Van is like . . . how you say . . . a sauna in this weather.'

'And me bet you have a lot of them parcel to deliver.'

The courier nodded in agreement.

'I start at five this morning and won't be done until after six tonight.'

Hubert tutted his disapproval and wondered how it had taken him until now to make the connection between 'the eastern Europeans' certain newspapers loved to complain about and his own situation all those years ago. It was the same story, only with a different cast of characters. People from one land coming to another because of the lack of opportunities in their own, working all the hours in the sort of backbreaking jobs the natives didn't want to do. Day after day facing all manner of hostilities, wondering if they'd made a mistake leaving home.

'Damn people working you to the bone like that! It's not right. You know what you need? A drink.'

The young man raised an eyebrow and so Hubert qualified his offer.

'What me mean is you need a soft drink, although I bet if you weren't driving you could murder a nice cold beer.'

'Drink would be nice but I have no time. I am running late already. Maybe I get drink later.'

Hubert became incensed on the man's behalf.

'You is a human being not a damn parcel delivery machine! Come in and let me fix you a drink.'

The young man appeared grateful and puzzled in equal measure.

'Thank you, very kind, but I must—'

'What happen if you dehydrate so much that you fall unconscious at the wheel?' interrupted Hubert. 'You kill yourself and a whole heap of people just because of one tiny drink? Me can't have that on me conscience! No, you let me give you a drink, and then you can get on your way.'

The young man thought for a moment and then nodded as though something else had occurred to him.

'Okay, thank you. I will have very quick drink. But first, please, please can I use toilet? I needing pee for an hour now and am about to burst!'

Hubert ushered the young man inside, pointed him in the direction of the bathroom upstairs and then went to the kitchen to prepare him a drink. Taking out a pint glass from the cupboard, he half filled it with ice cubes, topped it up with pineapple juice and handed it to the parcel courier when he appeared at the kitchen door.

The young man received it gratefully and promptly drained the glass in several large gulps.

'Thank you Mr . . .'

'Bird,' said Hubert, refilling the man's glass. 'Hubert Bird. And what's your name?'

'Emils,' replied the young man. 'Emils Skuja.'

Leaning against the sink with a mug of tea, Hubert asked Emils where he was from.

'I come from Aglona in Latvia. Is very beautiful. Is famous for Basilica. You know it?'

Hubert shook his head.

'Geography has never been my strong point.'

Emils smiled.

'I very glad for sat nav! London is so big. Is easy to get lost here.'

Hubert chuckled. 'Me been here nearly sixty years now and I still get lost sometimes. Tell me, how long have you been in this country?'

'Eight months. I come for work.'

'That's why me come too nearly sixty years ago now,' said Hubert. 'Things tough back at home?'

'My father, he drank too much,' said Emils. 'He died when I was fifteen. My mother she is cleaning houses to get money but she doesn't get paid very much. Also she looks after my little brother Maksims, who is not well. My big sister Dagnija, she tries to help but she is married with three little kids, so it is hard for her. So I come to England to send money home to help my family. My brother's medical bills are very big. I have to work many jobs to help out. I work for parcel courier in day, sometimes barman at night and every other weekend I am kitchen porter at big country hotel near Sevenoaks. By the time I pay for rent, tax and petrol and send money home, I have not very much left.'

'So you just work, work, work, all the time?'

'Mostly, yes. But when I have free time I bake. Cakes, biscuits, bread, mostly Latvian recipe but I start to do more English. I share house and kitchen is not very well . . .' He searched around for the right word. '. . . maintained. The cooker is old and sometimes does not work. But I make do. Last week I make coffee and walnut cake. My housemates say it was best they had ever eaten.'

'Is your mother a good cook?' asked Hubert.

'The best,' said Emils proudly. 'One day I will cook her recipes in my own bakery. It will be called Emils' and will sell the best Latvian and English cakes.'

Hubert tapped his stomach playfully.

'Well, as you can see me like a good cake so if you ever need anyone to sample your wares you know where to—'

Hubert was cut off by a shrill electronic staccato coming from the phone poking out of Emils's top pocket.

'That will be base wanting to know where I am. I will have to go.'

Dodging past Puss as she emerged from the living room to see what all the fuss was about, Hubert led Emils to the front door, where he shook his hand.

'Well, it was lovely to meet you.'

'You too, Mr Hubert.'

'And any time you're passing and you need the loo or a quick drink you jus' knock the door, okay?'

As Hubert watched Emils's van screech off from the other side of the road he couldn't help thinking that if only the young man had been fifty years older, and in possession of a Freedom Pass, with a few more interactions like that, he might possibly have made himself a new friend.

16

Then: April 1959

Joyce slipped on her overcoat, paused to look around the room to see if there was anything she'd forgotten and then, scooping up baby Rose from her makeshift bed constructed from the bottom of a chest of drawers, closed the door behind her and carefully descended the stairs.

As she bent to lower Rose into the battered pram that Gus had managed to find for them from a friend of a friend, she felt a twinge in her back that made her wince. Hubert would be cross if he knew she was going out today, especially as he'd made her promise that she would rest until her back was better, but he'd looked so tired this morning, so utterly exhausted that she knew she couldn't wait another day. After he'd left for work she'd got herself and Rose ready and then, taking the slip of paper she'd hidden under clean nappies in the wardrobe, on which she'd scribbled down the address of a local childminder, she'd made up her mind that this was the day she would set the wheels in motion for going back to work.

'Going anywhere nice?'

Joyce turned around to see Mrs Cohen, their landlady, dressed in a pale blue housecoat and carrying a dustpan and brush.

'Morning, Mrs Cohen. Just taking Rose out for a quick stroll.'

'Oh, how lovely,' said Mrs Cohen. She put down the things in her hands, came over to the pram and beamed down adoringly at Rose. 'She's such a beautiful little character, isn't she? Always got a smile on her face, just like her father.'

They chatted for a short while, mostly about Rose but a little about the health of Mrs Cohen's elderly bedridden husband, Isaac. He wasn't well, she said, he was coughing constantly and every morning when she awoke, the very first thing she did after opening her eyes was check to see if he was still breathing.

'And when I find he is,' she said, 'I thank God for another day with him and then I get on with my chores.' She smiled, leaned down and kissed Rose on the cheek. 'Have a good time both, and come and tell me all about it over a cup of tea when you get back.'

'We will,' said Joyce and then, opening the front door, she came back around to the pram and began the mammoth task of manoeuvring it outside.

Following the wedding, Joyce and Hubert had decided they needed to move before the baby was born, but finding a new place had proved difficult for a couple like them. Some landlords made their feelings plain with signs posted in their front windows but others were more subtle, showing Joyce a room that became mysteriously unavailable the moment Hubert made an appearance. And of those landlords that remained, most were put off by the prospect of a new baby being in the house. Finally, they had come across the place they were in now, which was as run down as they came, especially as Mr Cohen wasn't able to maintain it as he once had. But what it lacked in finesse was more than made up for by the presence of the kindly Mrs Cohen, who, though getting on in years herself, worked tirelessly to keep it as clean and as tidy as she could manage.

After the wedding, Hubert had left Hamilton's in search of a bigger wage packet and had found work at a small car parts factory in Vauxhall. At the weekends he and Gus picked up extra money working for a painting and decorating firm and twice a week he went to night school to train as a plumber, as he'd heard the money was good with all the new houses being built. Joyce had hung on at Hamilton's for as long as she could, ignoring the whispers and gossip she overheard, until one day Mrs Critchlow pulled her aside and gave Joyce her marching orders, commenting spitefully that, 'Hamilton's isn't the sort of place for someone like you.' Desperate to put by as much money as she could, Joyce had picked up work here and there doing everything from cleaning to clothing repairs, but the closer she got to her due date the less inclined people were to employ her and now with rent to find, food to buy, bills to pay, and only one wage to cover it all, money was tighter than ever.

The childminder's was a fifteen-minute walk away on the other side of Brixton. Joyce didn't really like the area; it was dirty, down-at-heel and could at times be dangerous, especially for people like her and Hubert. Since all that nasty business in Notting Hill with the dreadful murder of that poor Antiguan chap and the trouble that had followed back in the summer, Joyce had felt uneasy and when she was out with Hubert she was alert for signs of trouble. She hated Teddy boys and everything they stood for and would cross the road to avoid them whenever she could. This wasn't Bromley, that was certain, and despite having spent the first twenty-one years of her life desperately wishing she could leave it behind and see more of the world, right now all she wanted was to go back.

She missed her family, her mum especially. The labour had been difficult and at its worst she had called out for her mother several times, and in the delirium that followed had even imagined she was there in the room with her and the midwife. They'd named the baby Rose after Joyce's mum and given her the middle name Lillian after Hubert's and although it had been a joy to finally hold her daughter, she couldn't help thinking about the difficulties that lay ahead.

The hardest time during her ten-day hospital stay hadn't been the late-night feeds, the nappy changes or the seemingly constant crying, but rather the empty seats around her bed at visiting time as she watched other women being fussed over, surrounded by family and friends. Gus and Lois had visited a few times and of course Hubert came whenever he could between jobs and night school, but it had been hard those first few days and not a single night went by without Joyce crying herself to sleep. At times she had almost wished she'd never met Hubert, that she had carried on with her life as it was before, working at Hamilton's, seeing friends of a weekend, having nothing more pressing to worry about than what to wear on a trip to the pictures or to a dance at the local swimming baths. Whenever she had these thoughts, however, she would look down at Rose sleeping in her arms or over at Hubert, so tired from his day at work that he was almost asleep in the chair, and she would think to herself: this is what love is. It's a husband willing to work himself to death to provide for his family; it's a child that is part her, part Hubert and all wonderful. They were a unit, a single entity bound together for ever. 'It won't always be tough like this,' she would tell herself. Better days lay ahead, she was sure of it.

Reaching her destination, Joyce took out her slip of paper and double-checked the address before knocking on the door. It was a tall, honey-coloured three-storey terrace that had seen better days. The top-floor windows were boarded up, and the windows of the second-floor bay were barely covered by a ragged set of greying net curtains. The lower bay was better kept but only marginally so, and it was this Joyce assumed was the location of the childminder's, an assumption confirmed by the sound of children's voices coming from within.

A stocky middle-aged woman came to the door.

'Hello,' said Joyce. 'I'm looking for Mrs Travis?'

The woman studied Joyce critically.

'You've found her, love.'

Joyce's heart sank. At the prices this woman was charging, Joyce hadn't exactly been expecting a Norland nanny but this was too much. With her dour expression, greasy hair and cigarette dangling from the corner of her mouth, Mrs Travis wasn't someone she would naturally leave her daughter with. But beggars couldn't be choosers. Anyway, perhaps the stained overalls she was wearing concealed a heart of gold.

'I'm Mrs Bird,' said Joyce brightly. 'We spoke on the telephone. I'm in need of a childminder.'

She held out her hand but the woman just ignored it, and said, 'It's two and six a week, food not included.'

'Oh,' said Joyce, taken aback. 'Is it not possible to see your premises?'

The woman shrugged.

'You can do what you like, love.'

Parking the pram and taking out Rose, who was fast asleep, Joyce followed Mrs Travis into the gloomy hallway, where they turned left into a ground-floor flat. The light wasn't much better here, but resisting the urge to turn around and leave, Joyce continued to the front room. Here there were half a dozen children in various states of undress. Some were playing on a tatty rag rug, others stood staring at Joyce, their dirty faces regarding her inquisitively, while in a corner, a child no older than Rose lay fast asleep in an old washing basket.

'Is this everything?'

Mrs Travis was confused.

'How do you mean?'

'I mean is this the only room? Is there a garden at least, so that they can get some fresh air when it's fine?'

The woman shook her head.

'What you see is what you get.'

Rose began to grizzle and so Joyce shifted her in her arms and loosened the blanket covering her. As if suddenly conscious of her need to make a bit of an effort, Mrs Travis took a step forward and started to arrange her expression into something resembling a smile. But then Rose wriggled, the blanket fell away from her head and the woman recoiled, her face twisted in disgust.

'You didn't say nothing about having one of them!'

Joyce felt herself rile.

'Having one of what exactly?'

'One of them black babies,' she spat. 'I don't have none of that in my place. Go on, get out of here before I get my husband on you.'

Joyce stood her ground.

'You make me sick. And I wouldn't leave my child here if you paid me!'

'Well, you make me sick an' all,' snarled Mrs Travis. 'Having a baby with one of those darkies. You ought to be ashamed of yourself!'

It was only after the fact Joyce realised that she had raised her hand and struck the woman, and it was only the resultant cry the other woman let out as they stood looking at one another that brought her to her senses. Turning on her heels, Joyce left the flat, bundled Rose back into the pram and hurried away as the woman stood shrieking all manner of abuse after her from the doorstep.

That evening, Joyce was so pleased to see Hubert when he came home from work that she flung her arms around him the moment he walked through the door. Hubert made a joke about wishing he could always have a welcome like this but Joyce couldn't even raise a smile. Instead she began to cry as she told him what had happened.

'I just don't understand how people can say such cruel things about an innocent baby, of all things,' she concluded. 'It's just so wrong!'

With fists clenched, Hubert stood up and demanded the woman's address but instead Joyce placed a calming hand gently on his shoulder.

'Don't, it'll only make things worse. You can't reason with people like that and it'll be you that ends up getting into trouble.'

'So what do you want me to do, Joyce? Just stand back and let them say what they want about our precious daughter?'

'Of course not.'

'So what, then?'

'Trust me it's already been dealt with.'

Hubert cocked his head on one side.

'How you mean?'

Joyce sighed and felt her cheeks flush with embarrassment.

'I chinned her. Right on her stupid face. No one talks about my baby like that!'

The look of surprise on her husband's face was so comical that Joyce began to laugh, and soon the two of them were doubled over in mirth.

'Joyce Bird,' said Hubert between fits of laughter, 'featherweight champion of the world!'

Later that night as they lay in bed, Hubert shattered from an evening at night school, he turned to her.

'Joyce, you know you can't pick a fight with everyone who has something to say about us, don't you?'

'I know,' she whispered in the darkness. 'There's too many of them, and not enough hours in the day.'

'It's funny,' said Hubert. 'Until me came to this country me went my whole life thinking me was just plain old Hubert Bird and then me come and find that actually me the devil himself.'

Joyce bit her lip. Sometimes she was so ashamed of this country she called home, she could cry.

'I bet you wish you'd never come sometimes.'

Hubert fell silent, clearly struggling with his answer.

'If me being honest me do sometimes,' he said eventually. 'But then me think about you and Rose, and the wonderful life we're going to have together and me say to myself, "Hubert Bird, what are you talking about? You is the luckiest man alive."'

17

Now

It was mid-afternoon and Hubert was in the park pushing Layla on the swings while her mother watched.

'Just three more pushes now from Granddad Hubert,' said Ashleigh, 'and that's your lot, okay, darling? We've got to get home.'

Layla jutted out her bottom lip at the prospect of having her fun curtailed.

'Don't be sad, little girl,' said Hubert. 'You might only have three more pushes left but me promise you they'll be good ones!'

As they left the park, Ashleigh regaled Hubert with yet more anecdotes about her job at the vet's. She told him about a tortoise with an injured foot, her shock at the huge mark-up on all the medicines and her difficulty with the office printer. In the middle of a tale about a very posh lady who'd brought in her Labradoodle with a case of chronic flatulence, Ashleigh stopped and pointed.

'I think that bloke over there is trying to get your attention.'

Ahead of them, a blue and white transit van was pulled up in the bus lane, and the driver was leaning out of the passenger window waving frantically.

'That'll be Emils,' explained Hubert as they walked towards the van. 'Him a Latvian parcel courier.'

As is often the way with these things, since their first meeting Hubert had bumped into Emils everywhere he went. One time while on his way to the supermarket he had spotted him collecting parcels from the newsagent's. Another, he'd been coming out of the dentist's and had nearly jumped out of his skin when Emils's van had pulled over suddenly so that he could show Hubert a photo on his phone of a birthday cake he'd been paid to make. And just yesterday on his way home from the pet shop, Hubert had almost walked into him coming out of the front gate of number sixty-five. Each time, no matter how busy Emils was, he always seemed keen to chat and pass some time with Hubert.

The two men exchanged greetings.

'I have important question to ask,' said Emils. 'What are you doing Saturday night? Latvian friends of my uncle who are living in England are getting married on Saturday. And I make the wedding cake for their reception at . . .' He paused, consulting his phone. '. . .Bromley Working Men's Club. It is a beautiful cake. Tastes wonderful. I want you to come to wedding as my guest, and taste my beautiful cake, and meet Latvian people.' The young man beamed a huge smile at Hubert. 'It will be my way of saying thank you to you, Mr Hubert, for your kindness with the pineapple juice.'

Hubert felt suddenly uncomfortable at the prospect of spending an evening in the company of an entire roomful of strangers. It was all very well trying to be more open on a one-to-one basis but a stranger's wedding? He wasn't at all sure he was ready for that.

'Really, Emils, there's no need to thank me,' said Hubert. 'No need at all.'

'I disagree,' said Emils. 'You do nice thing for me, so I do nice thing for you.' He glanced at Ashleigh and Layla and smiled. 'You can bring friends too. The more the merrier.'

'I've never been to a Latvian wedding before,' said Ashleigh. She self-consciously ran a hand over her hair. 'And you know me, Hubert, I love cake.'

He really didn't want to offend Emils or disappoint Ashleigh but this whole thing was making him feel very uncomfortable indeed.

'What about the bride and groom? Are you sure them won't mind?'

'I save them hundreds of pounds by only charging them cost price for cake,' said Emils. 'The least they can do is let me bring my own guests.' He shrugged and added, 'Anyway, is Latvian wedding, everyone is welcome at Latvian wedding!'

When Hubert answered the door to Ashleigh the following Saturday afternoon he barely recognised her. She was wearing a glittery purple dress with matching shoes and her hair was done all fancy, as if she'd just walked out of an up-market salon. Layla wore a sparkly silver dress accessorised with a sequinned hair bow and silver ballet shoes. They both looked delightful.

'Yeah, I know,' said Ashleigh, seeing the surprise on Hubert's face. 'We do scrub up well, don't we? And I'm not going to lie, Hubert, so do you.'

Hubert felt himself blush but he wasn't about to correct her out of some sort of misplaced humility. It had been a long time since he'd had anywhere special to go and even longer since he'd been to a wedding reception, so in spite of his reservations about the event he'd been determined to look his best. Two hours he'd spent in front of a full-length mirror trying on different permutations of the contents of his wardrobe, asking Puss for her opinion as she lay watching him from the comfort of a pillow. In the end they'd mutually decided on the navy-blue suit he'd bought for his and Joyce's fortieth wedding anniversary. It had been altered several times over the years to accommodate his burgeoning waistline but even so looked good as ever. He finished off the outfit with an expensive floral silk tie that Rose had bought for his seventieth birthday, a pair of patent-leather dress shoes and a light grey trilby, set at his usual jaunty angle.

Part of the reason Hubert had put so much effort into his appearance was that he felt as though he had a lot riding on the evening ahead. The clock was still ticking on Rose's arrival. In just two and a half months his daughter would be home. And despite attendance at an open day at the bowls club, engaging his white-haired postman in conversation and chatting with a fellow pensioner in the local Sainsbury's, he was yet to make a single age-appropriate friend. This wedding then, with its gathering of multiple generations, was perhaps his last hope. If he was lucky he might be able to snag a Latvian grandfather or even an aged uncle. But really he was open to any old man, so long as he could befriend them in time for Rose's visit.

Bromley Working Men's Club was only a short taxi ride from Hubert's house but the journey provided more than enough time for Ashleigh to relay everything she had managed to learn about Latvian weddings during an afternoon trawling the Internet. She informed him about something called a 'capping ceremony' and how apparently it was customary for the groomsmen to kidnap the bride and only return her once the ransom of a round of drinks had been paid. Hubert was sceptical of her findings, however, and even when she showed him an article on her phone, his only comment was, 'If anybody had tried to steal my Joyce on our wedding day, me would've boxed them ears!'

Arriving at the club, Hubert, despite Ashleigh's protests, insisted on paying the taxi fare. Once inside the building, they were immediately greeted by the sound of music. On the stage in the function room there were accordion and fiddle players dressed in strange costumes playing some sort of up-tempo folk song and a young woman singing into a microphone in Latvian while encouraging the audience to clap along. The dance floor was packed with a mix of giddy children jumping up and down, middle-aged women waving their hands in the air and young men, a little worse for wear, with their arms wrapped around each other as they sang along with the music at the tops of their voices. It was, thought Hubert, unlike any wedding reception, Jamaican or English, he'd ever been to.

'I don't know about you,' said Ashleigh, 'but I feel a bit like we've just landed on another planet!'

Hubert opened his mouth to reply but then felt a firm hand on his shoulder and turned around to see Emils. Divested of his blue and white uniform and wearing a smart leather jacket, crisp white shirt and tight jeans, he looked like an off-duty premier league football player.

He embraced Hubert as if they were long-lost friends. 'Mr Hubert! I'm so glad you came! And you bring your lovely friend too!' He smiled in Ashleigh's direction before bowing theatrically and kissing her hand. 'Welcome to Latvian wedding. Mr Hubert's friend, you look very lovely indeed!'

Hubert had never seen Ashleigh blush, nor had he witnessed her being lost for words and yet, thanks to Emils, she did both right in front of him.

'That's . . . that's . . . very kind of you to say,' she said, once she'd finally managed to recover herself.

'I only say what is true,' said Emils, and then he gave yet another bow for the benefit of Layla. 'And this young lady must be the princess of the ball! You are very beautiful, your royal highness!'

Layla's eyes opened wide with delight and it was immediately clear that Emils had charmed her as much as, if not more than, her mother.

'Now you are here,' said Emils, 'I will get you to meet real live Latvians!'

Without pausing, Emils began a whirlwind of introductions.

'This is my close friend, Mr Hubert, his beautiful neighbour, Ashleigh, and her daughter Layla, who is an actual princess,' he said each time he managed to collar some passing stranger. 'They are good people. And this is first time at Latvian wedding.'

While everyone greeted them warmly, Hubert couldn't help noting with dismay that they were all youngsters like Emils and Ashleigh. Thankfully, however, he was soon introduced to the bride's great-uncle. He had short white hair and spoke heavily accented English and was, Hubert quickly discovered, a cricket fan too. But no sooner had Hubert struck up a conversation with him about the state of the current West Indian squad than the man's wife interrupted them. 'Janis,' she said excitedly, 'come meet my second cousin Ingrida. I haven't seen her since we both left the old country fifty years ago!' Before Hubert knew what was happening, Janis was whisked away, leaving Hubert alone.

Conscious of the fact that as the only black face in the room he was beginning to attract attention, Hubert scanned the crowd for Ashleigh and spotted her chatting happily at a table with Emils. When it came to matters of the heart, Hubert would never have claimed to be an expert – that had been more Joyce's thing – but even so, he was pretty sure that Ashleigh was keen on Emils and suspected the feeling was mutual. Reluctant to play the third wheel, he briefly considered calling a taxi to take him home but reasoned that he might as well have a quick drink first and perhaps sample a plate of the tasty-looking food stacked up on tables along the edge of the room.

There were three women working at the bar: a young girl with blue hair and several piercings, a middle-aged woman wearing a permanently doleful expression and an older lady with softly waved white hair. As Hubert waited to be served he couldn't help thinking that he recognised the eldest of the trio, but given how many people he'd chatted to over the past few weeks, he reasoned that this wasn't much of a surprise.

He was about to order a Guinness from the young girl with the piercings when the older lady suddenly intervened.

'I'll take this one, pet,' she said to her colleague. She smiled at Hubert. 'Hello, stranger, I bet you don't remember me.'

Hubert racked his brains.

'You work in the post office?'

She shook her head and gave him a playful smile.

'The dentist?'

'Wrong again. But here's a clue for you. How's that lovely great-granddaughter of yours?'

All at once, Hubert recalled both the woman and his lie.

'You're the lady from the park who spoke to me when I was out with Layla! Me thought me recognise you!'

The woman smiled, clearly pleased that he remembered her, albeit with a little prompting.

'The name's Jan. What can I get for you, love?'

'Pleased to meet you, Jan, me called Hubert, Hubert Bird. A Guinness would be nice.' He handed her a twenty-pound note from his wallet. 'And make sure to have one for yourself.'

As she brought his drink they got chatting and Hubert didn't leave the bar for the rest of the night. While Jan served customers he sipped on his pint, and when there was a lull at the bar they chatted about their lives. Hubert learned that she was seventy-five and lived alone in a flat on the other side of town. She didn't have much in the way of a hobby but she did like gardening, even if for her that meant just filling up the various pots and containers on her balcony with colourful plants and flowers.

She'd been officially retired for the past fifteen years but had worked most of that time doing a few shifts a week at the club – less for the money, more for the company and a reason to get out of the house.

'The days ain't half long sometimes when you're on your own,' she said. 'There's only so much cleaning and tidying you can do and you get sick of talking to yourself after a while. So working here has been a bit of a lifesaver really.'

In return, Hubert answered her questions and much to his surprise found himself telling her about growing up in Jamaica, moving to England and of course about Joyce.

'Me have a daughter, Rose,' he concluded, 'she a professor of politics and lives in Australia. Oh . . . and me have a cat called Puss, who costs me a fortune in vet's bills. And that is pretty much it.'

'And what about that gorgeous great-granddaughter of yours?'

Mortified, Hubert closed his eyes for a moment and decided he had to nip this in the bud straight away.

'About that . . . the day we chatted . . . well, the child I was looking after . . . she's . . . she's not my great-grandchild exactly, she's actually my neighbour's little girl.'

Jan laughed.

'Well, I can't say I didn't have my suspicions, what with her blond hair and all!'

'Me don't know what me was thinking to say that sort of nonsense. Me didn't mean to lie, it's just that at the time it seemed easier than the truth.'

'Which is?'

'That the child's mother was desperate and needed someone

to look after her and me couldn't say no. Me hope that doesn't change your opinion of me.'

Jan smiled.

'You helped a neighbour in need. In my book that's a good thing.' Jan disappeared for a moment to serve a customer but when she returned, her expression was thoughtful.

'How do you fancy going out sometime? I've been meaning to go to that posh garden centre – what's it called again? – Ketner's, that's it. We could make a day of it, get some nice plants and then maybe have a spot of lunch?'

Hubert was intrigued. Finally his efforts at being more open were paying off. Of course, he had imagined if his mission tonight was successful that his new friend would have been a man. Still, beggars couldn't be choosers. After all, here was an actual pensioner offering a hand of friendship. Or had he got it wrong? Hubert wasn't interested in romance. And he suddenly panicked that a single man chatting in the manner he had might have given the woman the wrong idea.

'You mean . . . you mean . . . as friends, of course?'

Jan cackled with laughter.

'No, as lovers! Of course, as friends! It's like I said to you earlier, I'm not interested in any of that funny business any more. More hassle than it's worth. I'm just suggesting a trip to a nice garden centre out in the sticks, and maybe pie and chips in the café afterwards. It'd break up the week nicely, would a jaunt like that.'

'It does sound good,' said Hubert carefully. 'And it would be nice to get a few more interesting plants for the garden.'

'You needn't look so worried!' teased Jan. 'I'm done with romance, Hubert. All I need these days are my soaps, a good murder mystery to curl up with on a rainy day and some quality company every now and again. So what do you say?'

18

Then: December 1961

Between work and fatherhood Hubert couldn't remember the last time he'd been to the Princess Club, let alone out on a Saturday night, but tonight was Gus's birthday and he was here to celebrate big time. Dressed as sharp as a razor and feeling positive about life, Hubert descended the familiar steps into the depths of the club and as he opened the doors was immediately hit by a thick fug of warm air smelling of sweat and tobacco smoke. They were playing his song of the moment, 'Donna' by the Blues Busters, which he took as a good omen. Tonight was going to be one to remember.

Ordering himself a Guinness at the bar, Hubert scanned the room looking for Gus and Lois. They'd been together over three years now, which was for Gus something of a record. Hubert guessed that with his friend now earning good money working on the underground and Lois having started her first teaching job, they would be tying the knot any day soon.

Spotting a free table, Hubert had sat down but was soon on his feet again, having finally caught sight of Gus.

'Gus, man! Happy birthday to you!'

Gus shook Hubert's hand and gave him a half embrace.

'Good to see you, Smiler, man. Where's Joyce?'

'She sends her apologies. Rose kept her up last night with a bad cold and she's still not right, so Joyce didn't want to leave her with the neighbours.' He scanned the room for Lois. 'Where's your lady? At the bar?'

Gus shook his head, his expression ominous.

'Let me get a drink . . . and I'll tell you everything.'

His friend disappeared off to the bar, returning minutes later with not only a Guinness for himself but also two shots of whiskey, one of which he slid across the table to Hubert.

'To your good health!'

Gus raised his glass and, encouraging Hubert to do the same, downed the contents in one go. Then, slamming his empty glass on the table, Gus said, 'Now we can talk.'

He told Hubert that he and Lois were no longer together and described how things had come to a head the night before.

'Now she's got this job, she's thinking about next steps . . . and for her that means tying the knot.'

'And what's so wrong with that?'

Gus kissed his teeth.

'Smiler, you know me, I'm not the settling kind. I don't like to be boxed in and it felt like everything Lois was doing was about building a great big box to keep me in.'

Hubert sighed but said nothing. How long and how hard had his friend pursued this woman he'd called a goddess, only to cast her aside for some imagined idea of freedom? Gus had been happy with Lois, that was plain for anybody to see, and now here he was throwing it all away for nothing.

'What,' said Gus after a while, 'you not going to say anything? You not going to try and talk me out of it?'

Hubert shook his head.

'Gus, man, me friends with you long enough to know you're going to do what you're going to do regardless of what anybody has to say.'

He picked up the Guinness he'd been sipping while listening to his friend retell the entire sorry episode and drained it in two gulps.

'Now, it's your birthday and me don't want to upset you but you is a fool, fool man for letting that woman slip through your fingers.'

He set down his empty glass.

'You want another?'

Gus chuckled. 'Smiler, man, you vex like a bull on milking day! Get me a Guinness and another whiskey chaser, I think I'm going to need it.'

For the rest of the evening the two men talked about Jamaican politics and the prospect of independence from the UK, Joyce's thriving childminding business, the sacrifices involved in saving for a new home and what they would do if they won fifty thousand pounds on the pools. The only subject they were both careful to avoid was Lois and the spectacular mess Hubert thought Gus was making of his life.

Around midnight Hubert made his excuses and prepared to head home, just as Gus began making eyes at a beautiful girl across the room.

'You sure you won't stay, Smiler? She might have a friend?'

'No, thank you. Me leave you to it.'

Gus laughed.

'Of course, unlike me you is a family man.'

It had sounded more like a dig than a compliment but Hubert let it go. Aside from anything else, they'd both had a little too much to drink and couldn't be held responsible for the words that left their lips. Gus's comment, however, stayed with Hubert as he made his way through the late-night streets of Brixton back home to Joyce. Was being a family man really such a bad thing? Gus had spoken about it as if it was a trap but Hubert didn't feel trapped at all. He wondered if he was wrong in his thinking. Should he be longing for freedom like his friend? But as he put his key into the door of his lodgings and made his way past Rose's pram and up the stairs to their room, he decided that Gus was talking a load of old – what was it that Joyce always said? – claptrap. He laughed to himself. That was right. Gus was talking claptrap!

Making a mental note to tell Joyce about this moment in the morning, he opened the door quietly and was surprised to see their bed empty. Joyce was sitting in a chair by the fire, the glowing embers casting shadows across her face. Even in the dim light he could see that her cheeks were wet with tears. Panicking, his eyes darted over to the cot in the corner of the room. Hubert had lost count of the times he read in the papers about young children dying from all manner of diseases.

'Joyce, darling, what's wrong? Is it Rose? Is she worse?'

'She's fine. She ate well and went to bed no problem.'

The dead weight on his chest lifted.

'Then what?'

'It's Mum . . . she's . . . she's passed away.'

Sobering up in an instant, Hubert knelt down in front of his wife and, taking her hands into his own, listened carefully as she told him what had happened. How, after Rose had fallen asleep exhausted, she had climbed into bed only to be woken moments later by a knock at the door. It was Mrs Cohen with a message that there was someone on the phone for her. Dressed only in her nightgown, Joyce had taken the call in Mrs Cohen's flat. It was her sister on the line calling with bad news: their mother had suffered a fatal heart attack.

He held her tenderly.

'Oh Joyce! Me so sorry, darling, so sorry indeed. But at least it was quick and she didn't suffer.'

Joyce sobbed hard for a moment.

'That's exactly what Peggy said. And I'd take comfort from it but for the fact that it all happened a week ago. Can you believe it? Mum's been dead a whole week and the only reason I know is because Peggy finally developed a backbone and told me, even though my brothers had warned her not to. Peggy said she thought it wasn't right, that no matter what had happened she was my mum too.' More tears welled up in Joyce's eyes. 'The funeral notice went in the paper today. I think that's why she told me. She was worried I'd see it. She said: "I still don't agree with what you did but I couldn't let you find out like that."'

'We'll send flowers,' said Hubert. 'Whatever the cost we'll send flowers, the biggest and the brightest and the best.'

When Joyce spoke, a new note of determination had crept into her voice.

'No, no we won't. I *will* go to the funeral. And I *will* see my mother off properly and then, and only then, will I wash my hands of my family once and for all.'

Hubert studied her in silence, a thousand arguments as to why this was a terrible idea running through his brain. But his wife's mind was made up, and really the only question that remained was whether he was going to let her go alone.

'Fine,' said Hubert at last, 'what you say goes. But know this, where you go, me follow, so if you're going to your mother's funeral, then me going too.'

There was never a good time of year for a funeral, thought Hubert as he and Joyce stood outside the church in Bromley, but mid-December had to be the worst. The weather was bleak and cold, the skies dark and foreboding and yet the joy of Christmas, with its focus on family and fun, was only just around the corner, strangely at odds with the solemnity of the occasion and the mourning clothes they both wore.

He stared intently at Joyce's anxious face.

'Are you ready?'

'As I'll ever be.'

She gave a little shake of her head to shift a stray strand of hair out of her eyes, then with her back straight, marched up the path towards the imposing wooden doors of the church.

Desperate to cause as little disruption to the proceedings as possible, they waited until they heard singing before entering and slipping into an empty pew at the back, well away from the immediate family and prying eyes. The moment everyone took their seats, however, they realised that their endeavours had been futile. One head turning and noticing Hubert was quickly followed by another: a chain reaction, until finally the message reached the front pews. Much to the surprise of the vicar, who had just begun his opening remarks, Joyce's father stood up, turned and glared towards the back of the church, quickly joined by his sons George and Eric. A ripple of confused whispers spread through the congregation, necks straining, heads turning this way and that to get a better look at the only black face in the room.

Hubert felt sick with nerves; there was no telling where this would end up but it certainly wouldn't be anywhere good. Just as he leaned across to whisper into Joyce's ear that they should go, she rose to her feet and stood, back straight, chin up, wearing that same look of steely determination she'd had when she'd announced her plan to attend.

Before he knew what he was doing, Hubert was on his feet too, taking Joyce's hand and holding it tightly in his. As he met the gaze of first Joyce's father and then each of her brothers, Hubert told himself he was ready for whatever happened next. As far as he was concerned, his wife's battles were his and that was just the way it was and would always be.

The stand-off felt as if it would go on for ever, as the two warring parties refused to give in, even as the vicar ploughed on with the eulogy, but then Joyce's father finally turned and sat down, his two sons quickly following suit, and then and only then did Joyce and Hubert take their seats. After a short while the commotion subsided, people's focus returned to the coffin at the front of the church, and the service continued uninterrupted.

Hubert hadn't been to church since leaving Jamaica, even though in every letter his mother wrote she encouraged him to do so. Friends and neighbours often invited him along but Hubert always declined. He read his Bible from time to time and said his prayers every evening and that was more than enough for him. That said, he couldn't help thinking how it was odd that his first experience of church in England wasn't for a Sunday-morning service but rather for the funeral of a woman he'd never met.

This vicar with his large nose and wispy white hair was unlike any preacher Hubert had ever known. The feeble attempts to render the hymns were nothing in comparison to the raise-the-roof singing back home and the message, some vague idea about Joyce's mother being in 'a better place', didn't bear any resemblance at all to the impassioned fiery sermons about the urgent need for repentance and the glorious promise of salvation he'd experienced at home, which never failed to get people on their feet praising. Perhaps it was the weather, thought Hubert, made all the worse by this cold stone building, which for all its stained glass and polished brass felt empty of the love of God. Then again, he considered, as the vicar drew his thoughts to a conclusion, maybe it was the English themselves that were the problem. Their reserve, their fear of emotion, as though to express any, even at a time like this, would be shameful somehow. For the first time in his life Hubert felt sorry for them, the people of the mother country, the people who didn't know how to feel.

They left before the final hymn had finished, Joyce leading him by the hand oblivious to the scandalised faces she was leaving in her wake, and once outside she linked her arm through his, let out a deep sigh and leaned her head on his shoulder as they made their way back to the train station.

That evening, as they lay on the bed, with Rose, now two, lying between them studying the pages of a picture book, Joyce turned to Hubert, eyes brimming with tears, and out of nowhere said, 'I've been thinking: I want another baby. I want Rose to have a brother or sister, so that when we're gone she won't be all alone in the world.'

Hubert nodded thoughtfully before replying with a smile.

'Me think that sounds like a wonderful idea.'

19

Now

It was mid-morning and a smartly dressed Hubert had been just about to go out when Ashleigh had dropped by with Layla on her way to the shops to see if he needed anything.

'You're going on a date!' Ashleigh exclaimed, wide-eyed, when Hubert told her of his plans for the day. 'Hubert Bird, you saucy old thing! You pulled the barmaid from Bromley Working Men's Club!'

Hubert frowned so fiercely that his eyebrows pushed together to form one long, untamed mono-brow.

'It's not a date. We're . . . we're . . . just friends.'

'Like I'd quite like to be *friends* with Emils, you mean?' teased Ashleigh.

'No, not like that,' protested Hubert, who had endured constant questions from Ashleigh about Emils ever since the wedding. 'Me made it plain when we made the arrangements that me not interested in anything romantic and she said that was fine.'

'I bet she did,' said Ashleigh in a manner that made Hubert suddenly feel a lot less certain.

'What? You think . . . you think she's lying?'

'Put it this way, when I went on my first date with Layla's dad the first words I said to him were "I'm not looking for a relationship." Cut to six months later and I'm moving to London to be with him! Truth is, Hubert, when a woman goes on a date and specifically says it's not a date, it really is a date. And when she says she's not looking for a relationship, she's not telling the truth. She is, but doesn't want to scare you off by being too keen too early. Plus, let's face it, you really are quite the catch. Of course she wants to be with you.'

'So what do you think me should do then? Call it off?'

'What do you want to do that for? I clocked her when I ordered a drink. She's a right cracker!'

Hubert pulled out his handkerchief and wiped away sweat both real and imaginary. He didn't want a relationship. Though she might not be here any more, Joyce was still his girl.

'Me . . . me . . . don't want . . . me don't want anything like that.'

'Well, if you're really not interested in her that way, Hubert, then make sure you're totally honest with her, because one thing you've got to know about us ladies is that we're eternal optimists!'

Despite Ashleigh's teasing, Hubert was convinced that he had nothing to fear from spending the morning with Jan. This, he reasoned, was simply two people in need of company, nothing more, nothing less. But on the bus journey out to Ketner's his resolve began to give way and when he saw Jan dressed up and waiting next to a tall potted palm it all but disappeared.

She was wearing a busily patterned cerise pink top and trouser combo with cream open-toed sandals. Her hair seemed bigger somehow, more voluminous and carefully arranged. Did she think this was a date? Or were these just the kinds of clothes she wore when she wasn't walking through parks or working behind a bar?

'Hello, Jan,' he said stiffly. He wanted to leave it there and not mention anything about her appearance but it felt rude not complimenting a lady on her outfit.

'You look nice,' he said, reasoning it was a suitably chaste thing to say.

'Do I?' She sounded delighted. 'I've had this outfit for years but haven't ever got round to wearing it.'

Hubert sensed the situation called for at least one more compliment before they could change topics. He thought of the most neutral thing he could say.

'The colour . . . it really suits you.'

'I wasn't sure when I picked it up in Marks's but then I got it home and loved it. But thank you for noticing, Hubert, that's made my day!'

Reasoning that things would be less uncomfortable if they were looking at plants rather than one another, Hubert suggested they go inside and gestured towards the door in a 'ladies first' manner, which Jan seized upon immediately.

'Oooh, a gentleman! Such a rarity these days.'

Desperate not to say anything that might add to his charms, Hubert clamped his mouth shut and followed after her.

Much like Ashleigh, Jan was a talker, a fact that Hubert, who was feeling somewhat lost for words, was grateful for. As he pushed their shared shopping trolley, they trailed up and down the outdoor maze of roses and shrubs, climbing plants and orna-mental grasses, bedding plants and bamboos, with Jan chatting all the way. She spoke about how lovely the bees were, dipping in and out of pale pink foxgloves, which somehow led her to comment on the stiffness of her knees during rainy weather and then, out of nowhere she revealed that in the sixteen years she and her ex-partner were together he had never once bought her flowers.

'So he wasn't the romantic type, then?' asked Hubert.

Jan frowned.

'He was more what you might call the punching type.'

Hubert shook his head in disgust as they came to a halt in front of trays of lobelias: sky blues, deep purples and snowy whites.

'He hit you?'

Jan slid a tray of plants on to the trolley, their baby-pink flowers just beginning to open. She met Hubert's gaze for a moment, offering a barely perceptible nod.

'He was a drinker. Not that it's any excuse mind. But it did bring the worst out in him.'

If there was one thing Hubert deplored it was men hitting women. To him women were, and would always be, the fairer sex and men's role was to protect them.

'Well, that is terrible. Where is he now?'

'Six foot under. The drinking got him in the end.'

'Cirrhosis?'

Much to Hubert's surprise, Jan giggled.

'No, the 182 to Beckenham!'

Hubert wasn't sure whether she was joking.

'Really?'

'I know it sounds like a punchline but yes, it's true. He was hit by a bus on his way to the offy. I know I shouldn't laugh but it tickles me even now. It couldn't have happened to a nicer fella!'

As they continued past collections of outdoor shrubs and ornamental trees, Jan told Hubert more about her past. She'd left school in Bromley at fifteen to work in a car parts factory, which was where she had met her husband, Keith, who was ten years her senior. She hadn't liked him to begin with but, having always considered herself quite plain and ordinary, had been flattered and eventually succumbed to his advances. She was seventeen when they married and by twenty had two children, a boy and a girl. Although life was hard, with money being in short supply, she'd been fairly happy until one day out of the blue she'd returned home from taking the children to school to find bailiffs waiting on their doorstep. Keith, she later discovered, had developed a significant gambling habit, running up the kind of debt that cost them their marriage and their home. Alone and with two small children, she moved back in with her parents and swore off men for good.

'It didn't last long, mind.'

They were now standing near the doors leading back into the garden centre, looking at some pre-potted hanging baskets.

'I was young, I suppose, and wanted my chance at a happy ending. And that pretty much explains how, after one bad relationship after another, I finally ended up with Ray, whose idea of communication was to use his fists.'

Hubert helped Jan lift one of the hanging baskets down on to their trolley.

'Life can be really tough sometimes,' he said.

Jan nodded.

'And don't I know it.'

After paying for their goods they made their way to the restaurant. Hubert chose pie and chips while Jan opted for the battered fish with new potatoes and a side salad, bought with the help of a two-for-the-price-of-one voucher plucked from Jan's purse.

As they sat eating at a table overlooking the car park, Hubert picked up their earlier conversation.

'And what about your children? Are they doing well?'

Jan shrugged.

'I think I'd be the last to know. My son Alan's up north near Leeds and my daughter Lisa got married for the third time to a bloke down Bristol way a few years back. Between them they've got six kids, and seven grandkids, and – this is no word of a lie – unless they want something, I don't hear a single word from them from one year to the next.'

Hubert tutted in disgust while Jan ripped open a sachet of salad cream and squirted it on to the side of her plate.

'Kids,' she said, spearing a new potato on her fork and dipping it into the salad cream, 'you raise them the best you can, make all the sacrifices in the world, give them all the love in the universe and all they do is break your heart.'

After lunch they called for a taxi to drop them home, and telling the driver to wait, Hubert helped Jan carry her bags to the main entrance. As they prepared to part, Hubert reflected on their time together. He'd enjoyed himself and Jan, true to her word, hadn't seemed to want anything more than a bit of company.

'Well, it's time for me to say goodbye,' said Hubert. 'Me had a really good time and if you'd like to, I think we should do it again sometime if you're free.'

'I'd love to,' said Jan. 'I'll give you call later in the week.'

On the journey home, Hubert was so happy that he even started humming a little tune. He couldn't believe it. After all this time, after all this effort it was looking highly likely he'd have at least one real friend to introduce to Rose. Of course, there'd be no escaping the fact that she'd be annoyed when she finally found out there was no Dotty, Dennis or Harvey. But surely Jan would go some way to making up for his deception. He was sure that Jan and Rose would get on well together. Perhaps so well that Rose might forget about being angry with him.

After dropping off his new plants at home, Hubert headed straight out to the supermarket. There were a few things he needed to tide him over for the next couple of days and as he was feeling so positive he reasoned he might even add a few treats to his basket. As he wandered around the aisles he picked up a packet of posh chocolate biscuits here, a travel-sized bag of Glacier Mints there and even some fancy cat food for Puss.

Entering the wines and spirits aisle, Hubert spied a small bottle of Captain Morgan rum on offer and his eyes lit up. How long had it been since he'd enjoyed a tot of rum? Years. He eagerly reached out to take one off the shelf but before he could pick it up, a voice from behind him called out: 'Hubert Bird! Well I never!'

He spun around to see a curvaceous black woman. She was wearing a short-sleeved leopard-print blouse and tight leather trousers, but the thing that really caught his attention was her elaborate wig. It was long, swishy and all black except for a wide blond streak running down one side.

'Bernice Taylor!' greeted Hubert. 'How long has it been?'

Bernice slapped her ample thigh in delighted outrage.

'Too long, Hubert Bird, far too long!'

Bernice was the considerably younger ex-wife of Hubert's old drinking pal Mister Taylor. With her booming laugh and outrageous manner, most people (including Mister Taylor himself) had a bit of a love-hate relationship with Bernice. Back in Jamaica, however, Hubert had grown up with at least half a dozen aunties of a similar persuasion and therefore had something of a soft spot for her.

'So tell me, Hubert Bird, you still live in Park Avenue?'

'The day me leave that house it will be feet first.'

She raised a painted-on eyebrow.

'You no remarry yet? It's not good for a man of your years not to have a wife!' She lowered her voice and added conspiratorially. 'And I hear about your sad news, Mr Hubert. Such a shame, such a shame, life can be so—'

Hubert cut her off quickly.

'Thank you for your concern, Bernice, but I'm fine.'

'Of course, of course,' said Bernice and deftly changed topic. 'So tell me, you still keeping company with them bad breed from the Red Lion?'

Hubert sighed.

'Them all move on.'

'You not even see Gus any more? You two used to be thick as thieves.'

'It's my fault really. Me didn't keep in touch. The other day me went all the way over to Brixton to see him but me think him must have moved, taken ill or even passed away.'

Bernice's eyes widened.

'Mr Hubert, Gus Campbell isn't dead, he's still in Brixton! Or at least he was two weeks ago.'

Bernice explained that her aunt's daughter had for a long time lived on the same street as Gus, and while visiting her to celebrate her sixtieth birthday, she had spotted him walking out of his ramshackle flat looking like a tramp.

'I never see such a thing in all my days! Him was wearing raggedy clothes and looked like he no wash in weeks! I try to say hello, but him walk right past me as if he no hear me.' She shook her head sadly. 'Such a shame to see him in that way! He was such a fine-looking man in his day.'

Hubert didn't know what to think. The details of her story certainly seemed to add up. But what could have happened to turn his oldest, closest friend, who had always been the smartest dresser and most house-proud man he knew, into such a state?

'You certain it was Gus you saw?'

'As sure as I'm talking to you.'

Without another word, Hubert set his basket on the floor and began walking towards the exit as Bernice called after him.

'Mr Hubert! Mr Hubert! Are you not going to give me a proper goodbye?'

Hubert called over his shoulder.

'Sorry, Bernice! Another time! Right now me have somewhere to be!'

20

Then: August 1964

Hubert closed the wardrobe door and scanned the room they had called home their entire married life.

'I think that's everything.'

Joyce wiped away a tear.

'It's funny, isn't it? All the nights I've spent dreaming of a place of our own and yet here I am getting upset about leaving this one.'

Hubert put an arm around her shoulder.

'There's a lot of happy memories in here, that's for sure. But don't forget about all the lovely ones we're going to make in our new place.'

He kissed her cheek tenderly.

'Let's collect the children from downstairs and say our goodbyes.'

Getting a place of their own had been something Joyce had set her mind on from the day Rose was born. She had always wanted a garden for her daughter to play in, a proper kitchen to cook in and space for them all to grow, and with the arrival of David two years earlier, the need had become even more pressing. To begin with, Hubert had suggested they might look for somewhere in the area, perhaps as far out as Clapham, but Joyce had been adamant she wanted to head back to Bromley.

'I had such a lovely childhood there,' she'd said, 'and the schools are wonderful.'

In her heart of hearts she knew this wasn't just about giving their children an idyllic start or even a good education, it was about staking a claim on a piece of what was after all her home town. It was her refusing to be driven out by ignorance and hostility, it was her refusing to be beaten.

Hubert hadn't argued the point. As much as he liked Brixton, he was far from convinced it would be the best place to bring up a young family. They had discussed the fact that it would be difficult not just for Hubert, but for the children and Joyce too, moving to an area like Bromley where they'd stick out like a sore thumb. Ultimately they'd reasoned that as they were going to stick out wherever they were, it might as well be out in a leafy Kent suburb.

They found the children playing shops in Mrs Cohen's front room, the old lady pretending to be the customer and making them giggle with outlandish requests. It was good to see her so happy after losing her husband the year before. She loved Rose and David like the grandchildren she never had, and was always spoiling them with sweets and homemade cakes.

Mrs Cohen caught sight of Joyce in the doorway.

'Is it time already?'

'I'm afraid so. Come on, you two, it's time to go.'

David, with his chubby cheeks and wild mass of dark curls, shoved out his bottom lip angrily. Rose, smartly dressed in her Sunday best dress, put a comforting arm around her brother's shoulders. They reminded Joyce of her own childhood. How she had always been the one to calm down her younger brother Eric. David resembled him a little, the shape of his eyes, the slope of his chin, even sometimes the way he laughed. Rose, on the other hand, strongly featured Hubert's younger sister Cora, or at least that's how it seemed from the single photograph Hubert had of her.

'We'll see Nana Cohen again soon,' said Joyce in a placatory tone as the children began to whine. 'We're not moving that far away.'

Hubert appeared and gave Mrs Cohen a hug, thanking her for all she had done for them over the years. Everything from renting them a room when no one else would, through to allowing Joyce to continue using her downstairs rooms for her childminding business. In short, she had been a lifesaver and they would both miss her very much.

'You take care of yourself and this lovely family of yours,' said a tearful Mrs Cohen. Then with a twinkle in her eye she added, 'And don't forget your promise to look at the sink in number ten. The tenant in there says the tap's dripping so loudly that he keeps dreaming it's raining in his room!'

Hubert agreed to look at it as soon as he could and then, scooping up the children in his arms, left Joyce to say her farewell in private.

Joyce hugged Mrs Cohen tightly.

'Thank you. Thank you for everything.'

Heading outside, Joyce joined Hubert and the children in the council van Hubert had borrowed from work. The sum total of their possessions was stacked in the back, and as Joyce climbed into the passenger seat she couldn't help but feel they were embarking on the biggest adventure of their lives.

Park Avenue was a wide tree-lined road made up of a mixture of 1930s semis and dilapidated Victorian villas, of which number fifty-one was a rather down-at-heel example. It sat next to a rickety wooden Salvation Army hall and had been lived in, since being built, by an elderly lady who had recently died after being bedridden for the last ten years. The roof leaked, the garden was overgrown, and the paint on all the woodwork had faded and was peeling so badly it was hard to imagine what colour it had once been. Its saving grace was that it was cheap, and as so few people were interested in it and the old woman's family were desperate for a quick sale, Joyce had pounced on it.

Catching sight of something, Rose pointed excitedly to the tree in front of the house that was now their home.

'Look, Squirrel Nutkin!'

'Maybe there's a Mrs Tiggywinkle in the garden,' said Joyce. 'Perhaps we'll put a saucer of bread and milk out tonight if we have time and if you're lucky she might come and say hello.'

The unpacking didn't take long. They'd bought a few items

of second-hand furniture, beds, a table and chairs, and a cottage suite, all of which were being delivered that afternoon, so for now they focused on opening all the doors and windows and clearing out as much of the rubbish that had been left behind as they could manage.

They worked hard until midday when Hubert suggested they have fish and chips for lunch as a treat. Taking the van, he left Joyce cleaning the front windows, perched on a stepladder they'd found in the shed, while the children played hide and seek in the back garden.

He'd been gone fifteen minutes, and she was nearly finished with the windows when she heard someone call to her and turned to see a middle-aged woman laden with shopping bags standing by the front gate.

'Just moved in?'

Joyce put down the cloth and bottle of Windolene and, wiping her hands on her apron, climbed down the steps and walked up to the gate.

'Today actually. I'm Joyce Bird, pleased to meet you.'

The woman put down her shopping bags and they shook hands.

'Irma Cook. I live up the road with my George. We've been saying how nice it would be for a young family to move in and take care of the old Partridge place. Have you come far?'

'Not too far but I was born and bred on just the other side of Bromley so it really does feel like I'm coming home.'

'I bet it does. We'll have to have you and your husband over for a cup of tea sometime.'

'Ooh, yes, that would be lovely.'

'My George works for the council. What line of work is your husband in?'

'He's a plumber,' replied Joyce. 'He does a lot of work for the council himself at the minute but he's hoping to set up on his own someday soon.'

Mrs Cook raised an eyebrow.

'Well, he'll find no end of work around here, I can tell you.

Last year we were looking for a plumber to do our bathroom – it's not been touched since before the war – and the fella we finally got in cost an arm and a leg and took for ever to do it.'

'Well, at least now you know where we are if you need anything doing in the future.'

Mrs Cook was about to reply when Rose appeared at the front door holding the hand of David, his small face wet with tears, his knee scraped and bleeding.

'It wasn't my fault,' protested Rose, leading her limping brother down the front path to the gate. 'I told him to slow down but he wouldn't listen and tripped over.'

Joyce whisked a tissue from her apron pocket and dabbed at David's knee until he'd calmed down. Drying his eyes, she turned around ready to introduce the children to their new neighbour, but Mrs Cook was nowhere to be seen.

'Are you looking for the lady you were talking to, Mummy?' asked Rose. 'She pulled a funny face like this . . .' She screwed up her own face as if she had a sour taste in her mouth. '. . . when she saw me and David and then she walked away.'

'Did she now?' Joyce was angry with herself for having let her guard down. Five minutes they'd been here and already it was happening. 'Well,' she said, striving to put a smile on her face as Hubert pulled up in the van, 'it doesn't look like she'll be getting any chips then.'

In the end the beds didn't arrive until the Monday morning and the table and chairs were delayed until late the following Thursday. Despite all the setbacks and unpleasantness Joyce was determined not to let anything spoil their happiness.

On the Friday morning, just before she and Hubert set out for work she suggested that they throw a housewarming party that weekend.

'You get in contact with Gus and ask your friends from work,' said Joyce, 'and I'll do the same with mine. Warn them it won't be anything too fancy, just a bit of food and a few drinks to christen the house.'

Hubert thought it was a great idea and the two of them spent most of Saturday making preparations for the party, sometimes helped but mostly hindered by Rose and David. By the time the evening rolled around, the kitchen table was groaning with food, and Hubert had set up a respectable bar in the garden in the dwindling heat of the day.

Gus was first to arrive, along with his latest girlfriend, a gorgeous girl from St Kitts, who clearly adored him.

Joyce kissed him on the cheek.

'Hello, Gus, and who's this lovely young lady?'

'This is Irene. Irene this is Joyce, Hubert's good lady.'

Although Joyce chatted to Irene while Gus went in search of Hubert, and tried her best to sound interested, her heart just wasn't in it. She still missed Lois, and although Gus had been out with some lovely girls since, none of them ever stuck around long enough for her to get to know them properly. She wondered whether he would ever settle down, and occasionally even worried that he might lead her husband astray. Hubert, however, always managed to allay her fears. 'You think me want to be like Gus?' he would say incredulously, before bursting into laughter. 'No, thank you, that life is not for me!'

While Gus went to talk to Hubert in the garden, Joyce showed Irene around the house, describing all the plans they had for the place, until another knock at the door signalled the arrival of more guests. There were friends both black and white they'd made while living at Mrs Cohen's, families they'd become close to after Joyce had minded their children, and many others they'd collected across their six years together. As they all flooded into the house carrying various gifts and platters of food, Joyce couldn't help but wish her mum were still alive, that she could've seen how happy she was with Hubert, how wonderful her grand-children were and how much they had achieved over these past few years. She had even written to Peggy, in part to invite her along today, but mostly to tell her that she was back in Bromley, but in the end she had screwed the letter up, recalling that in six years she hadn't even received so much as a Christmas card from her sister.

As she took people's coats and pointed them in the direction of the food and drink, Joyce realised that she didn't need to show her family she was doing well. She didn't need to prove to them somehow that she had made the right decision in marrying Hubert. The happiness she felt right now was testimony enough.

Even though the party went on until late, Joyce was up at the crack of dawn the following morning tidying up. Later, while Hubert took the children to the park at the top of the road, she made her first ever full Sunday roast in the temperamental gas oven the old lady's family had left behind.

They ate their meal sitting at their new kitchen table, Rose diligently consuming everything that was put before her, David picking at his food like he always did, throwing half of it on the floor and getting most of the rest in his hair, Hubert enthusing over every mouthful, even the charred roast potatoes and soggy cabbage. This was her family, thought Joyce. This was her home, where she and Hubert would raise their children and grow old together.

The next morning they were both up early, Hubert off to start work on a new housing development site over the other side of town and Joyce to get the kids up and ready to take them with her to work in Brixton. As she left the house she noticed a single piece of mail sitting on the doormat, which she scooped up and placed in her pocket and didn't get chance to read until they were sat on the train. The absence of a stamp should have set her alarm bells ringing but naively she'd thought that perhaps it might be a housewarming card from one of the neighbours she'd yet to meet. She took a thin cream sheet of paper out of the envelope and unfolded it. Scribbled across the middle of it in block capitals were the words, 'Nigger lover go home.'

21

Now

By the time Hubert reached Brixton he'd conjured up all manner of theories as to how Gus might have ended up in the state Bernice had described. One strong possibility was that Gus had succumbed to dementia and had no one to look after him. Or perhaps he'd got together with the wrong sort of woman and she'd taken him for everything he had. Maybe he'd developed that glaucoma and he literally couldn't see the mess he was in. Whatever the reason, one thing was certain: Gus Campbell needed a friend.

Reaching Gus's front door, Hubert knocked firmly on it and when there was no response began shouting at the top of his voice through the hole in the UPVC door that was all that remained of the letterbox.

'Gus, man, it's me Hubert! Open up the door and let me in!'

Nothing. He listened carefully but unlike the time before he couldn't even hear a TV. Perhaps this time around there was no one home. Perhaps Bernice had got it wrong. Perhaps Gus was alive and well and living somewhere nice that was the complete opposite of this mess.

He knocked on the door again, calling out through the letterbox.

'Gus, man! It's me, Hubert! Open up and let me in!'

Hubert was so busy banging on the door that he didn't notice the dark figure that appeared several feet behind the frosted glass until a low, deep baritone voice from inside growled, 'Go away!'

It was Gus. Hubert was sure of it. He would know his old friend's voice anywhere. And as he peered through the glass at the blurry outline behind it, he was certain. He bent down and peered through the letterbox. It was Gus, but not the man he remembered. This version was wearing a green T-shirt splattered with food stains and navy tracksuit bottoms out of which poked gnarled unshod feet. What was left of the hair on his head was the same pure white as his matted beard. It was just as Bernice had said: the man was a state.

'Gus, man, it's me, Hubert! Hubert Bird! Don't leave me standing out here like a fool! Let me in!'

There was a silence and then a voice spoke.

'H-h-h-ubert?'

Hubert bent down to peer through the letterbox again.

'Yes, Gus! It's me, man. Let me in.'

Another long silence, then the same voice spoke tentatively.

'Sm-sm-smiler?'

'Yes, man! It's me! Open up, old friend.'

'I thought . . . I thought you were dead. I thought you must be dead and gone.'

Hubert's heart suddenly felt heavy.

'Not dead . . . at least not yet. Just let me in so we can talk, okay?'

There was a long silence, then Gus spoke again.

'I can't . . . Smiler, man . . . you need to go . . . just go and forget you ever come here.'

'No, me not going anywhere until you open this door and that's a promise.'

Another long silence but this time Gus came close enough to the glass for Hubert to almost make out his face.

'Hubert Bird, it's good to hear your voice, man.'

'Then let me in!'

'I can't.'

'What you on about? Just open the door.'

'Smiler, no bother make me explain. I just can't.'

'Gus, you can't make your old friend come all this way on a train just to turn around.'

There was a pause, followed by what to Hubert's ears sounded like the beginning of laughter.

'Tell me, Hubert Bird, you still smile like the morning sun?'

'Yes, but me have to put me teeth in first!'

Gus laughed a deep raspy laugh and came even closer to the door.

Hubert could feel his heart racing. He was close, really close.

'Come on, man, you can do it, just open the door and let me in.'

With bated breath, Hubert watched as Gus's hand slowly reached up to the lock, slid back the chain and opened the door. Following Gus's shuffling figure across the hallway and into the living room, Hubert was shocked to see that his friend's home was exactly like the man himself: a mess. There were piles of bin bags in the hallway, towers of books and old newspapers on the floor in the living room and apart from a tatty old armchair positioned opposite the TV, the only available place to sit was on the sofa next to two empty Calor gas canisters. Although Gus could see Hubert's struggle as he perched gingerly on the edge of the scruffy brown sofa with rips in its fabric covered over by gaffer tape, he made no attempt to address the situation.

As they sat in silence, Hubert took in the room. There was definitely a story here but the only way he was going to hear it was if his friend chose to volunteer the information, and Hubert guessed this wouldn't be any time soon.

Gus made no attempt to make conversation. Instead he sat staring at the TV, even though it was switched off. Hubert used the time to take in more of his surroundings. The room was decorated exactly as he remembered from his days when he was a regular visitor. There was the glass cabinet Gus had bought from a small ad in the local paper; there was the dark brown sofa suite that Hubert could remember being delivered; and on the wall above the fireplace were framed photographs of Gus's parents, Samuel and Vernia. The only things that were new to Hubert were the TV, the mess, and the degree to which everything in the room, including Gus, seemed to have faded over time.

'So tell me, Gus, man,' said Hubert when he could stand the silence no more, 'how you been keeping?'

Gus said nothing, so Hubert tried again.

'Come on, Gus!' He spoke a little louder this time in case his old friend's hearing had deteriorated. 'Me ask, how you been keeping?'

'Me heard you the first time.'

'So why you no say nothing?'

Gus fell silent. Hubert wondered if he had offended him but then he spoke again.

'I don't hear nothing, not a damn word from you for five years and you think we can just pick up as if nothing happened?'

Hubert sighed.

'Come on, Gus. You know what happened. Me just couldn't . . . couldn't be around people . . . it wasn't you . . . me know you tried.'

'I call, I come by your house, I try everything and not a word from you!'

'Me know. It was my fault. And me sorry. But me here now and me want to help you.'

'Help me with what?' His voice was heavy with disdain.

Determined not to antagonise the man any further, Hubert surveyed the room again, hoping Gus would do the work for him, but he said nothing.

'Look,' said Hubert finally, 'me can see things aren't right. We all need a little help from time to time.'

Gus gave a short, bitter laugh.

'And you the man to give it? I don't see you for years then out of nowhere you just show up on my doorstep and tell me you're going to help me? Don't make me laugh! I don't need your help, Hubert Bird! I don't need anyone's help and if that's all you came round here to say, then you can go!'

'But Gus, man, you can't—'

Gus picked up the remote next to him and switched on the TV, cutting off Hubert midsentence. Hubert wanted to box his friend's ears. He raised his voice so he could be heard over the closing credits of some property programme or other.

'So you not going to talk about this?' Gus remained silent,

eyes fixed to the screen. 'Man, me come all this way just to see you and this how you want to leave things?' Still silent, Gus turned the TV volume up even louder.

Hubert got to his feet. He didn't want to leave his old friend in this pigsty but he didn't want to get into a fight with him either.

'Fine,' yelled Hubert, fighting to be heard over the TV. 'Me going to leave you alone but this is not the last word on this, Gus Campbell. Me and you have been friends too long for that!'

Ashleigh dunked her biscuit in her tea.

'And he kicked you out just like that?'

Hubert sighed.

'Him didn't kick me out as such. Truth is me don't think he's got the strength to kick his way out of a wet paper bag at the moment, let alone anything else. Him just made it clear that he wanted me to go and so what else could me do? Me take myself up and left.'

It was just after lunch and Hubert was sitting at his garden table with Ashleigh, who had dropped in after work having picked up Layla from nursery. Layla was plucking daisies from the lawn and handing them to her mother, who was piling them up next to her tea, while Puss lay stretched out lazily on the patio next to them sunning her belly.

Hubert hadn't planned on telling anyone about his friend's plight – it seemed like a betrayal somehow – but it was weighing so heavily on his mind that the words came out before he'd known what he was saying.

'So, what do you think's happened for him to get like that?'

'Me don't know. Me really don't know.'

Ashleigh took a sip of tea.

'And he's got no family?'

'Maybe a few distant relatives dotted here and there. Me pretty sure he had an auntie and a couple of cousins living up north at one time. But his auntie will be long gone by now and his cousins . . . well, you know how it is . . . people move on and get busy with their own lives.'

'He never married?'

Hubert laughed, fondly remembering the Lothario figure of his youth. After a while, however, it faded, only to be replaced by the unkempt man he'd left behind in Brixton.

'He was never one to settle down,' said Hubert. 'He came close once but he let her slip through his fingers, fool that he was.'

'That's so sad. And he's got no kids or anything?'

'Not that me know of. Him never wanted to be tied down.'

'So he's all alone in the world. That's proper heartbreaking that is. How come you lost touch with him? Did you have a falling out or something?'

Hubert thought for a moment, recalling those days when Gus would ring, would come by, would bang on the door and shout through the letterbox to get his friend's attention, just as Hubert himself had done yesterday.

'No, love,' said Hubert sadly. 'We didn't fall out. Me just . . . me just wasn't very much of a good friend back then.'

Hubert could tell that Ashleigh wanted to ask more questions but he wasn't in the right frame of mind to answer them, so he stood up and walked down to his shed, returning with a small plastic pot.

'Here you go,' he said to Layla. 'You can put your mum's flowers in here.'

Back in his seat at the garden table, he sat with Ashleigh watching Layla at play, neither of them speaking. He sensed that Ashleigh was aware this was difficult for him to talk about and was relieved that when she returned to the subject, she did so in more general terms.

'There are so many lonely people around these days,' she said. 'I see it at the vet's all the time: old dears whose only friend in the world is their pet and who want nothing more than a little chat when they pop in for worming medicine or whatever. The world is moving so fast and no one's got time to stop these days. It's sad really. I read a thing in the paper last week while I was having my break at work. Apparently, loneliness is a bigger killer than cancer. Can you imagine that?

There's a bigger killer than cancer in the world and no one's doing anything about it.'

'Well, that's the thing,' said Hubert. 'Whose job is it? It used to be the family all looking out for one another but it's not like that any more. It used to be you at least knew your doctor, but these days you're lucky to get an appointment, let alone see the same GP twice. It used to be your neighbours kept an eye on you but people like to keep themselves to themselves now. It used to be that you belonged to a community, but really, is there such a thing any more? Now it's more like every man for himself.'

'Well, someone should do something,' said Ashleigh. There was a crack in her voice and tears in her eyes. 'I'm sorry,' she said, aware that Hubert had registered her upset. 'It's just that the idea of Layla growing up in a world like this is so upsetting. If things are this bad now, what will they be like when she's got kids of her own? I want something better for her, more hopeful.'

That evening Hubert sat alone in his living room thinking not only about Gus, but also about Ashleigh. Her words had really resonated with him. She was right. Someone should do something about this loneliness problem. It wasn't right to just let things deteriorate further. It wasn't good to leave so many people struggling alone. Something had to be done, but the question was what, and by whom?

22

Then: April 1972

As the plane's wheels touched down on the tarmac of Kingston's Norman Manley Airport there was a spontaneous eruption of applause and whoops of delight, the loudest of which came from ten-year-old David. His big brown eyes were wide with excitement and his head twisted this way and that trying to get a peek through one of the windows. Not for the first time, he loudly voiced his disappointment that all four of them were stuck in the middle of the plane. 'Can we get window seats on the way back?' he pleaded. 'We'll see, son,' said Hubert, trying to sound like a sensible grown-up, even though he himself had found it hard to contain his excitement, never having been on a plane before. 'And if not, maybe we can have a word with one of the stewardesses and see if they'll let you have a little look in the cockpit.'

David's eyes grew even wider as he contemplated the possibility of such a wondrous thing. As the plane taxied to a halt, his imagination sparked and crackled with increasingly fantastic scenarios, which culminated in him being allowed to fly the plane while the captain stood by admiringly.

David's excitement worked its way down to his feet, which were currently kicking the back of the seat in front of him.

'Well,' said Joyce. 'You certainly won't be allowed back on the plane at all, let alone to fly one, if you don't stop that and sit properly.'

'Here you go, David,' said Rose kindly.

She offered her brother one of the sweets she'd saved from when the air stewardess brought around a basket of them prior to landing. 'Have this, and if you're good I've got another one in my pocket for when we get off the plane.'

Hubert and Joyce exchanged glances and smiled. It had been her idea they should all visit Jamaica together but it had been his decision as to whether it would happen. The list of reasons not to make the trip had been long and at the top was the sheer expense, the children's seats alone costing over five hundred pounds.

In addition to all this, Hubert had to turn down three weeks' worth of work, money they could ill afford to lose. Then there was the worry of Joyce having to leave the nursery in the hands of the girls she'd been training up these past few months. All in all, on paper it had seemed like a terrible idea, but Joyce had made a convincing argument for now being the moment to go. 'There's never a perfect time for this sort of expense,' she'd argued. 'But the children are old enough to travel now, your mum's in good health and I know if I was her I'd be desperate to see my grandchildren. We're always being sensible, Hubert, maybe just this once we can throw caution to the winds.'

She was right, of course. With one thing and another he had been putting off even thinking about going back home to visit for the past ten years, but now was the time. After Joyce lost her mother, he was more than a little aware that he couldn't take for granted that everyone and everything he'd left behind in Jamaica would always be there. As it was, his sister Vivian had moved to New York with her husband and was working as a teacher, and even his little brother Fulton was a grown man now, with a family of his own, living in Vancouver, carving out a good career for himself as a policeman. Things had changed, people had grown up and moved on, and if he waited any longer, who knew what would be left.

That same weekend, they'd visited the travel agent's on the High Street and after he'd put down a deposit for the airline tickets, he and Joyce had taken the children out for an ice cream in the park and told them the good news. 'We'll get to meet our grandma for the very first time,' said Rose, while David's main concern was that they would be travelling by plane. 'I can't wait,' he said excitedly, unaware, Hubert noted, that his ice cream was dripping down his hand. 'We're going on a plane! We're going on a plane! And if we crash we'll get to use a parachute too!'

As row after row of passengers filed off the aircraft, Hubert had been so busy making sure that they had left neither carry-on luggage nor children behind that he was completely distracted as he stepped out on to the metal steps only to be hit by a blast of hot humid air that was like a punch in the face. When he'd left Jamaica he'd never imagined a day might come when he would forget what real warmth felt like and yet here he was, dressed in a totally unsuitable jacket for the weather, sweat already forming on his brow and upper lip as he guided his son and daughter carefully down the steps to the tarmac.

Collecting their suitcases, they found a water fountain for Joyce, who was already struggling with the heat, before making their way to the arrivals hall. Hubert was struck by the sight of so many black people all in one place: black people in police uniforms, black people serving behind the counters in the numerous kiosks around them, black people doing every job at every level. He had almost forgotten what it was like not to be the odd one out, he had almost forgotten what it was like to be just one of the crowd.

He began scanning the hall for the familiar face of his sister, which was, as it turned out after fourteen years away, not quite as familiar as he'd imagined it would be.

'Cora!' exclaimed Hubert when he finally found her. 'Me would walk right by and not give you a second glance. You've grown up!' Gone were the gangling arms and awkward legs of the teenager he'd left behind, and in their place were the long and slender limbs of a woman. Wearing a pale blue cotton summer dress and straw sunhat, she looked just like a younger version of their mother, tall and elegant but at the same time not someone to be underestimated.

Cora laughed, hugged her brother, then stood back to look at him. 'And you've grown wide!' she teased, poking a finger into the side of his belly. 'Joyce must be feeding you up real good.'

Hubert made the introductions and Cora embraced her

sister-in-law, then the children, with the same warmth and delight she'd shown to her brother.

'It's so good to finally meet you all,' she said, taking hold of one of the suitcases. 'Hubert always writes so fondly about you, and in such detail that me feel like me already know you.' She leaned down and stage-whispered for the benefit of the children. 'And your grandmother is beside herself with excitement to meet you two! Let me warn you now, you are about to get spoiled!'

Leaving the relative cool of the airport terminal, Hubert and the rest of the family followed Cora across the car park past clutches of white holiday makers, bored-looking taxi drivers and unashamedly vocal tour guides trying to drum up trade for boat rides around the island and sightseeing bus trips.

Finally, hot and sweaty from the scorching midday sun, they reached a battered white pick-up truck.

'It's Lloyd's,' said Cora as Hubert began loading the suitcases into the back. 'My tiny car wouldn't be able to fit you all plus luggage unless we strap this one to the roof.' She tickled David's tummy. 'You two go up front, and the kids can sit in the back.'

Joyce shot Hubert an anxious look.

'They'll be fine,' he reassured her as the children eagerly scrambled in amongst the luggage. 'We used to ride around in the back of trucks all the time when we were kids. Plus Cora is an excellent driver. Has been since she was Rose's age.'

Cora laughed. 'Me haven't lost a single one of my nephews and nieces yet. And me not about to start now!'

As they drove through the streets of Kingston, past makeshift stalls at the side of the road selling all manner of things from straw hats and handbags to fresh coconuts and iced drinks, Hubert marvelled at how little things seemed to have changed. Yes, there were more cars on the roads and more tourists than he recalled, but the essence of the place, its heart and soul, seemed to be the same. And as they left Kingston in the direction of Spanish Town his eyes were drawn towards the Blue Mountains, at once so familiar and yet still able to inspire awe. He chastised himself for having left this visit so long when it was clearly just what he needed. He could feel the damp of England evaporating from his skin, and the deep chill of the season he'd left behind thawing from his bones. This was what he'd been missing all these years, even though he hadn't known it.

As they pulled up the dirt track that led to the house, past tall lines of breadfruit trees, scattering whole flocks of wandering chickens pecking hopefully at the baked earth in front of them, past goats chewing joylessly at thistles sticking out of the bushes, Hubert delighted in the reaction of his family. Joyce's laughter, the children's gasps of wonder, the collective awe at the sights and sounds that had seemed so commonplace to him growing up. It was a joy to be able to set all this before them like a feast and watch as they devoured every morsel.

Hubert was not one for tears but when he saw his mother standing on the front porch, hastily removing her apron and fixing her hair, he felt a lump in his throat so large he could barely swallow it down. In his memories his mother was always so slim and youthful, but the woman before him, with a thickened waist, patches of white hair, and the beginnings of lines forming around her mouth and eyes, was not the woman he'd left behind. And yet she was unmistakably his mother, from her dark brown eyes now brimming with tears through to the warmth of her smile that had provided so much comfort in his youth. They embraced for the longest time, as if trying to make up for the past fourteen years of separation, and she only released him in order to take hold of Joyce, in whose ear she whispered, 'Thank you for taking such good care of my son.' After that she moved on to the children, planting a kiss on each of their cheeks before taking them both by the hand and demanding that they tell her every detail of their journey.

The afternoon that followed was one that the children, in all the years that were to come, would never forget. Eating their first coconut, fresh from the tree, its white flesh all jelly unlike the dried stuff they had enjoyed at home. Seeing chickens roaming around the back of the house, unhindered by cages or fences, and looking on later with a mixture of horror and delight as their grandmother, armed with a razor-sharp machete, dispatched one with a single stroke, ready to be plucked and prepared for their evening meal. Sucking on sugar cane, its sweet juice so abundant that it ran in rivulets down the sides of their chins, while riding on the back of a donkey led past fields of corn by their Uncle Lloyd, a man so big with a voice so deep that they both reasoned he had to be a giant.

By the time their grandmother summoned them for dinner, as they ran around the backyard trying to catch lizards soaking up the last of the early evening sun, they were so grubby and dishevelled that they reminded Hubert of him and Vivian when they were young. Joyce, however, was horrified at the state of them and spent a fruitless ten minutes trying to smarten them up for the dinner table in a house that had no running water or mains electricity. Still, Hubert could tell just from looking at them as they all squeezed around the table, the children sitting on upturned fruit boxes, that everything they were experiencing, whether good or bad, was making an impression on them, etching itself permanently on to their memories. Gus had visited home the year before last, and other friends had all been back too over the past five years, but whether single or married, they had all, for reasons of economy, made the journey alone.

Hubert, however, was now glad that he waited, because thanks to Joyce and his children, he was seeing his country of birth through their eyes and not his own, seeing all the wonderful delights of rural Jamaica as if for the first time. Fresh fruit growing on trees that belonged to no one dotted along the roadside, flowers so bright and vibrant that they almost hurt your eyes to look at growing on scrubby untended pieces of land, and wildlife so fascinating and diverse, from the hummingbirds feeding on nectar to spiders as big as your fist, all without the bars or strengthened glass of a zoo.

After the meal and using what little light remained of the day, Hubert, Joyce and the children walked the five minutes to where his father Theodore was buried. It was on a quiet, elevated spot on the southernmost edge of their land, overlooking a stream and the valley below. Hubert hadn't been a frequent visitor to this place even when he lived here, but for reasons he couldn't vocalise he felt the need to show the children the last resting place of their grandfather. Rose and Joyce very sweetly picked a posy of brightly coloured wild flowers, full of yellows, oranges, reds and purples, and gently laid them on the marble tablet in front of the headstone.

David stared up at Hubert, his eyes questioning.

'What was he like? Was he fun?'

Hubert nodded, even though it wasn't quite as simple as that, given the troubles his father had lived through.

'He . . . he did his best. And you can't ask for more than that, can you?'

Thinking about what Hubert had said, Rose traced her fingers across the lettering of the headstone.

'When I grow up and have children of my own, if I have a boy I think I'll call him Theodore, it's a nice name.'

'That's lovely,' said Joyce. 'Theodore is a nice name.'

They stood in silence for a moment until David heard something in the bushes behind them. Desperate to see his first ever mongoose, he raced off, closely followed by Rose, leaving Joyce and Hubert alone.

'It's so lovely seeing them so free and happy here, don't you think?' said Joyce as she and Hubert walked along hand in hand.

Hubert didn't respond. He was too busy thinking about the past, his own childhood, and trying to make sense of it.

Joyce nudged him gently.

'Penny for your thoughts?'

Hubert blinked several times, as though waking from a dream.

'Sorry, love, were you saying something?'

'Not really, what was it you were thinking about?'

Hubert didn't know what to say. He tried not to think about the past if he could help it, but coming back here with his family after so long away had brought a lot of long-buried memories to the surface.

As though reading his mind, Joyce said, 'You never really talk about your father. How old were you when he passed away?'

He thought for a moment about that day, the day when his mother told him that his father, a man he barely knew, had taken his own life.

'Fifteen,' said Hubert.

Joyce squeezed his hand tightly.

'Oh Hubert, I'm sorry.'

'Me too,' replied Hubert. 'Me too.'

23

Now

The next morning, following a restless night, Hubert woke early and after breakfast and feeding Puss, got dressed and left the house. On the way to the train station he called into the Tesco Metro and bought a small bunch of pink carnations that he tucked under his arm and a pack of barley sugars for the journey. At the station he boarded a train to central London, and twenty-three minutes later was gathering his things together and joining the throng making its way to the underground. Hubert made the short journey to Westminster on the District Line and as he took the escalator up to street level he tried to read the advertising posters on the wall next to him, but it was as if they were written in a foreign language. Who or what was a Zoopla? What exactly was an O2 or indeed a 'vitamin concept'? Hubert suddenly felt like he was really getting old, like he was a relic from the past, like the world was racing ahead and leaving him behind.

Emerging into a busy mid-morning in central London, Hubert took a moment to get his bearings. To his left a man selling fruit and vegetables from a stall was busy crushing empty boxes, straight ahead of him snaked three long lines of traffic and to his right sat a homeless man begging, legs covered with a filthy sleeping bag. Hubert took a five-pound note from his wallet and placed it in the cap at the man's feet, then, crossing the road, made his way towards Westminster Bridge.

Gaggles of tourists were taking photographs of themselves on the bridge using the Houses of Parliament as a backdrop while hurried office workers strode past them purposefully. No one paid Hubert the slightest bit of attention as he slowly made his way to the middle of the bridge and gazed over the parapet, taking in the view.

The Thames, he thought as he removed the carnations from underneath his arm, wasn't a pretty river, certainly nowhere near as attractive as any of the big rivers back home in Jamaica. It was, however, a grand river, he decided. One that was impossible to ignore. This was a river that kings and queens had sailed down, that famous artists had painted, and that rich men paid millions to live next to. But more importantly than all of these things was the fact that this river, this bridge on which he was standing, had borne witness to his first date with Joyce all those years ago. And it was here, rather than her grave in Bromley cemetery, where he came when he wanted to feel close to her, or like now needed an answer to a question weighing on his mind.

Removing the cellophane from the flowers, Hubert lifted a single bloom to his nose and inhaled deeply. He'd hoped to catch a scent of heady sweetness but disappointingly it didn't smell of very much at all. Possibly it was Hubert's failing – old age seemed to be diminishing each one of his five senses every day – but it could just as easily have been the flowers themselves, grown in a test tube or something. Next time, he thought, he would search out a little florist's like the one he used to buy Joyce flowers from in Bromley to see if they had better stock. Regardless of their smell or lack thereof, Hubert decided it was the thought that counted and so, pressing the flowers briefly to his lips, he said quietly: 'For you, my love.' Then, holding the bouquet out over the water, he released his grip and as it fell through the air then finally into the river below, Hubert thought about Joyce, their life together and how, even now, nearly thirteen years on, he still missed her with every fibre of his being.

He stayed on the bridge long after the flowers had been swept away by the current. He thought about the questions he had come to ask, and he thought about the answers Joyce might have offered had she been there with him, and by the time he was ready to leave he knew, if not exactly what he should do, then at least the direction he needed to be going in.

On his return home, Hubert felt lighter and more focused than he had done in a long while. So when Ashleigh came round later that afternoon and said she'd had some thoughts about what they'd been talking about the day before, Hubert had wanted to tell her that he had been doing some thinking of his own. He could see that she was excited, however, and so let her speak first.

Reaching into her bag, she proudly produced a bright yellow A5 sheet of paper. Slipping on his glasses, he read it aloud:

> Do you think loneliness is a bad thing? Do you wish you knew more of your neighbours? Did you know that loneliness is a bigger killer than cancer?
>
> If you've answered yes to any of the above then here's your chance to stop being part of the problem and start being part of the solution! Come and join the Campaign to End Loneliness in Bromley!
>
> First meeting, Friday 1 June @ Bromley Library Community Room @ 7.30 p.m.

'The Campaign to End Loneliness in Bromley,' read Hubert again. 'Me never heard of them.'

'That's because they don't exist yet,' said Ashleigh cryptically.

'How you mean?'

Ashleigh took the flyer from Hubert's hand and held it aloft gleefully.

'Because I made it up last night on my laptop and printed it out at work this morning! The idea came to me in a flash. I was thinking about your friend and everything we talked about, and then I got thinking about my situation and how different it would be if I didn't have you to talk to. That's when it hit me . . . you remember I said that somebody ought to do something about this loneliness problem? Well, I got to thinking, what if that somebody was us? Me and you, Hubert? Because that's what's wrong with the world, isn't it? Everyone's always passing the buck or shifting the blame on to someone else. But what if we stopped thinking about problems like loneliness as someone else's thing to sort out and started taking responsibility for it ourselves? It's like my nan always used to say, "Ash, if you want a job doing, roll up your sleeves and get stuck in!"'

'So let me get this right . . . you . . . you . . . want us to set up a . . . campaign group?'

'Well, I think they're called pressure groups these days. But yeah, we'd be like CND or Greenpeace or Surfers Against Sewage . . . but, you know . . . for lonely people in Bromley.'

'But this sounds like an awful lot to take on,' said Hubert, thinking not just about Ashleigh but about Rose. He now only had two months left in which to make some more new friends. No time at all really, if he was to have any hope of sorting out his life so that his daughter wouldn't have to worry about him. Yes, he'd made some headway with Jan, but that was about it. With Gus being the way he was and everyone else having vanished off the face of the earth, he'd have to get his skates on.

'Haven't you got enough on your plate as it is? Just a few days ago you were telling me that you hadn't got time to do all your housework. Where are you going to find the time to . . .' He glanced at the flyer again. '. . . end loneliness in Bromley?'

Ashleigh seemed a touch affronted.

'Firstly, I only said that about the housework because when you came in for a cup of tea that day the flat was a tip and I didn't want you thinking we lived in a pigsty. Secondly, I won't be ending loneliness in Bromley on my own because you'll be helping me . . .'

'To end loneliness in Bromley?'

Ashleigh nodded confidently, which made Hubert feel uncomfortable. He didn't like the sound of this at all.

'Don't you think we should start with something . . . me don't know . . . smaller?'

'Hubert, I know it sounds like a crazy idea and when I was making the flyer, even I thought it seemed a bit bonkers. I mean trying to "end loneliness in Bromley", it sounds completely ridiculous, doesn't it? But then so did sending people to the moon and freeing that Nelson Mandela fella and having a computer in your pocket that you can watch telly on. Everything new sounds ridiculous until someone makes it happen. And like someone posted on Instagram this morning: "Even the longest journey starts with a single step."' She paused briefly, scanning Hubert's face in an effort to gauge his reaction. 'Listen, I know this seems crazy and I know you probably won't want anything to do with it, but I think this is really important not just for people like me, or like your friend Gus, but for everybody who's ever felt—'

Hubert interrupted.

'Yes.'

The word was out before he'd had time to stop it.

'What do you mean "yes"?'

It was a good question. Admittedly a plan like Ashleigh's hadn't been what Hubert had in mind when he said to himself that something needed to be done about the issue of loneliness. At best her idea sounded like the kind of hare-brained scheme that would cause more problems than it solved. But in the absence of any other kind, what choice was there? What was it people used to say? 'If you're not part of the solution, you're part of the problem.' Hubert didn't want to be part of the problem. Not any more.

'Me want to help you end loneliness in Bromley.'

Ashleigh pulled a face. This clearly hadn't been what she'd expected to hear from him at all.

'You mean you don't think it's a daft idea?'

'What? Helping lonely people? There's nothing daft about that, darling. Nothing daft at all. Count me in.'

She rested her hand on Hubert's arm.

'Wow, Hubert. I thought you were going to say no.'

'Well, the thing is,' said Hubert, 'it's like me said, me been doing some thinking of my own and it seems me sort of come to the same conclusion as you. You see, Joyce was of the same mind as your grandmother. If someone told her she couldn't do something, she would find a way to do it anyway. She wouldn't have just stood by and let things go down the toilet like they are.

She would've been in the middle of things, trying to make a difference. And me want to do the same.' Hubert drew a deep breath and wondered once again what he was getting himself into. 'Granted, until you arrived this morning me didn't have any idea where to start, but me think you're right . . . ending loneliness in Bromley seems as good a place as any.'

24

Then: August 1975

The saloon bar of the Old Duke in Brixton on a Tuesday evening wasn't exactly the most happening place to be. There were a smattering of customers – all men, all the wrong side of forty – most at the bar with a pint, smoking and reading dog-eared newspapers, while a few others played darts or dominoes or simply sat staring into space. It felt like a place where men came to escape their troubles, leaving them stacked neatly at the front entrance ready to pick up again on their way out.

'Smiler, man,' said Gus, as the two men sat in their usual corner nursing half-drunk pints of Guinness. 'You've barely said two words the entire evening. Are you going to tell me what is plaguing you or do I have to drag it out of you?'

Hubert shook his head as if trying to rouse himself from a dream.

'What you say?'

'Cha, man! You really is somewhere else tonight.'

Hubert took several large gulps of his drink as though trying to fortify himself.

'Me sorry, man, it's not you. It's just that me got . . . well . . . a lot on my mind.'

Gus left it a minute, hoping that his friend would elaborate without the need for further prompting, but when Hubert said nothing, Gus was unable to let it go. 'Hubert Bird,' he said sternly, 'it's been a long day and my body is dog tired, so either tell me what's going on right this minute or let me leave so I can go to my bed.'

Hubert's whole heart ached with all this sorry business.

'Enough, Gus, man, me tell you everything.'

Ever since Marianne had made the invitation over a pot of tea at their usual café the Friday before, Hubert had been trying to work out exactly how he had got himself into this mess. It wasn't as if he had been looking to have an affair, in fact he'd always thought people who did were weak-willed and feckless. Cheating on your wife wasn't exactly the hardest thing in the world – especially if you still had your looks – but staying faithful, doing the right thing not just by your wife, but by your children too, that was the tricky thing. That took strength, discipline and determination – values that Hubert had always held dear.

Hubert hadn't felt himself since the sudden death of his mother back in February. It had all happened so quickly; one minute he was reading a letter from her in which she spoke of feeling under the weather following a bout of flu, and the next he was receiving a call in the middle of the night from Cora with the terrible news that their mother was gone.

Joyce told him that he should fly home for the funeral no matter what the cost, but Hubert had reasoned that the money would be of more use sent to Cora to help pay the funeral expenses and ease any financial burdens that had come from caring for their mother during her final days. So instead of grieving for his mother in person, he tried his best to do so from a distance but it was hard not knowing what he should be feeling, what he should be doing. He'd been fifteen when he'd lost his father but as he'd rarely been around, the loss hadn't had a great deal of effect. Besides, the man had been in such torment that his passing had almost been a blessed release. This was different, he knew that, but he couldn't bring himself to feel it, to understand what was going on deep within himself.

Joyce had tried her best to comfort him, knowing only too well what it was like to lose a parent, but whether out of a desire to appear stronger to his family than he actually felt, or his own natural reticence, Hubert found it impossible to open up to her. Instead, every time she asked how he was, he would assure her he was fine, that he was getting on with life, that he didn't need to talk, that he would be okay if he just kept busy.

The kids hadn't helped matters. Rose had some boyfriend that neither he or Joyce approved of, and his constant fear was that she would get into trouble and throw away all the opportunities he and his wife had worked so hard for her to have.

David, meanwhile, seemed to be struggling to keep up in school. He'd just scraped into grammar school and although he loved playing rugby and any other sport for that matter, he was finding the academic work difficult and his school report had not been good. Sometimes it seemed to Hubert that the only place he felt sure he knew what he was doing, where he felt confident, where he could find a little bit of peace, was at work, and it was here that he first met Marianne.

Hubert was now working in the maintenance department for a big housing trust in south London. It was for the most part a supervisory role, allocating all of the jobs that came in day by day, but every now and again they would be so overrun with work that Hubert himself would step in and it was a day like this when he was called to a job at a new block of flats in Camberwell.

At first, he barely noticed Marianne, a single mother with two school-age children. But then the issue had proved to be more complicated than he first thought, involving return visits over several days, and the two eventually got to talking as she brought him cups of tea and biscuits every hour on the hour.

Over the course of the job, Marianne told him all about her childhood in rural Ireland. How she'd escaped the confines of country living for London as soon as she could. Her first few months had been tough, working all the hours she could to make ends meet. Then she'd met the man who was to become the father of her children, and for a while things had been good. But one day he left for work and never came home. After lots of anguish and frantic searching, she discovered that he had in fact returned to Liverpool and the young family he'd never told her about.

Spurred on by her frankness, Hubert found himself talking too. Not just about his own journey to this country but also the recent passing of his mother. Talking to Marianne was different to talking to Joyce somehow. He didn't have to worry about what she would think of him, or how she would react to anything he said. He could just talk.

Even though he had mentioned having a wife and children several times, when the job ended and she suggested that they might keep in touch, Hubert had found himself agreeing, reluctant to give up the small oasis of calm he had found for himself. Despite not telling Joyce about Marianne, this had all seemed harmless enough to begin with, even when their ad hoc arrangement became a regular weekly occurrence.

One day Marianne told Hubert that her children would be away visiting her sister for the weekend and invited him over for dinner. It was then Hubert knew he could no longer fool himself that this was as innocent as he had pretended. Despite the casual nature of her invitation, Hubert was well aware what would happen should he accept. At the time he had told her he would need to check his schedule and that had been the last time they had spoken.

'Well, well, well,' said Gus as Hubert finished speaking. 'I did not see that coming.'

Hubert shifted uncomfortably in his seat.

'Me neither. This sort of thing . . . well, you know . . . it's just not me.'

Gus laughed.

'You can say that again! All these years I hoped you'd rub off on me but it's looking like it's the other way around.'

Hubert nodded, acknowledging the truth of his friend's statement. Gus was, after all, something of an expert in this field, two-timing, three-timing girlfriends and even messing around with married women on occasion. Hubert had always held a poor opinion of his friend's activities and yet here he was, about to go down the very same road.

'Gus man, tell me what to do. Me can't sleep, me can't eat, thinking about it all. Me sure Joyce knows something is up.'

'But strictly speaking you haven't done anything wrong yet . . . have you?'

'Of course not!'

'Then what's to worry about? Just don't go.'

Hubert sighed.

'But that's just it. Me seriously thinking about it.'

Shocked to hear the words coming from his own lips, Hubert suddenly felt his mouth become dry. He picked up his drink to slake his thirst and ended up draining the glass completely.

Gus shook his head mournfully.

'Smiler, you is not built for this kind of thing. You is a good man. You is a family man. You were never like me, always chasing after the girls them, so don't start now. Think of everything you built up these past twenty years. Think of Joyce, think of Rose, think of David. You have too much to lose to risk it all on one night of foolishness.' Gus drained his glass too and then stood as if making ready to go to the bar to get them another round. 'I know you must think I'm nothing but a hypocrite, given the way I carry on with the women them, but my advice to you is don't do this. Don't do it at all, because if you do you're going to make a whole heap of trouble for yourself. A whole heap of trouble.'

Hubert spent the next few days in a state of complete turmoil. He felt as if his guilt were written all over his face and any time Joyce asked him what was wrong it was as if she'd read the words written there and was waiting for an explanation. He found it almost impossible to concentrate at work, and driving back from a job he had almost killed himself and two of the lads he worked with by failing to give way at a junction and careening straight across the road, only narrowly missing a bus heading straight towards them. At night he was so fearful of talking in his sleep that for three days in a row he deliberately stayed up late on the pretext of watching a film on TV, only to fall asleep on the sofa and stay there until morning.

When Joyce reminded him that she was taking the children up to Manchester for the weekend to visit Mrs Cohen's niece, Ruth, Hubert took this as a sign – whether from fate, or from the devil, he wasn't sure – that he should go through with meeting

Marianne. The following day, after waving them off at the station, he returned home, had a bath, slipped on his best suit and a brand new tie he'd been saving for a special occasion and drove over to Camberwell.

On the way, Hubert tried not to think about anything. Not the chicken, rice and peas Joyce had left him in the fridge to tide him over while she was away. Not the hug Rose had given him before getting on the train, nor David's last-minute appeal to stay at home and keep his dad company. Instead he tried to focus on the journey and the fact that once he'd done this thing it would be out of his system, in the past, left behind once and for all so that he could get on with the business of being himself again.

Hubert's heart was racing as he pulled up across the road from Marianne's flat. Switching off the engine, he sat for a moment trying to calm himself down, watching people come and go about their business, kids playing football on the street, or riding up and down the kerbs on their bikes. It all seemed so normal, so ordinary, none of it a fitting prelude to such a monumental act of betrayal. Hubert wanted empty streets, dark skies, perhaps a thunderstorm. He wanted heavy rain, harsh winds that chilled you to the bone and not a single person in sight. But what he got instead was a fine summer's evening in London, which oddly made what he was about to do seem all the more terrible.

Taking his keys out of the ignition, he caught sight of the half-empty packet of Wrigley's Juicy Fruit chewing gum lying on the dashboard. David had left it on the back seat the other day and Hubert had tutted when he'd found it, having told the kids off a hundred times about leaving their rubbish in the car. He'd tossed it angrily on to the dashboard, meaning to take David to task about it when he got home. But there it had remained, baking in the summer sun, and now here it was a week later, an old forgotten pack of chewing gum belonging to his son, the son that he'd had with the wife he was about to betray.

Hubert took the chewing gum and placed it in the glove box, out of sight, out of mind. He reached for the door, then stopped when he realised there was a problem. He felt as though he was stuck in his seat, glued in position, as though a force greater than himself was keeping him in place. His body simply didn't want him to go through with this. The longer he sat there, the more he realised that Gus was right. He wasn't this kind of man. This wasn't the sort of thing he did. He had too much to lose to risk it all. He loved Rose, he loved David, but most of all he loved Joyce, and the thought of what he had been about to do to her was enough to make him feel sick to his very soul.

Starting the engine, Hubert made his way back to Bromley, uttering all manner of promises and vows under his breath about how things would be from now on. He would never again take his family for granted, he would be the best father he could be and would love Joyce with all his heart and strength forever more.

The following weekend, while the children were out with their friends, Hubert asked Joyce if she fancied an ice cream and a walk in the park. As they sat side by side on a bench near the children's playground, lamenting how long it had been since either Rose or David had shown an interest in such places, Hubert decided this was the moment to bare his soul. To tell his wife everything.

'Joyce?'

'Hmm,' she replied, her eyes closed as she sat, like a sleepy cat enjoying the warmth of the sun.

'Me have something me need to tell you—'

Without opening her eyes, she cut him off.

'Don't . . . don't say another word, Hubert. Not another word. Just tell me that whatever it is, it's over.'

Hubert bit his lip. She knew. She must have known all along.

'It never really even started.'

With her eyes still closed, she reached over and took his hand and together they listened to the sounds of the children playing, of the sparrows chirping in the holly bush behind them, of the distant chimes of the ice-cream van, and made a wordless agreement never to speak of the matter again.

25

Now

It was twenty-nine minutes past seven in the evening on the day of the inaugural meeting of the Campaign to End Loneliness in Bromley. Hubert, Ashleigh and Jan were standing at the front of the community room of the library, staring at forty empty chairs.

'This is a disaster,' said Ashleigh. 'An absolute disaster. No one's coming. It's just going to be me, you, Jan and two family-sized packs of Hobnobs. Even Emils hasn't turned up like he said he would. I can't believe I forked out for a babysitter for this!'

Hubert was torn. On the one hand he didn't want Ashleigh to be disappointed, but on the other he couldn't help feeling that it was probably all for the best.

'Maybe we should hang on a little bit longer,' Hubert said, in an effort to sound encouraging. 'You never know, some people might be stuck in traffic.'

'The meeting's supposed to start in less than a minute,' snapped Ashleigh uncharacteristically. 'There's no traffic jam. No one's coming, that's all!'

Hubert, keen to say something comforting, opened his mouth to reply just as the door at the rear of the room swung open to reveal an elderly lady dressed, in spite of the pleasant weather, in a thick, navy-blue padded jacket, brown trousers, boots and a transparent rain-hood.

'Is this where the meeting is?' she barked. 'It says so on this leaflet!' She waved one of Ashleigh's yellow flyers in the air as if they'd demanded proof.

'You're in the right place, love,' said Jan.

'So I haven't missed it then?' she asked, looking round the empty room.

'No,' said Jan, 'we're just running a bit late, that's all. You're right on time. Take a seat and I'll sort you out a cuppa. What's your name, love?'

'Maude,' said the woman gruffly. 'I take three sugars in my tea and I'll have a couple of those biscuits as well, while you're at it.'

While Maude got herself settled and Jan sorted out her drink, the door swung open again, this time revealing a short, balding, slightly overweight man who appeared to be in his mid-fifties. He was wearing faded black jeans, scuffed Dr. Marten boots and a T-shirt with a picture of the current leader of the Labour Party on it looking distinctly like Karl Marx.

'Sorry I'm late,' he said. 'I'm Tony. I would've been here earlier but just as I was finishing my shift, I found a man fast asleep in the biography section and couldn't wake him up for love nor money.'

'You work here in the library?' asked Jan.

Tony nodded. 'Part-time,' he said. 'For my sins. The rest of the time I work on my novel.' He pointed to a flyer on one of the chairs. 'It was me who pinned one of these up on the library noticeboard. I thought I'd come along and add my two penn'orth.'

'I hope he was all right,' said Maude anxiously, as Jan handed her a cup of tea.

'Who?' asked Jan.

'The man who fell asleep in the biography section. I've done it myself a few times and it can be quite a shock to the system when you wake up to find you're not in your own bed!'

'He was fine,' said Tony. 'A few too many glasses of pop at the pub next door, if you know what I mean.'

Just as Hubert was beginning to wonder if anyone else would turn up, the door opened once again and in strode two women, one of whom Ashleigh greeted warmly.

'Hi, Randip,' she said, running over to hug the plump Indian woman Hubert recognised from the vet's. 'I'm so chuffed you came.'

'Well,' said Randip, 'it's for a good cause, isn't it? And anyway,

I can watch *EastEnders* on catch-up, so it's not like I'm missing out on anything.'

Ashleigh walked the woman over to meet the others. 'This is my friend Randip from work,' she explained. 'Randip, this is Hubert and Jan.'

'And I'm Fiona,' announced the woman who had come in at the same time as Randip. She was tall and smartly dressed with fire-engine-red hair cut into a sharp bob. 'I picked up one of your leaflets in the hairdresser's the other day and I thought it was a marvellous idea.'

At first glance Hubert thought she seemed middle-aged, but on closer scrutiny concluded she was somewhat older and that her youthful appearance was down to her hair, the trendy horn-rimmed glasses and bright plastic jewellery she was wearing.

'Take a seat,' said Hubert, feeling that he ought to show willing, 'and Jan will sort you out a drink.'

Suddenly the doors swung open again and Emils burst in, red-faced and panting, still wearing his blue and white courier uniform and holding three large Tupperware boxes.

'Have I missed meeting?' he asked. 'Traffic in Bromley is nightmare.'

'You haven't missed anything,' said Ashleigh, brightening considerably. 'We haven't started yet. The important thing is you're here now.'

'Thank you,' said Emils, and then he surveyed the room before announcing, 'I made cupcakes for meeting: chocolate and coffee, lemon meringue and salted caramel. Where should I put them?'

'I'll sort those out for you,' said Jan, taking the boxes from him. 'You sit yourself down and I'll make you a drink. You look like you could do with one.'

As Emils took a seat Ashleigh turned to Hubert and said excitedly: 'I can't believe it, people are actually coming! This hall could be full if it carries on like this!'

Hubert remained sceptical and sure enough, although by ten to eight several cups of tea and coffee had been drunk and a good number of Emils's cakes consumed, after that first flurry no one else appeared. And so, having discussed her plan with Hubert, Ashleigh asked Emils to help her make a small circle of chairs at the front and position the portable whiteboard to the side of her, and then called the meeting to order.

'Good evening, ladies and gentlemen,' she began nervously. 'I'd like to welcome you all to the very first committee meeting of the Campaign to End Loneliness in Bromley. The plan tonight is to . . . is to . . . is to . . .'

Ashleigh's hands were shaking and her face was so pale Hubert thought she might be about to faint. At pains not to draw attention to himself but unable to just sit and watch her struggle, Hubert stood up and put a comforting arm around her shoulder.

'You can do this,' he whispered in her ear. 'Just take a deep breath and have another go.'

'Sorry,' she said as Hubert returned to his seat. 'I'm not very good at public speaking . . . speaking normally I can do 'til the cows come home, but the minute I've got an audience I get nervous.'

'Don't worry, love,' said Jan. 'You're doing brilliantly.'

'Absolutely,' said Fiona. 'You're doing very well, my dear.'

'You are wonderful,' said Emils and it sounded so much more like an assessment of his feelings towards her than a word of encouragement that everyone looked at him briefly before turning their attention back to Ashleigh.

'Thank you, Emils,' said Ashleigh, blushing. 'And everyone else too. I'll try again, shall I? Good evening, ladies and gentlemen, and welcome to the very first committee meeting of the Campaign to End Loneliness in Bromley. For those of you who don't know me, my name's Ashleigh. I'm a single mum, I work part-time at the vet's and I'm fairly new to the area. And this,' she said, gesturing to Hubert, 'is my neighbour and good friend, Hubert Bird. Hubert has lived in Bromley for over fifty years and it's the two of us who had the idea to start this campaign. So that's us,' she said, looking expectantly at the faces looking at her. 'As there aren't that many of us, how about we go around the room and everyone introduce themselves and say a bit about why you're here tonight.'

There was a bit of an awkward silence as people shuffled uncomfortably in their seats, nobody wanting to be the one to go first. When it became obvious no one else was going to volunteer, Fiona cleared her throat and said, 'Good evening, everyone. My name's Fiona and I suppose I'm here because my husband died last summer, six months after we both retired, me from a thirty-year career as a teacher at a private girls' school and him after forty years in finance. I've found that because I look after myself and keep myself busy, people often assume I'm never lonely, but that couldn't be further from the truth. The reality is that losing Geoff has hit me hard and I'm just not used to spending hours on my own. So if I can do anything to stop people feeling the way I have at my worst, then I'd like to do it.'

'I know exactly how you feel,' said Randip shyly after a moment. 'It's been three years since my husband left me and even though my kids are good at keeping in touch, they have their own lives. Sometimes there are these long stretches of time where I feel like I don't belong anywhere. If it wasn't for work, I think I'd be completely lost.'

There was a long silence, so long in fact that for a moment Hubert wondered whether anyone would speak again, but then Tony shifted in his chair, coughed several times and then began to speak.

'Actually, it was a bit like that for me,' he said. 'After my relationship broke down . . . well . . . I soon realised that I didn't actually have any friends of my own. It was odd, a bit like not realising you've lost a limb. It was as if one day I had a busy social life and the next, it had all disappeared and I was stuck at home with only Radio Four for company.' He paused and stared into his mug. 'I had a bit of a breakdown, I suppose . . .' he said quietly. 'But I'm on the mend now . . . that's why I thought I'd give today a try.'

There was a brief pause while everyone reflected on Tony's words and then Emils spoke.

'It can be very lonely moving far from your family to a different country,' he began as everyone turned to look at him. 'The house where I live is full of immigrants like me and sometimes, when we are all in our rooms, it feels like we are all being lonely alone. When Mr Hubert told me about this I thought to myself, '"Yes, Emils, this is something you should try to help with."'

As soon as Emils finished speaking Jan sniffed self-consciously and then said, 'The only reason I still work part-time at my age is to get me out of the house and enjoy a little bit of company. If I didn't, I doubt I'd see anyone for days on end.'

Maude nodded vigorously and through a mouthful of cupcake said, 'Back in January when there was all that ice about, I went two whole weeks without talking to another human being. It was horrible. Really lonely.'

The room fell silent again and Hubert took the opportunity to think about the strangeness of life with its ebb and flow, people drifting in and out, lives filling up and emptying seemingly at random.

'Thanks, everyone,' said Ashleigh, getting to her feet again. 'As someone who arrived in Bromley only recently without knowing a single soul aside from my baby daughter, I really get what you all said. What's clear is that we're all here because loneliness is a big issue, which, as I said in our flyer is a bigger killer than cancer. And—'

Ashleigh stopped mid-sentence as Randip raised her hand.

'I don't really want to be that person, Ash,' she began, 'but are you sure about that?'

'What?'

'About loneliness being a bigger killer than cancer.'

Tony nodded. 'She's got a point. While I get what you mean, it isn't right. According to what I read on Google, scientists think loneliness might be a bigger killer than obesity or possibly smoking but definitely not cancer.'

'Okay fine,' said Ashleigh. 'It's a bigger killer than obesity and smoking.'

Tony put his hand up and pulled an apologetic face. 'Technically that should be "a bigger killer than obesity *or* smoking", not the two combined.'

'Okay,' said Ashleigh, trying not to sound exasperated, 'let's just say then that it's a bigger killer than obesity *or* smoking, which means that it's really bad, okay? Are we agreed?'

To Ashleigh's huge relief, everyone in the circle nodded.

'Tonight,' continued Ashleigh, 'we're all here because we want to do something about it. So here's the plan: firstly we need to nominate a president to be our spokesperson and the face of the campaign. Then secondly we need to come up with some ideas on how we're going to end loneliness in Bromley.'

'About that,' said Fiona, raising her hand. 'Ending loneliness in Bromley is quite an ambitious undertaking, isn't it? I was just wondering whether it might be wiser to have a rather more modest aim. After all, Bromley is quite a big place and loneliness is quite a complicated problem.'

'I was thinking something similar,' said Tony as others nodded in agreement.

'Me too,' said Randip, 'I like the sound of it, but . . . look at us, we're just a handful of ordinary people sitting in a room at the library that's far too big for us. It's not like we're really going to be able to end loneliness, is it?'

Hubert found himself getting annoyed. Ashleigh needn't have gone to all this effort making flyers and organising a meeting. She could've easily been out getting drunk every weekend like other young people her age. But instead she'd spent both time and money trying to make a difference to the community in which she lived. He didn't care if anyone thought that the campaign was pie in the sky. Sometimes, thought Hubert, you have to try the impossible to work out whether it is impossible. Sometimes, as his Joyce used to say, instead of waiting around for somebody else to do something, you have to be that person. Sometimes you just have to go big or go home.

It was only when everyone in the circle started clapping that it dawned on Hubert that the thoughts he'd been voicing to himself had actually been shared with the whole group.

'Well,' said Fiona, 'I don't know about everyone else but I certainly know who I'm voting for president.'

'Me too,' said Maude, as the others nodded in agreement. 'I had a black gentleman as a lover in the late Sixties. Very handsome he was too.'

There was a stunned silence until Ashleigh, keen not to dwell on Maude's revelation, said briskly, 'Right then, all those in favour of Hubert being made president of the Campaign to End Loneliness in Bromley please raise your hand.'

Five arms shot up in the air and the only two that remained down belonged to Hubert and Tony, although Tony's only stayed down for a moment.

'So it's unanimous then,' said Ashleigh, turning to beam at Hubert. 'If you accept the nomination, Hubert Bird, you are now officially our campaign president.'

Hubert didn't know what to think. Yes, he had wanted to do something to help Gus and people like him, but he'd been convinced that Ashleigh's idea would fall flat on its face. He certainly hadn't had designs on even being the campaign's secretary, let alone president. But as he took in their expectant faces and saw the expression of elation and relief Ashleigh wore, he didn't have the heart to let them all down or to burst her bubble. And he'd meant everything he'd said, hadn't he? This was a good thing Ashleigh was trying to do. And even if it failed, if the whole thing came to nothing, then at the very least all the people sitting in this room would be, for a time anyway, a lot less lonely.

26

Then: September 1978

Hubert and Joyce had been talking in the kitchen when the shouting had begun upstairs. It was generally Hubert who dealt with altercations between Rose and David, and so taking the stairs two at a time, he burst into Rose's bedroom to find his children squaring up to one another, faces inches apart, yelling the most venomous of threats. The moment Hubert entered the room, however, the shouting stopped and they each took a step away from the other, as though a bell signalling the end of round one had just rung, although they continued to shoot each other furious looks from their respective corners.

'If this is about damn bedrooms again, me going to be seriously vex!' snapped Hubert. He didn't like losing his temper but he would if the situation required.

Neither said a word, thereby confirming Hubert's suspicions.

'Well?' he demanded. 'What's all this damn noise about?'

David's broad shoulders sagged, signalling defeat.

'I don't see why she's still got the bigger room when she's not even going to be living here.'

'Because I'll be coming back during holidays,' defended Rose, 'and I'll still need my desk and all my things.' She appealed to her father. 'Dad, tell him.'

Hubert turned to his son and sighed.

'Boy, what me already said about Rose's room?'

David shrugged, an action that infuriated Hubert.

'What happen? You deaf? What did me say about Rose's room?'

'That . . . that . . . nothing is changing for the time being.'

'Exactly. So why you in here bothering your sister?'

David shrugged again.

Hubert barked, 'Me waiting for an answer!'

In an instant David flipped from sullen to incensed, and desperate for a release, he kicked the corner of Rose's bed.

'Because it's not fair! She always gets everything she wants. She's your favourite!'

Before Hubert knew what he was doing, he had lifted his hand ready to strike his son. He couldn't remember the last time he'd smacked either of his children, but this past year David had been sorely trying his patience and today of all days he'd just had enough.

'David! Go to your room this instant!' ·

All three spun around to see Joyce in the doorway wearing a look of fury to match Hubert's. For the first time in a long while David didn't argue with his mother and instead, grateful to be out of his father's reach, he left the room, slamming his door shut with such force the whole house shook.

Joyce turned to Rose, her expression softening.

'Almost done packing, love?' Rose nodded. 'Good, well why don't you help your dad put the rest of the things in the car and I'll go and talk to your brother?'

Today was a momentous day for the Birds: Rose was off to university, the first member of either branch of the family ever to do so. Hubert and Joyce had been so proud when she'd received her A-level results back in August, neither of them fully realising just how quickly she would be gone. It was as though one moment they were celebrating her success with a family meal at a country pub, and the next they were collecting boxes from the supermarket in which to pack her belongings for the five-hour drive to Durham.

Hubert observed that each member of the family had taken the news that Rose would be leaving the home in their own unique way. Rose herself had been fizzing with excitement from day one, a whirlwind of activity ever since, purchasing new clothes and shoes and restyling her hair in a bid to have her reinvention as a sophisticated woman of the world complete before her arrival in halls.

By contrast, sixteen-year-old David, whose behaviour had been going steadily downhill for the past few years, spiralled off into a steeper decline. Besides the constant arguments with his sister, there had been a number of incidents over recent weeks where he'd defied his parents and stayed out far later than he was allowed, and just last weekend he'd been brought home by the police after he and his so-called friends smashed up a bus shelter.

It wasn't as if Hubert and Joyce were strangers to teenage rebellion – at her worst, Rose had been quite the handful – but this was different. It felt less like a phase and more like it was becoming a permanent state of affairs, and neither parent was sure what to do for the best. They'd tried punishing him, they'd tried reassuring him he was loved, reminding him everybody made mistakes and it was in his power to turn things around, but nothing worked. It was as if Rose's success had only confirmed his belief that he was and would always be a failure.

For her part, Joyce had focused on practical arrangements: making her daughter a new bed-set, gathering together a box of kitchen utensils, taking her shopping for things she might need and helping wherever and whenever she could to tick off items from Rose's ever-lengthening to-do list that was pinned to the cork board in the kitchen. Hubert, however, could see past all the busyness to what was really going on: she was scared, really scared of letting her daughter go off into a world that she knew had the potential to be dangerous; of the house that would keenly feel the lack of Rose's calming presence; of the idea that her daughter might never properly return home.

Over the past few weeks, Hubert had tried to talk to his wife about it all several times but she always brushed aside his comments with a breezy, 'Oh, I'm fine,' or 'There's nothing to talk about.' Of course, what she really meant was, 'I don't want to talk about this because talking about it will only make it real.'

Hubert didn't really know what he felt. He couldn't have been more proud of his daughter and all that she had achieved, from getting into grammar school through to appearing in the local paper with her outstanding A-level results. It was all he'd ever wanted for his children, that they work hard, do well and move up in the world. But then, he couldn't imagine what this place would be like without Rose. Would this still feel like a family home when one of its members was missing? Could the Birds still function like a unit when a quarter of their number was living over three hundred miles away? How would those who remained rub along in this new arrangement when David, who at sixteen was already so spiky, difficult and hostile, became the sole focus of his parents' attention?

This was uncharted territory for Hubert. With friends like Gus, who at forty-two was still footloose and fancy free, and the rest of the Red Lion stalwarts, none of whose children were university bound, he had no one to consult for advice. All Hubert wanted was that Rose might enjoy this next chapter of her life but also that she might not forget them, that she would remember this would always be her home, and no matter what happened in the future, he and Joyce would be there to love her, hold her, pick her up and dust her off whenever she needed it.

By the time Hubert and Rose had finished loading the car, Joyce had worked her calming magic on David, who appeared, scowl-free, holding a Tupperware box of cakes his mother had baked the night before. 'Mum says these are for you,' he said, handing them to his sister. 'She's baked some extra for the journey and even made some of the coconut ones especially for me. You can have one if you want.'

Rose smiled, the relief plain on her face that things between her and her brother were back to normal.

Thanks,' she said, taking them from him and putting them on the back seat of the car, 'if you're lucky I might let you have one of mine.'

As Hubert sat in the car waiting for Joyce to lock up the house, he watched Rose and David in the rear-view mirror. Rose, her hair styled in a fashionable Diana Ross afro, was wearing a denim jacket over a striped V-neck sweater, every inch the chic young woman she wanted to be. David, meanwhile, had borrowed one of Hubert's old trilbies and wore it angled so sharply that it was a miracle it hadn't slid right off his head. He'd teamed it, Hubert observed, with a white T-shirt and black leather jacket in a bid to look cool and tough.

How could his two babies both look so grown up when it had only been yesterday that they would crawl into his lap to watch TV? It didn't seem possible, and yet here he was, about to set one of them on a journey that would take her who knew where? Time seemed to be racing past, the clock ticking two beats for every one, and Hubert sometimes felt like he couldn't keep up. Before he knew it, David would be leaving too, whether to university as Hubert hoped, or off pursuing dreams of his own, and then it would be just him and Joyce again, like it had been in the early days. But that time felt so long ago, it might as well have happened to another person. He wasn't that young man any more and Joyce wasn't that young woman. They were different, they were parents and had been for so long now that it was almost impossible to conceive of a life when they were anything else.

'Right then,' said Joyce as she slid into the passenger seat next to him, filling the footwell with yet more bags and Tupperware boxes full of food. 'Let's get going. We've got a long journey ahead.'

With delays on the motorway it was mid-afternoon as they pulled up outside the university accommodation office to get directions to Rose's halls and collect the keys to her room. Joyce and David stayed in the car while Hubert and Rose joined the queue that had formed outside the office. There must have been a hundred parents standing with their nervous-looking offspring: some appeared well-to-do, others rather less so; some were tall and athletic looking, others short and dumpy; but the one thing they all had in common was the colour of their skin.

As they waited their turn, spontaneous conversations between different sets of parents striking up all around them, Hubert wondered what he would say if he were ever included. If they told him they worked in banking, would he be honest and tell them he was a plumber, albeit one who now supervised the work of others, or would he make something up so as not to embarrass

Rose, who was already looking anxious at the prospect of anything happening to make her stand out more than she already did? As it was, there had been no need to worry, as they stood in line for a good twenty minutes and no one addressed him at all.

Eventually, armed with keys and a map, Hubert and Rose returned to the car, where Joyce and David were already tucking into some of the sandwiches Joyce had packed. Rose was mortified. 'What if someone sees you?' she said, ducking down in her seat. Joyce laughed, 'Well, I'd offer them a sandwich. There's plenty to go around.'

Rose's room was on the second floor and looked out across a lake that had geese and ducks on it. It was small, with a single bed against the wall, a desk under the window and a tiny sink and wardrobe at the other end of the room. Despite the view Hubert thought it resembled a prison cell, but Rose couldn't have been more delighted. While he and Joyce concentrated on unpacking her things, she focused on decorating. As she pinned up posters with bold political slogans and artfully arranged her books and cassettes, she chattered away to her brother about the welcome event planned for that evening.

All too quickly, the last things were unpacked, her bed made, curtains fixed, suitcases emptied and stowed away, and soon there was nothing left other than to say goodbye as Rose walked them back to the car.

'Now you will remember to eat properly, won't you?' said Joyce, adjusting Rose's collar.

'Of course I will, Mum. You know me, I love my food.'

Joyce forced a smile.

'I know you do, love, it's just . . . it just—' She burst into tears. Hubert's heart went out to his wife as he comforted her. She'd kept such a tight lid on her emotions but was struggling at the final hurdle.

'Oh, Mum.' Rose hugged her mum fiercely. 'I promise I'll be fine.'

Joyce reached for the tissue she'd tucked up her sleeve in preparation for this moment.

'Of course you will. I worry that's all. It's just what mums do.'

When Joyce eventually calmed down, Hubert took his turn to say goodbye to his daughter. He wanted to leave her with words of wisdom, something that would echo down the ages and give her comfort and certainty whenever such was required. All he could manage, however, was a bear hug and an assurance that if she ever needed anything, all she had to do was pick up the phone.

Due to their later-than-expected departure and several patches of congestion on the return journey it was almost midnight by the time they reached home. Joyce went to bed first, complaining of a headache, and was quickly followed by David and then finally, once he'd locked up the house, Hubert. Heading upstairs, he noticed David's light still on and decided to check in on him.

'You okay, son?'

David nodded sleepily and put down the music magazine in his hands.

'I can't believe I've got football in the morning. And it's an away match so I'll have to be there for eight. It'll kill me.'

Hubert smiled.

'You'll be fine. I'll give you a lift, if you like.'

'Thanks, Dad.'

David yawned and reaching across, switched off his light and wished Hubert a good night.

Standing in the darkness, Hubert was desperate to say more to his son. He wanted to assure him that Rose wasn't his favourite, that he loved them both equally, that he loved him more than words could ever express, but David was already fast asleep and snoring softly.

As Hubert left the room his gaze was drawn to Rose's door across the landing. Before he really knew what he was doing or why, he reached for the handle but the moment he touched it was shaken by a wave of sadness so overwhelming it brought him to his knees. Sitting with his back pressed against the wall outside her room and biting down hard on the sleeve of his shirt in order to dampen the sobs erupting from him, Hubert thought of his late mother. He wondered whether she too had experienced this same searing pain as she'd waved him off on the boat that would take him thousands of miles away from her to England.

27

Now

Hubert opened his front door.

'Morning, Jan, all ready for a day of spreading the word?'

Jan pointed down at her feet, clad in pristine white trainers.

'I am now. I picked these babies up yesterday because I thought to myself, if I'm going to be stomping up and down Bromley High Street all day handing out leaflets then I'm going to need something comfy. What do you think?'

Hubert nodded admiringly, then hitched up one of his trouser legs a fraction to better display his own sporty footwear.

'Rose bought these for me must be ten years ago now. She said me needed to do more exercise and that these would help. Me just keep them in their box on top of the wardrobe until now, but me knew they'd come in handy one day.'

Sensing that something interesting was going on, Puss made an appearance at the door and began winding herself around Hubert's legs mewling loudly.

'Come in, Jan, me almost ready but me need to put down this one's lunch before we go, in case we back late, although knowing her, she'll probably scoff the lot down the minute me back is turned!'

'Ooooh!' exclaimed Jan, following Hubert along the hallway into the kitchen. 'You've got a lovely home here.'

'Thank you,' replied Hubert, trying his best not to feel too self-conscious that Jan was now in his home. Before now they'd always met on neutral territory and he hoped she wouldn't take this as a signal that their relationship was somehow escalating to another level.

'To be honest, it's too big for me now.' He reached into a

cupboard and took out a pouch of cat food for Puss. 'Me probably should've moved somewhere smaller a long time ago, let one of these growing young families have it, but me too old to leave here now. Selfish really.'

Jan pulled a face. 'Nonsense. Your home is where your heart is and I can see that a lot of love and care has been put into this place over the years.'

Hubert scraped the food into Puss's bowl and like a flash she pounced on it and began gobbling it down.

'Well, I never,' said Hubert, scratching behind the cat's ear as she ate, 'anyone would think me never feed you! You had your breakfast less than an hour ago!'

Hubert gave Puss one last stroke, told her to behave herself and then, grabbing his jacket, hat and umbrella, set out with Jan.

The idea to spend the morning handing out flyers and recruiting potential volunteers to help with the campaign had been one of many to come out of that first meeting at the library just over a week ago. Whilst they had been only a few in number, when it came to how they might go about ending loneliness in Bromley they were brimming over with ideas. By the end of the evening Ashleigh's whiteboard was crammed full of suggestions that had ranged from the sublime to the ridiculous. Everything from holding a welcome party for local refugees (Fiona's idea) through to creating a saucy charity calendar featuring members of the committee in various states of undress while looking lonely (Maude's proposal). Of the handful of viable suggestions, there emerged several favourites:

1. The creation of a map, either physical or virtual, of existing clubs and activities within Bromley to show people what was already on offer.

2. Draw attention to gaps in provision for the lonely and encourage the formation of new groups to meet these needs.

3. The holding of an Anti-Loneliness week featuring a series of events to raise awareness of issues relating to loneliness in Bromley.

4. A party to launch the Anti-Loneliness week to be held at the community centre (with invitations sent out to Ed Sheeran, Meghan Markle and Adele).

5. A publicity campaign to be held as soon as possible to recruit more volunteers, engage public support and raise the campaign's profile within Bromley.

As meetings go, it was far more productive than either Hubert or Ashleigh had imagined it would be, and by the end of it they had unanimously decided to start with the publicity campaign. To this end, Ashleigh had persuaded the vet's to sponsor the production of a thousand flyers and it was these that the committee was meeting to distribute in the town centre.

Alighting from the bus, Hubert and Jan made their way through town to the front entrance of Primark to meet the rest of the committee. Present was Maude, once again dressed inappropriately for the season. She wore a brown fur coat, fur-lined boots and a baseball cap emblazoned with the legend, 'I'm the boss'. Next to her, Fiona and Randip were deeply engaged in conversation while Emils helped Ashleigh separate flyers into piles as Layla looked on from her pram.

'Morning,' said Hubert, 'lovely to see you all! We all feeling good?'

Hubert was more than a little aware that as president it was up to him to motivate the rest of the committee and he did want today to go well. What's more, if they managed to get more people involved then hopefully he could hand off his role as president to someone more suitable, thus giving him the freedom to focus his attention where it was needed: Rose's upcoming visit.

'Right then,' said Ashleigh, 'who are we waiting for?'

'Just Tony,' said Emils. 'He must be running late. I deliver parcel to the library yesterday and he said he was definitely coming.'

'Well if he's not here by—'

Hubert stopped, distracted by a small commotion further up the road.

Everyone turned to see a man in a polar bear costume striding along the pavement towards them, crowds of bemused Saturday shoppers parting before him. The bear walked right up to where the committee were assembled, came to a halt in front of Hubert and Jan and then took its head off.

'Morning guys,' said Tony, face flushed and hair awry. 'What do you think?'

Hubert was confused.

'Me don't understand. Who you meant to be?'

'I'm a polar bear,' explained Tony. 'And this is marketing.'

'Marketing?' repeated Hubert.

'To help us get our message across. It's the library's. It used to be the story-time bear but too many of the kids got scared by it, so it just ended up in a cupboard. I thought it would help draw people's attention to us and get them talking.'

Fiona laughed and gestured over Tony's shoulder to where a group of giggling teenage girls were taking photos of him with their phones. 'Well, it's certainly doing that.'

'Good thinking, Tony,' said Jan, and Hubert nodded, even though he thought the bear looked a little flea-bitten.

'Well,' said Ashleigh. 'The important thing is that we get the message out to everyone and if this helps then I'm all for it.'

She began handing out the piles of leaflets and clipboards.

'As discussed at the meeting, the main thing we want to achieve today is to let people know about the campaign and get down the contact details of anyone interested in joining us. So, let's get to it. Good luck, everyone!'

At Ashleigh's command the committee members paired up and went to stand in their designated positions. Randip and Fiona headed off to stand outside TK Maxx; Ashleigh and Emils to the front of the Glades shopping centre; Maude and Tony outside the main entrance to Marks & Spencer and Hubert and Jan in front of the big Sainsbury's.

It was only when he and Jan were in place that it occurred to Hubert just how nervous he was about facing the general public. After all, it was one thing to pass the time of day with someone, but it was quite another to attempt to recruit them into volunteering their time and commitment.

'Is this about Brexit?'

A silver-haired middle-aged woman dressed in flared jeans and open-toed sandals examined the leaflet Hubert had given her. Hubert swallowed hard, then cleared his throat.

'No, it's about loneliness.'

She scrunched up her face.

'What you handing out leaflets about loneliness for? If you're going to be handing out leaflets about anything, it should be Brexit.'

Hubert didn't quite know what to say to that, so instead he just smiled pleasantly and hoped she would walk away, but she seemed to take his silence as an invitation to continue talking.

'So, what about loneliness then?'

Hubert cleared his throat again.

'Everything you need to know is on the leaflet.'

'I know that but I want to hear it from you.'

'Well . . . it's about loneliness,' repeated Hubert. 'And what a big problem it is these days. The aim of the campaign is to put an end to loneliness in Bromley once and for—'

The woman snorted. 'You want to do what? End loneliness in Bromley? I'm not being funny but how's that going to happen, then?'

Hubert considered her question carefully.

'Hard work and a lot of determination.'

'Hmm,' said the woman. She handed the leaflet back to Hubert. 'That's what they said about Brexit and look where that's got us!'

Thankfully for Hubert, not every person he spoke to was as sceptical. While some just took a leaflet and smiled politely, others seemed genuinely interested and even agreed to leave their contact details. Most, however, just ignored both him and the leaflet in his outstretched hand walking past hurriedly as if he wasn't there.

Around one o'clock, with several piles of leaflets still left to distribute, Hubert and Jan met up with the rest of the team on some benches just down from Primark. As they all sat down, the news about that morning's efforts was mixed. Fiona and Randip had done well, not only getting rid of a considerable number of their flyers but also collecting over two pages of contact details. Maude and Tony had been less successful, losing half their leaflets after Tony chased some boys who had thrown a milkshake at him. They'd also failed to collect any contact details, due mostly, Tony confided while Maude was out of earshot, to his billing partner's habit of thrusting the clipboard under people's noses and saying in a threatening tone, 'Give me your email address!' Ashleigh and Emils's efforts had fared better, not least because Emils had approached a group of young Latvian men and persuaded them all in their mother tongue to sign up, while Ashleigh with the help of Layla had been able to charm quite a number of pensioners who had all wanted to stop and admire the little girl.

As those who had brought their lunch with them began to eat, the others, at Hubert's suggestion, headed towards McDonald's. As they made their way up the street Jan pushed Layla along in her stroller, chatting to Hubert, while Ashleigh and Emils decided to make the most of the short journey by carrying on handing out flyers. While some were received gladly, others were immediately discarded and as they walked, Hubert checked over his shoulder and was disappointed to see a trail of leaflets blowing about behind them. The truth was, most people didn't seem to care about the campaign or the issue of loneliness. Hubert couldn't find it in himself to get angry with them, however, because, he acknowledged, not so very long ago he too had been just the same.

Outside McDonald's, Jan lifted Layla out of her pushchair while Hubert tried in vain to collapse it. In need of help, he glanced around for Ashleigh, only to discover that she was across the road with Emils talking to a group of homeless men sitting on some benches outside a disused bank. There were three of them in total, one with matted brown hair, wearing a stained T-shirt and ripped jeans, another with a bald head covered in tattoos, and a third with light brown skin and long black dreadlocks with touches of grey at the temples. All three were drinking strong lager straight from two-litre bottles and were in such a sorry state they could barely sit up properly, let alone hold a conversation.

Without a word to Jan, Hubert rushed across the road and, grabbing Ashleigh by the arm, tried to pull her away.

'Hubert!' cried Ashleigh in astonishment. 'What are you doing? I'm just giving these guys some leaflets.'

When Hubert let go of her arm he found that he was shaking. 'You're wasting your time with these kind of people. Don't get involved!'

Ashleigh was horrified. 'What's gotten into you? They weren't being horrible or anything. I was just telling them about the campaign.'

'Drunks like them! Swigging from bottle in the middle of the day! It's a disgrace! They don't care about anything but themselves.'

'Is okay,' said Emils. 'Yes, they drunk, but they not hurting anybody, Mr Hubert, I assure you. I would not let anyone hurt Ashleigh.'

'And anyway, Hubert,' added Ashleigh, 'it's people like these guys who really need this campaign. It must be ever so lonely living on the streets.'

There was real disgust in Hubert's voice when he spoke.

'Lonely? Don't give me that! Look at them, leavings of men the lot of them! If it was up to me they would not be allowed to mess up the street like that. Me would lock up the whole bunch and throw away the key!'

'Hubert,' said Ashleigh, 'you can't really mean that surely?'

'Me do,' snapped Hubert. 'Every last word!'

'Hubert, I can't believe you're being like this,' chided Ashleigh. 'These are people just like you and me, and they need our help. You can't talk about sweeping the homeless off the streets like that, it's horrible!'

Hubert pointed at the man with dreadlocks, who was so intoxicated he could barely keep his eyes open.

'See that one there? That one's my son, my only son, and him dead to me! So, don't you go telling me what me can and cannot do! That boy disgust me!'

28

Then: July 1981

'Do you think this is a bit what the royal wedding will be like?' whispered Joyce, unwrapping a mint and handing it to her husband.

Hubert discreetly slipped the sweet into his mouth and then lifted his gaze, taking in the huge stained-glass windows and vast stone columns that held up the imposing vaulted ceiling with its intricate web of carvings.

'To be honest,' he whispered, lodging the mint in the side of his cheek for a moment, a smile playing on his lips, 'me think St Paul's Cathedral might be a step down after this! If Lady Di had seen this place she would have insisted on dragging the whole troop of them up here!' He pointed to the magnificent circular stained-glass window in front of them. 'Just look at that thing, it really takes your breath away. Who wouldn't want to get married here?'

'And to think, our little Rose is having her graduation here!'

'Congregation,' corrected Hubert, pointing to the order of service in his hand. 'This place so posh them even make up them own name for things that already got names!'

Today was Rose's big day. After three years of essay writing, late nights in the library and countless hours spent with her nose stuck in books, she was finally being rewarded with her degree, her ticket to a world of success and happiness. A ticket that, to Hubert's mind, meant all the more in the light of the troubles that had plagued the area they had once called home. Troubles that were now spreading across the country. Regardless of who was at fault, seeing Brixton on fire like that had broken Hubert's heart and as far as he was concerned, the further Rose was away from such problems the better.

Hubert and Joyce had been overjoyed when she'd called to tell them her results, that she'd been awarded a first and had been accepted on to the master's programme to study Politics and International Relations. Hubert hadn't known at the time what one might do with such a qualification, but he trusted his daughter knew what she was doing in a world that was so alien to him. All that mattered was that she had done well, that she was happy and had a bright future ahead of her.

'I wish David was here,' Joyce sighed, as a couple of latecomers appeared at the end of the pew, forcing everyone to shuffle up two seats. 'It feels wrong being here without him. This is a big family moment.'

'I know,' said Hubert. 'But the last thing we all need is another row. All we can do is hope and pray that he'll find his way somehow.' He couldn't help but frown at the thought of his son, who claimed to be too busy to attend his sister's graduation. This in spite of the fact that since leaving school two years ago, he had done nothing other than drift from one low-paid job to another, leaving himself plenty of time, Hubert thought, to get into all kinds of mischief. At the height of the rioting Hubert had even wondered if David had got himself tangled up in it, but although he kept erratic hours, he seemed uninterested in the whole business whenever Hubert brought it up.

Having finished his mint, Hubert was about to nudge Joyce for another when there was a loud blast from the huge organ pipes at the front of the cathedral that reverberated around the building, and the other parents around them began rising to their feet. Joyce and Hubert stood too, and as the organ continued playing, they turned to see the university's white-haired chancellor, dressed in all his finery, leading a procession of similarly gowned academics through to the front of the chapel. Following on behind came the students, dressed in their black gowns and mortarboards, sporting their faculty colours.

Reaching down into Joyce's handbag, Hubert took out the brand-new camera he had purchased especially for the occasion and trained it on the passing parade, ready for the first sight of

Rose. She had warned him beforehand not to embarrass her by taking photos during the ceremony and for the sake of peace Hubert had agreed. But that was then, before he realised just how much his heart was bursting with pride. He couldn't let this moment pass undocumented, he wanted to capture every second and not miss a single thing.

He'd taken two or three shots before she noticed him, and even when she did, rather than scowling as he'd imagined, she just rolled her eyes and flashed them both a huge smile.

Joyce cried when it was Rose's turn to receive her degree but Hubert just couldn't stop smiling, and as they both clapped, it was all he could do not to yell at the top of his voice, 'You see that gal there? That's my daughter!'

Afterwards, as they waited for Rose, Hubert was still on a high, unable to stand still for more than a few moments, desperate to give his daughter the hug of her life. Scanning the crowds, he was so focused on the graduates congregated around the front of the cathedral that when he felt a tap on his shoulder he nearly jumped out of his skin.

'Rose!' reprimanded Hubert, 'you trying to kill me? My heart is already beating fit to burst with all the excitement.' Throwing his arms around his daughter, he hugged her tightly, and as she let go to do the same to Joyce, he noticed a tall, handsome young man with sandy-coloured hair lingering a few feet away, looking uncertainly in their direction. This must be the boyfriend, thought Hubert, vaguely recalling the dog-eared Polaroid Rose had propped up on her bedside table when she'd come home for Christmas. They'd yet to meet him, but Hubert couldn't think of a conversation he'd had with her in the past six months where his name hadn't been mentioned.

Hubert held out his hand to the young man.

'You must be Robin,' he said as the boy stepped towards him, 'me . . . I mean *I'm* Rose's father and I'm very pleased to meet you.'

'Pleased to meet you too, sir. I've been looking forward to meeting you for such a long time. Rose has told me so much about you.' Robin had an accent that made him sound like a minor member of the aristocracy. Was this why of late Rose had started to sound quite plummy?

'So lovely to finally get to meet you,' said Joyce. She shook Robin's hand warmly. 'And, of course, congratulations!'

Robin darted a confused glance at Rose.

'She means on getting your degree,' she said quickly.

'Ah, of course, thank you, Mrs Bird. I wouldn't have been able to get through any of it without Rose's support. She's been marvellous.'

They chatted for a while, mainly about the splendour of the ceremony and setting, before Rose whisked Robin away, saying something about needing to have some photos taken.

'Well, he seemed nice,' said Joyce.

'Hmm,' said Hubert pensively, 'me suppose so.'

'And he was so polite and well spoken.'

'He certainly was,' said Hubert, still thinking.

'Do you think we ought to invite him to come along with us for lunch?'

'We could do but he probably already fixed up something with his own parents.'

'Wouldn't hurt to ask though, would it?'

Hubert didn't reply, concentrating instead on his coalescing thoughts as he watched Rose and Robin posing for photographs with their friends. They took numerous shots in various poses, culminating in them all throwing their mortarboards in the air. Throughout, Hubert remained thoughtful, mulling over their earlier conversation and that look the two of them had exchanged. Something wasn't quite right here, something was going on Rose wasn't telling them, something big.

Rose and Robin returned, forcing Hubert to shelve his musing for a moment. They chatted some more about the day and their plans for the evening, then Rose fell suddenly quiet, before taking Robin's hand and clearing her throat as if about to make an announcement.

When Rose spoke, there was something about the timbre of

her voice and the look in her eyes that convinced Hubert he knew what she was about to say.

'Mum, Dad.'

'Rose Lillian Bird,' he said stiffly, 'please tell me you're not in the family way.'

The effect of Hubert's words was immediate. It was difficult to work out who was most shocked. Rose gasped, Robin blushed scarlet to the roots of his hair and Joyce covered her mouth with both hands.

'Dad! Why would you say such a thing?'

'Because me can tell that something isn't right.'

'Of course I'm not pregnant!'

'Are you certain?'

'Dad!'

'Well, if you're not pregnant then what is it?'

Rose sighed heavily in defeat and, reaching inside her gown, pulled out a diamond ring on a chain around her neck.

'We're engaged, Dad. It only happened last night and I've been dying to tell you since you got here but I was waiting for the right moment.'

Robin stepped forward.

'But, of course, if you think it's a terrible idea and decline to give your blessing then we give you our word that we'll wait. I've plenty of job offers to consider at the moment and perhaps once I've secured a position you'd feel happier about the situation. As you know, Mr and Mrs Bird, Rose is an amazing girl and I just didn't want to let her slip through my fingers.'

Hubert looked at Joyce, and while he could see that she was just as stunned as he was, he was also aware that she too was recalling the moment he proposed all those years ago. Their own engagement had caused so much trouble, so much heartache, and he knew that neither of them wanted to show even a shadow of that same reaction to their beloved daughter.

'It's wonderful news,' said Joyce, 'absolutely wonderful! Isn't it, Hubert?'

Hubert reached out to shake the young man's hand again but

then thought better of it and instead gave him a hug. What a day this was turning out to be.

'Welcome to the family, Robin,' he said. 'Me hope you will both be very happy.'

In light of this announcement their plans for lunch were reconfigured to include not only Robin but also his parents, Mr and Mrs Callaghan.

The Callaghans were a smart, professional couple from the Sussex borders. He was a tall, solid-looking man with a firm handshake and owned an engineering business making parts for small aircraft. Mrs Callaghan was a petite, glamorous blonde whose life revolved around her husband, the tennis club and her local embroiderers' guild.

While they were clearly as taken aback by the engagement as he and Joyce had been, Hubert was relieved that they showed no signs of prejudice towards Rose. In fact, they seemed to go out of their way to demonstrate how much they liked her, not only constantly engaging her in conversation but also inviting her to join them on holiday to Italy in August.

Although things were noticeably better than they had been back when Hubert first arrived in England, that didn't mean racism had suddenly disappeared overnight. It was still there every day in newspaper headlines, in the stereotypes appearing on TV, in the assumptions strangers made about people who looked like him. The only difference with this kind of racism was that it was marginally more likely to result in graffiti scrawl across a family's front door than a physical attack or a beating. Instead it remained an ever-present background noise that, from time to time, if the situation allowed, could be tuned out for a moment's respite.

While relieved that Rose and Robin wouldn't be facing the opposition he and Joyce had experienced, Hubert was unsure how he felt about this new development. It wasn't until he and Joyce were in the car on the way home later that afternoon, stomachs full of steak and red wine, that he finally gave voice to his feelings.

'Well, me know me said it a lot today but me certainly wasn't expecting that.'

Joyce continued staring out of the window at the passing scenery.

'Me either. She looked so happy though, didn't she?'

Hubert smiled.

'Like she wanted to burst into song!'

'And he does seem like he adores her.'

'True,' said Hubert. 'He did have the look of a man in love.'

'But?'

Hubert laughed. Joyce had effortlessly seen through his efforts to remain upbeat.

'You know me too well.'

'He loves her, he comes from a nice family and he's got excellent prospects. What's your objection?'

Hubert thought carefully before answering. His list of reasons was extensive: they were too young, Rose had a career to think of, they were from different backgrounds. But he could overlook all of this if he could shake the fear that this young man, pleasant though he seemed, was one day going to break his daughter's heart.

Hubert was reluctant to give voice to his fears.

'I don't know. Maybe it's just that she's my baby girl and nobody, not even Prince Charles himself, is going to be good enough for her.'

It was late by the time they reached home and although they had hoped David might be in so they could tell him the good news about his sister, the house was shrouded in darkness and he was nowhere to be seen. These days he often stayed out late and while Joyce constantly begged him to call and let them know where he was, invariably he wouldn't and they would both spend a fitful night worrying, ears straining for the sound of his key in the front door.

As Joyce brushed her teeth, Hubert closed the curtains in Rose's room as he always did. Taking a moment to look at her things, the books on her shelves and the posters on her walls, it dawned on him that now she was engaged she may never come home to live again. That this room, once her refuge from the world, might finally be handed to David, if he even wanted it any more.

Joining Joyce in the bathroom, Hubert reached for his toothbrush just as the phone rang. They exchanged anxious looks, neither one of them fully confident that this was just a wrong number. As he went downstairs to answer it Hubert hoped that it was nothing more serious than Rose checking to see they'd arrived home safely, but the moment he heard a male voice at the end of the line, a voice belonging to a stranger, a cold fear overcame him. In that instant he knew this must be about David.

'Hello, sorry to call so late but I wonder if I might be able to speak to a . . . Mr Hubert Bird?'

Hubert swallowed hard.

'Speaking.'

'I'm Dr Murray from Westleigh Hospital, and I'm calling about your son, David. He was found collapsed in the street. He's stable now but he's going to need to stay with us for a few days.'

Hubert felt sick. He'd read about a recent spate of racist attacks in the area and prayed that David hadn't become the victim of one.

'What happened? Did someone hurt him?'

There was a pause before the doctor spoke.

'I'm afraid to say we think it might be solvent abuse.'

29

Now

By the time Hubert arrived home, having stormed off following his outburst, he was more embarrassed than angry. Why hadn't he just pretended not to know David? It wouldn't have been hard, given that the truth was he didn't really know who his son was any more and hadn't for a very long time. Instead he'd made a fool of himself and now everybody would be asking questions, questions he didn't want to answer, questions that would hurt even to consider.

Letting himself inside the house, Hubert went straight to the kitchen, filled the kettle with fresh water, and set about making a cup of tea. As he reached a mug down from the cupboard Puss came in through the cat flap and began mewling loudly. Hubert glanced at her dish, now empty, and tutted.

'You hungry?'

Puss regarded him hopefully.

'Well, tough, you shouldn't have been so greedy and eaten your lunch as a mid-morning snack!'

Puss continued to mew but Hubert noted that she had made an attempt to look suitably chastised and so, feeling more soft-hearted than usual, reached into her food cupboard and took out a packet of her favourite flavour of Dreamies. She gobbled them up greedily from her bowl, purring between mouthfuls while Hubert scratched behind her ear.

As Hubert straightened his back, the kettle came to the boil and as he reached for the tea bags, the doorbell rang. He remained still, hoping he'd misheard. When it rang again, however, there was no mistaking it.

Much as he wanted to ignore it and wait for whomever it was

to go away, he knew that he couldn't. It would more than likely be one of the members of the committee. Probably Ashleigh. He didn't want to worry anyone and after all, he'd agreed to be the campaign's president and the last thing someone in his position should do was leave those relying on him in the lurch.

Hubert opened the door and was surprised that rather than Ashleigh, it was Jan standing on his doorstep. She looked worried, and was pink in the face.

For a moment neither of them spoke, then finally, a little breathlessly, Jan said: 'You left this on Layla's buggy.' She handed Hubert's umbrella to him and then glanced up at the sky. 'You might need it if you plan on going out later.'

'Thank you,' said Hubert. 'It's very kind of you to go to the bother.'

There was a long pause and then Jan spoke again.

'Everyone was worried about you, you know? They all wanted to come and make sure you were all right, but I told them it might be best if it was just one of us. You know, so you didn't feel overwhelmed. It was a toss-up between me and Ashleigh – that girl really does think the world of you – but in the end, I came because Ashleigh had to get Layla back home for her nap.'

'Thank you, Jan. Me think it probably would be a bit much if everyone was here.' He paused, watching as a few drops of rain started to fall. 'Come in out of that. Me just about to have a cup of tea. You want one?'

Jan followed Hubert into the kitchen, where she sat down gratefully at the table. Aware of the heavy silence between them, he flicked on the radio, hoping it might make things feel less awkward, but somehow the sound of people arguing on *Any Questions* seemed to make things worse. Finally, with a pot of tea made and having spent far too long arranging biscuits on a plate, Hubert took everything to the table.

'Well, it's really coming down now,' said Jan, glancing towards the kitchen window. She helped herself to a custard cream. 'I hope the others don't get soaked.'

Hubert sat down in the chair opposite Jan.

'It's just a shower. It'll be over before you know it.'

Jan took a bite of her biscuit, chewed it slowly then swallowed.

'Still, it'll be good for the plants.'

'Yes,' said Hubert, wishing things would somehow get back to normal between them. 'That's true.'

There was another long, awkward pause, then Jan said, 'Hubert, I don't mean to pry but about earlier . . . you don't have to tell me anything if you don't want to. But I just want you to know that if you need to talk, I'm here to listen.'

'That's a very kind offer, Jan,' Hubert replied, having not quite realised until now just how grateful he was to have company. 'And one day me will be ready to tell you everything, okay? But the truth is, this afternoon has left me pretty shook up and me just don't feel like talking about it yet. One day me will, just not now, not yet.'

A whole myriad of emotions swirled around inside him. He hoped Jan might be satisfied for the time being with the little he had offered.

'Of course. I won't bring it up again unless you do and I'll make sure all the rest of the campaign know not to bother you about it either.'

'Thank you,' said Hubert, and the swell of emotion he felt made the words catch in his throat and for a moment he feared the whole story of David might spill out of him like so much floodwater.

Jan stayed for another cup of tea and a few more biscuits, and by the end of their time together, the earlier awkwardness had all but disappeared. As Hubert walked her to the front door once again, he was overcome with gratitude for her companionship.

'You is . . . you is . . . what me call a good friend, Jan.'

'It was nothing. Us old folks have got to stick together.'

Hubert smiled.

'Less of the old. Me still feel like a spring chicken inside!'

Halfway down the path Jan stopped.

'So, I'll see you Wednesday for the follow-up committee meeting at Ashleigh's?'

Hubert detected a note of uncertainty in her voice.

'Yes,' he said breezily, not wanting to worry her any more than he had already, 'me see you there.'

In the days leading up to the meeting, in an effort to keep from fretting about facing everyone for the first time since his outburst, Hubert kept busy. He mowed his lawn, spoke to Rose, did his shopping and caught up with all his jobs around the house. To a degree it worked, and he neither worried about the meeting nor thought about David, but then when Wednesday evening came around and he found himself pressing the buzzer to Ashleigh's flat, he felt his earlier anxiety return.

Ashleigh greeted him with a hug.

'It's so good to see you. I've been dying to pop round but Jan said you needed some space. Are you okay now?'

He nodded sheepishly.

'Good, then we'll say no more about it. Everyone's already here, so I'll sort you out a tea and then we'll get started.'

When Hubert entered Ashleigh's tiny living room, everyone greeted him warmly but made no mention of Saturday's episode. Fiona, Tony and Randip, who were squeezed together on the sofa, chatted to Hubert briefly about the fruit trees in his garden they'd been admiring earlier from Ashleigh's kitchen window. Jan, who was sitting on a dining chair in the corner of the room, struck up a conversation with him about the latest plot twist in *EastEnders*, while Maude was thankfully prevented from saying anything inappropriate by Emils, who was perched on a step stool next to her armchair, plying her with a fresh batch of cupcakes. They were all clearly making such an effort to put Hubert at ease that by the time he had a cup of tea in his hands, he almost felt as if Saturday hadn't happened.

Ashleigh addressed the room.

'Right, first item on the agenda: Feedback from Saturday's publicity drive. Who wants to start?'

When no one volunteered, Ashleigh made eye contact with Tony.

'Tony, you said you would count up all the potential volunteers who put their names down on Saturday. How many have we got?'

He pulled out a scrap of paper from his jacket pocket.

'Er . . . six . . . and I'm pretty sure two of the names I've got down are made up, that is unless there really is a Mr and Mrs Seymour Butts.'

'Four? Is that all? I thought Randip and Fiona got a whole stack before lunch?'

'We did,' said Randip, 'but then I left the clipboard in McDonald's and by the time I realised and went back for it, it had gone.'

'I don't want to be that person,' said Tony. 'But we could get done by the data protection police for a gaffe like that.'

'I'm really sorry,' said Randip.

'It's fine,' said Ashleigh, 'it's not the end of the world. Fiona, did we at least manage to get rid of most of the leaflets?'

''Fraid not,' said Fiona. 'We've got two carrier bags' worth left over and there were so many on the floor afterwards that I wouldn't be surprised if we were fined by the council for littering.'

'Great,' said Ashleigh despondently. 'Did we get any good feedback from people on the street?'

'Not really,' said Jan. 'Most of the ones I spoke to seemed to think it was an okay idea but weren't interested in getting involved.'

'Same here,' said Tony. 'Although, to be fair, it was pretty hard to hear what anyone was saying from inside my bear suit.'

'People kept thinking I was trying to get them to give to charity,' said Emils, 'so they avoided me.'

'Maybe next time we should give out cakes,' said Maude, her mouth full of lemon and blueberry muffin. 'People like cakes.'

'So, what we're essentially saying is we've wasted a Saturday morning and over a hundred quid's worth of the vet's money they gave us for flyers, and all we've got to show for it is four extra volunteers and a possible fine for littering?'

'Hold on,' said Hubert, seeing the dismay on Ashleigh's face. 'Let's not get downhearted. It's still early days. We all spoke to people who thought it was a good idea, so maybe we just try again this Saturday. Set up a stall or something, maybe a few balloons, you know, make it look appealing.'

Emils raised his hand.

'I can make cake. Not enough for all of Bromley but some to attract people to stall.'

Ashleigh wasn't convinced.

'I don't think a stall and a few cakes are going to cut it. I don't know, maybe we're wasting our time. It's like everything else, people want something doing, they just don't want to do it themselves.'

'Well, we're all here and we want to do something,' said Jan defiantly.

'I know, Jan, but there aren't enough of us. We wanted to put on a show, to do something really big to get Bromley's attention. We just can't do this without more help. We'll have to put on our thinking caps again.'

Tony made a suggestion.

'How about a bit of direct action? You know, stage a sit-in at the town hall. It might attract a bit of media interest.'

'I can't set foot in the town hall,' said Maude. 'I've been banned! I've got it in writing that if I go within fifty feet of it they'll have me arrested! I don't want to go to prison at my age.'

For a moment Hubert considered asking Maude for more details but thought better of it.

'I could see what other costumes we've got in storage,' said Tony. 'I'm pretty sure there's an ostrich somewhere but there might be a rip in one of its legs.'

Fiona spoke up.

'We could try collecting signatures again. But this time in the form of a petition to present to the government. Apparently if you get over one hundred thousand signatures it can be considered for a debate in parliament.'

'It's a good idea,' offered Randip. 'But how are we going to get a hundred thousand signatures when we struggled to collect just a handful of names last time?'

'And how long would it even take to get that many signatures?' said Jan. 'More than a couple of Saturdays going around Bromley town centre, that's for sure.'

Ashleigh got to her feet.

'Guys, we're in danger of getting depressed by the whole thing, or at least I know I am. Why don't I put the kettle on, make us all a nice drink and we'll come back and try and dig out the flip-chart paper from the last meeting and see if there's any ideas on there we've missed.'

'Good thinking,' said Tony. 'And in the meantime I'll have a search around the Internet and see if I can find out how to add an online petition to our Facebook account.'

'Great idea,' said Ashleigh. 'How many friends have we got?'

Tony checked his phone.

'Two . . . and one of those is a porn site. Still, better than nothing.'

As Ashleigh disappeared into the kitchen, the living room filled with chatter. Some began checking things on the Internet, others brainstorming new ideas, and in the case of Maude, asking Emils whether he had any more cake.

When Ashleigh returned to the room, her face was pale with shock and she was staring at her phone open-mouthed.

'You okay?' asked Hubert, getting to his feet as the rest of the room turned to look at Ashleigh. 'You don't look right.'

'I . . . I don't feel right, either,' said Ashleigh. 'We've just had a bit of a weird email to the committee's account.'

'Weird how?' asked Hubert.

'Weird in that it's from a journalist at the BBC. You're never going to believe this but . . . *London Tonight* wants to put us on the telly!'

30

Then: March 1989

Joyce twisted the tissue she was holding in her hands, refusing to make eye contact with her husband.

'I just can't do it,' she said, her voice barely a whisper. 'Not today.'

Hubert sat down in the empty chair next to her and rested a comforting hand on her shoulder. She'd been quiet since they'd woken that morning but he'd thought it was just the prospect of the day that lay ahead.

'You not feeling well?'

She shook her head.

'No, it's not that. I just can't face it, Hubert. I thought I could but I can't. Just go without me.'

'But he'll be expecting you.'

'I know,' said Joyce. 'But I'm just not up to it. I'm sorry. Tell him I love him and that I hope he's doing well and that not a moment goes by when I don't think about him.'

'And when him ask where you are?'

Joyce thought for a moment.

'Tell him the truth: that I couldn't face it, that this was one time too many, that my heart's broken enough as it is. Tell him that no mother, no matter how loving, wants to visit her only son in a drug rehabilitation centre on his birthday of all days. It would tear me apart.'

Angry tears sprang to her eyes, one after another, and she dabbed each one away with her tissue before standing up and gesturing towards the hallway.

'His presents and cards are in a bag by the front door.'

She bent down and kissed Hubert on the cheek.

'Drive safely, won't you?'

As she left the room he listened as she made her way upstairs into the bathroom, where she closed and locked the door behind her.

At the bottom of the stairs Hubert stood listening to the sound of his wife crying, then turned around, scooped up his car keys and hat from the hallway table and the bag by the front door and left.

This was David's sixth time in a drug rehabilitation centre in the past eight years. The first time had been when he was hospital-ised following his collapse from inhaling solvents after Rose's graduation. That whole episode had been such a shock for the family, none of them having had the faintest idea that David was involved in anything of that nature. He'd always been headstrong and rebellious, but nothing out of the ordinary, no different to other boys of his age, or so they had thought. So to see him lying in a hospital bed, all sorts of tubes sticking out of his arms, left, right and centre, looking so small and weak, had been nothing less than devastating.

A grilling of David's friends had revealed the true extent of his drug use: how since leaving school, as well as smoking and getting drunk like everybody else, David had begun abusing solvents. At first it had been an occasional thing, but over time it became something that he was doing more or less every day, and no matter what his friends said, David refused to give up.

Hubert had relayed all this information to their family GP, Dr Marlow, who had been wonderful, going above and beyond to get David into a centre that would treat him for his addiction and help him turn his life around.

As soon as David was well enough to leave hospital, Hubert had driven him to the south London unit, where he had stayed for six weeks before returning home. Convinced that he was cured, Hubert and Joyce did their best to put the experience behind them, and as David, helped by Gus, secured a job working for London Underground his future had looked brighter. But then just eighteen months later, after moving out to live with a girlfriend, David relapsed and was booked in for a second stint in a rehabilitation centre, this time in Sussex.

So began the cycle of recovery and relapse, hope and disappointment that was to continue over the next eight years. Spells spent in various treatment centres around the country, both state-funded and later paid for by Hubert and Joyce with savings they had once hoped their son might use to put down a deposit on a home of his own, just as they had helped his sister and her husband to do. And as the pot of money dwindled, so too did Hubert and Joyce's hopes that David might recover for good. Not that they would ever say this to him, or for that matter to each other. Instead, each time, they would assure one another that this time would be different.

They'd only found out about this most recent relapse when Julie, David's current girlfriend, who he lived with in Bournemouth, had called to say that he was in hospital, having accidentally overdosed on heroin. Fearing for their son, Hubert and Joyce had rushed to his bedside once again and this time, determined that it would be the last, had, with Rose's help, researched facilities that might cure David for good. The Cedars, set deep in the Dorset countryside, had come out tops, with a price tag to match. Its programme was tougher than any they had encountered so far, with patients having no contact with the outside world for the first two months of their stay, but its success rate seemed to justify this extreme measure. David had been booked in on a cold, wet day in the middle of January and today, a cool but bright spring day in March, was the first time they had been allowed to visit him. That it was also David's birthday was a poignant coincidence, one that Hubert thought he could live with if it meant that at least his son was getting better.

With traffic, the journey took Hubert just over three and a half hours to complete. He'd whiled away most of the drive listening to music on the tape player in his car, some Motown, a bit of Sixties soul and a compilation Gus had made of blue beat and ska tunes. Gus's tape reminded Hubert of happier times, when he had been young and carefree. Back then he could never have imagined that one day those very same songs might form the soundtrack for a journey such as this. Back then the only thing on his mind had been Joyce.

Perhaps if David had met someone like his Joyce he wouldn't be in this mess. Perhaps he, like Hubert, would've married and settled down, spent his life working hard for his family instead of getting mixed up with all this nonsense. Then again, perhaps it was being born in this country that was to blame. People back home in Jamaica couldn't just sit around on their backsides and get money from the government and use it to get off their faces. Not to say that there that weren't drunks and so forth back home, but certainly when Hubert was growing up it was rare to see someone like this. The fact was, if you didn't work you didn't eat, and maybe that was enough to keep people out of trouble.

As he pulled up in front of a long, white-washed farmhouse set in the prettiest location you could ever hope to imagine, he thought how much Joyce would enjoy being out in the country-side like this, miles away from anything. Getting out of the car, Hubert stood still and listened and no matter how hard he strained, found it impossible to hear anything other than birds singing and lambs bleating in the distance. It sounded like peace, real peace. A place where a broken soul could heal. If anywhere in the world was going to cure David, it would be here.

Clutching the bag with the cards and presents inside, Hubert made his way to an informal reception area where he was met by a woman with wild frizzy hair and small round spectacles, who introduced herself as one of the centre's staff members. She led him through the house and back outside to a worn wooden picnic table that overlooked a large pond with a family of ducks swimming across it.

'Just wait here and I'll go and get David for you.'

Enjoying the warmth of the hazy mid-morning sun on the back of his neck, Hubert noticed a number of people dotted around the grounds. Some were occupied repairing a post and rail fence, others sat in small groups or pairs holding cups of tea and chatting, while one or two worked on a vegetable garden to the side of the house.

At first glance it was impossible to tell which were staff and which were patients or 'guests', as the centre's literature referred to them, but on closer scrutiny, observing their body language and general demeanour, Hubert guessed that most of them were in fact actually here to receive treatment, just like David.

Deliberating whether to arrange his son's presents on the table for him to open there and then, or to leave them in the bag for later, Hubert heard a sound behind him and turned to see David walking towards him. He was thin and drawn, but looked a million times better than he had in hospital. His hair, now in dreadlocks, was held back from his face with a sweatband, and he was wearing a navy tracksuit top with jeans and scruffy white trainers.

He mumbled a greeting to Hubert as he climbed on to the bench on the opposite side of the table. The two sat in silence, David constantly playing with an ornate silver ring on his finger, all the while blinking in the sunlight as though this had been the first time he'd been outside all day.

'Where's Mum?' he said eventually. His voice was slightly slurred and uneven and Hubert wondered what cocktail of medication they had him on this time.

'Your mother wasn't feeling too well. But she sends all her love and of course wishes you a happy birthday.'

David nodded, but his eyes glazed over almost as if he'd forgotten asking the question.

'Rose called last night too. She and Robin wished you a happy birthday, and them say you're still welcome to stay with them when you finish up here.'

David said nothing.

'You want me tell them all that you send your love?' prompted Hubert.

David nodded again. 'Yeah, tell them that.'

There was another long silence. A small group of residents headed indoors and one of them called to David, who waved in response. 'So tell me,' said Hubert when he realised that his son wasn't going to say anything, 'how you settling in? What the place like?'

David scratched the back of his head absentmindedly. 'It's fine.'

'And you feel like you're getting better?'

A pause, several blinks of the eye and then, 'Yeah, definitely.'

'What kind of thing you have to do here?' asked Hubert, struggling to keep the conversation going. 'Me saw some people mending the fence. Is that the sort of thing you get involved in?'

'They . . . they . . . keep us busy. We . . . we . . . all have to help around the place.'

'Sounds good. Your grandmother always used to say, "The devil make work for idle hands."'

David yawned and stretched like a cat.

'Late night?'

'I . . . feel like I'm always tired these days. Even when I've just woken up.'

'That'll be the country air,' said Hubert, trying to make light of the matter. 'None of those city fumes getting in your lungs!'

David didn't respond.

They continued like this, Hubert asking question after question, with David offering one-word answers or nothing at all for a good twenty minutes. Eventually Hubert gave up trying and instead they sat in silence, enjoying the peace and the sunshine.

When a gong sounded David said, 'It's the lunch bell,' and without any further comment stood up as if to leave.

Hubert couldn't believe it. He'd driven all this way to see his son for the first time in two months on his birthday of all days and this was all he was getting? It seemed wrong. Very wrong. But he didn't know what he could do.

He reached under the table and handed the bag with the presents and cards to David.

'For you, son, from all of us. Happy birthday.'

Without acknowledgment, David accepted the bag, then began walking away. Something about this moment made Hubert feel that this was the end. As if his son was going to spend the rest of his life walking away from him. In that moment he realised he couldn't let this happen without asking the one question he needed an answer to.

He called out after David.

'Just answer me this one thing: is this our fault? Did we make you this way?'

It was the question he and Joyce had tortured themselves with most over the years. Had they been too strict with him or not strict enough? Had their expectations been too high or too low? Would things have been different if they'd stayed in Brixton or moved right out of London to live somewhere like this in the countryside? Could they have saved him if only they'd been more observant when he was younger, or been quicker to condemn his actions when he was older? These endless musings were enough to drive anyone over the edge, and all the more so when they were being asked of the two people who loved the boy most in the world.

For once, David seemed as if he was actually considering the question but then he lifted his gaze from his feet to Hubert and without another word, walked away.

31

Now

'So what them say?' asked Hubert.

'Was she posh?' asked Jan. 'They're always posh them BBC types.'

'Are they going to mention us on the news?' asked Fiona.

'Hold your fire, everyone,' said Ashleigh, resting her phone on Hubert's kitchen table. 'Let me just catch my breath and get my thoughts together for a minute.'

'Come on,' said Hubert, pulling out a chair for Ashleigh. 'Sit down and take your time.'

It was the morning after the committee meeting where Ashleigh had relayed the exciting news about the BBC. Following an exchange of emails a time had now been arranged for Ashleigh to talk to the journalist, and while the whole committee had been desperate to be in on the conversation, in the end, due to their various commitments, only Hubert, Jan and Fiona were available. The journalist had called Ashleigh on her mobile, as arranged, just after ten and she'd disappeared into Hubert's front room to take it, emerging over half an hour later, by which time Hubert, Jan and Fiona were bursting with questions.

'Right,' said Ashleigh, scooping up Layla, who had just run in from the garden, proudly carrying a fistful of dandelions that she presented to her mum. 'It's basically better than we could ever have hoped. This journalist's family lives in Bromley and she was visiting on Sunday when she saw a leaflet that her mum had been given by one of us while out shopping. Anyway, she loved the idea behind the campaign and so yesterday she pitched it to her boss – that's journalist talk for telling her about it – and her boss liked it too, so she contacted us. Anyway, I've told her all about the committee, how we got started and what our aims are and she loves it, and she's pretty sure that they'll be able to do a three- or four-minute piece about us on *London Tonight!*'

'That's amazing,' said Fiona. 'To think what it would cost for prime-time publicity like that and here we are getting it for free.'

'I always watch *London Tonight,*' said Jan. 'I like that fella, the one with the bright ties who they get to do the funny stories. Maybe they'll send him and we'll get to meet a real celebrity! Oh, when are they thinking of filming? I'm not due to get my hair done until next week. That said, I suppose I could give Bryony a call and see if she can squeeze me in sooner. She might do if I tell her I'm going to be on the telly.'

'Well, about that,' began Ashleigh. 'The thing is, they don't want all of us, apparently it gets too complicated if there are too many voices. They only want one of us talking on camera.'

'Who do they want?' asked Fiona. 'You?'

'No,' said Ashleigh. 'They want Hubert.'

Hubert sat up in his chair. 'Them what?'

'They want you to be the one who talks about the campaign,' repeated Ashleigh. 'When I was telling her about everyone, I mentioned that you came over from Jamaica nearly sixty years ago and she got really excited. She started talking about the Windrush generation and how you'd make a great "angle" for the piece.'

Hubert pulled a face. The last thing he wanted was to be on TV. Apart from the embarrassment of speaking in front of a camera, what if Rose or someone who knew her saw the programme and she found out that, far from being the life and soul of the party, her old dad was on TV wittering about lone-liness? No, he definitely couldn't do it.

'Can't Fiona do it?' suggested Hubert. 'She's been a head teacher. She's used to getting up and talking in front of people.'

'I would happily volunteer,' said Fiona. 'But I can see what the journalist is saying. There are so many news stories competing for airtime these days and if you don't have an angle, the story and the message it's carrying can easily get lost. With Windrush being in the news, not just because of its upcoming anniversary but also because of the scandal, it's adding another layer, a greater dimension to our story.'

Hubert could see her point. He'd been following the story of how the government had been treating people like him ever since it had first been on the news. And although he felt outraged and disgusted by the whole sorry business, he wasn't sure this was enough to persuade him to get in front of a camera.

'But me no feel right about it,' he said. 'It's just not me. Tell them Fiona will do it and see what them say.'

'The thing is, Hubert, I knew this would be how you'd react and so I told the woman that you're quite shy and don't really like the limelight, but reading between the lines I think she was trying to say that if you couldn't do it, then there was a pretty good chance we wouldn't get on.' Ashleigh sighed and put a hand on Hubert's shoulder. 'If you really don't want to do it, don't. We'll just have to find another way to get people interested in the campaign.'

An hour later, having come no closer to a decision, the others left, giving Hubert some time to mull over the situation alone. Sitting at his garden table, a freshly made mug of tea in front of him, enjoying the warmth of the mid-morning sun against his skin, Hubert considered the options open to him. On the one hand he could be firm in his refusal, but this would mean letting down the committee for a second time in less than a week. But if he agreed to be on the programme, then he would not only have to talk into a camera, which was a dreadful enough prospect on its own, but he would run the risk of Rose finding out the truth about him.

He was, he noted with deep despondency, damned whatever he did and closing his eyes, he wondered once again what his dear Joyce might have advised him under such circumstances. 'Well, I wouldn't have got myself into this predicament in the first place!' he could almost hear her saying. 'Just like cheats, liars never prosper. That said, what's done is done and sometimes you've just got to make the best of how things are.' Hubert smiled, feeling a sense of comfort settle on him as he imagined his wife sitting

by his side as they'd done at this very table many times over the
years. The moment he opened his eyes, however, that sense of
comfort vanished, leaving behind the sorrow of losing her as keen
as it had ever been, while at the same time handing him a new
sense of clarity, a better understanding of the way forward.

Returning to the house, he picked up his phone and dialled
Ashleigh's number.

'Hello, Hubert. Can't talk long, I'm just off to work. Everything
okay?'

'Everything is fine. Call that journalist. Me changed me mind.'

Over the next few days, Hubert thought about picking up the
phone to tell Rose about the filming, reasoning that he could
explain it away as something he was helping a friend with.
However, the thing that stopped him was the further lies that
would be required to make this new story believable. Who was
the friend? Why had they asked him to help? What did a social
butterfly like her father know about the subject of loneliness?

Thankfully, before he'd had chance to change his mind, the
day of the filming arrived. Having only ever seen TV crews on
the news when they were huddled together in front of a politician
or a scandal-hit celebrity, Hubert was somewhat disappointed
when the journalist arrived at his house a little after midday,
accompanied only by an extremely tall man carrying a number
of metal cases.

'Hi,' said the journalist. 'I'm Verity and this is my cameraman,
Hugh. You must be Mr Bird.'

'You can call me Hubert.' He gestured towards Fiona, Ashleigh
and Jan, who had all come to offer their support. 'And this is
the committee . . . well, at least those who could make it today.'

Verity offered the others a polite smile before asking Hubert
if she and Hugh could have a look around the house to see where
it would be best to set up. They were gone a good ten minutes,
during which time Hubert made a pot of tea for everyone in an
effort to calm his nerves and Maude polished off an entire plate
of biscuits.

'I think we're going to set up in your front room, if that's okay,' explained Verity. 'It's such a sweet room, just like my grandparents', plus the light in there is really good.'

It took a good half-hour before they were ready to start filming and Hubert had to wear a microphone on the lapel of his jacket, just like the newsreaders on TV. The questions Verity posed were straightforward. She asked how long it had been since Hubert had lost Joyce, what his life was like living alone and how he'd come to get involved with the campaign.

Hubert had tried his best to be truthful, even though at times, particularly while talking about his experience of loneliness, he had felt uncomfortable. But there was a warmth about Verity that had put him at ease, so he'd answered her questions as best he could, trying all the time to turn the subject back to the campaign and what they hoped to achieve.

With the main interview over, Hugh asked if he could take some footage in a few different locations, explaining that these would be edited in later. He filmed Hubert in his garden watering his hydrangeas, standing at the sink washing up and sitting in his armchair pretending to watch television.

The following evening, when Hubert would normally have been eating his dinner with Puss curled up on the sofa asleep next to him, he was instead round at Ashleigh's again with the other members of the committee squashed around him, all angling for a clear view of the TV set.

So far they had sat through news items on a fire at a local tyre factory, the police reopening of an old murder case, a local school threatening to close early on Fridays due to budget cuts and now the building of a new online retailer's depot promising to bring over fifteen hundred jobs to the south-east.

'I bet we're next,' said Ashleigh. 'Local news always starts with the depressing stuff and finishes with the stuff that's supposed to make you smile. That's got to be us.'

Hubert tried to join in with the light-hearted chatter going on around him but his heart wasn't in it. He was too scared that he was about to make a fool of himself and even more terrified that his daughter might see him doing it. He felt so sick with nerves that all he wanted was to get up and leave, but then the room erupted into huge cheers as Hubert saw himself on the screen.

Given how much they had filmed, Hubert was surprised by how little of it they had used. None of the stuff in the garden appeared, for example, but the fake committee meeting Verity had proposed, complete with cameos from Jan, Fiona and Ashleigh, had featured heavily.

Once the piece was over, Ashleigh turned off the TV and everyone gave Hubert a big round of applause.

'You were brilliant, Hubert,' said Ashleigh. 'Absolutely amazing.'

'You look like film star, Mr Hubert,' said Emils, patting him on the back.

Jan gave Hubert a peck on the cheek.

'You'll have all the ladies after you now!'

'Splendid job,' said Fiona. 'You acted like a real professional.'

Hubert didn't know what to feel or what to think. He just felt shell-shocked and the whole thing seemed unreal.

Maude started a round of, 'For he's a jolly good fellow' and everybody bar Tony, who was staring at his phone, joined in. Before they could get to the 'and so say all of us' refrain, Tony yelled, 'I can't believe it!' at the top of his voice.

'What?' asked Ashleigh.

'Our Twitter feed. You know how last time we checked we only had two followers? Well, look at it now.'

Tony held his phone out so everyone could get a better look at the screen. Even without his glasses on or, for that matter, any real idea what a 'Twitter' was, Hubert could see that something was happening.

'Our followers,' said Emils. 'They're shooting up!'

'It's the same for Facebook too,' said Tony. 'Our numbers are going through the roof! A photo I posted on the group page of us all has got over three hundred likes and that's within the last five minutes! This is it, guys, this is what we've been waiting for! We've gone viral!'

32

Then: September 1996

Rose was sitting in her bright yellow Beetle, the one she'd bought six years earlier as a thirtieth-birthday present to herself. She peered up at her parents' house and felt like a failure. A complete and utter failure. Ordinarily the journey from Manchester to Bromley to visit her parents was a joyous one filled with the wonderful expectation of being simultaneously spoiled and heralded, an experience she appreciated all the more the older she became. Today, however, was different. After years of being their golden girl, of making them proud, of doing the right thing, she was finally going to disappoint them.

It had been on the cards a long time but she and Robin were getting divorced. It wasn't anybody's fault. They'd just got married too young. They weren't the people they'd been when they first met at university, they'd both changed over the years, sculpted and formed by the things that had happened to them: career failures and successes, ill health and family problems, fertility issues and affairs on both sides. It all added up to a recipe for disaster, a parting of the ways. An ending. The Victorian terrace in Didsbury they'd bought for a song when it had been a wreck had sold almost overnight and the thought of remaining in the place they'd once called home felt too much to bear.

With her share of the money from the house sale and a year-long research grant, she was free from the confines of a teaching post for a while and the decision had been easy: she would get all of her things put in storage, escape to her parents' home back in Bromley for a while, lick her wounds, and then begin the work of mapping out the next stage of her life.

Not wanting to attract the attention of the neighbours, Rose climbed out of the car and, locking it behind her, made her way quickly up the path. Reaching into her handbag, she fished out her keys and opened up the front door. Once inside, she stood for a moment in the hallway listening out for signs of life, and hearing the sound of a tap gushing water in the kitchen, she made her way down the hallway, knocked once on the pine door and entered the room.

'Rose!' exclaimed Hubert as he turned towards the door, kettle in hand, wearing a look of complete surprise. 'What you doing here?'

Steeling herself, Rose walked over to her father, kissed his cheek and forced a laugh. 'Good to see you too, Dad!'

'Of course me always glad to see you,' said Hubert, putting down the kettle on the kitchen counter. He gave her a proper hug. 'Me just wasn't expecting you, that's all. Where's Robin? Parking the car?'

Rose shook her head. She felt sick with nerves.

'No, Dad, I left Robin at home.'

Hubert kissed his teeth, his mind clearly stuck on the topic of the street being overcrowded. 'Parking around here is getting to be impossible!' he opined. 'Since them damn people knocked down the old Salvation Army place next door and built those flats, every man and his dog is parking him car left right and centre.'

Rose forced another smile. 'I managed to get a cracking parking spot right outside the front of the house.'

Hubert laughed.

'The neighbours must have known you were coming. So poor Robin is on his own?'

Rose nodded. 'Yes, Dad, it's just me.'

He gave her a peck on the cheek.

'"Just me," she says, as if she's nobody special!' He gestured to an empty chair at the kitchen table. 'You sit yourself down. Let me tell your mother you're here, then I'll make you a nice cup of tea and you can tell me all about the exciting things you've been up to.'

Hubert bustled out of the room, leaving Rose alone in the kitchen. She took a deep breath and closed her eyes, savouring the familiarity of it all. The ticking of the clock over the kitchen window, the sound of the kettle bubbling away, the lingering smell of a Saturday-morning fry-up in the air, combined with the scent of the same brand of lemon washing-up liquid they had always used. This was home and always would be, no matter how old she was or how many years she had lived away.

The kettle came to the boil but there was still no sign of her parents, so Rose got up and made three mugs of tea. She'd been trained from a young age in the art of making the perfect brew the Bird Way: mugs warmed first with a splash of hot water, tea bag in, then each filled to within half an inch of the top, allowing room for the perfect quantity of milk to be added after a good two-minute steeping.

Placing the steaming mugs on coasters on the kitchen table, Rose opened the cupboard above the bread bin, took out the biscuit barrel from the shelf where it had always lived, placed it on the table and then resumed her seat, wondering what was taking her parents so long. Usually whenever she arrived home her mother was first on the scene, almost as if she'd sensed her daughter's presence before she'd even arrived.

'Here she is,' announced Hubert as he entered the room followed by Joyce.

As she went to embrace her mother, she noticed there was something different about her but couldn't quite put her finger on what it was.

'Sorry to drop in unannounced like this.'

Joyce glanced at Hubert.

'Weren't we expecting you?'

A puzzled look crossed Rose's face.

'No, Mum. It was a last-minute thing.'

'Well, it's always lovely to see you, love, no matter what the reason.'

They sat at the table and as her father grilled her about the journey down from Manchester, with special emphasis on how impatient drivers seemed to be these days, Rose took the opportunity to study her mother.

Although they spoke on the phone every week, it had been almost six months since her last visit for her father's sixtieth and something had definitely changed. At first, Rose thought it might be that she'd lost weight, as she'd felt thinner when they'd hugged. Mum had been on a diet of one kind or another for as long as Rose could remember, but none had ever had a noticeable effect. Clearly whatever she was doing was working, perhaps a little too well.

Rose also noted that her mother appeared not to be wearing a bra. For a woman who had always extolled the virtues of the need for good support, this seemed distinctly odd. Then again, there could be a whole host of reasons for it. She could have been in the middle of changing outfits when Rose arrived. Or perhaps her favourite one had broken and the spare was just out of the wash and drying on the line.

There was another change, however, and perhaps it was this that had startled her the most, she now realised: her mum wasn't wearing make-up. Having always been the sort of woman who appeared first thing in the morning fully groomed and ready for the day ahead, it seemed strange to see her at midday still barefaced. Of course, it was her decision and Rose herself had never been a huge fan of make-up, limiting herself to a sweep of mascara or dab of lip gloss when the occasion required, but with her pale skin, the lack of colour made Joyce look tired and old, even though she was not yet sixty.

In and of themselves, these were tiny things, and to a casual observer would have no significance at all, but to Rose, who had always been close to both her parents, these were signs of something gone astray somehow, in a way she couldn't articulate. Perhaps her mum selling the nursery last year had had a greater effect on her than Rose had realised. Then again, maybe she just wanted a day off and as someone who had arrived unannounced, who was she to judge?

In contrast, her father was the same as ever, although he had a little more white in his hair and had clearly put on an extra pound or two. But in his regular weekend uniform of navy-blue corduroy trousers and checked shirt, he could have been any version of himself from the past twenty years.

Her father gestured to her with the mug in his hand.

'So come on, tell us how that man of yours is doing? Any more trips to foreign parts? We nearly called you the other day, actually. Your mother and I heard him on the radio again . . . last Wednesday I think it was. Talking about something to do with trade agreements or some such. Whatever it was, it certainly went over my head! But he sounded very intelligent, didn't he, Joyce?'

Joyce nodded. 'He's got such a lovely speaking voice.'

This is it, thought Rose. Now is as good a time as any to tell them the truth about her and Robin. She opened her mouth to speak, but the words that sprang from her lips weren't the ones she'd been planning.

'What's wrong?'

Her dad was confused.

'How you mean?'

Rose glanced briefly at her mum before returning her gaze to her father.

'Something's going on. Something's not right.'

For a moment Rose thought her parents weren't going to respond, but then the doorbell rang and her father, wearing what to Rose seemed like an expression of relief, got up to answer it.

Joyce stood up, mug of tea in hand.

'Do you want a brew, love?'

Rose glanced down at the steaming mug in front of her, still too hot to drink.

'No, Mum, I haven't started this one yet and you've barely touched yours.'

Rose watched as Joyce gazed absentmindedly at the mug in her own hands as if seeing it for the first time.

'Silly me, don't know what I was thinking!'

Returning to the room, Hubert sat back down at the table, picked up his tea and turned to Rose.

'It was the milkman come for his money. So, you were telling us about Robin.'

In that instant it all made sense. The changes in her mum's appearance, the time it had taken her to come downstairs and her mum's odd question. Now Rose thought about it, she'd spent far more time talking to her dad on the phone over the past few months than her mum, who always seemed to be in the middle of a tricky household task or on her way out to meet friends, whenever she called.

Rose stood up.

'Dad, can you help me get something out of the car?'

'Of course, love. Let me just get my shoes.'

They headed towards the hallway, Rose trailing after her father so that she could close the door to the kitchen behind her.

As Hubert reached for the catch on the front door, Rose stopped him and indicated towards the front room.

'Actually, could we just go in here for a moment. There's something I need to talk to you about.'

Hubert looked worried.

'What's the matter, darling?'

She gestured to the room again.

'In here. Let's talk in here.'

They entered the front room, the room that reassuringly never seemed to change. The same furniture, the same family photos on the mantelpiece, the same china in the cabinet that never saw the light of day.

Sitting down on the sofa, she patted the seat next to her.

'What's this about, Rose? You've got me worried.'

She took her father's hand.

'How long, Dad?'

Hubert frowned.

'How long what, darling?'

'Don't play games, Pops. How long have you known that Mum has dementia?'

Rose watched the dilemma play out across her father's features. The desire to protect her from the truth matched with the relief of no longer having to hide it any more.

Finally his shoulders slumped and he let out an audible sigh and avoided her gaze by looking down at his lap.

'Six months . . . or thereabouts. It's hard to say because she was so good at hiding it at first. She'd forget things while out shopping but blame it on not having made a list. She'd get words wrong but say she was just tired. Then I started to find things in the strangest of places, house keys in the shoe-cleaning box, an open bottle of milk in the cupboard instead of the fridge, her shopping money in the bread bin.'

'And did you think something might be wrong?'

'At first I thought maybe it was just her adjusting to being at home after working all these years. You know . . . a different daily routine throwing her off kilter . . . but then she went out one day all the way to the post office and back again in her slippers . . .' He paused, struggling to continue. 'You should have seen them. It was raining and they were filthy, but she was walking around the house as if she didn't know the difference.'

Rose hugged him tightly, her heart breaking.

'Oh Dad, you should've told me. You shouldn't have tried to deal with this on your own.'

'Me didn't want to worry you, darling. Anyway me kept . . . me kept . . . hoping she might get better.'

'But you must know she won't get better, Pops. You must know this isn't the sort of thing people get better from.'

He shook his head.

'She'll be fine with me, darling. Me look after her.'

'And what happens when she gets worse? Dad, you can't do this on your own. Have you even seen a doctor?'

Hubert sighed.

'She's too young to have that dementia thing. Me ask Gus about it and one of him neighbours' mother has it and she's in her eighties. Dementia is an old person's disease and just look at her, your mother's not old, is she?' His voice cracked. 'She not even sixty, Rose. This was supposed to be our time. We were going to do all the things we'd always talked about doing. We were going to travel, and me was going to show her all the places she had always wanted to go and now . . .'

He stopped and as Rose hugged him again, tear after tear began to fall. It was horrible seeing him like this. She wanted to be strong for him, as strong as he had always been throughout her whole life, in the face of blatant racism, money worries, and the endless trouble with David. Despite her determination, however, she couldn't hold back her own tears any longer.

'We'll get through this, Pops,' she said. 'We'll get through this together.'

33

Now

'You want me to do what?'

Hubert stared hard at the young man in front of him. He was wearing a faded raggedy T-shirt and absurdly tight bright red trousers and green shoes. In spite of the clipboard and the fancy headset microphone contraption he was wearing, he didn't look old enough to have a job, let alone the authority to tell anyone where they should be going in a TV studio.

'I need to take you to make-up, Mr Bird.'

'Make-up? Me don't understand. What kind of place is this?'

'It's a TV thing, Hubert,' explained Ashleigh. 'Isn't it, Josh?'

The young man with the clipboard shot her a grateful smile. 'That's right, Mr Bird. It's just because of all the cameras and the lights. It's not lipstick and mascara or anything . . . just a touch of powder to take the shine off you. It won't take long, I promise, and I'll bring you straight back here to the green room afterwards.'

Reluctantly Hubert got to his feet. When he'd agreed to being interviewed on *This Morning*, no one had said a word to him about wearing make-up like that Boy George fella that Rose used to like back in the Eighties. Still, there was no point making a fuss, this was simply too big an opportunity for the campaign to miss.

'Are you sure you don't want to swap places with me, Ashleigh?' said Hubert, not for the first time. 'Me could stay here and look after Layla while you get your make-up done instead.'

'We've been through this a million times, Hubert! You're the face of the campaign. You're the one they want to hear from. Now go in there and have your make-up done and I'll be waiting here for you when you get back.'

Following the young man along the corridor, Hubert was led to a small brightly lit room dominated by a huge dentist-style chair facing a long illuminated mirror, in front of which was spread a vast array of pots and palettes of make-up.

'Hello, love,' said a bubbly young woman. She had dyed silver hair cut into an angular bob. 'I'm Zara, and I'll be doing your make-up this morning. Not that there's a lot to do. You have the most amazing skin and cheekbones to die for! Anyway, take a seat and I'll give you a quick powder.'

The past couple of weeks had seemed to Hubert like a dream and he fully expected to wake up at any minute. That first appearance on *London Tonight* had led to an article in the *Evening Standard*, which had been picked up by the *Daily Mail*, and after that things had snowballed out of all control. Soon the committee were receiving requests for interviews with Hubert every other day and, fearful that any further exposure would lead to Rose discovering what he had been up to, Hubert tried his best to dodge the limelight by suggesting that other members of the committee might like to take their turn with the press. But as the researcher from the *Today* programme explained when he'd asked if she might like to talk to Ashleigh instead: 'I'm afraid that wouldn't work for us, Mr Bird. All our listeners will know you as the Windrush Pensioner declaring war on loneliness. To all intents and purposes, you are the story!'

And so Hubert felt he had no choice but to let himself be swept along by it all, and just hope beyond hope that neither Rose nor any of her friends would find out about it. Each time she called, Hubert's heart would be in his mouth, fearing that he'd been found out. Why was her father, who barely had a moment to spare between social engagements, the spokesperson for a campaign to end loneliness? Why was he telling the media about how hard things had been since losing his wife? Why was she learning the truth about how empty his life was from a news article emailed to her by a well-meaning friend? But the castigation he dreaded never came. Each time Rose called, all she spoke about was how excited she was about her visit, how eager she was to give him a hug and spend some proper time with him. 'I know it sounds strange,' she'd say, 'but it feels like it's only now I'm coming home that I'm realising just how much I've been missing you. I can't wait to see you, Dad, I can't wait until we're together again.'

The request from the people at *This Morning* had come a week ago, and although Hubert had been reluctant to do it, feeling like he'd already pushed his luck far enough, the excitement of the committee and Ashleigh's insistence that this was too big an opportunity to turn down meant that once again he felt he couldn't say no.

True to her word, the make-up woman hadn't made him look like a clown but, with judicious application of a bit of powder here and there and the trimming of a few unruly eyebrow hairs, had made him look presentable.

'Thank you, darling,' said Hubert as she removed the protective gown from around his shoulders. 'You've done a good job.'

'It's easy when you've got a good canvas to work with. Good luck today, I think it's a really good thing you're doing.'

Back in the green room Hubert found it busier than when he'd left it, as more guests had arrived in time for their appearance on the show. There was an Eighties pop star plugging her latest comeback album, an actress from one of the soaps Hubert occasionally watched and a glamorous-looking beauty expert who Hubert discovered through Ashleigh was on the show to talk about the latest trends in eyebrows. They were an odd bunch but Hubert found them quite friendly, and even the Eighties pop star, who had seemed a little offish at first, once warmed up was happy to pose for a photo with Hubert, which Ashleigh then tweeted to all the campaign's followers.

Every few minutes or so, the young man in the tight trousers would appear at the door to take one of the guests up to the studio, and in what seemed like no time at all, Hubert, Ashleigh and Layla were the only ones left.

'There's a lot of waiting around in this TV business,' remarked

Hubert, helping himself to his fourth Danish pastry of the morning. 'Not that I'm complaining, if they're going to feed us this well!'

No sooner had he taken a bite of his cinnamon swirl than Mr Tight Trousers appeared at the door. 'They're ready for you now, Mr Bird.'

Hubert stood up, noticing for the first time just how nervous he was. It had been one thing being filmed in his own home by the local news but it was quite another to be live on national TV.

'You'll be fine,' said Ashleigh, as though reading his mind. She brushed stray pastry crumbs from the lapels of his jacket and straightened his tie. 'Forget about the cameras and the lights and all that, and just chat to them like they're ordinary people and you'll absolutely smash it.'

Everything that followed on from his goodbye with Ashleigh happened so quickly Hubert didn't have time to let his nerves get the better of him. It seemed as though one minute he was sitting on the sofa with people he'd only ever seen on the TV, and the next it was all over and the young man with the tight trousers was escorting him back to Ashleigh and Layla.

'You were amazing,' squealed Ashleigh, 'an absolute superstar. And that's not just my opinion either. My mum and her mates texted me the whole way through it and they totally loved you. I think half the village was stuffed into her front room cheering you on.'

'That's nice,' said Hubert. 'Although me been thinking, it's all very well doing these TV and radio things and it's nice that we've got lots of people on that Twitter thing you talk about and the Facebook as well. But what we really need is actual people who want to get stuck into all the work we've got ahead of us.'

Ashleigh seemed slightly crestfallen.

'I know, you're right. It's easy to get carried away, just because we've had all this attention. I suppose the important thing is what happens next.'

Hubert handed Layla a biscuit from a plate on the table.

'Exactly,' he said. 'The committee needs more help if we're going to make a splash and get regular events up and running.'

'Well, let's cross our fingers for tonight's meeting,' said Ashleigh. 'And hope that this time around, we won't be faced with another room full of empty chairs.'

It was mid-afternoon when the car *This Morning* had booked for them dropped Hubert and Ashleigh home. Carrying a sleeping Layla in her arms, Ashleigh whispered to Hubert that he should come to hers for lunch so that they could watch the show again, but Hubert politely declined. 'Me think the little one has got the right idea,' he said, gesturing to Layla. 'Me going to have a quick brew and then take a nap, this day has taken enough out of me as it is.'

With an empty mug next to him and a contented Puss on his lap, Hubert settled back in his chair and waited for sleep to come. He was bone tired but his mind was full of thoughts about his day so far, about the TV appearance, about what if any difference it might make.

Most of all, he couldn't stop thinking about Rose and wondering yet again if she'd hear about his brush with fame and the reasons behind it. He'd already made up his mind that he would tell her about it once she was here. That way he'd have the chance to explain himself to her face to face, to make it clear how it had happened.

It wasn't a conversation he wanted to have over a phone line. But she would be here in just over four weeks and he didn't want her to hear about it from anyone else before he'd had chance to explain. He tried to reassure himself that as she hadn't been aware of anything so far, there was no need to assume that an appearance on a single TV show would make any difference, but try as he might, he just couldn't shake his need to be sure. If he wanted a nap any time soon he was going to have to call her.

'Rose, it's Dad here,' he said when his daughter finally answered.

Rose laughed.

'Pops, why do you think that after all these years I'm not going to recognise your voice? Is everything okay? You don't usually call at this time.'

Hubert pressed his free hand to his chest. He could feel his heart pounding.

'Yes, everything is fine, darling. Me just . . . me just wanted to say hello, that's all.'

'Are you sure? There's nothing wrong? This isn't you panicking about my arrival again, is it? It's sweet that you want to meet me off the plane but I'm fine to get a taxi from the airport and I don't like the idea of you hanging around Heathrow when there could be delays.'

'It's not that. I was just worrying, I suppose . . .' He paused, unsure how to turn the conversation towards where he wanted it to go. 'Tell me, Rose, you don't do that social media thing me hear about on TV, do you?'

'Why, are you getting all techie, Dad? Have you finally decided to join the twenty-first century and get a mobile phone?'

'No, no, no, me just mean . . . well, do you do that Twitter thing me hear about?'

'Yes, but for work mainly. Lots of academics use it now. It's a good way of raising your profile, keeping in contact with colleagues and peers and checking in on who's doing what where, that sort of thing.'

'And . . . you know, have you ever gone viral?'

Rose laughed.

'No, Pops, never, I think the most likes I ever got for a tweet was about how comfortable the pillows were in a hotel I was staying in. I think I got about sixteen then. Why do you ask?'

'No reason.'

'Okay.'

She sounded sceptical.

'It's just, well . . . do you ever see things that go viral?'

'What sort of things? Dancing cats, dresses that people think look different colours to how they really are, monkeys wandering around in IKEA?'

Hubert had no idea what she was talking about. 'Are these viral things?'

'They can be, but generally speaking I'm too busy to pay them much attention. Usually I post one or two things a day if I'm at a conference, add a few hash-tags and then forget all about social media until the next time I need to post something.'

Hubert felt a wave of relief flood over him. 'So, you don't spend too much time on it?'

'Not if I can help it. So you don't need to worry about me. I bet you've been reading an article about the harmful effects of social media, haven't you?'

'You guessed it,' said Hubert, glad to have been provided with an excuse. 'Guilty as charged.'

'Well, I might not be a teenage girl but it's always nice to know that even though I'm long in the tooth, my dad still worries about his little girl.'

With his mind now at ease, Hubert managed a good two-hour nap before waking up to the sound of Puss mewling because she was hungry.

After feeding her, he set about making his own dinner, which he ate in front of the TV, and then went upstairs to spruce himself up ready for the meeting that evening. He was waiting by the door when Ashleigh arrived with Layla asleep in her pram, and together they made their way to the library. Ashleigh was chatty as ever, telling Hubert about all the calls she'd had from friends back in Wales, how many likes his photograph with the Eighties pop star had garnered, and how excited she was about the meeting tonight. 'I've got a really good feeling about it,' she said as they walked. 'I've watched your bit on *This Morning* at least half a dozen times now and I have to say that if I wasn't already on this committee, I'd definitely be coming tonight. You made it sound wicked!'

Hubert chuckled but he didn't share Ashleigh's optimism. He'd been around long enough to know that the world moved very quickly on to the next big thing, that today's news was tomorrow's fish-and-chip wrappings. It was one thing for people to think that what the campaign was up to was worthwhile, but it was another altogether for them to leave the comforts of their living rooms after a hard day at work and attend a meeting.

As they walked up the road to the library, Hubert crossed his fingers – the last thing he wanted was for Ashleigh to be disap-pointed – but within seconds of reaching the car park, it became clear that on this occasion luck wasn't needed. The car park was full, and the entrance hall and the community room itself were packed to the rafters with people wanting to join the campaign.

34

Then: September 1997

All around their table in the Red Lion there was laughter. Hubert was laughing so much tears were running down his face; Mister Taylor was wiping the beer from his jacket that he'd spluttered over himself the minute Gus had delivered the joke's punchline; a barely-able-to-breathe Teetus was banging the table with the flat of his hand with delight; Biggie Brown was holding his sides as if he literally feared he might burst if he didn't; and Oney, clueless as ever, was asking everyone around the table to explain the joke to him.

Drying his eyes, Hubert got to his feet.

'Right then, before me laugh meself into a heart attack, let me get some drinks in.'

After he'd taken the orders, he turned to walk to the bar and Gus called for him to wait so he could give him a hand.

It was a Saturday, so the bar was crowded with lunchtime drinkers, and unlike its days as the Old Duke when it used to be their regular, it was now bright and airy, with cream walls and sanded pale wooden floorboards. Its clientele had changed too over the years; now instead of being the haunt of just old men and smokers, there were groups of young people, both black and white, all chatting, drinking and eating, giving the place a relaxed and friendly vibe.

Getting together for a drink at the Red Lion on a Saturday afternoon was something that had been going on for a couple of years now. At first it had just been Hubert and Gus catching up with each other once a month, but then Gus had invited along some of the men he worked with at London Underground: Biggie Brown, who Gus had lived with briefly when he first came to

England, and Oney, who was from Trinidad. Then Hubert invited Teetus, a guy from Spanish Town who he'd become friends with during his time at the council, who in turn had brought along Mister Taylor, who he'd known since his days in the West India Regiment, and finally this circle of old friends, all West Indians who had come to England in the Fifties and Sixties in search of a better life, was complete.

'You know, Gus, man,' said Hubert as they stood at the crowded bar, 'these get-togethers are really good for the soul. Me can't remember the last time me laugh so hard.'

Gus patted his friend on the back.

'It's been good to have you back these past few months, Smiler. It hasn't been the same without you. How are things with Joyce, by the way? Any better?'

Hubert shrugged. He hadn't really spoken much to anyone about the speed of Joyce's decline over the past year.

'About the same, really. Some good days, some bad. Rose is a real help, though.'

It was an understatement really. While Hubert insisted on doing more or less everything for Joyce, from helping her to dress and doing her hair, to organising and administering her medication, to calming her down when she became distressed, there was still so much to do and Rose did it all. Driving them to and from hospital appointments, helping to keep up with the housework, dealing with all of the miles of red tape that come part and parcel when someone you love can no longer look after themselves.

'She's a good one,' said Gus, 'no mistaking. That husband of hers must have been a fool to let her go.'

Hubert kissed his teeth. The very thought of that boy made him angry. Picking up with a new woman and getting her pregnant, when the ink on the divorce papers wasn't even dry! He deserved a good thrashing for that kind of behaviour, and even at sixty-one, Hubert felt he was just the man to give him one.

'Don't get me started,' said Hubert.

He caught the barmaid's eye as she finished serving a couple in front of them and gave his order, telling her to have one for herself.

'Anyway, how are things with you and what her name again . . .?'

'The lovely Dominique,' said Gus with a flourish.

Hubert recalled their most recent conversation about Gus's ever-changing love life. This girl was in her thirties, had two teenage boys and was old enough to know better than to get involved with someone like Gus. But, thought Hubert, there was no telling some people.

'That's the one. So, how's things going?'

'I moved in with her last month,' said Gus, almost gleefully. 'She makes all my meals, washes all my clothes and doesn't even ask for rent. Meanwhile, I'm letting my place out to a fella from work for a couple of months, so for the first time ever I'm rolling in it!'

Hubert laughed.

'You should've said that before me pay for the whole round!'

'Listen,' said Gus, 'I might be grey up top but I've still got all my marbles!' He laughed, fully expecting Hubert to join in, but when he didn't he immediately realised his mistake. 'Smiler, man, you know I didn't mean . . . well . . . you know.'

'Of course, don't worry,' said Hubert. Even he found it difficult to think of his wife this way, so it should come as no surprise when other people forgot too.

The barmaid finished pouring their drinks and Hubert gestured towards them. 'Come on, then,' he said, 'if we take any longer over these there's going to be a riot.'

Hubert stayed for another hour with his friends before leaving them playing dominoes, in order to go home to Bromley. When he came into the house, he found Rose in the kitchen listening to the radio and making preparations for the evening meal. There were sliced peppers lying in a row on the chopping board, a glass bowl full of diced onions and a full bag of rice next to her.

'Oh Rose! Me told you me get dinner sorted when me come in.'

Rose smiled.

'I thought you could do with a day off. Anyway, I like cooking.'

'What are you making?'

'A red pepper risotto,' said Rose. She reached down a large casserole dish. 'We had it a few weeks ago, remember? Mum really enjoyed it.'

'And me too,' said Hubert. He filled the kettle and took out three mugs.

Rose glanced at the mugs.

'Mum's asleep in the front room at the minute. Dozed off in the middle of the afternoon film and I've just had a cup. But you go ahead. There are some new biscuits in the barrel. I got those chocolate ones from Marks & Spencer that you raved about last time. How are all the boys? Did you have a good time?'

'Them all fine,' replied Hubert. He rooted around in the cupboard for the new biscuits and helped himself to one. It tasted so good he immediately reached in for another. 'Nothing much to report. Them all said to send you their best.'

As Hubert made his tea and Rose carried on with her cooking preparation they chatted for a while, making light of Gus's new living situation, speculating about how long this one would last and wondering if the next one he met would be even younger. Finally, having exhausted the comic potential of his friend's love life, Hubert helped himself to another couple of biscuits, took up his mug and made his way to the front room.

The TV was still on but Rose had turned the volume right down, so that all that could be heard was the gentle snoring of Joyce. She was fast asleep on the sofa, her chin resting on her hand. She seemed peaceful, a fact that Hubert was grateful for, as she'd spent another restless night sitting up in bed, unable to settle, convinced as she was that it was daytime and she had washing to put on the line and ironing to catch up on.

It had been almost a year since Joyce had been officially diagnosed with early onset dementia, a year in which Hubert felt as if not only his world had been turned upside down, but also that of the Bird family as a whole. It had now been two years since any of them had seen or heard from David, the longest they had gone without contact. For all they knew, he could have completely turned his life around and be living happily by the sea, or lying dead in a ditch somewhere. It was the not knowing that was the most painful thing, the hope sometimes as painful as the despair.

Then there was poor Rose, no children, newly divorced, with an ex-husband about to start the family she had always wanted for herself, stuck in Bromley helping to look after her mother when she should've been living the wonderful life she truly deserved. Even though he loved having her around, Hubert had continually reminded her from the day she moved in that this should only be a temporary arrangement, that he fully expected her to move on, with both her life and career, and her mother's illness shouldn't stand in her way. Rose had paid lip service to this idea, occasionally applying for this job or that, but with the anniversary of her arrival approaching, Hubert couldn't help feeling that perhaps she was losing confidence and the longer she stayed the more difficult she would find it to leave. Perhaps, somehow, she felt it was easier to stay at home looking after her mother than to be back out in the world starting her life all over again.

Then finally there was Joyce, his beloved wife. He was slowly losing part of her every day. Her long-term memory was in perfect condition: Hubert only had to mention the foul child-minder woman Joyce had punched all those years ago for her to go into a detailed rant about the incident, and remark how if she ever saw her again she'd do the same. Her short-term memory, however, was far more shaky, and she had difficulty recalling even the most mundane of details, like what day it was, what she'd had for breakfast, even sometimes whether or not she'd eaten at all.

She knew Hubert, though, called him the love of her life, and she recognised Rose too, although from time to time she seemed to forget how old she was, and would ask her how school had been or if she had seen her brother's football boots. David was a particular source of angst for her at this time, and she would often stand by the window expectantly and explain that he should have been home by now as it was long past his bedtime. She would also sometimes sit in his old bedroom, now made up as a guest room, and even though it had long since been redecorated, his posters taken down, his sporting trophies in boxes in the loft, she would sit on the bed as though lost in thought as she remembered the room as it used to be.

Hubert sat with Joyce while he drank his tea and when he finished, he got up, found the remote control and switched off the TV. Even though the volume had been barely audible, its absence seemed to rouse Joyce from her slumber.

At first she was startled and confused but, on seeing Hubert, immediately recovered herself and beamed a smile at him.

'Hello, handsome. Have I been asleep long?'

'Not long. You feel rested?'

'Enough to dance all night. Are we going to the Princess Club again? I like it there, you can really let your hair down.'

'We can if you like, my love,' said Hubert. He had learned over the past year that sometimes it was kinder to let her version of reality go unchallenged than to constantly be reminding her that she was wrong, that her brain was playing cruel tricks on her, that this wasn't 1958, 1961, 1972 or any other year she cared to conjure up.

'I'd like to very much. I've got some new shoes that will be just the ticket for that sleeveless dress I made.'

'Sounds lovely, my dear,' said Hubert and he took her hand. 'Me think me wear that suit you always like to see me in.'

'Oooh, yes! And that lovely yellow tie your mum bought for you. Such a pretty lady, she is. I can't wait until I get to meet her.'

'She'll love you. I've told her all about you in my letters.'

With eyes full of adoration, Joyce fixed her gaze on Hubert.

'Have you really? What did you say about me?'

'Me told her that me have just met the most wonderful English girl and that me think she might be the one!'

Joyce smiled sadly.

'I wish I could tell my mum and dad about you. I know they'd love you if they were only willing to put aside their prejudices, my brothers and sister too. What is it with people that they just can't be nice to one another?'

'Me don't know,' said Hubert. 'It's just one of those things.'

'Well, it shouldn't be,' said Joyce firmly. 'What should it matter to anyone what colour my boyfriend's skin is? It's just silly when you think about it. I mean, I once liked a boy at school who had red hair and no one batted an eyelid about that.'

She paused, thinking.

'George Timmins his name was, lived two roads down from us, he did, his dad was our postman.'

She smiled, and for a moment he wasn't sure whether she was still thinking of this red-haired boy or had moved on to something else.

'I love you, Hubert Bird, I really do. And I'm not going to let anyone stand in the way of us being together.'

'Me either,' said Hubert, looking into her eyes and for a moment seeing not only the Joyce right in front of him but also the girl he'd fallen in love with back at Hamilton's all those years ago. 'Me love you, Joyce Pierce.'

He leaned forwards and pressed his lips against her cheek.

'Me love you from the tips of your toes to the top of your head and what's more, me always will.'

35

Now

'Would you like to come through? Councillor Pemberton will see you now.'

Getting to their feet, Hubert and Ashleigh exchanged nervous glances as Councillor Pemberton's PA gestured to the door behind her.

Ashleigh straightened her skirt.

'What do you think?' she whispered. 'Do I look like someone you'd take seriously?'

Hubert nodded solemnly, even though he was of the opinion that if 'serious' was the look she was going for, then she might have been better off not accessorising her smart business suit with a Minnie Mouse hairclip.

'It was the only one I could find in the flat that wasn't broken,' she said, noticing Hubert's eyes lingering on the top of her head just a moment too long. 'And this bit of hair just won't behave itself.'

'Me think it's very you,' said Hubert diplomatically.

'Thanks, Hubert.' She gave her companion a cursory once-over. 'And as always, you look very dapper. We make a cracking team, don't we?'

'That we do. That we certainly do.'

It had been a little over a week since the second public meeting of the campaign, which had been so oversubscribed it had been standing room only. It seemed that not only had the publicity worked, but Hubert had been wrong about people's reluctance to turn 'likes' into action. By the end of the night they had completely run out of sign-up sheets and now had an army of volunteers, both young and old, willing to help out with whatever was needed.

Amongst the committee, there was a new sense of excitement

about their mission: suddenly this wasn't just an airy-fairy idea but something real and tangible, which was actually going to happen. Even the normally cynical Tony remarked at the end of the evening, 'This must be what it feels like to witness the beginning of a revolution.' And just when it seemed things couldn't get any better, a bearded man in an ill-fitting suit approached Hubert and introduced himself as a representative of their local councillor. 'Mr Pemberton's really keen to meet with you,' he said, handing Hubert a business card, 'he's been following your story from the beginning and wants to know what he can do to help.' One telephone call and the swapping of a shift with Randip later, and now here they were in the plush interior of Bromley Town Hall.

'So pleased to finally have the opportunity to meet you both!' said Martin Pemberton. He got up from his chair and walked around the large, ornately carved mahogany desk. He was a silver-haired man with tired eyes and a ready smile and seemed genuinely pleased to see them. 'You've certainly been putting Bromley on the map this past month, haven't you?'

'Well, to be honest, it's mostly been Hubert. The media can't get enough of him. Did you see him on *This Morning* the other day? It was all I could do not to scream when I saw him on the sofa next to Phil and Holly! Couldn't believe it, like!'

'I know,' said Councillor Pemberton, 'very impressive, and I've seen and heard all the other press you've been doing too. It really has been exciting to watch and I want to assure you it hasn't gone unnoticed by council members. We've been trying to get in contact with you for weeks now because we want to know what we can do to support your very worthy campaign. You've been the subject of a great number of discussions in chambers and we're all very keen to do everything we can to help.'

He gestured for them both to take a seat and returned to his position behind his desk, took out a notepad from a drawer and opened it up to a fresh page.

'To cut to the chase, the reason I asked you here today is simple: I want to find out what we here at Bromley council can do to help support your campaign.'

A bewildered Hubert turned to Ashleigh for guidance, only to find that she was already staring at him. He cleared his throat and tried his best to sound businesslike.

'When you say support . . . How exactly do you mean?'

'Exactly what I said. Your campaign has really struck a chord, not just with the people of Bromley but also further afield. Loneliness is a nationwide problem, and I think a people-focused response like yours could be the answer we've all been looking for. I couldn't be prouder that it's constituents in my borough that have come up with it and we want you to know we're right behind you. And we also want to offer practical help. What would you say your most pressing needs are at the moment?'

'Well . . . well . . .' said Ashleigh, finally finding her voice, '. . . to be honest pretty much everything. None of us have ever done anything like this before. To begin with we had some quite grand plans, which we'd scaled back over time, but now things have taken off we might need to have another think. I mean we had booked a room in the community centre, but I don't think that's going to cut it now.'

'So which venue would you prefer?'

Ashleigh and Hubert exchanged looks again.

'Well . . . Hubert and I were talking on the way over and we were thinking . . . well, we were thinking maybe somewhere outside like . . . Bromley Park or the rec ground for example. You know to give the whole thing . . . I don't know . . . a "Live Aid" sort of festival sort of vibe.'

Councillor Pemberton jotted something down on his notepad.

'And then,' said Ashleigh, warming to her theme, 'there would be a whole week of anti-loneliness events around the local area. Things like "Get to know your neighbour" meet-ups, coffee mornings and refugee welcome events. Basically anything and everything to get people out of their homes and talking to each other.'

'Sounds really exciting,' said Councillor Pemberton, adding yet more notes to his pad. 'These are all things we can definitely help you with.' He considered the pad for a moment. 'When ideally are you thinking about for everything to happen?'

Hubert thought for a moment. He didn't want to be busy with campaign business when Rose was fresh in town.

'Perhaps somewhere towards the end of August?'

Ashleigh nodded in agreement.

'The bank holiday weekend would be perfect. Bank holidays always put people in a good mood.'

Councillor Pemberton drummed his fingers on his desk thoughtfully.

'Well, I'll be honest, for large events like this we normally plan at least a year in advance. But I suppose we really do need to capitalise on the momentum you've established. It'll be a push, but let me speak to some people and I'll see what we can do.'

They chatted about their hopes for the launch day for a good amount of time, but then Councillor Pemberton's secretary entered the room to inform him that his next appointment had arrived. After shaking hands, all three agreed to keep in touch and then Hubert and Ashleigh were led out of the room.

Ashleigh was wide-eyed.

'I can't believe it. Did that really just happen?'

Hubert laughed.

'It doesn't seem real, does it?'

'This is too amazing for words. I can't wait to tell the others so we can celebrate. This is really happening, Hubert. We really are going to end loneliness in Bromley once and for all!'

'So you're saying the council's actually going to put its money where its mouth is for a change?' asked Tony, as those of the committee who could make it sat in the beer garden of the Three Horseshoes having a celebratory drink.

Ashleigh took a sip of her white wine spritzer.

'Well, them and some local businesses apparently. He said we should carry on fundraising as every bit helps but yeah, it looks like things have really taken off and we can do everything we've planned and maybe even more besides!'

'It all feels rather surreal,' said Fiona. 'Who'd have thought that anyone would end up taking our little campaign so seriously?'

Ashleigh wiped a dribble of juice from Layla's chin, before sending her for a walk around the garden with Jan.

'Well, I always did. It's like we said at the beginning, "Go big or go home". . .well, it's certainly gone big, hasn't it?'

Fiona laughed.

'I'll say.'

'They're only doing it to make themselves look good, though,' said Tony. 'It's what politicians do: jump on good causes and take all the credit. You'll see.'

'They're a right lot of sneaky beggars,' said Maude, slamming her hand down on the table so forcefully that she nearly knocked over her pint of Guinness. 'And they keep forgetting to empty my green bins! It's a disgrace!'

Fiona took a sip of her Campari and soda.

'Oh, don't be such a couple of old moaners. Anyway, who cares why they're doing this when the only thing that matters is helping those in need? This campaign is already having such a wonderfully positive effect. Only yesterday a neighbour who has barely said more than two words to me since she moved in three years ago actually stopped to have a chat. Granted it was because she'd seen me with you chaps in the local paper but still it's something, isn't it?'

'I think you're right,' said Ashleigh. 'I was talking to one of the mums at Layla's nursery the other day and out of the blue she started telling me about how there was a local campaign group trying to end loneliness and what a good idea it was. And I totally blew her mind when I said to her, "Yeah, I know, I helped start it!"'

As Jan and Layla returned from their stroll, Fiona proposed a toast.

'To the campaign! May it bring an end to the spectre of loneliness in the borough of Bromley and beyond, once and for all!'

As the afternoon wore on, one by one the committee members started to disperse, eventually leaving Hubert and Jan alone at the table.

'You're quiet,' said Jan. 'Everything all right?'

'Me was just thinking.'

'Anything in particular?'

Where to begin? thought Hubert. Should he confess his worries about Rose's impending arrival? Tell her about how he had lied to his daughter for years? Reveal how he had made up fictional friends called Dotty, Dennis and Harvey and regaled Rose with their antics week after week?

Should he tell her of his concerns about how Rose might react when she learned the truth? How she would almost certainly give up her career and her life in Australia just to look after him? And how hurt she would be if she ever found out that he had been speaking to all and sundry about his loneliness without ever once mentioning it to her? Should he even, and Hubert was very doubtful about this, tell Jan how his feelings towards her had changed of late? That perhaps he wanted them to be more than friends? Should he share with her how happy the idea of them being together made him, while at the same time how guilty he felt even entertaining this thought after a lifetime spent loving one woman?

Hubert sighed, as he realised that although he had many worries, the one that seemed to be most pressing was the question of Gus.

'Me was thinking about my old friend. You know the one me tell you about who living like a tramp in a broke-up flat in Brixton? With all this chat me been doing about ending loneliness in Bromley, me can't help feeling a bit of a fraud. How can me be preaching to other people when me oldest friend in the world is living like a hermit?'

Jan thought for a moment.

'Then do something about it!'

'Like what?'

'It's easy to waste a lot of time trying to think of a perfect solution to a problem. But sometimes the only thing you can do is cross your fingers and have a go.'

Hubert was sitting in Gus's living room. It was tidier than last time, but only marginally so. The two empty Calor gas canisters had been shifted from the sofa to the floor and a rip in the side of Gus's armchair had been fixed using silver duct tape. Gus himself, however, was still as shabby as ever. Despite the warmth of the day, he was wearing a frayed brushed cotton shirt under a stained navy-blue jumper, his greasy-looking jeans wearing thin at all the usual stress points.

'So, what you call this again?'

Gus was looking at the contents of the burger box on his lap.

'Them call it a bacon burger with cheese. You see it has bacon, a burger and cheese in it. I tell you, man, it's delicious!'

Gus lifted the burger out of its container and sniffed it suspiciously.

'No bother skin up your nose like that! Me tell you it's real tasty! To be honest, me wasn't sure my first time either but then me have a taste and since then me never look back!'

The idea to surprise Gus with a McDonald's had come to Hubert as he'd sat on the train to Brixton following his conversation with Jan. He'd thought about perhaps buying Gus some new clothes or toiletries, but he was all too aware of how such gifts might cause offence. Then when a young man, dressed head to toe in sportswear, boarded the train and sat across from Hubert eating a chicken burger, its aroma filling the carriage, he knew exactly what he would do to cheer up his old friend.

Hubert watched in eager anticipation as Gus took a tentative bite of his burger and chewed it slowly.

'It dry,' said Gus.

Then, without a shred of self-consciousness, he wiped his mouth and beard free of stray ketchup using the sleeve of his jumper.

'Then take a sip of your drink, man!' urged Hubert.

Gus picked up the drink from the table next to him.

'And what you say them call this again?'

'A strawberry milkshake. It like them take a bowl of ice cream, melt it, then pour it into a cup.'

Gus lifted the drink to his lips and tentatively took a small suck on the straw. At first there was no change in his expression, but then he took a second long slurp, followed quickly by a third even longer one. Hubert was convinced he could see the trace of what might have been a smile playing across his old friend's lips.

'So, what you think?'

Gus pulled a face.

'It cold.'

Hubert kissed his teeth.

'Me know that, you dumb fool! Me mean the taste.'

Gus took another sip, then shrugged.

'I've drunk worse things.'

Hubert laughed and recalled with perfect clarity a moment from the old days he hadn't considered in decades.

'Remember that first cup of tea me make for you when you came to see me in my new lodgings?'

Gus nodded slowly.

'It was . . . it was . . . nasty.'

He stopped for a moment as though he too had travelled back in time.

'What was it that I said to you? We used to laugh about it all the time.'

'You said . . . you said . . . I remember now . . . you said, "Smiler, this damn tea so weak it nearly a fortnight!" Man, we laugh long time about that.' This time Gus gave Hubert a full, if somewhat toothless, smile, and in that moment Hubert knew that his plan was working.

Each time he had been to see Gus before now, he had come wanting something from his friend: the first to renew their friendship for Rose's sake and the second to find out what had gone so wrong in his old friend's life. This time around he wanted it to be different: he didn't want anything from Gus other than to share a meal and remember the old days. Hubert had been prepared to sit in silence while Gus ignored both him and the food. This then was a pleasant surprise, a glimmer of how they used to be and, he hoped, a spark that might reignite the fire of their friendship.

36

Then: September 2005

Hubert checked his watch. How long had he been sitting here like this? He looked at Joyce lying in the hospital bed, her features obscured by an oxygen mask, her frail body swamped by the checked blue gown they had put her in, almost as if he were expecting her to answer his unspoken question.

He needed to call Rose, he thought. He needed to let her know what was happening. But that meant going to the payphone and the last thing he wanted was for Joyce to wake up, as she did from time to time, and find him not there. But the call needed to be made, sooner rather than later, and so, very gently Hubert let go of Joyce's hand, laid it carefully by her side and then poked his head out of the door.

It was mid-morning and Hubert knew that the nurses would all be busy doing their rounds, looking after the helpless, doing what they could do to alleviate the suffering of those in need. He felt bad even thinking of asking for help from them when they were all so run off their feet, but then he thought of Joyce and knew there was no other option.

'You okay, Hubert?'

It was Sampaguita the lovely Filipino nurse, who the night before had brought him some tea and toast when she'd discovered he hadn't eaten all day.

'Me need to make a phone call but me don't want to leave Joyce on her own. Me know you're all busy, but is there any chance someone could come and sit with her? Me promise not to be long.'

'Of course,' said Sampaguita. 'You make your call, take as long as you like.' She held up the thick wodge of orange folders in her hands. 'I was looking for a quiet place to do this paperwork anyway.'

Hubert thanked the nurse profusely and without delay hurried up the corridor to the payphones at the end of the ward, and it was then that he realised he didn't have any change. Cursing himself for not thinking of this earlier, Hubert got the lift all the way to the ground floor and then out to the WRVS shop. The pink-haired middle-aged woman behind the counter waved the moment he walked in.

'Oh, hello, Hubert, haven't seen you for a while. What can I get you?'

'Anything, me just need some change for the telephone, and me need it quick.'

He grabbed a banana, a packet of mints and a knitting magazine, and placed them on the counter. The pink-haired woman, who was usually so chatty, seemed to pick up on the urgency of the situation and quickly rang the items up on the till, handing Hubert so much change for his twenty-pound note that his pockets bulged. She didn't even make a fuss when he left all of his purchases behind on the counter.

Returning to the lifts, Hubert made his way back up to the third floor only to find a young man wearing a black and grey tracksuit with matching trainers using the phone. He thought about waiting but the young man didn't seem in a hurry, then he thought about asking him why he wasn't using one of those damn mobile phones everyone was always glued to these days but decided against it, as the last thing he needed was trouble. Instead he made his way up to the next floor and was relieved to find the payphone there was free. Digging into the inside pocket of his jacket, Hubert took out his reading glasses and slipped them on, before fishing out the wallet from his back pocket and retrieving Rose's number.

Rose hadn't wanted to tell Hubert about the job offer she had received from the University of Melbourne but when he'd spotted the letter in the post addressed to her, franked with an Australian postmark, he had asked her about it and the lie she had attempted to tell him had been so flimsy, he had seen straight through it. With prompting, she had gradually revealed the truth of the situation: she had been offered what amounted to her dream job, but only if she was prepared to move to the other side of the world.

'Of course, I'm not going to take it,' she'd said. 'I'm not about to abandon you and Mum when you need me most.'

'You're not abandoning anyone,' Hubert had reassured her. 'You've been here nearly eighteen months now, you've helped me and your mother more than we could ever thank you for. This is your time now, Rose. After all that horrible business you went through with Robin, and Mum's illness, it's about time you had some good news.'

The discussions had gone on for a week, with Rose coming up with every excuse under the sun to stay. Finally Hubert put an end to it.

'Rose, me love you, but if you don't write and tell them that you want this job this very minute, me do it myself!'

That had been the spring of 1998, and although she'd been gone for seven years now, she'd returned home every Christmas and summer holiday without fail.

Her last visit had been only a matter of weeks earlier, which was partly why, even when Joyce was rushed into hospital five days ago with breathing difficulties after developing pneumonia following a chest infection, he hadn't suggested she come home. Anyway, over the past year they had been in the same position at least half a dozen times, Joyce gravely ill, Rose ready to jump on a plane to be by her side, only for her to rally at the last moment.

Even after all these years of Rose living in Australia, Hubert still marvelled at the technology that meant a person could sound crystal clear, as if they were in the very same room, and yet be the best part of ten thousand miles away. As he waited, listening to the sound of the ringing tone, he wondered what invention they might be dreaming up next. Maybe there would be moving pictures, like talking to a TV screen, or some sort of teleportation device where you could be with your loved ones in an instant just by calling them up.

It would be half past nine in Melbourne, thought Hubert. If Rose was home she might still be working, even though he was forever telling her that she needed to rest. She didn't have a man in her life at the moment, at least not as far as Hubert was aware. There had been someone a few years back, and once or twice he had even joined her on one of her visits home. Hubert couldn't recall his name now. He had been nice enough and was clearly smart and well read, but over time she stopped mentioning him, and so Hubert stopped asking.

These days, Rose seemed happy enough on her own. She had lots of friends, a successful career, a lovely home and even a swimming pool. Hubert couldn't see a reason why not having a man should make any difference. As far as he was concerned, she'd won the lottery.

'Hello, Rose Bird speaking.'

Even under the circumstances it was lovely to hear her voice, well spoken and yet warm and calm, undoubtedly English, but with the tiniest hint of Australian creeping into her vowel sounds.

'Rose, it's Dad here.'

Her voice brightened immediately.

'Pop! How are you? How's Mum doing?'

'Me is fine. Or at least as fine as can be expected, but Rose your mother . . . she . . . she . . . well them just tell me she hasn't got long left.'

He thought of the poor young doctor who had been sent to break the news less than half an hour ago. How kind he had been, how genuinely upset he had seemed that there was no longer anything to be done to make Joyce better.

Hubert relayed the little he knew to his daughter.

'But I don't understand. I thought it was just a chest infection. She's had them before and got better with antibiotics, why not now?'

Hubert desperately shovelled more coins into the voracious belly of the telephone.

'Because she tired, Rose,' he continued. 'She's been fighting nearly ten years now, ten long years of this disease eating away at her. I know it's hard, my love, the Lord knows it's hard, but it's time to let Mummy go.'

Hubert tried his best to comfort his daughter but with ten thousand miles between them, there was little he could do other than listen to the sound of her heart breaking. Finally, as Rose sobbed, the beeps sounded, signalling their time was up.

'Tell Mum to hang on for me,' said Rose before they were cut off. 'Tell her to hang on and I'll be on the first flight over.'

Returning to the ward, a little slower, a little heavier, a little more broken than before, Hubert entered Joyce's room to find Sampaguita chatting to his wife and holding her hand.

'Here he is,' said the nurse cheerily. 'I told you he wouldn't be long.'

Joyce mumbled something as he and the nurse exchanged places.

'She said, thank you very much for looking after her,' he explained and then paused as Joyce mumbled again. 'And she said to tell you that you've got a lovely smile.'

Once they were alone, Hubert told Joyce that Rose was desperate to see her and was on her way. When she muttered something that Hubert felt sure was their son's name, he assured her that David was on his way too, even though Hubert had no idea where in the world he was, or even if he was still alive. Hubert remained by her side as she slipped in and out of consciousness, talking softly about things he hoped would reassure her, never once letting go of her hand.

Later, when the nurses came to change and wash Joyce, Hubert returned to the WRVS shop and got himself some more change, this time to use to call their family and friends. He called Cora in Jamaica, asking her to pass on the news to Vivian and Fulton. He called Gus, who fell into a deep silence at the news.

'She's one in a million, your Joyce,' he said, and promised to let all of the boys from the Red Lion know. 'Give her my love and if you need anything, Smiler, anything at all, just call.'

Finally, Hubert called Eileen, Joyce's oldest friend and her very first employee at the nursery, now living in a tiny village in County Clare with her daughter. He broke the news as gently as he could and asked her to let all of those who knew and loved Joyce know what was happening. At the end of the call, Eileen tearfully assured him that he had done an amazing job looking after his wife over these past ten years.

'It was an honour and never a chore,' Hubert replied, fighting back tears of his own.

And he meant it too.

Caring for Joyce had been much more than a fulfilment of some sort of duty. Instead it had been a daily expression of his love for her, and he knew without a shadow of a doubt that she would have done the same for him had the tables been turned.

At the time of their wedding, lots of people had doubted whether the marriage would last, the odds being so stacked against them, but what they didn't know, what they couldn't know unless they were in Hubert and Joyce's shoes, was that even though they had been married in a down-at-heel register office in Brixton rather than a fancy church, even though there had been no big wedding party, no lavish gifts, no honeymoon, they had meant every single word of their vows: *'For better for worse . . . in sickness and in health, 'til death us do part.'*

Visiting time that afternoon was a flurry of activity, with a steady stream of people come to pay their last respects, so much so that by the time the bell rang, Joyce's hospital room looked like a florist's. She'd been barely conscious for most of it, her papery eyelids fluttering open and closed from time to time, but now that it was just the two of them again, she seemed more peaceful, more like she was just enjoying an afternoon nap.

Rather than dragging, the hours seemed to fly by, so much so that it seemed to Hubert as if one moment he was being asked what he would like for lunch, and the next it was pitch-dark outside. During this time he chatted to Joyce, recalling fond memories of their forty-seven years together, or sat quietly, saying nothing and holding her hand. Occasionally he even sang softly to her, songs that he knew she would enjoy, a bit of Frank Sinatra, a touch of Ella Fitzgerald and, of course, Nat King Cole. His voice wasn't brilliant these days, if indeed it ever had been, but it was enough to help put a smile on his face in these dark times and although it may just have been a trick of the light, he felt sure it made Joyce smile a little too.

He didn't remember falling asleep but he woke with a start in the chair by the bed and realised he must have nodded off. It took a moment for him to remember where he was and another to realise that Joyce's hand was cold. He stood up and leaned towards her, terrified at what he might discover, even though he'd known this moment would come. Seeing that she was no longer breathing, he panicked and, desperate for a little bit more time with his love, he reached across to press the button to call the nurse but stopped at the last moment. He'd become so accustomed to seeing Joyce in distress or pain and now here she was looking so peaceful, so serene, finally free from the prison of this terrible disease. Sitting back down, he took her hand and pressed it to his lips.

'Thank you, Joyce Pierce,' he whispered. 'Thank you. For everything.'

37

Now

Hubert and Jan were looking through the glass of the double doors to the main hall of the community centre where the weekly session of the O-60 was already in full swing.

Hubert turned to Jan.

'You okay?'

'To be honest, I'm feeling a bit nervous. Silly, isn't it? Worrying about what a bunch of strangers are going to think of you.'

'It's not silly. Me know exactly how you feel. But at least we have each other to lean on, eh? At the worst we can have a cup of tea and then leave.' And with that, Hubert pushed open the doors and they both strode into the room.

What with Rose coming in just over a fortnight and all the preparations for the campaign launch and week of activities, the idea of making a return to the O-60 Club hadn't been on Hubert's radar at all. He'd made his peace with the fact that he wouldn't be able to present anything like the life he'd pretended to have to Rose. Jan would be it, his one and only age-appropriate friend. But then something odd happened a few days ago while accompanying Jan to the post office to renew her passport.

'You've written your name wrong,' he'd said, pointing to the box on the first page of the form that she'd asked him to check over as they waited in the queue.

Putting on her reading glasses, Jan peered down at the form and laughed. 'That's no mistake. It's my given name. My mum wanted to name me after a friend of hers at nursing college but my dad wasn't keen, so the compromise was they'd put it down on my birth certificate to keep Mum happy but the name everyone called me was actually my middle name.'

'So your real name's not Jan?'

'Well, not officially, no, and it's caused the odd problem over the years cashing cheques and the like, but I can't think of myself as anything else.'

'So . . . your real name is . . . Dorothy?'

Jan gave him a strange look.

'Are you all right, Hubert?'

Hubert laughed so hard that he had to lean on Jan for support. After all this time, after all this searching, he'd actually had a 'Dotty' right in front of him.

Jan was mildly affronted.

'What's so funny?'

'You wouldn't believe me if me tell you,' said Hubert, once he'd recovered himself. But as he mulled it over that evening, he couldn't help thinking that perhaps this was a sign. Not that he should continue his lies to Rose, but rather that somehow he had been given an opportunity to do the very thing he should have done all that time ago. Even if he miraculously found himself a 'Dennis' and a 'Harvey' to go with his 'Dotty' he'd still tell Rose the truth, because that was what she deserved. But given that it had been his first lie about going to the O-60 that had forced Hubert to spin such an elaborate web of deceit, it now seemed fitting that he take this last opportunity to finally put things right.

The hall was just as busy as it had been on Hubert's first visit, if not a little more so, although the activities on offer appeared not to have changed a great deal. The only differences Hubert could see were that the table-tennis table had been replaced by a small portable badminton net and at the opposite end of the room there was a game of darts in progress.

Suddenly the confidence Hubert had mustered for Jan leached away, leaving him temporarily frozen to the spot. He didn't know what to do first or who to approach. Should they join those sitting at the tables doing a jigsaw to the left, or the group having a cup of tea to the right, or something else altogether? Of course, the moment Jan plumped for the jigsaw table was the exact one

Hubert decided to go for the tea and coffee stand and as they still had their arms linked, it was almost as if they were improvising their own moves to the line dancing going on at the far end of the room.

They were saved from any further embarrassment, however, by a voice calling out from just behind them and as they turned, they saw a tall woman with mousy-brown hair, wearing a short-sleeved lemon dress. She was carrying two portable hot water dispensers, one in each hand.

'Hello there!' she said cheerily. 'Welcome to the O-60! The name's Audrey, I'm club secretary. I'd shake your hands but I'm afraid mine are a bit full at the moment. I just nearly killed myself struggling to get through those blasted doors.'

'Let me help you,' said Hubert. Glad of anything that might lessen his feeling of awkwardness, he took the dispensers from her. 'Just point me in the right direction and me take these where you want them.'

Audrey gestured towards a row of three trestle tables, with biscuits and cakes at one end and a collection of tea bags and coffee jars at the other.

'You're a lifesaver,' said Audrey. She removed the empty dispensers to give Hubert room to put down the fresh ones. 'Thank you so much, Mr . . .'

'Bird,' said Hubert. 'But there's no need for mister, you can call me Hubert.'

She smiled and her eyes crinkled slightly as though she were trying to recall something as she shook his hand.

'You look familiar. Have you been to the O-60 before?'

'No,' said Hubert, keen to leave his alter ego, the Windrush Warrior, to one side for the moment. 'First time for me.'

Audrey turned to Jan.

'And you must be . . . Mrs Bird?'

The words caused Hubert a mini coughing fit.

'Ooh no!' said Jan quickly. 'We're not married.'

'Well,' said Audrey. 'I've always said it's only a bit of paper, after all!'

'No,' said Hubert emphatically, looking at Jan in horror, and this time, even through all her make-up, he could see that she'd turned crimson. 'She means we're just friends.'

'Ah,' said Audrey, 'of course! Sorry for the crossed wires! You must think me very dense!' She grabbed a cup and saucer and, with a somewhat theatrical flourish, turned to Hubert and Jan. 'Let's get you both some drinks sorted and I'll introduce you to the rest of the gang. Now who's for tea and who's for coffee?'

Following Audrey's introductions, Hubert and Jan worked on a five-thousand-piece jigsaw with Sue, a former school cook, Barbara, a retired publican, and her husband Cliff. Half an hour later, after making themselves another drink, they sat and enjoyed a piece of cake with Margaret and Colin, who had recently moved to the area to be closer to their family. Following on from this, they played a few hands of whist with Alfredo, a former landscape gardener, and his brother, Enzo, a retired builder. After which, they ended up having a good chat with Gordon and Marion, ten-year veterans of the O-60 and the most terrible gossips you could hope to meet.

Bolstered by Jan's company, Hubert was considerably less nervous than he had been on his previous visit and, with her by his side, tried his best to bond with all of these people, even to the extent of choosing to overlook a few comments from Cliff about his problems with 'the Polish'. Even so, Hubert struggled to find much common ground beyond the usual chat about gardening, public transport and the weather.

He could tell just by looking at Jan that she was feeling the same, and her usual bubbly personality was somewhat muted. As midday approached, with just an hour of the session remaining, Jan whispered in Hubert's ear, 'This isn't for me,' and Hubert was just about to reply, 'Me neither,' when a couple he'd seen earlier taking part in the line dancing session came over to introduce themselves. The man was a few inches shorter than Hubert, had close-cropped white hair and was wearing a short-sleeved checked shirt and navy-blue shorts. The woman by his side was small with peroxide-blond hair and an open, friendly face.

'Had to come over and say hello,' said the man, shaking Hubert's hand. 'Since the moment you stepped in here, me and my partner have been racking our brains trying to think where we know you from and it's just come to me: you're that bloke off the telly and in the papers, aren't you?'

Hubert squirmed with embarrassment.

'Yes, that's me.'

'What was it they called you again? That's it . . . the Windrush Warrior! The pensioner declaring war on loneliness!'

'I feel quite giddy getting to meet you in person,' said the woman. 'We both saw you on the sofa with Phil and Holly. We said at the time we thought you were fantastic.'

'I'm Bob, by the way,' said the man, 'and this is my partner Anita. We're so pleased to meet you.'

Hubert introduced himself and Jan, careful to point out as he'd had to do all morning that they were friends and nothing more.

'This place can feel a bit overwhelming the first time you come, can't it?' said Anita.

Bob laughed.

'I hated it so much the first time, I wanted to leave straight away.'

'Me too,' said Anita. 'They all seemed to know each other, didn't they, Bob? And it was hard to feel like you weren't intruding.'

'That's right,' said Bob. 'But it's like anything, the more time you give it, the better it gets.'

'I wouldn't know what to do with my Wednesdays now if this wasn't on,' said Anita. 'Pretty quickly you learn who you get on with and who to avoid, and they do some cracking trips.'

'Oh yes,' said Bob. 'We went for a tour round a brewery the other week. Brought a few souvenirs home from that excursion, I can tell you!'

'Tell me, Jan,' said Anita. 'Do you like *Corrie*?'

'Like it?' said Jan, her face lighting up. 'I love it.'

'Well the Club's got a trip planned in September to Granada

Studios where they make it! Have you been? It's fantastic. There are still some places left on the coach, if you fancy it.'

Spurred on by Bob and Anita, Hubert and Jan not only signed up for the trip but also put their names down for the Christmas meal, as Anita explained that even this early there were only a few spaces left.

After helping themselves to another cup of tea, Hubert and Jan sat down and chatted more with Bob and Anita. Hubert learned that although Bob, originally from Melton Mowbray, was a diehard Leicester City fan, he was not averse to watching cricket and had also spent some time in Barbados with the engineering company he'd worked for most of his life. This revelation led to all manner of discussions about life in the Caribbean, conversations that sadly were cut short by Audrey's announcement that their time in the room was over, as the Zumba Mums had already started to arrive.

As they helped clear the room and pack the equipment away, Hubert couldn't help thinking that after all this time, after all this effort, he was very close to having found himself the two extra friends he needed to present to Rose. So they were called Bob and Anita rather than 'Dennis and Harvey' and yes he might have to drag himself all the way up to Manchester on a coach to see a film set for a soap opera he had no interest in to do it, but the important thing was that he would have friends, real live friends, to introduce to his daughter when she arrived.

'We should go out for lunch some time,' said Jan. 'Me and Hubert had a very pleasant meal at Ketner's Garden Centre recently, do you know it?'

'Know it?' said Anita. 'We love it. In fact, they've just sent us a couple of two-for-one vouchers if you're interested.'

Jan laughed.

'I love a good bargain! What do you say to lunch next Tuesday?'

Hubert felt like a different person as he and Jan sat on the bus home. He felt lighter, like a weight had been taken off his shoulders. Finally he could relax and really look forward to Rose's visit. Granted, he'd still have a lot of explaining to do, about his deception and, of course, about his involvement in the campaign, but now he'd managed to put together, at least in part, some of the life he'd been pretending to have, and surely that had to count for something.

'It's been a good day, hasn't it?' said Jan.

They were now standing at the bus stop around the corner from Hubert's, waiting for the 105 that would take Jan home.

Hubert felt almost unable to contain his relief.

'It's been wonderful. Thank you so much for coming with me. Me couldn't have done it without you.'

Jan beamed at Hubert.

'I enjoyed it. Normally things like that aren't my cup of tea, but going with you made all the difference.'

The roar of an engine in the distance alerted them to the approach of Jan's bus and as it drew closer, Hubert bent to give her a kiss on the cheek as had become their custom. At the last moment, however, she turned her head and planted a lingering kiss right on Hubert's lips.

'I'll . . . I'll . . . see you tomorrow,' said a flustered Jan as they parted. 'Seven o'clock at Fiona's house, isn't it?'

'Yes,' said Hubert, trying his best to regain his composure as the bus pulled up next to them. 'Me think that's right.'

Before he knew it, Jan had hopped on to the bus and as he watched it disappear, Hubert tried his best not to think about what had just happened, and failed. He'd liked the idea of taking things further with Jan but the reality filled him with a mixture of such strange emotions – happiness, guilt, fear and self-loathing – that he didn't know what he thought any more. No, he would have to do a better job of keeping a tight lid on his thoughts until he'd opened up his front door, slipped off his shoes and made a brew. He needed proper thinking time. This was too much for him to take in at the moment.

The minute he opened his front door, his Yale key still in the lock, Hubert sensed that something wasn't quite right. The air in the hallway felt different somehow and there were sounds coming through the house that shouldn't have been there. Withdrawing his key from the lock, he moved further into the hallway and as he glanced through the open door of the front room, the fear that had been growing with each passing moment was confirmed by the smashed china, the overturned bookcase, the framed pictures lying shattered on the floor. He'd been burgled.

38

Then: October 2005

Hubert took a freshly laundered handkerchief and handed it to his daughter.

'Come on, darling, don't get upset. Me will be absolutely fine. Me promise.'

Rose held the handkerchief up to her nose and then smiled through her tears.

'Even after all these years you still dab cologne on your hankie like a proper gent!'

'Well, that's because me never know when me going to meet a damsel in distress!'

'I just hate thinking of you on your own, Pops. Maybe it's not too late. I could change my ticket, tell the university I need a bit more time here.'

Hubert rested his hands on her shoulders.

'Darling, darling, you've put off your flight twice now as it is! And that university of yours has been very good to you already. As much as me would love you to stay for ever, you need to go back to work, get on with your life. You need to go home.'

It was five thirty in the morning and Hubert and Rose were standing in an area just in front of passport control at Heathrow Terminal 3, saying their goodbyes. All around them, people were preparing for journeys that lay ahead. Some were drinking over-priced coffee from the nearby concession, others were stocking up on last-minute essentials like magazines and chocolate bars, while others anxiously checked their watches and phones as they awaited the arrival of travelling companions. In the midst of this hubbub, however, Hubert and Rose were an island of stillness as he tried his best to persuade her to leave, while she just as fiercely argued the case for staying.

It had been a little over six weeks since a heartbroken Hubert had picked his daughter up from this very airport and taken her home. Six weeks during which he had buried the love of his life while trying his best not to fall apart. In the end, he remained strong through the whole ordeal not for his own sake, but for Rose. Though she was now well into her forties and knew more about the world and how it worked than he would ever know, to him she was still his little girl, a little girl who needed looking after, protecting and shielding from the vagaries of this life. Therefore, no matter how much he missed Joyce, no matter how much the prospect of living life without his beloved filled him with dread, he would never allow the grief he felt to totally subsume him. No, he would be strong for Rose always. He would be there for her whenever she needed him. This was his job. Having already lost one child through circumstances outside of his control, he wasn't about to lose another. Rose was his flesh and blood, his pride and joy, and his last living connection to Joyce.

'But there's still so much that needs doing,' Rose persisted.

'Like what? You've more than taken care of everything. Me could never have got through these past weeks without your help. Never. And if you think for a second that me don't want you here then let me tell you you're wrong. Me would love to have you here all the time, Rose. But you know as well as me that your mother wouldn't want the two of us moping about the place and making it untidy! She would want us out there living our lives to the full. She was so proud of you, Rose, we both are, and you have worked too hard for too long just to give up on everything now to come home and rot. You're nearly a professor! My little Rose a professor! Me can't wait for it to happen. You're nearly there, my girl, you're nearly there. Don't give up now!'

Rose fell silent and for a moment Hubert was convinced he'd won her over, but then she sighed heavily, bit her lip and tried a different tack.

'Okay then,' she began, 'you win for now but how about this? How about you changing your mind about coming to live with me for a few months? How great would that be? I know you'd love the weather and seeing all the sights and meeting new people. It could be a new lease of life for you.'

'Me definitely look into it,' said Hubert, keen to show willing. 'You know me always wanted to see a kangaroo in real life.' He stopped and chuckled. 'The Red Lion had kangaroo burgers on the menu once and Shorty bet me that me wouldn't eat one so me did.' Hubert laughed and then screwed up his face comically. 'It tasted a bit like beef but not as nice, so me said to myself next time me see one of them creatures it had better be alive!'

Unable to resist the effect of her dad's humour, Rose laughed for a few moments but then eyed him thoughtfully as though something had just occurred to her.

'Okay, I think I've got a solution,' she said as a gaggle of boisterous young men dressed in straw hats, shorts and espadrilles walked past them, 'I'll get on this plane on one condition and one condition only.'

'Name it.'

'You have to promise that you'll pick up your life again. Start seeing all the old friends you lost touch with while looking after Mum, you know Uncle Gus and that crowd of reprobates you used to meet at the Red Lion. They were all so wonderful at the funeral, said so many kind things about both you and Mum, and they said how much they've missed you these past few years. I can't think of any group I'd rather have looking out for you. So that's my offer: I'll get on the plane if you promise that the first thing you do when you reach home is phone them and make some plans to meet up. Do we have a deal?'

Gazing at his daughter in wonderment, Hubert couldn't help thinking what a fine young woman she had become. She was kind and considerate but tough when she needed to be. She was hard working and diligent too, and judging from the friends who had called and sent cards following Joyce's passing, still had an active social life. She was everything he and Joyce had hoped she would be and it felt good to be loved by her. This last reason alone felt like all the motivation he needed to carry on, to keep on trying, to strive to find meaning in life now that Joyce had gone.

'Me promise it will be the first thing me do,' he said and, grinning, he lifted one hand in the air and placed the other across his heart. 'Scout's honour.'

True to his word, Hubert called Gus that evening and after a long chat told him that he would be joining him and the rest of the gang at the Red Lion. Gus had been over the moon and said he would call everyone to make sure there was a full turnout. And so it was that two days later Hubert walked in to the Red Lion for the first time in eight years.

'Smiler, man!' called Gus as Hubert scanned the unfamiliar room for his friends. Once again, the pub had undergone a makeover and this time the theme seemed to be taking things that would ordinarily have been dumped in a skip and attaching them on to the walls. There were kitsch Sixties-style reproduction paintings everywhere, old-fashioned adverts for corsets and cough syrups adorning the bar, and all the light fittings resembled the kind of thing he and Joyce had thrown out in the Seventies. But the bones of the place were unchanged and the sight of the old gang gathered around a table made him feel as if he'd come home.

Once Gus had set him up with a pint of Guinness, Hubert settled back in his seat and enjoyed the banter. Although his friends had all made the effort to drop by from time to time over the years, they'd always come individually or in pairs at most, not wanting to disturb or disrupt the careful routine Hubert had constructed for Joyce. So it had been a long time since they'd all been together like this, laughing, joking, teasing one another mercilessly, and Hubert realised just how much he'd missed it.

'So, Smiler,' said Mister Taylor, returning to the table with another round of drinks, 'you want to hear my big news?'

'Don't tell me!' said Hubert, recalling Mister Taylor's perennial declaration that he was done with this country and was moving back to St Kitts. 'You finally bought your ticket back home?'

'Not quite, but me getting there. Me bought some land to build a house through my sister's husband and him organising a builder for me. He sent me the plans the other day – it's going to be a palace!'

'Palace!' scoffed Gus. 'More like a pigsty! Tell me, Mister Taylor, how you know that man isn't just spending all your money on rum and sending you pictures of a house him get out of a magazine to keep you happy?'

'That's why me have me brother-in-law keeping an eye on things,' countered Mister Taylor. 'Him a big man with a neck like a bull, so if that builder give him any problem him give him a good hiding!'

'And if him brother-in-law won't box his ears,' said Teetus, barely able to keep a straight face, 'him sister will! Mister Taylor showed me some photos of her. Me not saying she fat but even her passport photo had to be taken with a wide-angle lens!'

At this, the whole table burst out laughing: Gus had tears running down his face, Biggie Brown was having a coughing fit after his beer went down the wrong way, Oney, who rarely, if ever, understood a joke, was chuckling heartily, and even Mister Taylor joined in.

'Just you wait,' said Mister Taylor when the laughter had finally subsided, 'when me sitting in the sun on my veranda, sipping on a nice glass of rum, while you lot are back here battling through the rain of yet another English summer, you'll be laughing on the other side of your face!'

The rest of the afternoon continued in a similar vein: pints of Guinness, joking, laughter, ribbing and gossip, until finally in the late afternoon they all went their separate ways. Feeling pleasantly merry but far from drunk, Hubert caught the train back to Bromley and passed the time thinking about Mister Taylor and his plans to return to the West Indies.

Since settling down with Joyce, it had never seriously occurred to Hubert to return to Jamaica. After all, with even Cora having moved to America, there was no one from his immediate family still there and he'd now lived far longer here in England than he had in the place he was born, and for all its faults he was glad to call it home. Still, with the winters being so cold and the summers not much better, it was tempting to imagine what it might be like to pack his things, sell up and buy some land back home like his old friend so often talked about.

He could settle somewhere nice, not far from his mother's farm, which had long since been sold, or even get somewhere on the coast so he could enjoy the views. In this modern age it would be as easy for Rose to fly to Jamaica as it was to come to England, and every visit would be far more like a holiday for her if they could stroll along the beach of an evening.

By the time he reached Bromley, Hubert had built up such an elaborate picture in his imagination that he had almost made up his mind to go through with his plans. And as he turned up the collar of his coat against the cold and made his way through the centre of Bromley, he couldn't help thinking that this time next year he could be living back in Jamaica. After all, with Joyce gone and Rose in Australia, what was really keeping him here?

39

Now

'Looks like they got in over the fence at the end of the garden,' said PC Pancholi, gratefully taking the tea from Hubert. 'The house at the back of you is empty, so chances are no one will have seen them. Still, it might be worth knocking on the neighbours' doors just to make sure.'

'You think you'll catch them?' asked Hubert.

The two officers exchanged glances and then PC Pancholi spoke. 'It's rare but not impossible. Sometimes we get lucky and catch them in the act, other times we nick them for one thing and then find their homes stuffed with stolen goods. To be honest, there's just no telling. But I assure you we'll do our best and when things have calmed down and you've had a chance to tidy up, I'll give you a call, let you know where we are and you can give us the details of what's missing.'

'Meanwhile we'll sort you out a crime number,' added PC Enfield, 'and if you're lucky, either today or tomorrow one of our SOCOs will be along, although I wouldn't hold your breath as they're backed up from here to Timbuktu.'

Hubert thought for a moment, mulling over likely suspects for the crime he had suffered. 'Do you think it was kids?'

PC Enfield shrugged. 'It's impossible to say, kids, career criminals, drug addicts . . . the list is endless.'

Drug addicts. Hubert's mind immediately leaped to David. Was this his son's doing? Would he really stoop so low? It wasn't beyond imagining. He'd stolen from friends and neighbours in the past, along with money from Hubert's wallet or Joyce's purse. But surely even he wouldn't do something like this? Hubert had seen him, though, hadn't he? That day in Bromley when they were handing out leaflets. Perhaps seeing Hubert had triggered something in his mind. Maybe when he was drunk or on something, the idea of coming home to get what he needed for his next fix had presented itself to him.

'Are you okay, Mr Bird?' asked PC Pancholi. 'You've gone very quiet.'

'Me fine. It's just . . . it's just . . .'

The doorbell rang.

'Do you want us to get that?' asked PC Enfield.

'No, thank you,' said Hubert. These two young people had earned their break. 'You finish your tea. Me deal with it.'

Hubert went to the door and opened it to find an anxious Ashleigh looking back at him.

'Are you all right? Randip was just dropping by mine with some campaign stuff when she saw the police car outside your house and I came round straight away. Is everything okay?'

Hubert shook his head, trying his best to keep hold of his emotions.

'What's wrong, Hubert? What's happened?'

'Them filthy buggers rob me!' His voice cracked as hot angry tears began rolling down his cheeks. 'Them take Joyce's wedding and engagement rings! The very last bit of Joyce me have and them take it!'

It had been just over an hour since Hubert opened his front door and made the terrible discovery that the home he had worked so hard for, the home where he'd raised his family and nursed his wife, had been violated by strangers. Shaking with fury and fear, he'd reached into the umbrella stand for his walking stick, the one he only ever used when his knees were really playing up, and raising it above his head as if brandishing an axe had crept into the chaos of the front room, checking first behind the door and then behind the sofa. With his heart pounding, he had moved down the hallway to the living room, which was in a similar state of disarray. His TV was still there, probably too heavy for them to carry, but all the drawers in the sideboard had been emptied out on to the floor, scattering a lifetime of bills and paperwork across the carpet.

In the kitchen he'd discovered how they had gained entry. The back door was wide open and shards of glass were scattered everywhere, the floor, the table, even the sink. Gripping the walking stick even tighter than before, Hubert had raised his eyes to the ceiling, fearing the intruders might be upstairs. He would beat the living daylights out of them if they were still there. He would beat them and beat them until they begged and screamed for mercy and then he would beat them some more. This was Hubert Bird's house, this was his home, and he and Joyce hadn't worked their fingers to the bone over all those years just to let some thieving lowlifes break in and take whatever they wanted.

Aware of every loose floorboard and creaking tread, Hubert had navigated his way up the stairs and, after pausing on the landing, had tackled his own bedroom first. His chest of drawers had been emptied and the contents of his and Joyce's wardrobes strewn around the room. Checking the rest of the upstairs, Hubert satisfied himself that he was alone, but the relief he felt was immediately replaced by dread as he caught sight of one of Puss's toys abandoned next to the radiator in the hallway. Walking back through the house, Hubert had desperately called out her name, reassuring himself that even if they'd seen Puss they wouldn't have hurt her. All they wanted was money or things they could sell. But then he remembered all the horrible stories he'd read in the paper, all the terrible things he'd heard on the news about people being cruel to poor animals and he could barely breathe, such was the horror he felt in the pit of his stomach.

The moment he saw Puss wandering in from the garden, wearing a look on her face as if to say, 'What's all the fuss about?', Hubert had whisked her up into his arms, held her as tightly as he dared and, no longer able to hold back the tidal wave of emotion, he had finally given in, letting it wash over him, sobbing bitterly into her soft, warm fur.

Hubert hardly remembered what he said to the operator when he'd dialled 999, but the moment he put down the receiver he suddenly saw things he hadn't noticed before. The twenty-pound note that had been on the side table with his shopping list ready for the morning was gone, the list abandoned on the floor. A sudden dread struck Hubert as he thought of all the other things they might have taken, and with a cry he had rushed back upstairs.

As he entered the bedroom his eyes had darted to the empty space on Joyce's bedside table where her wedding and engagement rings usually sat, in front of his favourite photograph of her. It was a colour picture, taken when Rose had booked a surprise session with a photographer as a present for their thirtieth wedding anniversary. Now the frame was face down on the floor and no matter how desperately Hubert searched, there was no sign of the rings. It had slowly dawned on him that they hadn't just fallen on the floor or rolled under the bed but had been stolen. At this realisation, a fresh wave of grief had crashed over him, causing him to sink heavily on to the bed, his head in his hands, his heart breaking.

'I'm so sorry this has happened to you, Hubert,' said Ashleigh, setting a fresh mug of tea in front of him. The police officers had left, Hubert had calmed down, and now it was just the two of them sitting at the kitchen table. 'I hate that there are such horrible scumbags in the world. Why have people got to be so cruel? I mean, what have you ever done to anyone to deserve this?'

'Them all just filthy animals!' said Hubert with a conviction that came from the very core of his being. 'Breaking into people's home, taking them things and all for what? So them can buy drink or drugs? Not even food because them hungry, but drink and drugs!' He shook his head sadly. 'Me tell you, this whole world is going to the dogs!'

'I know it feels like that at the moment, Hubert. But people aren't all bad. Think about everyone we've met doing this campaign, for instance. There are some wonderful people out there and we can't ever forget that, because that's how the bad guys win, isn't it?'

Hubert didn't reply, but that didn't mean he agreed with her. Right now he felt like the world was past saving, beyond redemption.

'As soon as I finish my tea,' said Ashleigh, assessing the room, 'I'm going to settle you down somewhere and crack on sorting this place out. Sitting looking at this mess isn't going to help anything, is it? The sooner I get things back to normal the better, eh?'

Hubert said nothing.

'And while I think about it, I'd better call someone to get your back door sorted before it starts to get dark. Have you got a number for your insurance people? I'll give them a ring first.'

Hubert gestured over his shoulder towards the hallway. 'It's in the living room in the sideboard drawer that them tip all over the place.'

Ashleigh got up from the table and left the room, returning moments later waving a manila folder on which was written: 'IMPORTANT INSURANCE DOCUMENTS.'

'You're so organised that even in that mess it was pretty easy to find. I'm just going to give them a call. Shouldn't be too long.'

She disappeared out of the room once more, leaving Hubert to consider the lengthening shadows creeping their way across the kitchen cupboards, heralding the close of the day. Would he feel safe sleeping here come nightfall? Would he dare for a moment to close his eyes, knowing how easy it was for strangers to enter his home? His earlier bravado with the walking stick now struck him as almost comical. What could he, an eighty-four-year-old man, really do to defend himself against a single intruder, out of his senses and beyond all reasoning, let alone two or a whole gang of them? For the first time ever, he didn't feel safe in his own home and what made it worse was that he wasn't sure he ever would again.

When Ashleigh returned, it was to ask him to speak to his insurer to confirm that he was happy for her to sort things out for him. Once he'd handed the phone back, he sat and finished his tea quietly in the kitchen and five minutes later she announced,

'Whatever you're paying for that insurance, it's well worth it. They're sending a bloke round now to board up the back door and they've promised you'll have a new one by Monday at the latest, and they're posting out claim forms, which should be here for Tuesday. And don't worry, I'll help you fill those in.' She paused and added brightly. 'So that's something, isn't it?'

Hubert said nothing. He and Joyce had spent their whole married life paying for insurance they had never claimed on, and the fact that he was doing so now gave him no comfort at all. They must have spent thousands over the years, no doubt paying for some fat-cat CEO's yacht somewhere, and now he'd finally made a claim, these same people who were being so helpful would no doubt put up his premiums to compensate. Thieves, the lot of them! One lot break into your house and the other suck the money straight from your bank account!

Finishing his tea, Hubert stood up and rinsed out his mug, and as if responding to something he'd said, Ashleigh remarked, 'Good idea, Hubert. I'm going to give Randip a call and see if she's all right to hang on for a bit with Layla while I make a start tidying up.'

Insisting that Hubert let her get on with things alone, Ashleigh supplied him with the pen and pad he usually used for shopping lists and suggested he write down everything that was missing. Starting upstairs in his bedroom, Hubert wrote the words, 'Wedding ring' and 'engagement ring' and then just sat on the bed staring out of the window. He didn't know how long he sat there. What roused him from his stupor was the sound of a van pulling up in front of the house, followed by the chimes of the doorbell.

'It's the bloke from the insurance come to secure the back door!' called Ashleigh up the stairs, but Hubert didn't respond. Instead, picking up the pad, he got up from the bed and continued cataloguing missing items. He had barely managed to add half a dozen things to his list before Ashleigh shouted that the man was all done and needed Hubert's signature before he left.

Slowly, carefully, clutching on to the banister, Hubert made his way downstairs, feeling with every step as if he had aged twenty years. He scrawled his name at the bottom of the form attached to the workman's blue plastic clipboard, saying nothing in response to his constant stream of cheery chatter. Once he'd gone, Ashleigh's phone buzzed.

'It's Randip. She's got to get off. Listen, Hubert, why don't you stay the night at mine? You can have my bed and I'll get in with Layla. She'll love that. I don't like the thought of you being here on your own until everything's properly sorted.'

'Me not going to let them chase me out of my own home. That is not going to happen.'

'Of course not. It's just for the night. While you get over the shock, that's all. You'll have a new back door in a day or so and maybe we can get them to add a few extra security measures while they're at it, just to be on the safe side like. We'll have you back here before you know it. It'll be like nothing's happened.'

'No, thank you. Even if they come again with more besides, me not going anywhere.'

'But Hubert—'

'Me said no!'

'Okay, okay, you're right. You shouldn't have to leave your home. How about I get Layla and bring her round here? I could pick up fish and chips for us all.'

'No, thank you. You've already done plenty to help me. Anyway, the last thing me want is for that lovely child of yours to see what them animals do to my home.'

'She's only two. She won't even notice.'

'No, you go and be with her. Me fine.'

'Okay, you win. But at least let me call Rose for you and let her know what's happened.'

Rose, thought Hubert. *She wants to call Rose.*

'No,' said Hubert. 'You're not calling Rose.'

She reached across and placed a hand on his arm. 'Hubert, listen to me. I know that you don't want to worry her but she's your daughter. I know if something like this had happened to my mum, I'd be gutted if she hadn't told me. Let's call her together, I can reassure her you're fine and tell her I'm looking after you.'

Hubert shook his head but said nothing.

'Look, I promise it'll be fine,' persisted Ashleigh. 'She'll be here the week after next anyway, so it's not as if she won't find out. Plus, you never know, she might be able to bring her flight forward or something. They can do that sometimes, especially if it's an emergency like this is.'

Hubert shook his head again but still said nothing.

'Come on, Hubert,' said Ashleigh, 'help me out here. I can't just leave you like this. You don't have to do anything at all, just tell me where her number is and I'll do the rest.'

Hubert's eyes began to fill with tears but he said nothing.

'Oh Hubert!' said Ashleigh gently as she rubbed his arm. 'Please don't get upset. It's the shock hitting you, that's what it is. I'm sure if you talk things over with Rose you'll feel much better.'

Hubert felt as if his very foundations were crumbling and with them the scaffolding he had erected to keep his walls in check all these years. This was it, he slowly came to realise, the end of everything that had kept him standing. It was time, time to face the truth.

'You can't speak to Rose,' he said quietly.

'Because of the time difference? I'm sure she'll understand.'

Hubert shook his head.

'Is she away or something? If you've got a mobile number, I can call her on that.'

Hubert turned to face Ashleigh, eyes overflowing with tears.

'You can't . . . you can't call her. My beautiful Rose . . . she dead.'

Ashleigh covered her mouth with her hand as she attempted to take in what he had told her.

'Oh, Hubert, how terrible! What happened?'

'She was in an accident.'

Ashleigh shook her head in disbelief.

'Oh, this is awful. You must be devastated. Here's me wittering on about insurance claims when you've been dealing with this. When did you find out?'

Hubert struggled to find the words, and then struggled further to find the strength to say them.

'Five . . . five years ago,' he said. 'She died five years ago.'

40

Then: November 2012

Hubert was in the kitchen making breakfast – bacon, eggs, plantain, mushrooms – just like he used to back in the old days. The radio was on but the volume was turned down so low it was really nothing more than a murmur.

The kitchen door opened and David stood in the doorway, blinking uncertainly as though not quite sure where he was. He was still wearing the greasy-looking jeans and stained T-shirt from the night before, but the vomit-splattered hoodie he'd been wearing was now washed and drying on the radiator in the hallway. Catching a whiff of his son's stench, Hubert tried not to recoil. He didn't want to scare him off. He didn't want to give him an excuse to run away. For now, he just wanted to give him a good meal, help fill out his emaciated frame and put some colour in his cheeks.

He'd been on his way home from an afternoon with his friends in the Red Lion when he'd spotted David. In high spirits after a session of Guinness, laughter and dominoes, there had been nothing more pressing on Hubert's mind than picking up a few bits of shopping to tide him over the weekend. Standing in the long queue at the tills of the Tesco Metro round the corner from his bus stop, an odd feeling had come over him as if he had forgotten something important. And it wasn't until he reached the front of the queue that it hit him; the issue wasn't with items on a forgotten shopping list, it was the man, the one he'd passed begging outside the very shop in which he was standing.

Crying out in anguish, Hubert had dropped the things in his hands and bolted to the entrance, only to find the beggar in exactly the same position as when he'd first seen him. He was slumped to one side, only barely conscious, with an empty coffee cup in front of him containing a handful of copper coins. Despite his matted hair, unkempt beard and slight frame, now that he was really looking there was no mistaking him. He was older, greyer, more haggard than his fifty years should've made him. But nonetheless, it was David. It was his son.

'Me wake you?' asked Hubert.

David said nothing and instead ran his fingers over his dreadlocks pensively. Hubert was shocked by how much his son now resembled Hubert's own father. He not only had his grandfather's high cheekbones and strong chin but his eyes also wore that same lost and haunted expression Hubert remembered so well.

'Me was trying me best not to make any noise.' He smiled and added, 'Then again, maybe it was the smell of bacon that woke you. You used to love a good bacon sandwich.'

David hovered in the doorway.

'How . . . how did I get here?'

'Take a seat,' said Hubert, 'and me tell you.'

David didn't move.

'But I don't understand how I got here.'

Hubert could see his son beginning to get quite unnerved.

'Do I live here?'

Hubert shook his head.

'Me found you yesterday evening. You . . . you . . . weren't well.'

Hubert recalled the night before. His horror at realising that he'd walked past his own flesh and blood, his only son, and hadn't recognised him. He hadn't seen him in such a long time, hadn't been able to find out how he was or where he was living. For years he hadn't known whether David was alive or dead, still struggling or back on his feet. Nothing for all this time and then suddenly there he was, less than a fifteen-minute drive from his own home, begging outside a supermarket.

'Me slip a taxi driver an extra twenty pound and he help me get you home,' explained Hubert, glossing over the details. How he'd desperately tried to move his son on his own, only to have to enlist the help of a passing stranger to get him to the roadside so that they could hail a taxi. How three had refused to take them because of the state David was in.

'I . . . I . . . don't remember,' said David, but still he didn't sit down.

'He was a decent fella, the taxi driver. He helped me get you home,' continued Hubert, again sparing David the details. How, because of the stink rising from his son, they'd had to drive with all the windows open. How halfway home David had been sick over himself and they'd had to pull over and wash him down with a bottle of water the cab driver had in the boot. How with the man's help he had manoeuvred his son up the stairs to his old bedroom, careful to place him in the recovery position in case he was sick again. How Hubert, worried for his son's welfare, had sat in a chair by his bedside the entire night, only leaving half an hour ago to make him breakfast.

'I . . . I . . . need to go,' said David, but he didn't move.

'Okay, son, but at least have a little something to eat first.'

Finally David sat down at the table, whether lured by the smell of bacon or hit by a wave of exhaustion it was hard to tell. Hubert was simply glad he had.

'Won't be long,' he said gently.

As quickly as he could manage, he finished preparing the breakfast while simultaneously making two mugs of tea, and within a few short moments the whole meal had come together.

Hubert placed the dishes in front of David so that he could help himself, and for a moment his son just stared at the food. So Hubert decided to plate some of it up for him and this seemed to do the trick. Picking up the bacon with his fingers, David began to eat greedily, using a slice of buttered bread as a shovel to scoop up mouthfuls of beans, tinned tomatoes and mushrooms. He ate quickly and furtively, as though any moment someone might take his meal away, and when Hubert loaded his plate up for seconds he ate it in the same manner, washing each bite down with a gulp of hot tea.

Hubert didn't say a word as David devoured his meal. Instead he pretended to concentrate on his own plate, all the while stealing surreptitious glances at his son. Did he already know that his mother had passed away? Was this why he had yet to ask about her whereabouts? Or was he still so out of it from the drink and drugs he had consumed the night before that it hadn't even occurred to him that she wasn't here?

If David didn't know, Hubert was going to have to tell him. He had no idea how he might take the news. Would he be indifferent or would he be devastated? Either way, his reaction would be heartbreaking to witness. But he had no idea where his son had been all these years and no idea when he might get another opportunity to speak to him. It was now or never.

'David,' said Hubert as his son polished off the last of his food. 'Me have something me need to tell you.'

He didn't respond and instead stared at the empty plate before him. Hubert wondered what, if anything, remained of the little boy who used to beg to be read to, the one who used to imitate his dad's every move, the child who wanted to grow up to be just like his father. Was he still in there somewhere, hidden in some deep recess? Or had he been long since swallowed up by his demons? His son was like a zombie, a member of the living dead: he didn't seem to be able to think, to feel or even be aware of what was going on around him.

'David,' said Hubert again. 'David, please look at me.'

Slowly, very slowly his son lifted his chin up a few degrees.

'It's about your mother . . . me think you ought to know that she . . . she . . . well, she passed away. She didn't suffer and me was with her when she passed. And she loved you, David. She loved you with her whole heart and everything she had to give. We both did . . . still do. And there isn't anything me won't—'

David stood up suddenly from the table, avoiding all eye contact with his father. 'I . . . I . . . need to go.'

Hubert felt an ache in his heart and a cry catch in his throat. 'Please, son . . . please don't go. Let's forget about the past. Let's make a fresh go of things. This is still your home and me still your dad. Let me help you, please, son, let me help you.'

'I . . . I . . . don't need your help,' stuttered David as he left the room. 'I . . . I . . . don't need anyone's help. I . . . I . . . just need to go.'

Hubert followed after him, watching impotently as his son grabbed his still-damp hoodie from the radiator, opened the front door and then stepped out into the bright daylight.

Following him down the front path, Hubert called after him. 'David! Son, come back! Please, me begging you, don't leave!'

But David kept on walking and Hubert could do nothing other than finally allow the wellspring of sorrow that had been bubbling within him all night to finally break free.

Over the next few days, Hubert tried everything he could think of to get David off the streets. He called the police, social services and even the Salvation Army, but the answer was always the same. Unless David himself asked for help, there was nothing they could do. Grief-stricken and powerless, Hubert couldn't even bring himself to go anywhere near the town centre, in case he saw his son.

For weeks he shopped in a different supermarket, visited a different library, and even made up excuses to Gus and the rest of the Red Lion crowd as to why he couldn't join them. Finally one day, having thought of nothing but David, Hubert could stand it no longer. He caught the bus into town and made his way to the spot outside the Tesco Metro, hoping beyond hope that his son might still be there. He would do everything in his power to talk sense into him, to make him come home, to encourage him to seek all the help he needed to get back on his feet. But he was nowhere to be seen.

For a moment Hubert's spirits lifted. Perhaps he'd had a change of heart, had sought help for himself and was now living in some sort of sheltered accommodation, trying his best to get better. But as he turned to go, he caught sight of a figure lying slumped on a bench across the way. With a sudden, urgent lurch of his heart, he realised who it was. Hubert was desperate to pick him up, to take him home, to look after him once again, but in that moment he knew what everyone said was true: David was never going to change unless he wanted to.

Bereft at this realisation, Hubert turned around and made his way inside the supermarket, where he picked up crisps, fruit, sandwiches, a bottle of water and some deodorant. Loading the items into a carrier bag, he left the store, made his way back over to David and, without a word, placed the bag by his sleeping son's side.

For the next six months Hubert made this same pilgrimage every time he visited the town centre, taking food and clothes to his son. When it was cold he would deliver duvets and jumpers, when it was raining he would leave him with waterproofs or an umbrella. Even if David was awake, they would never speak. Hubert would simply leave the items and then go home.

Then one day Hubert spotted David begging outside Marks & Spencer and, as usual, picked up a few items of food for him, leaving them by his side before making his way home. That evening he hadn't had much of an appetite and so made himself a cup of tea and then settled down on the sofa, under the pretext of watching an old James Cagney film on cable. He hadn't seen *Angels with Dirty Faces* for years and had been quite looking forward to it, but within minutes was fast asleep.

Waking with a start an hour later, Hubert switched off the television and decided that he would get an early night. After giving his garden a good watering, as was his habit before bed, Hubert was about to turn off his hose when he spotted a shape near the rose bushes that ran along one edge of the lawn. As he got closer he saw it was a cat and, filled with annoyance that it might have been about to do its business on his property, he turned the hose on it and it ran off hissing like a mad thing.

Back inside, Hubert locked his back door, then headed upstairs to the bathroom to brush his teeth. Once in bed, he reached for the photograph of Joyce on his bedside table and kissed it lightly as he did every night, the cool of the glass lingering on his lips long after he had returned the frame to its usual place.

As he waited for sleep to come, he thought about the day and how it had unfolded. He smiled as he recalled how well his new wisteria was bedding in, tutted when he realised he'd forgotten to call the council about his missed bin collection. And frowned when he thought about the cat, and made a mental note to buy cat repellent from Homebase before it made a permanent toilet of his back garden. Then finally he thought about David, how thin he had looked, how drawn and tired, and racked his brains again, wondering what he could do to help his son.

After a while, he fell into a fitful sleep and was plagued by dreams of being chased by some anonymous figure. It was only when this figure was about to capture him that he woke with a start to the sound of his phone ringing.

41

Now

The light outside was fading fast. Normally around this time Hubert would be switching on table lamps around the house as a prelude to drawing the curtains. Instead he and Ashleigh were sitting at the kitchen table, both seemingly oblivious of the encroaching darkness as day finally gave way to night.

Ashleigh broke the silence.

'Hubert . . . I don't . . . I'm not following you. I think all this upset has made you confused. Rose isn't dead. She's coming over to visit.'

He shook his head.

'Me not confused, darling, me wish me was, but it's all true.'

Hubert told her about the call he'd taken late that fateful night five years ago from the Australian police. Rose had been on the motorway on her way home from a conference and a lorry coming the other way had blown its tyre, crossed the central reservation and smashed straight into her car, killing her instantly.

He told her how he'd always thought it would be David he'd get the late-night call about. Some policeman or social worker confirming that his son had finally destroyed himself. So to have it be Rose, Rose who had everything to live for, Rose who had always worked so hard and done the right thing, had nearly killed him.

He told her all about the living hell of the weeks that followed Rose's death. How desperately he'd searched for his son in order to tell him the terrible news. Finding David still living on the streets, Hubert had begged him to come back home but his son had refused. And hadn't even shown his face at the funeral.

He told her about the day he buried Rose. How packed the

church had been, full of his friends and Rose's, all rallying round, all coming together to say goodbye to his little girl.

He told her how on the night of the funeral he'd made the decision to eliminate David from his life for good. How he'd sat down at the kitchen table, surrounded by family albums, and cut his son out of every single picture – baby photos, school portraits, holiday snaps, the whole lot – and put the pieces in the bin.

He told her how, without the funeral to focus on and with everyone returned to their own lives, a terrible silence had descended on the house, a silence so profound that Hubert couldn't bear it. Perhaps this had been where the ringing telephone had come from, a desperate desire to combat the deafening nothingness of a life lived without his beloved wife or darling daughter.

'Me was in the kitchen washing up a few things the first time Rose called,' said Hubert, looking away from Ashleigh. 'When me pick up the receiver and she said hello, me was so shocked, so shaken that me almost dropped it. Me knew it couldn't be Rose. Rose was dead. But me so wanted it to be her that in the end it didn't matter. To be able to talk to her again, to hear her voice, to feel less alone, that was all me cared about.'

Hubert could feel Ashleigh's eyes on him searching for answers. Finally, he turned back towards her, ready for the questions that he knew would come.

'You think me lost me mind, don't you? Gone cuckoo. Completely gaga.'

'Of course not, Hubert. You were just missing her, that's all, and trying to cope as best you could.'

Hubert gave a mirthless laugh.

'For five whole years? Because that's how long me been talking to her on the phone. Once a week for five years. Maybe I am crazy. Maybe it's time them lock me up in a home with all the other crazy old people.'

'Oh, don't say that.'

'Why not? That's what happened to my own father. He was in and out of Bellevue Mental Hospital in Kingston him whole life until he finally killed himself.'

Ashleigh bit her lip and for a moment seemed as if she was lost for words.

'I had no idea about any of this,' she said, squeezing his hand. 'No idea at all.'

'Doesn't matter,' said Hubert. 'Chances are me taking after him. Chances are me not been right in me mind all along.'

'I don't believe that for a second,' said Ashleigh. 'What you're saying makes perfect sense. At least it does to me. I've lost count of the times I've nearly called my nan to tell her something funny or ask her advice. It just seemed so natural, especially after moving to London, as we were always talking on the phone anyhow. I suppose it was easy to imagine her still pottering about her little terrace doing all the things she used to do.'

'It was just so comforting,' said Hubert. 'Every week she would call like she always did, but the strange thing was, she didn't just say the things me wanted to hear. She would bully and badger me just like she did in real life. Telling me to eat properly, take my medicine, telling me not to mope around the house and watch TV all day. That's why me have to make up Dotty, Dennis and Harvey.'

'Who?'

Hubert shook his head.

'It's a long story.'

'And her coming over to visit?'

'That came completely out of the blue,' said Hubert. 'Deep down me knew it couldn't happen but me really wanted it to be true.' He turned to her, his face etched with sorrow. 'Now look me in the eye and tell me that me haven't lost my mind.'

Ashleigh said nothing, but Hubert could tell she was beginning to doubt his sanity and who could blame her? Here he was, confessing to making preparations for a visit from his dead daughter, who he'd been talking to on the phone once a week for five years. It was a wonder Ashleigh was still here, let alone worrying about him and holding his hand.

He turned his head towards the door and watched as Puss

strode into the room and settled herself on the vacant chair next
to him.

'Me just feel like such a fool. A stupid old fool who should
have known better.'

Ashleigh's phone buzzed.

'Oh, that'll be Randip wondering where I am. Let me just give
her a quick call and I'll be right back.'

She left the room, leaving Hubert to consider the future. No
more pantomime with the telephone, no more Rose, no more
fooling himself that his life was anything other than what it was:
day after day of emptiness. His mind flicked back to that moment
with Jan and the kiss they'd shared, a moment that now seemed
to belong to another time.

What had he been thinking? What had he thought it might
achieve? It had been a moment of madness no less deluded than
the phone calls from Rose. He was done with pretending. He
was done with opening doors and letting people in. All he wanted
now was to be left alone. All he wanted was to give up the foolishness of hope.

Ashleigh bustled back into the room.

'Sorry about that. Randip said she's made a call and can stay
with Layla as long as I need.'

Hubert stood up, shakily, feeling like he had not one single
ounce of energy left.

'Ashleigh, me want to thank you for all your time but me want
you to go now.'

'Layla's fine, I promise, really she is. She'll have a whale of a
time with Randip and anyway, right now the most important
thing is making sure you're all right.'

'Me appreciate that but me still want you to go. Right now,
me just want . . . me want to be left alone.'

Ashleigh tried everything she could think of to change Hubert's
mind, repeating her offer to stay with him or have him stay with
her, but he wouldn't hear of it and so finally she had no choice
but to accept his wishes.

'You will call me if you need me during the night, won't you?'

she said anxiously at the front door. 'I'll pop round tomorrow first thing to see how you're getting on.'

'No need. Me will be fine on my own.'

'Okay then,' said Ashleigh reluctantly. 'As for the committee meeting at Fiona's tomorrow, don't feel like you have to come. I can always swing by afterwards and fill you in.'

'Don't bother yourself. Me won't be doing that committee thing any more.'

'But why not?'

Hubert could think of a million reasons. Because he'd made a fool of himself. Because he didn't want to face Jan. Because he didn't want to have to explain everything to everyone all over again. But the biggest reason of all was the one that was most difficult to articulate: he'd had enough. Of being open, of being around people. He wanted to go back to how things used to be, before the committee, before Jan, before Ashleigh. Maybe if he hadn't opened the door to Ashleigh that day, if he'd just stayed safely on his sofa, stroking Puss and watching the world go by through the television screen, none of this would have happened and he'd still have Rose.

'It doesn't matter,' he said finally, bone tired and feeling every last hour of his eighty-four years. 'Me just not doing it. Me just want to be left alone.'

42

Now: Ashleigh, 3 August 2018

'Right, is that everyone?'

Ashleigh scanned her tiny living room, doing a quick head count. All were present apart from Hubert.

'Some of you will be wondering why the last meeting was cancelled and why we haven't been able to sort one out until now, especially with the launch day less than a month away.'

There were nods and murmurs from around the room, mostly from Tony, but a few from Maude and Fiona too.

'To be honest,' said Tony, shifting his weight on the sofa, 'I don't see any way we can pull it off this late in the day, even with the backing of the council.'

'Oh, don't be so negative, Tony,' said Fiona. 'I'm sure Ashleigh has a plan, don't you, dear?'

Everyone in the room turned their attention back to Ashleigh, and overwhelmed with self-consciousness, she coughed and took a sip from the glass of water on the coffee table in front of her.

'What's the hold-up anyway?' asked Tony. 'And where's Hubert?'

'He's not poorly, is he?' asked Maude. 'I had the most terrible diarrhoea last week, kept me running to the loo two days straight. I'm better now but at the time it was awful. Is it something like that Hubert's got?'

Ashleigh shook her head. 'I'm afraid not, Maude. I'm afraid Hubert's not himself at the moment: he was burgled a few weeks ago.'

A chorus of gasps and tuts rippled around the room.

'Poor Mr Hubert!' exclaimed Emils. 'Is he all right? Was he hurt?'

'Stealing from a pensioner!' gasped Maude. 'When they catch the culprits, they should string them up!'

'It's a terrible world we live in,' said Randip. 'Just the other week a ninety-six-year-old lady was mugged for her handbag just around the corner from me. They pulled the poor dear to the floor and she broke her hip.'

'Well, I'm pleased to say that Hubert wasn't physically hurt, as thankfully he wasn't in at the time, but I can't lie, it's really knocked him for six and I'm afraid he's decided to step down as president of our committee.'

'But he was such a marvellous spokesperson,' said Fiona.

'Plus, he's the face of our campaign,' said Tony.

Emils raised his hand as if he was in school. 'We should go and visit Mr Hubert right now and tell him how much we need him.'

'Austerity Britain,' said Tony dolefully, 'that's what's caused this. Universal credit and police cuts equals chaos!'

Pointedly ignoring Tony's remark, Maude called across the room to an unusually quiet Jan.

'You're close with Hubert. Can't you talk him round? We really need him.'

Jan shook her head sadly.

'I've tried visiting, calling and even dropped a note through his door but I've heard nothing.'

'Me too,' said Ashleigh. 'At first I was hoping he might get over it in a week or two, which is why I delayed this meeting, but I really don't think he's going to change his mind. The last thing he said to me was that he just wanted to be left alone.'

Ashleigh still couldn't shake the image of Hubert that day. It was almost as if he'd woken up as one person and gone to bed another. In the morning at Martin Pemberton's office he'd been his usual self, laughing, joking, full of life, looking years younger than his actual age. But that night in his hallway, as he'd made it clear he didn't want her there any more or to continue to be part of the committee, he'd seemed the opposite: old, frail, lost and lonely.

She felt terrible. This was all her fault. Pushing her way into his life, pushing him to start the campaign, to lead the committee, to appear on the radio and TV. She had meant it for the best, hoping that he might see in himself what she'd seen in him that first day, despite his efforts to keep it hidden: a kindness, a spirit of adventure, a strength. But she'd gone too far, asked too much of him, and this was the result.

She had tried to see him the following morning but although she'd rung the doorbell several times and even spotted the unmistakable outline of her old friend lurking behind the net curtain, he wouldn't answer the door. Calling Jan to let her know about the burglary, Ashleigh then enlisted her help and the two went round again that same afternoon and evening. Each time, however, Hubert ignored them, just as he went on to do every day of the week that followed.

Growing increasingly concerned but feeling unable to share the real reason for fear of breaking Hubert's confidence, Ashleigh had even considered calling the police but then one day, on the way home from work, she'd spotted him halfway down the road, laden with shopping bags. Even from a distance he seemed different, his shoulders stooped, his gait shuffling, all of which added to the impression of a broken old man. Desperate to talk to him, Ashleigh had called out his name but his only reaction was to dip his head down and increase his pace until, changing direction, he disappeared from view through his front gate. She'd been shocked by how much it had hurt and hadn't felt right since. She'd thought they'd be friends for ever.

'So, what are we going to do now?' asked Maude. 'Carry on or give up?'

Ashleigh cast a glance around the room, its air thick with the defeat and dejection of its occupants. She'd been dreading the prospect of this meeting all morning but there were things that needed to be said, decisions that needed to be taken.

'Well, that's actually one of the reasons why I called this meeting,' said Ashleigh. 'The fact is I couldn't have done any of this without Hubert and with him not being here, my heart's just not in it.'

'So you want to call the whole thing off?'

Ashleigh shook her head. 'That's not what I'm saying at all.'

'So, what are you saying?' asked Fiona.

Ashleigh sighed. 'That I don't want to do this without Hubert.'

There was a long silence while everybody considered her words and then finally Jan spoke up. 'But what about all the lonely people?' she said. 'What about all the people who need us? No one misses Hubert being here more than me, but his not being here is all the more reason for us not to give up, for you not to give up, Ash. People like Hubert – the ones who have been let down by life and feel like giving up – are the very ones who need this most.'

Randip nodded.

'Jan's right, our campaign has really captured people's imaginations. Just last week I heard two people talking about it in the vet's saying what a good idea it was. And those two people didn't know each other, so it's already sort of working. It would be a shame to give up now.'

Emils raised his hand.

'Ashleigh, our Facebook has sixteen thousand likes, our Twitter, twenty-five thousand and our GoFundMe page is now six thousand pounds over the ten-thousand-pound target we set. People really want this . . . they really need this.'

'It's true,' said Fiona, 'since your meeting with Martin Pemberton, not a single day has gone by when someone hasn't contacted us with either promises of support or donations for the launch day. I think that as much as we'll miss Hubert, we've come too far to give up now, and I think more than ever we need strong leadership, the kind that only you can give, Ashleigh.'

'But that's just it,' said Ashleigh. 'I'm not strong. I'm not confident. If I'm honest, I'm a complete mess. You should've seen me the night I first moved to Bromley, sobbing into my pillow like a baby all night, wondering what the heck I'd been thinking moving myself and Layla so far from the places and the people that we knew, I—' She stopped, suddenly overwhelmed, not only by what she was saying but also by the fact that just an hour ago she'd made up her mind to step down from the committee. It hurt too much to think of doing it without Hubert. Carrying on without him seemed like an impossible task and now they were asking her to take his place. She wasn't anything special, she wasn't clever like Fiona and Tony, creative like Emils or experienced in life like Maude or Jan. She was just a young single mum who had an idea that Hubert had helped turn into a reality. She couldn't do it.

'The thing is—'

Tony stood up.

'Before you say anything more, I want to say something. I always thought this mission of yours, while admirable, was too ambitious. I never thought it would get off the ground, that we'd raise any money, get the permissions needed for the launch party in the park, or even get people's support for what essentially is a crackpot idea. I mean, ending loneliness in Bromley, it's ridiculous! But credit where it's due, you not only got this off the ground, you've inspired people to believe that it's actually possible. Even, to be totally honest, an old cynic like me, and for that alone, I think we should carry on and see this through, which is why I'd like to propose a vote. All those in favour of making Ashleigh our new president raise your hand.'

Without hesitation everyone in the room, with the exception of Ashleigh, raised their hands. Maude even raised two.

'Motion carried,' said Tony, 'so what do you say, Ashleigh? Will you be our new president?'

Ashleigh sighed. How could she say no when all of these people were depending on her?

'Fine, I'll do it, but if we're really going to pull this off there's a lot of work we've still got to do. So make yourselves comfortable, grab a drink and a biscuit or nip to the loo if you need it, because this, guys, is going to be one heck of a meeting.'

It was ten o'clock by the time the meeting was finally over, and over the next hour everyone gradually drifted home, with the exception of Jan who, even after Emils had offered her a lift, had insisted that she'd stay behind to help Ashleigh clear up. In truth there wasn't much to do but Ashleigh hadn't protested, sensing that the real reason for Jan's reluctance to leave was that she wanted to talk about Hubert.

'There's something I think you ought to know,' said Jan, her hands knuckle-deep in suds as she washed up dirty coffee cups in the kitchen sink while Ashleigh dried. 'About Hubert and me,' she added, her cheeks flushing at the mention of his name.

'Go on, then,' said Ashleigh, wanting to be encouraging while at the same time being aware of Jan's discomfort.

'It's my fault Hubert doesn't want to be on the committee any more,' she said. 'That day we all went to the pub to celebrate that Martin Pemberton bloke getting behind the campaign . . .'

'Yeah,' encouraged Ashleigh, 'what about it?'

'Well . . . I think I might have had one too many, if you know what I mean . . . I don't know . . . it was such a lovely day, we were all in such good spirits and well . . . I went and made a right fool of myself.'

'Don't be daft,' said Ashleigh, 'you were playing with Layla for most of the afternoon. I didn't see you doing anything embarrassing.'

Jan's face went purple.

'I kissed Hubert.'

'You did what?'

Ashleigh nearly dropped the plate she was drying. She set it down on the kitchen counter and put an arm around Jan.

'I'm sorry, Jan,' she said, 'I didn't mean that to come out how it sounded . . . it's just . . . well . . . wow! You kissed Hubert? How did that come about?'

'We walked home together and it just sort of happened.'

'And he kissed you back?'

'Well, yes . . . no . . . I don't know. It all happened so fast it's hard to tell. But the thing is, he always made it crystal clear that he wasn't looking for any romance and I should've respected that. Instead I've ruined everything and lost one of the nicest friends I've ever had.'

Jan started to cry.

'I'm just a stupid lonely old woman.'

'There, there,' said Ashleigh, comforting Jan, 'I promise you, it's not your fault.'

'But it can't just be the burglary,' said Jan, 'that doesn't explain why he doesn't want to see any of us.'

'It's complicated,' said Ashleigh.

'What?' said Jan. 'Do you know something?'

'I can't say anything,' said Ashleigh. 'It's not my place. But I promise it's got nothing to do with you.'

Ashleigh could almost see Jan's mind whirring as she tried to read between the lines.

'Is it to do with his son? Or his daughter? Did they have a row or something?'

Ashleigh bit her lip.

'Jan, I've already said too much as it is. Just know that it's not your fault and to be honest, it's not Hubert's either. It's just one of those things, those terrible things that happen even to the nicest people.'

43

Now

'Hello, stranger.'

Bob stood to greet Jan, then called over to a woman who was busy making a round of teas at the refreshment table. 'Anita, look who it is!'

'Ooh, it's you, Jan! So lovely to see you! We were beginning to think you and Hubert had eloped!'

'Speak of the devil,' said Bob, craning his neck to look at the doorway behind Jan, 'where is that man of yours?'

Jan felt herself flush.

'He's not my man . . . We're just . . . we're just friends.'

'Oh sorry, I was only pulling your leg,' said Bob. 'Where is he, though? Nothing wrong is there?'

Anita was carrying a tray of drinks, which she set down on the table.

'Oh Bob. Stop grilling the poor woman and give her chance to take her coat off! You have a sit-down, Jan, and I'll pass you over a tea.'

Jan had only made the decision to come to the O-60 Club about five minutes before she put her jacket on and left the house. Prior to that her plans for the day had consisted of taking down and washing her net curtains, making a salad to eat while watching *Loose Women* and then perhaps a visit to the library to exchange the books she'd taken out the week before. Throw in an evening meal consisting of a Weight Watchers Salmon and Broccoli melt, followed by a night in front of the TV catching up with *Coronation Street*, *Emmerdale* and *Grantchester*, and that would have been the sum total of her day. And it was this real-isation, together with the fact that she hadn't spoken to anyone for three days, that had prompted her to set aside her fears and go back to the O-60.

Her primary fear was that people would ask her about Hubert, as she knew that their questions, no matter how well intentioned, might upset her. She missed Hubert. She really did. From the moment she woke up to the moment she fell asleep she felt an ever-present heaviness in the pit of her stomach caused, she was certain, by his absence. It seemed ridiculous, given the short time they had known each other, the stuff of teenagers, the melodrama of the TV soaps she loved so much. But this pain that she felt, this discomfort that she carried, wasn't just a figment of her imagination or part of a desperate desire to make her life more interesting than it was. It was real. And awful.

While she managed to sidestep the issue of Hubert's absence by telling them that he wasn't well, explaining away their recent lack of attendance at the O-60 with a vague mention of being away 'seeing family', she ran into trouble when Audrey came across waving a copy of the local free newspaper.

'Where's the man of the hour? I was hoping to get this signed!' she joked as the newspaper was passed around the small group.

'Jan's been telling us he's not well,' said Bob.

'Oh, that's a shame,' replied Audrey, 'he looks a million dollars on here. Look at that cheery grin, it's enough to put a smile on all our faces!'

Jan shifted uncomfortably in her chair and when the paper was finally passed to her, she had no choice but to sit and stare at the photograph of Hubert, even though she was finding remembering this happy version of him hard to bear. When the paper had told Ashleigh they were running a story about the campaign's launch day, she had told them specifically not to use photos of Hubert as he was no longer a member of the committee, but they seemed to have decided that he was too good a character to ignore and used it anyway.

Audrey took the paper back from Jan. 'Not long to go now until this big launch day of yours. Just under three weeks, isn't it? You must be very excited.'

Jan stood up.

'Actually, I'm supposed to be at a committee meeting right now. I don't even know how it slipped my mind. Must be old age, I suppose. So sorry to have to rush off like this.'

'Of course,' said Anita. 'It's important work you're doing. We'll certainly be there to support things, won't we, Bob?'

'Just try and stop us,' said Bob. 'And give Hubert our love. Perhaps we'll see you both at the next O-60 if you've got time.'

'Yes,' said Jan, putting on her coat, 'if we've got time.'

Leaving the community centre, Jan walked briskly across the car park so that anyone watching would think she was a woman with somewhere to be. But the truth was quite the opposite. She didn't want to go home. She couldn't go to Hubert's, and Ashleigh was at work. And much as she liked Maude and the others, she didn't feel like she knew them well enough to just drop round on the spur of the moment. Anyway, chances were they'd ask her about Hubert just like everyone else.

She thought about walking into town but there was nothing she wanted there, then she thought about just hopping on the next bus that passed by and seeing where it took her, but when she reached into her bag, she realised that she'd lost her bus pass somewhere. Ready to give up, to just cry in the street like a mad woman, she spotted a café and decided what she needed right now was a treat and, ducking inside, she joined the short queue at the counter.

'I'll have a slice of that one there,' she said to the young man at the till, pointing to a magnificent Black Forest gateau that seemed to consist almost entirely of fluffy whipped cream, shards of chocolate and oozing dark cherry compote. 'And a hot chocolate, please.'

'Would that be a regular or large hot chocolate?'

Jan briefly considered her Weight Watchers points.

'Large.'

'And would you like whipped cream and marshmallows too?'

She thought again about her Weight Watchers points, but she'd come too far to go back now.

'Yes, please, the works.'

As the young man handed Jan her change, she had a moment of inspiration. 'I don't suppose you've got a pen and piece of paper I can borrow have you, please, love?'

The young man searched around behind the till for a moment and then handed her a pencil and a sheet torn from a notebook. 'Will this do?'

'Perfect,' she said. 'Thank you so much.'

Carefully clutching her tray, Jan picked her way through a forest of chair legs, prams and errant toddlers to an empty table in the corner of the room. Taking a seat, she placed her items on the table and then slipped the tray on to the empty chair opposite. She considered the cake and hot chocolate, both laden with enough cream to block an artery, but tempted as she was, instead she picked up the pencil and began writing.

As she wrote, Jan thought about the first time she had met Hubert that day in the park. It had been such a gloriously sunny day, the kind that pulls you outside in spite of whatever plans you'd made. She had intended to do a little shopping and then perhaps find a café with some tables outside where she could have a cup of tea and do some people watching. The world and his wife must have had the same idea though, because after half an hour of looking, the only café she could find was full, apart from a table for four, which she would have felt selfish taking up on her own.

Instead she'd bought herself an ice cream from a newsagent, made her way to the park and eaten it on a bench overlooking the children's play area, which made her think sadly about her own grandchildren, and how lovely they had been when they were little. Now they were moody teenagers who never thought to give her a call, even though, it seemed, they lived their entire lives through their phones.

In an attempt to shake off the sadness that threatened to spoil such a lovely day, she had started strolling through the park, and it had been then that she'd spotted Hubert pushing Layla in her pram. At this point in her life Jan had found it hard to believe in love at all, let alone that such a thing might happen at first sight, but if she had done, this would've been it. It was such a lovely image, this elderly gentleman in charge of such a sweet child, and it instantly made her forget all the maudlin thoughts that had plagued her moments earlier.

While she had delighted in fussing over Layla, it had been Hubert who had really grabbed her attention. Who was this dapper West Indian gent? Why was he, and not his wife, looking after this lovely little girl? And how were they related? Was it a granddaughter? Or a great-granddaughter? Did he look after her all the time while her mum was at work or was this just a one-off, a proud grandparent showing off the next generation of his family to the world at large?

As she talked to him he had seemed awkward and embarrassed, which of course she now knew was due to the fact that he barely knew Ashleigh or her daughter. Back then she hadn't known what to make of it; all she knew was by the time they parted, she had been charmed.

When she'd seen him at the wedding reception at the social club it had felt like a sign, like fate was saying, 'Sorry for the past forty years of misery, Jan. To make up for it, here's that lovely fella you keep thinking about!' And he had been lovely, more relaxed and at ease than when they'd chatted in the park. And when she had suggested that they go out for the day, even though he made it clear it would only be as friends, Jan had thought to herself, 'Perhaps I am going to be allowed to be happy after all.'

Jan wrote of all this and much more on her piece of paper, trying to explain to Hubert just what meeting him had meant to her and how upset she was to have ruined it all, and how much she hoped that he would forgive her, forget everything that had happened and resume their friendship.

As Jan finished the letter, her phone rang. It was Ron, the manager of the social club, asking if she could cover a shift that afternoon, as Lisa who was supposed to be working had called in sick with a stomach bug. 'We've got the do for a funeral this afternoon, a young bloke it was, got drunk one night, went home on his own and they found him face down in the canal. Apparently they're expecting a good two or three hundred to turn out for it, so we're going to need all the help we can get.'

Jan told Ron she would cover the shift; after all it wasn't as if she had anything better to do. But as she got up from the table, leaving her cake and hot chocolate untouched, and tucked her letter to Hubert into her bag, she couldn't help thinking about the poor young man's funeral. She knew from her years of working at the club that whenever a young person died, the place was packed to the rafters with people come to pay their respects. It was the shock, she supposed. A sense of outrage at a young life ended too soon. It wasn't the same with the elderly. Just last month one of the club's regular members died at the age of ninety-one, and even though Ron had said that the family could have the room for free and the food at cost price, fewer than a dozen people turned up. It was heartbreaking to see a life summed up by an empty room and tables full of untouched finger food, and as Jan walked out of the café and into the warmth of the midday sun, she couldn't help but wonder how many would be at her funeral when the time came.

44

Now

Hubert poured lukewarm water from the kettle into the empty can of cat food, swished it around and then emptied the pitiful contents into Puss's bowl. When he'd taken this last tin of Whiskas from the cupboard, he'd hoped that by some miracle or other it would last perhaps another day or two. Clearly that wasn't the case.

Hubert wasn't at all sure about his ability to cope with an extended excursion from home. How long had it been since he'd last gone out? He struggled to recall. Had it been one week or two? Perhaps he should try to get into the habit of marking off the days on the calendar again. It was easy to lose track when you lived alone and had nowhere to be.

He stared down at Puss's bowl sadly. It had been his hope that the addition of a little water to the scrapings left inside the can might form something akin to a gravy she could enjoy. The grey liquid in which the scraps of food were currently floating, however, did nothing to enhance the meal at all. If anything he'd made it worse.

Shifting his gaze from the bowl to his pet, Hubert had no choice but to acknowledge the look of disgust on her face. It made him feel both guilty and annoyed. Guilty because he knew that meal-times were the highlight of Puss's day and annoyed because, unless she was partial to oxtail soup, which was the only other food left in the house, he was going to have to go outside.

Hubert huffed and slammed the empty tin can down on the cluttered kitchen counter. 'Now me have to drag me weary body to the shops just to get more supplies for you, your majesty! How your lot cope in the wild, me do not know!'

Leaving the kitchen, Hubert shoved his bare feet angrily into the first pair of shoes he came across on the shoe rack, which happened to be the trainers he'd worn when leafleting for the campaign. An image of himself and Jan on Bromley High Street handing out flyers popped into his head, and he immediately pushed it out before it had chance to settle. He didn't do the past, not any more. Hubert Bird lived in the present and right now he was getting ready to go outside.

He rummaged around on the hallway table for his keys but his search was hindered by the amassed contents of everything that had been posted through his letterbox over the past few weeks. There were unopened bills and letters, takeaway menus and leaflets advertising window cleaning all piled up in an untidy heap. Hubert finally found his door keys sandwiched between a free newspaper and a flyer for a carpet-cleaning service.

Slipping on a jacket, Hubert dropped his keys into its pocket and then grabbed the baseball cap he only ever wore for gardening, and as he slipped it on his head, he caught sight of himself in the mirror on the wall and barely recognised the reflection looking back at him. His transformation into an unshaven old man, with tired eyes and loose-fitting clothing, had been a gradual one. He'd stopped shaving because he couldn't see the point, his eyes were tired because he wasn't sleeping properly, and his clothing was loose because some days it felt like it was all he could do to feed Puss, let alone himself. Seeing his reflection, he couldn't help but acknowledge that his old self would never have dreamed of going out looking like this. Or, for that matter, staying in like it either. But these were different times, he concluded, he was living a different life now. A solitary life. One in which he only had himself to please.

Turning away from the mirror, Hubert went into the living room, picked up the remote and switched on the TV. It came on fairly loud, just how Hubert, with his hearing getting worse all the time, liked it, but he made it louder, loud enough so that any passing burglar keen to try their luck would be convinced that someone was in.

From the back room Hubert went to the cupboard under the stairs and took out his new shopping trolley. As practical as they were, he'd always hated the things, finding them cumbersome and overly feminine. But as he'd found out on his last shopping trip, when he'd bulk-bought cat food and other long-life staples for himself, hoping it might mean having to leave the house less often, carrier bags, even the bags for life, weren't designed for heavy loads and even if they were, his arms were no longer up to the job of lugging them home.

At the front door, Hubert confidently drew back the first of the newly installed deadbolts but when it came to the second set, he was more reticent. Did he really want to go outside? There must be something else in the cupboards Puss would eat. Perhaps something in the freezer? He vaguely recalled frying some fish just like his mother used to make, sometime at the beginning of the year, and freezing part of it to have another day. Had he defrosted and eaten it all? Or was there some still left that would mean he could put off this journey for just a little while longer?

Returning to the kitchen, he opened the door to the freezer and went through every drawer. But aside from the half-open bag of frozen peas and a carrier bag of blanched rhubarb, there was nothing Puss might actually consider consuming. So that was that. He had no choice. He would have to go to the supermarket.

Heading back to the front door, Hubert undid the bottom deadlock and then slid back the newly installed chain. Taking a deep breath, he then grabbed hold of the lock and opened the door. He was immediately met by a tsunami of fresh air that flooded into his nose, mouth and lungs, bathing every inch of him that was uncovered. It was in such sharp contrast to the stale musty air he'd grown used to that for a moment he just stood there, gulping down the stuff as though slaking a thirst.

Turning to the wall next to him, Hubert punched the code (the month and year of Joyce's birth) into the control panel of his burglar alarm, just like the installer had shown him three weeks earlier, and, waiting until it began beeping, he carefully pulled the door shut firmly behind him.

It felt odd being outdoors after so long inside; his eyes were so unaccustomed to the brightness of natural daylight that he had to squint, his skin so sensitive to the change in temperature and so unused to the warmth of the early-morning sun that he started to break into a sweat. Most striking of all, however, was the sheer scale and vastness of the outside world in stark contrast to the security and containment of the four walls of his home. Had the world always been this big? Its sky so limitless? And if it had, then how had he forgotten so quickly? Here was a world where anything could happen, he thought as he manoeuvred his shopping trolley outside. Here was a world he could never hope to control. Here was a world he would only venture into if it were absolutely necessary.

After rattling the door handle to make sure it was properly secured, Hubert double-locked the top lock and then turned the key in the deadlock before making his way down the path. The front garden was unkempt: there were flowers that needed dead-heading, the borders required weeding and the small lawn was in desperate need of a cut. It grieved him to see it in this condition, especially after all the years he and Joyce had tended it, but he couldn't risk gardening at the front of the house where someone might see him and want to start up a conversation.

At his front gate Hubert paused, scanning the street carefully in both directions. Primarily he was on the look-out for ruffians, thieves who might be lurking around the corner, watching to see which home might be vacant, but also he was wary of bumping into Ashleigh taking Layla to nursery, Emils passing by in his van or Jan making one of her detours. It was always easier to ignore people from behind his front door than it was face to face, just as it was easier to let the telephone ring unanswered and have letters sit unopened, rather than having to explain himself again and again to people who just wouldn't understand. Anyway, avoiding people was easy once you learned how, and with every day that passed it seemed to be getting easier.

After news got out about the burglary there had been a flurry of well-meaning visits and phone calls from every last member of the committee, even Maude. They'd all wanted to make sure that he was okay, to see if he needed help, to let him know they were thinking of him. And while he'd been grateful for their concern and hadn't wanted to hurt anyone's feelings, Hubert reasoned it would be better for everybody in the long run if he started as he meant to go on. He'd made his position clear to Ashleigh and he hoped his actions would do the same for the rest of the group: he'd got into this trouble by opening his front door and so from now on it made sense to keep it firmly closed.

So he ignored the pleas and cries through the letterbox from Ashleigh. He deleted the long and involved answer-machine messages from Jan without listening to them. The baked goods Emils left on his doorstep ended up untouched and stale on his kitchen counter. The cards from Tony and Fiona went unread into the recycling, along with the 'Beware of the dog' sticker Maude had pushed through his letterbox and her attached note saying, 'This will help keep the burglars away. Maude xxx.' He rejected it all because doing so was the only way he could see made any sense going forwards. He was done with being involved with the world any more than he had to be. From now on, it would just be him and Puss.

Nights were particularly difficult, especially before the insurance workmen came to put in the extra security measures. As each day turned to darkness every creak, every groan, every sigh the old house made caused Hubert to reach for the walking stick he now kept at the side of the bed. In the end, he gave up going upstairs at night and instead chose to sleep in the armchair in the living room, so that he might be ready to tackle any intruders before they knew what had hit them.

It was only after the workmen left, having installed at his request a burglar alarm, along with all the other locks, bolts and lights he'd wanted, that he finally began to relax. His home was finally secure. Nobody would ever again get in without his permission, he'd made sure of that.

At the bus stop an elderly couple dressed in matching shades of beige attempted to engage him in conversation. Apparently, rain was expected by midweek and wasn't it a shame to have to say goodbye to all this fine weather? Though Hubert nodded politely in all the right places, he didn't offer anything by way of return. As soon as the bus arrived he made sure to block access to the seat next to him with his shopping trolley, in case anyone else got it into their heads to try to pass the time of day with him. All he wanted, all he needed, was cat food, long-life milk and a few tins and packets to restock his cupboards. He wasn't interested in people or their stories. He just wanted to be left alone.

Hubert arrived at the supermarket, which was busy with mothers and their young children and pensioners like himself venturing out into the world to pick up supplies. Next time, he would try first thing on a Saturday morning when most people were still in bed, or perhaps early on a Wednesday evening when people would be settled in front of the TV. Being around people made him nervous, as though anything might happen at any minute, and he didn't like it.

Determined not to be distracted or waylaid by special promotions or discounts, Hubert grabbed a trolley, hung his shopper off the end of it and, going up and down the aisles, picked up everything he needed: baked beans, tinned carrots and potatoes, tins of soup, sweetcorn, fruit cocktail, evaporated milk, custard, rice, kidney beans, corned beef, tinned ham, sardines, tins of stewing steak and, of course, plenty of cat food.

As he made his way to the checkout, Hubert surveyed his trolley and couldn't help feeling a sense of satisfaction. This lot would see him and Puss right through the coming week and well into the one after, and if he was careful, perhaps even longer. That would be at least a whole week and a half in which he wouldn't have to leave the house, wouldn't have to see anyone, and instead could just sit safely at home with Puss and watch TV.

Hubert's cashier was called Lewis. He knew this because his

name was emblazoned in large white letters across a green name badge. Lewis had a big hole in his left ear that was the size of a ten-pence piece, a ring through his nose and tattoos that poked out beneath the short sleeves of his work shirt. Why did young people insist on mutilating themselves like this? Was it a fashion? What would they do when the fashion was over? Walk around with big holes in their ears and marks all over their bodies? Idiots, the lot of them, thought Hubert.

'And how's your day going, sir?' asked Lewis as he started scanning Hubert's shopping.

Hubert frowned. Before the burglary he might have indulged this question, even though it was clearly something Lewis had been trained to do by his bosses. Ask the customer how they are, make them feel valued and they'll keep coming back for more. It was nothing but a con trick, a way to win more custom. Lewis didn't care how his day was going and even if he did, Hubert didn't feel inclined to tell him.

Just as Hubert thought, the young man wasn't expecting a reply and didn't blink an eye when he failed to receive one. Instead, with a glazed expression, he began scanning Hubert's shopping and the rest of the transaction was conducted wordlessly, until the young man asked: 'Cash or card?'

'Cash, thank you,' said Hubert. He took out his wallet, counted the exact amount he'd been asked for and handed it over.

'Thank you,' said Lewis. Taking the money, he gave Hubert his receipt in exchange. 'Enjoy the rest of your day.'

Hubert didn't respond and left the shop pulling his trolley behind him, but it was only as he reached the bus stop that it dawned on him that this exchange with Lewis, awkward as it had been, was the longest he'd had with another human being since the workmen from the insurance company left nearly a month ago. Like a man in a boat without any paddles, he was gradually drifting further and further away from the shore and soon there would be no going back.

The relief Hubert felt when he finally reached home was palpable. With his heart racing, he opened up the front door, switched off the burglar alarm and quickly stepped inside, pulling his trolley behind him. Shutting the door, he bolted it behind him and breathed a deep sigh. He was home. He was safe. Nothing bad had happened. He was okay. He regarded his shopping, pleased at the thought of what his haul represented: a week, maybe two, of safety, the security of not having to be out there dealing with people again. But before he could take a step towards the kitchen to start putting it away, the doorbell rang. Ignoring it, he continued to the kitchen, but then he heard his letterbox open and a voice called out that was so familiar, it stopped him in his tracks. But it couldn't be him. It couldn't be real. And his heart filled with dread at the thought that the voices were happening all over again.

45

Now

'Smiler! Smiler, open up the door and let me in!'

He'd known the man for so long that Gus's voice was almost as familiar to him as his own, but Hubert knew it couldn't be him. The last time he'd seen Gus the man hadn't looked capable of crossing his living room, let alone London. No, this couldn't be Gus. But if it wasn't his old friend, what was it? His ghost? Had he died in that wreck of a flat of his and come back to haunt Hubert for being such a terrible friend?

Hubert recalled childhood stories of duppies, restless spirits sent by enemies using obeah, a sort of sorcery, but he didn't believe in ghosts or for that matter magic, black or otherwise. So if the voice didn't belong to a duppy, and it couldn't possibly belong to Gus, then the only explanation left was that Hubert was losing his mind again. Having conjured up Rose's voice on the telephone, now here he was summoning his old friend for company. He couldn't go through this again. Once was enough.

Desperate to do something to keep the madness at bay, Hubert yelled at the door: 'Go away! Me know you're not real! So just go away!'

There was a brief silence filled only with the noise of the blood rushing through Hubert's ears and the sound of his own heart racing. For a moment he believed he had banished the voice for good but then it called back in that same, low, deep baritone: 'Smiler, man, what you talking about? It's me, Gus, open up and let me in!'

It sounded so real, so much like his old friend that Hubert wanted nothing more than to open the door and find Gus standing there. He knew it couldn't be him, though, and what's more he knew he couldn't give in to the urge like he had last time. He had to be strong or they would end up carting him off to a mental institution, just like they had his father all those years ago. On the other hand, if he were to open the door and prove once and for all that there was nobody there, he would at least be able to dismiss it more quickly should it happen again.

Clenching his fists, Hubert inched his way to the front door and then, drawing a deep breath, pressed his eye up to the spyhole he'd instructed the workmen to install after the burglary. There was definitely a figure there, distorted by the fisheye lens, but whether it was really Gus or not, Hubert couldn't tell.

'Smiler, man, come now!' said the voice through the door. 'My bladder's full and I'm busting for the toilet so unless you want a puddle on your doorstep, let me in!'

Scared as he was, Hubert couldn't help but raise a smile. Real or not, this voice sounded so much like his friend that it was impossible not to be comforted. How long had it been since he'd felt like that? He reached a hand up to the latch and, resigned to his fate, opened the door to reveal Gus standing right in front of him. If this was his mind playing tricks, he thought, it would win every time, because this apparition looked and sounded as real as anything else in his life.

Despite the temperate weather, the figure was dressed in a woolly hat and a shabby overcoat, a newspaper sticking out of the pocket.

Hubert reached out and touched its arm. It felt real. It was real. This was Gus, his old friend.

'Gus, is it really you?'

The note of hope in Hubert's voice sounded strange to his ears.

'Yes, man!' said Gus. 'Yes, man, it's me!'

Gus hadn't been joking about needing the toilet and so after pointing him in the direction of the bathroom, Hubert headed to the kitchen and filled the kettle. By the time Gus came downstairs, Hubert had made them both a mug of tea and filled a plate with biscuits.

Sitting down at opposite sides of the kitchen table, the two men sat in silence, sipping tea and crunching biscuits one after the other, until Puss wandered in from the direction of the living room.

Gus raised an eyebrow. 'You have cat now?'

Hubert nodded. 'She called Puss.'

'I always thought you couldn't stand them.'

'Me too,' said Hubert, and he shrugged. 'What can me say? Life is full of surprises. Bit like you showing up here today.'

Gus nodded and finished chewing a mouthful of biscuit.

'Let me tell you,' he said, reaching for another, 'no one is more surprised than me, friend.'

'So, what bring you here?'

Putting down his biscuit, Gus reached into the pocket of his overcoat, pulled out a rolled-up newspaper and laid it on the table between them. It was a copy of the *Bromley Gazette* from two weeks earlier, and there on the front cover was a picture of Hubert and the rest of the committee, hands raised as if in mid battle cry.

Hubert smiled as he recalled the day the photograph was taken. It had been the week before the burglary in the midst of all the press attention the campaign had been getting. The photographer had latched on to the idea of them declaring war on loneliness and had requested that they all adopt battle stances. Hubert stood smiling but with an arm raised like a warrior; Ashleigh posed, mouth wide open, looking like she was in the middle of a war cry; Jan was holding her hands above her head as though she were about to execute a lethal karate chop, and Fiona, Tony, Maude and Emils stood behind them, fists up like boxers. As ridiculous as the photo had turned out it had, Hubert recalled fondly, been a good day with lots of laughter and excited chat. And for a fleeting moment he allowed himself to miss those times and the people he'd spent them with.

Hubert scanned the article's headline: *Big Day Approaches for Local Action Group Declaring War on Loneliness.*

'Where you find this? Brixton?'

Gus pointed to Ashleigh in the photograph.

'No, man. That girl there brought it to me just last week. She wanted me to come and talk to you. Said you were in a bad way.'

'Ashleigh came to you? How did she know where you live?'

'That's not important. What matters is that she was right. I can see just from looking at you that you're not yourself.'

'How much did she tell you?'

'Everything,' said Gus. 'About David, about the burglary, about Rose and the phone calls: everything.'

Hubert was quiet for a moment. He felt ashamed and embarrassed in equal measure.

'And me expect everyone is laughing at me. Stupid old fool, making out like his dead daughter is still alive.'

'Hush up!' exclaimed Gus. 'No one is laughing at you, least of all that young girl. I don't know why she thinks you're so special, but let me tell you, she does. That girl, well, she thinks the world of you, and she was so worried about you that she came to rattle the cage of an old man like me just to help you.'

'Me tired, Gus, man. So tired.' Even saying the words aloud felt like an effort. 'Them damn thieves coming in me house, taking Joyce's rings, rooting through me things . . . well, after everything else . . . it was . . . it was . . . the last straw.' He stared down at his lap, ashamed of what he was about to say next. 'You know, some days me don't even bother getting out of bed. Some days when me wake up me wish me hadn't. It's too much, Gus, this life is too much.'

The two men fell silent again while Puss, back arched, weaved her way around their legs, desperate for attention.

'After Rose died, Smiler, you weren't the same, and who can blame you? It was a terrible thing that happened. Something I wouldn't wish on my worst enemy, let alone my oldest friend. But when you cut yourself off, that left me cut off too. Over the years, every last one of the old Red Lion lot went their own way: moving out of the area, the country even, or getting sick and ending up in some home or other . . . or worse. Without you to see and do things with, I almost stopped going out altogether.

Then three winters ago, when we had that terrible snow and ice, do you remember it?'

Hubert nodded.

'The pavement outside my door was so slippy it was like a skating rink. Me had to put some sharp sand down just to make it to the gate.'

'Well,' said Gus, 'it was then it happened. I was coming back from the shops, lost my footing and mashed myself up so bad they had to take me to hospital in an ambulance. I smashed up my hip, my shoulder and lost a tooth too, and as I lay there day in day out while them fix me up, I got to thinking about how no one knows I'm here, and no one cares.' He stopped for a moment, as if struggling to find the words to carry on. 'Smiler, man, I should have married Lois, all them years ago. I should have married her when I had the chance. I should have been more like you and Joyce. Had a few kids, got myself a nice place, but instead all I did was carry on with woman after woman, never settling down, never taking life seriously, and now there I was, holed up in a hospital bed, watching all the others on the ward with them cards and visitors. All I could think was, that could've been me if I hadn't lived my life so selfish. What if I had been more like Hubert Bird? By the time I was well enough to go home, I'd all but given up on life. I stopped looking after myself, looking after my place, looking after anything at all. Instead I just sat there hour after hour, hoping each day that passed might be my last.'

He stopped again, removed his woolly hat in order to run a hand over his matted white hair.

'I thought I was dreaming that first day you came by. I thought you might be dead. That I'd never hear from you again. And then there you were, just like Lazarus, sitting in my living room as if the last five years hadn't happened.'

Hubert shook his head sadly. In all this time, all his grief, he'd never once spared a thought for how his behaviour after losing Rose had affected his old friend. But it had, in ways that Hubert would never have guessed, and he felt awful about it.

'Gus, man, me didn't know any of this. Me so sorry.'

Gus waved one of his large hands in the air, as if swatting away Hubert's apology like an errant bluebottle.

'Smiler, man, I'm not asking you to be sorry, I'm asking you not to waste your life by locking yourself away again. You have people who care for you, people who need you, people who are counting on you. I'm not sure what this campaign thing of yours is about. But you know what, that isn't the point. The point is you've got people fired up, Hubert Bird, you've got them all really fired up! Councillors and MPs listening to your every word, newspapers and TV people interviewing you left, right and centre and a big carry-on in Bromley Park on Saturday to set it all off. Don't you see, Smiler? You're hiding away from the world again, thinking it's the only way to live. But you and I both know that's not living, that's waiting to die. It's not what Joyce would've wanted for you, and it's not what Rose would've wanted for you either.'

Hubert didn't notice the tears until he accidentally brushed a hand against his cheek. Gus was right, he thought as he dried his face on his sleeve, neither Joyce nor Rose would ever have countenanced such behaviour. They were both fighters, right until the bitter end, unwilling to yield or give in to their circumstances, always striving to hold on to life and the riches it offered. What would they think, what would they say, if they could see him now? They would tell him he had to carry on, if not for himself then at the very least for the memory of them.

'I wasn't going to come, you know,' said Gus. 'When the young girl came, I told her there was nothing I could do, that you were your own person, that you were a grown man.'

Lifting his head, Hubert fixed his gaze on Gus.

'So, what changed your mind?'

Gus gestured towards the table.

'She left behind that newspaper. I didn't even think to touch it until last night. But when I read what you said about me, how you said that you weren't going to give up on me no matter how stubborn I was, no matter how awkward, that was when I knew I had to do the same for you. I had to help you, even if you didn't want to be helped. It's just what friends do.'

46

Now

It was morning and Hubert and Gus were sitting at the kitchen table, two mugs of tea and the remains of breakfast in front of them. Hubert was dressed in a smart pale blue shirt and what he liked to call his summer trousers, a pair of light beige slacks that Joyce had bought him for a holiday to Torquay they'd taken. Gus, meanwhile, who had not long woken up, was still wearing the pyjamas Hubert had loaned him the night before, the legs and arms of which were woefully inadequate cover for his long limbs.

Hubert picked up his mug and plate and took them to the sink.

'So, Gus, man, me going to have to get off now but me should be back sometime late afternoon. Help yourself to anything you want to eat, and there's plenty of hot water if you want another bath. If you want to watch some TV, use the long remote control to turn it on and use the one shaped like a peanut to change the channels.'

'Don't you worry about me, Smiler,' said Gus as Puss wandered in through the cat flap in the back door and made a bee-line for Hubert's guest. In one fluid movement, she leaped from the floor to Gus's lap and settled herself down, purring loudly. 'I've got this little lady to keep me company. You go about your business. I'll be fine right here.'

As Hubert brushed his teeth, he thought how good it felt having someone else in the house. It had taken Hubert a long time to talk Gus into the idea that he'd had: that they should become housemates again like they had been in the old days. 'You can't go back to that mess of a flat,' Hubert had reasoned, 'it's not good for your . . . what them call it now . . . your mental health. No, you need to stay here with me for a while, take David's old room, get yourself well again and then we'll see where we are. Come on, man, what do you say?'

'The two of us sharing a place again after all these years? Could be fun. We had some good times back in the day didn't we, Smiler, man? And at least this time around we don't have to share a bed!'

Rinsing out his mouth, Hubert dried his face with a towel and checked his reflection in the mirror. He looked more like himself, having shaved his beard off that morning following his shower, more like a man with things to do and places to be.

Downstairs, he sat on the bottom step to put on his shoes and then, standing up, he slipped on his jacket, put on his hat and, after calling a final goodbye to Gus over his shoulder, headed outside.

Within a minute or two of ringing Ashleigh's door buzzer, it became apparent to Hubert that she wasn't in. He checked his watch, wondering if she was at work and how she might feel about him dropping by to see her there. What he had to say to her felt urgent, but the last thing he wanted to do was get her into trouble when he'd caused enough as it was. As he weighed up his options, a middle-aged woman wearing a pink and black spotty dress came up the front path, carrying two heavy-looking shopping bags.

'You're Ashleigh's friend from next door, aren't you,' she said, and smiled. 'Are you looking for her?'

'Me was hoping to speak to her, yes. Me guess she must be at work or something.'

'Not today, I walked up the road with her and Layla earlier. They were off to the stay-and-play group at the big church opposite the petrol station.'

'Me know the one. Me go and see if me can catch up with her.'

'I saw you when you were on the TV with Phil and Holly that time,' said the woman. 'You were great. And I absolutely agreed with everything you said.'

Thanking her, Hubert made his way up to the main road and then, turning right, headed to the church. The main doors were closed when he arrived, but a quick glimpse through the windows that ran along the side of the building revealed that the room was full of young mothers with their babies and toddlers, along with the odd grey-haired grandparent with their grandchildren. They were all facing away from him, looking at a young woman dressed in rainbow-pattern dungarees, who appeared to be animatedly telling them a story. Hubert spotted Ashleigh and Layla sitting at the very front. He began waving but try as he might, he couldn't get their attention. But then the young woman in the dungarees pointed in his direction, causing everyone to turn around. Ashleigh's eyes widened when she caught sight of Hubert and, scrabbling to her feet, she ran towards the exit.

Hubert couldn't remember the last time he'd been hugged so tightly and for so long. Perhaps it had been at Rose's funeral, or Joyce's, but if it had he couldn't recall it. The fierceness of Ashleigh's embrace and the relentless nature of her tears reassured Hubert that he was forgiven for letting her down, for turning his back on the campaign. He couldn't help thinking about how easily he'd dismissed Ashleigh's friendship in their early days, how his focus on finding age-appropriate companions had blinded him to what was in front of his very eyes.

'Ashleigh, girl, me sorry, you've been nothing but a friend to me all along. And me sorry for acting the way me did, leaving everything all in your hands, shutting myself off, letting people down. Me been a damn fool these past few weeks, a damn fool and no mistake.'

Ashleigh stood back and wiped her eyes.

'Oh Hubert, don't be silly, of course you haven't let anyone down. You've been going through the mill, that's all. I'm just so glad to see you back out and about.'

'Well, it's all thanks to you. Me had an unexpected visitor yesterday. And don't pretend like you don't know who it was. Me nearly have a heart attack when me saw Gus on me doorstep.'

Ashleigh's hand went up to her mouth.

'So, he actually came? I hoped he might, but the way he was talking I was convinced he wouldn't.'

'Well, he did. So, thank you. Although me been racking my brains trying to work out how you did it.'

'It was all Tony's doing,' said Ashleigh. 'The only information I had was Gus's name and the area he lived in, but then Tony worked his magic with the electoral register and Bob's your uncle, I had an address.'

'And you went all the way to Brixton, and sat in that mess of a flat just for me?'

'It wasn't that terrible. But he's obviously in a bad way, poor thing. I've been trying to think how best to help him, but I reckon the last thing he'd want was social services getting involved.'

'Well, he's with me now and he'll be staying in David's old room for the time being. He needs to get him strength up, time to get back on his feet. And then we'll see what happens next.'

'Well done, Hubert. That sounds like the perfect solution . . . so, where does that leave you? Are you okay?' She took a step back and scrutinised him, shaking her head as she did so. 'You've lost weight. Have you been eating properly? I've been so worried about you these past weeks. Every time I've walked past yours I've wanted to knock on your door, see how you were doing . . . but at the same time I wanted to respect your feelings too.'

'Me know. And me didn't exactly make it easy for you and for that me sorry. You of all people didn't deserve to be shut out like that.'

'Don't you worry about me, Hubert Bird. I'm tougher than I look.' She smiled and hugged him again. 'So does this mean . . . you'll be coming tomorrow? That you'll still be giving your speech? I've got so much to tell you about the campaign and the launch and everything that's been planned. Councillor Pemberton and his team have been absolutely amazing, I can't fault them, they've taken our little idea and turned it into something really—'

Hubert held up his hand.

'Ashleigh, hang on. Me pleased to hear that everything is going well, and that's all credit to you and the rest of the committee, but hand on heart me can't say that me up to doing anything tomorrow. Now me sorry if that's not what you want to hear but it has to be this way. Me just not ready.'

'Of course, I don't like it but I understand. The important thing is that you're on the mend. But I can't lie, it won't be the same without you. Now, how about coming in for a cup of tea and a slice of toast with the toddlers? You might have to sing a few verses of "Wind the bobbin up", mind you, but I think you'll like it.'

'Sounds lovely, but me have one more person to see.'

'You mean Jan?'

'How she been?'

'She's okay, like me she's been worried about you. To be honest, I think she thinks it's all her fault . . . like she's done something wrong. She told me about . . . you know, you and her . . . and I tried to reassure her, but it was tricky because I didn't want to break your confidence by telling her everything you told me. So, I just explained that you were going through a bit of a rough patch and that it had nothing to do with her. Not sure she believed me, though.'

'You did the right thing, darling. And now it's time for me to make things right with her.' They hugged again. 'Me hope everything goes well tomorrow, me sure it will. And maybe when it's all over, if you have the time, you can pop by for a cuppa with Layla and tell me all about it.'

'It's a date,' said Ashleigh.

After telling Hubert that there would be a good chance of finding Jan in the community room at the library with the rest of the committee, putting together the last of the information packs for distribution tomorrow, Ashleigh kissed Hubert's cheek and went back inside the church.

He felt bad for not agreeing to attend the launch day, but right now it was more than he could face. He wasn't even sure he could cope with seeing the committee together in one room, with all the questions they'd have. He thought briefly about putting off seeing Jan until later when she was back at home. But Jan deserved an explanation for everything that had happened; he'd never wanted her to feel that any of this was her fault. And so, taking a deep breath, Hubert turned on his heel and headed in the direction of the library.

47

Now

The door to the community room was closed and Hubert reached out and grasped the handle. He could just about make out voices on the other side but had no idea who they belonged to. Steeling himself, he pushed the door open and just as he'd feared, everyone stopped what they were doing, turned and stared at him.

Jan, Tony, Maude, Fiona and Randip were all wearing bright yellow T-shirts emblazoned with the slogan **#knowyourneighbour** and sitting around a collection of tables strewn with leaflets, tote bags and pens.

'Hubert,' said Tony, unable to hide his surprise. 'What are you doing here?'

There was an awkward silence and then Fiona said, 'What Tony means to say, Hubert, is how glad we are to see you.'

'Yeah,' said Tony. 'What she said.'

'I told them you weren't dead,' said Maude. 'But they've all been going around with faces like you were.'

'No, we haven't,' said Randip. 'We were just missing him, that's all.'

Hubert shifted his gaze from Randip to Jan, who he hadn't even dared look directly at until now. She was covering her mouth with her hands, eyes wet with tears.

'Me sorry about . . . well, about everything,' said Hubert, quietly addressing the room. 'Me know that you all must feel like me let you down and me sure you have a lot of questions. But for now, would you mind if me just had a quiet word with Jan?'

'Of course,' said Fiona, standing up and taking her jacket from the back of a chair. 'We were all just going for a break anyway, weren't we?'

'Yes, we were,' said Randip, following Fiona's lead.

Maude, her face screwed up in confusion, opened her mouth to protest but was prevented by Tony, who put his arm out for her and said, 'How do you fancy a nice hot chocolate, Maude, on me?'

She eyed him suspiciously.

'With the cream and the little marshmallows?'

'With whatever you like.'

She gave him a wink so theatrical that it looked like she was having some sort of seizure.

'In that case, I am going for a break after all.'

One by one, they all left the room until finally Hubert and Jan were alone.

'So, you're better now?' asked Jan as Hubert sat down on one of the plastic chairs next to her. Now that she had recovered herself, there was an unmistakable frostiness in her tone.

'Jan,' began Hubert, 'you have every right to be upset. You've been nothing but a friend to me and me have behave . . . well, it can't have been nice for you.'

'You mean worrying about you day and night?' said Jan. 'You mean going over and over everything I'd said and done? You mean knocking on your door, calling you, even writing letters only to be completely ignored? No, it wasn't nice. It wasn't nice at all.'

'There is a reason, Jan, but that's no good excuse for the way me treated you.'

'Go on, then,' said Jan. 'Let's hear it.'

'My daughter Rose died,' said Hubert quietly. 'She died five years ago and me was such an old fool that me pretended to myself and the whole world that she hadn't.'

There was a moment of silence as Jan struggled to comprehend what she had just heard, and then without speaking, she reached across and took his hand in hers. As they sat together, her anger having melted away, Hubert told her everything about losing Rose, how he withdrew from life, about the phone calls.

'The funny thing was,' said Hubert, 'even though the calls weren't real, she would say exactly the sort of things my Rose would say. Bothering me about what me was eating, asking me whether me was getting enough exercise and even trying to sort out my social life. That's how Dotty, Dennis and Harvey came about.'

Jan raised an eyebrow, and Hubert sighed.

'Sometimes me forget who me tell what to,' he said, and then, taking a deep breath, he told her all about his fictional friends and the lengths he had gone to in order to be able to produce friends that he could present to Rose.

'So, you were trying to find a real-life Dotty, Dennis and Harvey?'

Hubert shrugged. 'It sounds ridiculous, now me said it out loud. But yes, that was the plan. Make friends with three pensioners, in the hope that she wouldn't be too angry with me when she found out that I'd been lying to her. But until you came along, the only friends I made were Ashleigh, Layla and Emils!'

'Only? What do you mean only? Have you any idea how much you mean to that girl? She thinks the absolute world of you, she does, and I'm not exaggerating. She's been so worried about you, I've lost count of the times I've had to comfort her.'

'Me sorry to hear that,' said Hubert, 'and yes me do know how much she cares for me. She's the reason me here right now. She dug up my old friend Gus, talked him out of his hovel of a flat to come and see me. He gave me a good talking to and now he's living in my spare room while he sorts himself out. Me went to see Ashleigh before me came here to thank her and apologise, and we're all good now. And me hope . . . well, it's my wish . . . that it might be the same with you too. Do you think that's possible?'

Jan sighed. 'Oh, Hubert. Of course it's possible. I don't think I could ever be angry with you for any length of time. But I can't just pretend that things are all right when they're not. I can't help thinking that part of you leaving like that was because of . . . well, you know . . . that day at the bus stop . . . what happened between you and me. It wasn't, was it?'

'No, of course it wasn't. But it is complicated. You see, Jan, Joyce and me were together for over fifty years, fifty years with a whole heap of ups and downs. Me wasn't always the perfect husband, but with my hand on my heart me can say that my Joyce was the love of my life, and for me there will never be anyone like her.'

Jan nodded sadly.

'Oh, I see.'

'No, you don't,' said Hubert. 'Until me met you, me hadn't even given romance a second thought. Why would me do that, when lightning never strikes in the same place twice? But then me got to know you, and me spend time in your company and well . . . all me can say is that you, Jan, you is a mighty fine woman, and me wish with me whole heart that me could be saying that me want us to be together. But right now, me not in the right frame of mind to think about such things. Me would ask you to give me time to sort myself out, but me would completely understand if you say no, if you say that's not for you.'

'Oh Hubert, the important thing is that you don't have to go through anything alone any more. You've got Ashleigh and Layla, you've got your friend Gus back on the scene, you've got all the committee, and last but not least, you've got a friend in me for life, if nothing else.'

They talked for a while longer, mostly about the campaign and how plans had changed. The venue for the launch day was no longer going to be Bromley Park but rather, due to a number of practical issues, the more expansive Queensmead Recreation Ground. 'It's going to be a lot bigger than we thought,' explained Jan, 'the local radio is going be there, there's going to be tables and tents for community groups and stalls too. Me and Fiona are going to help Emils with a cake stall and all the proceeds are going to be donated to the refugee centre.'

Hubert was taken aback by the scale of operations Jan was describing. 'That all sounds wonderful. Certainly a step up from a simple coffee morning!'

'It's going to be amazing,' said Jan. She paused. 'Are we going to see you there?'

Hubert shook his head. 'No, but me will be with you in spirit.'

He could see that Jan wanted to talk him around, but then thankfully Maude barged into the room holding her hot chocolate gleefully aloft, followed by Tony and Fiona, whose clutches she had clearly escaped.

Tony shot an apologetic look in Hubert's direction. 'Come on, Maude. I told you they weren't finished yet.'

'You're fine, Maude,' said Hubert. He patted her gently on the arm. 'Me got to push off now anyway.'

After kissing Jan goodbye, Hubert offered a wave to the rest of the committee and then headed home.

That evening, Hubert and Gus ate a meal on their laps in front of the television, commenting on the action unfolding on the screen between mouthfuls of food. Hubert couldn't help but note how good it was to have company at mealtimes again, someone to chat to apart from the cat.

That night, lying in bed, Hubert replayed the day's events in his mind, paying particular attention to his encounters with Ashleigh and Jan. He felt bad that he wasn't going to the launch, but it was all probably for the best. It certainly appeared as though the committee, with Councillor Pemberton's help, had everything in hand, and the last thing they needed was a doddery old man getting in their way.

When he finally drifted off, his sleep was restless and filled with strange and vivid dreams. Cora and David paddling in the stream at the edge of his mother's farm. Joyce picking flowers in a garden with Ashleigh and Layla. None of it seemed to make any sense, but all of it left him feeling unsettled long after he woke the next morning. That sense of disquiet followed him as he ate breakfast with Gus, dressed for the day ahead and even as he mowed the lawn. Finally, unable to stand it any longer, Hubert unplugged the mower with half the lawn still uncut and sat down next to Gus at the garden table.

'What's the matter, Smiler? You been up and down like that cat of yours all morning.'

'Me don't know. Me just can't seem to settle.'

'Maybe you sick. You have fever?'

'It's not that kind of feeling. It's . . . it's . . .me can't think what the word is.'

'You think it might be something to do with that thing happening in the park today?'

Hubert shook his head, perhaps a little too vehemently.

'It's not that.'

'Well, in that case, I'm all out of ideas.'

Kissing his teeth in frustration, Hubert got up from the chair, plugged the mower back in, and was about to start it up when he stopped and reconsidered Gus's comment. Could it be that his friend was right? Could his strange mood be connected to the launch party going on without him? He checked his watch. It was half past twelve and the day's events were supposed to start at one o'clock. It wouldn't do any harm if he took a little look, would it? He could just slip in unnoticed, see what was going on and leave before anyone spotted him. That way he could feel like he was supporting them somehow, rather than using up a whole lot of energy he didn't have, pretending that this was a day like any other.

He made up his mind. He would go. And abandoning the lawnmower, he rushed past Gus into the house, muttering something about needing to pop out, and still in his gardening clothes and without a single glance in the mirror, he headed straight out of the front door.

48

Now

Hubert couldn't quite believe how many people there were at the recreation ground. He'd never seen it so full. The place had been transformed into a temporary festival site, with a huge stage with a mammoth screen above it at one end, pop music blaring out from speakers either side. Around the edges, various charity and community groups had set up their stalls under gaily decorated gazebos, men and women in hi-viz tabards were strolling around, handing out the bright yellow tote bags Hubert had seen the committee filling at the library the day before, and right in the middle of it all was, it seemed to Hubert, something like the entire population of Bromley.

Positioning himself towards the back of the crowd, Hubert regarded the stage and saw on the screen the camera pan towards a gaggle of people in matching bright yellow T-shirts, who he recognised as the committee. Resisting the urge to wave at them, he watched as a young man, also wearing one of the yellow T-shirts, came on stage to enthusiastic applause. Hubert didn't recognise him, but then he overheard the family next to him remark that he was a local comedian who was acting as compère. The young man told a few jokes that Hubert didn't think were funny but the crowd seemed to find hilarious.

'And now,' boomed the comedian over the sound system, 'please put your hands together and give a great big Bromley welcome to Councillor Martin Pemberton!'

Councillor Pemberton's arrival on stage was met with mild applause, some booing and a solitary cry of, 'Bring back the weekly bin collection!' Ever the professional, Councillor Pemberton remained unfazed and began talking about the first time he heard about the campaign while speed-eating a microwave meal for one in front of the TV before heading out to a fundraising event for a local hospice. He described how the news item about the campaign had stopped him in his tracks.

'I felt these two people had really captured the spirit of Bromley, what this borough is about, what we locals are made of, and I knew there and then that I wanted to be part of it, and the rest of the council were in total agreement. What this group have achieved in such a short space of time is truly remarkable and it should inspire us all to become more involved in this wonderful community of ours. So, without more ado, please let me introduce you to local resident and vice president of the Campaign to End Loneliness in Bromley, Ashleigh Jones!'

This time around, the welcome from the crowd was noticeably warmer, and amongst the clapping and cheers there were even one or two good-natured whoops of support as a clearly nervous Ashleigh walked to the microphone in the centre of the stage. A hush descended over the audience.

'As you can probably tell,' she began, glancing at a piece of paper in her hand, 'I'm not from round here . . . I'm actually from north London . . .' A ripple of laughter ran through the crowd. 'But seriously, I'm from a tiny village in south Wales, and when I moved down here three years ago I didn't know anyone apart from my boyfriend at the time. It was really difficult at first, and I missed home loads, but then the relationship broke down and I can honestly say I've never felt more alone in my life.'

At this there was a small chorus of sympathetic noises from the audience and Ashleigh took a moment to compose herself before continuing.

'I moved to Bromley only five months ago, looking for a fresh start for me and my little girl, Layla. I wanted us to have friends and be part of a community, and so the day I moved in I made up my mind that I was going to get to know my neighbours. You'd think it would be straightforward, but in this day and age people don't really talk, even when they live next door to each other. So, when I knocked on my neighbour's door to introduce myself, I don't mind telling you my knees were knocking too. I won't lie, it wasn't brilliant at first, and it didn't help matters that after the third time I said hello to Hubert, I needed a favour. He could have said no, he could've said he was busy but do you know what? He didn't. He said yes. And that one act of kindness, that willingness to help, well, it meant the world to me. It was the beginning of a friendship I wasn't expecting and I know he wasn't either, but it's a friendship I needed and one I wouldn't be without.' She paused, glanced at her paper and then with a shrug shoved it into the pocket of her denim jacket.

'I had a whole bunch of other stuff I wanted to say to you all,' she continued, 'stuff about how the campaign came about and what it all means to those of us on the committee, but there's someone really special missing today and I'd like to talk more about him instead.' A picture of a grinning Hubert taken from the local newspaper flashed up on the huge screen above Ashleigh's head. 'This is the neighbour I was telling you about, his name's Hubert Bird and without him, none of this would've been possible. I'm so sad that he's not here today and I know he'd be here if he could, but he's been going through a bit of a rough time lately and—'

As Ashleigh stopped to dry her eyes and apologise for getting upset, Hubert began to notice people turning to look at him and back at the screen, as if confirming his identity, and in no time at all a wave of recognition had travelled through the crowd. Making the most of the silence from the stage as Ashleigh gathered her thoughts, a young man shouted at the top of his voice, 'He's here, Hubert Bird is here!' and before he could make an escape, Hubert saw a cameraman coming towards him and the footage he was filming appeared on the big screen.

'Bloody hell!' yelled Ashleigh, pointing up at Hubert's face on the screen as the cameraman descended on him. 'Hubert, it's you! I knew you'd come.'

Hubert wanted to disappear. If it wasn't enough that his panic-stricken face had been blown up on the screen for all to see, the crowd were also now chanting his name in a bid to get him to join Ashleigh on the stage. He was suddenly conscious of his shabby gardening clothes and was overcome with an urge to disappear, but before he could make his move, one of the stewards stepped forwards and began escorting him through the crowds. With every step he took, the chants seemed to get louder, and now strangers were patting him on the back like they knew him and shouting words of encouragement. Nearing the stage, Hubert was led past the security guards at the barriers to stairs at the side of the stage, where Councillor Pemberton was waiting.

'Mr Bird, I'm so pleased you could make it after all,' he said. 'It would be my honour to help you on stage.'

The crowd was still chanting his name as Hubert followed Councillor Pemberton up the stairs, and they exploded into a cacophony of cheers and applause as he walked over to join Ashleigh, who flung her arms around him and stepped back to look at his face anxiously.

'Are you okay? I know that this must be a bit much. It's just that I was so glad to see you. I didn't have time to think it through.'

'Me all right,' said Hubert. 'A bit taken aback but with you here, me will be okay.' And holding hands the two walked up to the microphone together and eventually the noise of the crowd died down.

Looking out across the crowd, which seemed even bigger from this elevated vantage point, Hubert took a deep breath. Until this moment, the largest number of people he'd addressed in his life were the forty or so members of his class when he was a schoolboy back in Jamaica. He had no idea what he was going to say or how he was going to express all of the feelings he was wrestling with. He didn't know where to start, or where he'd end up, and then he remembered something Joyce would say to the children when they were small and so desperate to tell her a story about their day that they would stumble over the words.

'Just take your time and start at the beginning.'

And so that's what he did. He told the story of a young man

who travelled halfway around the world, leaving friends and family behind in search of work and a better life. He spoke about the desperate loneliness he felt living in a country that at times made it plain that it didn't want him or his kind here.

He talked of finding love in the most unexpected of places, of a marriage that made him a better man and of a family that gave him a purpose. He described the devastation of losing a son to drugs and his beloved wife, first to dementia, and then to pneumonia. And he talked about how his world fell apart following the tragic loss of his only daughter just five years ago.

'Me thought me was beat,' he said, 'that me had enough of life, that nobody needed me. And me let that bitterness and that sorrow eat me right up inside.'

He paused and considered the crowd properly for the first time since he'd begun speaking, and was surprised to see that they were hanging on his every word.

'And me probably would've stayed like that until my dying day,' continued Hubert, 'but then out of the blue there was a knock at my door and that's when me met someone who changed my life.' Ashleigh squeezed his hand. 'You see, the key to helping other people out of them loneliness is nothing more difficult than good old-fashioned perseverance. It's not always easy, me know that, but you've got to be willing to keep doors open, to carry on trying even if it doesn't look like it's working. You've got to refuse to give up on people, even if them given up on themselves.' He paused again, reflecting on just how lonely he'd been all those years, how cut off from the rest of the world.

'When Ashleigh came up with the idea to end loneliness in Bromley, one of the committee members remarked that perhaps we should set our sights a little bit lower. "After all," this fella said, "it's not as if we really can end loneliness in Bromley for good. That's just pie in the sky!"'

A peal of good-natured laughter rang out from the crowd.

'But the thing is,' continued Hubert, 'if you had told me a year ago that me, Hubert Hezekiah Bird, an old man from a small town in Jamaica, would be standing on a stage in a park in

Bromley talking to a whole heap of strangers, me would have said that was pie in the sky too!' Another ripple of laughter ran through the crowd, peppered with some cheers. 'And that's the funny thing about life. Extraordinary things can happen to ordinary people like you and me, but only if we open ourselves up enough to let them.'

49

Now

The assembled crowd let out a deafening cheer and Hubert stood, hands shaking, heart racing, eyes brimming with tears, and gave everyone looking on a wave. It had been an amazing experience. Something he would never have imagined he could do, but something he would never forget as long as he lived. How he wished Joyce and Rose could see him now. How he wished they could be with him to share this moment.

On behalf of the Borough of Bromley the compère thanked Hubert, and Ashleigh then announced the next act, a local dance troupe made up of tiny girls dressed in matching sparkly outfits who were already waiting in the wings. As he followed Ashleigh off the stage, Hubert turned and gave the crowd a final wave and, for a fleeting moment, thought he saw David. But before he could be certain, the flock of girls rushed past him to take up their positions and by the time Hubert looked back, David, if indeed it had been him, had gone, swallowed up by the sea of people. For a moment Hubert remained frozen to the spot, desperately scanning the crowd, hoping for another glimpse, but then Ashleigh appeared by his side, hugging him and guiding him down the steps towards the backstage area.

'Are you okay? For a minute there you seemed a bit lost.'

It had most likely been wishful thinking on his part, reasoned Hubert, so there was no point telling Ashleigh about seeing David. And if it wasn't, if that had been his son, then at the very least he hoped he knew just how much he loved him and how desperately he wanted him to be well.

'Me fine,' said Hubert after a moment. 'Me was just a little distracted, that's all.'

The next hour was a flurry of interviews for local and national newspapers, TV and radio. Each organisation wanted to hear Hubert and Ashleigh's story and for them to distil their solution to the problem of loneliness into a snappy sound-bite. They were photographed shaking hands with members of the public and posing next to local dignitaries. In one shot, Hubert and Ashleigh were even hoisted into the air by a Bromley-based rugby team who had pledged one hundred free tickets to their next match for anyone who was lonely.

Eventually, however, the journalists and their camera crews, photographers and sound technicians drifted away, leaving an exhausted Hubert and Ashleigh free to go and get themselves a cup of tea. Heading to a tent that Ashleigh referred to as 'the green room', the pair were met by raucous applause the moment they walked in.

'That was outstanding, guys,' said Tony. 'Absolutely outstanding.' He shook their hands and slapped Hubert on the back, grinning from ear to ear.

'You were wonderful,' added Fiona. She kissed Ashleigh and Hubert on the cheek as everyone gathered around. 'You both came across brilliantly.'

'You were amazing,' said Emils. 'I was standing next to a group of young school kids and they were all shouting your name, Mr Hubert, like you were a movie star!'

'And that moment when you came on stage, Hubert,' said Randip. 'It was just so unexpected. I was in floods of tears.'

'You did very well,' said Maude. 'And I particularly like your new look, Hubert. Normally you're a bit too trussed up for my liking.'

'Thanks,' said Hubert as his eyes searched the tent.

'You looking for Jan?' asked Emils. 'Layla was desperate for wee so Jan took her. They should be back soon.'

Hubert breathed a sigh of relief. For a moment, he had worried that Jan had deliberately absented herself as he had arrived. As someone put a cup of tea in Hubert's hand, he searched around for somewhere to sit down. Spotting an empty chair, he went to take a seat but before he could do so, he felt a tap on his shoulder.

'Sorry to bother you,' said a steward, 'but there's someone at the security barriers claiming they're a relative of yours and they're desperate to talk to you.'

Hubert's heart raced. It had to be David. It had been his son that he'd spotted in the crowd, after all.

'Let him through,' said Hubert. 'He's my son.'

The young man looked at Hubert, confused.

'Er . . . actually it's a girl, a young girl, mid to late teens.'

'Oh,' said Hubert. 'Let me come and find out who she is.'

Hubert followed the steward to the security barrier where there was indeed a young woman waiting for him. She had dark brown hair tied back in a ponytail, clear skin, a pleasant smile, and looked like one or other of her parents might be Chinese. She was wearing a light grey hooded top, ripped black jeans, black suede trainers with a logo on them and was carrying a bright yellow rucksack. Hubert didn't know this young lady from Adam, and he couldn't imagine for a second why she might think they were related.

The steward beckoned to his colleague to let her through the barrier.

'You okay, dear?' asked Hubert. 'This young man says that you want to speak to me.'

The young girl beamed at him. 'You're Hubert Bird, yeah?'

Hubert nodded.

'And you were married to Joyce Anne Pierce, yeah?'

'Yes.'

'Well, the thing is I recently found out that my great-grandma Peggy was your wife's sister. Which, I think, makes me your sort of great-grandniece or something.'

Hubert blinked hard as he recalled the one and only time he'd spoken to Joyce's sister, on his wedding day when he'd begged her to come and celebrate with them. And now here, all these years later, was one of her descendants standing right in front of him.

'You're Peggy's great-granddaughter?'

The girl nodded. 'My name's Melody, Melody Chen, and I

just really wanted to say sorry to you, on behalf of all my stupid family. We saw you in the paper, that's what made Mum tell me everything about what happened back then, you know, how they all treated you and Joyce. It makes me sick even thinking about it. Anyway, I know I'm too late to say all this to Great Auntie Joyce, and that's really sad, but I just wanted to say that I'm sorry my mum's side of the family were such idiots. Would you like to like to come round to ours for tea one day or something? Have you got a mobile?'

Speechless, Hubert shook his head and so she slipped the rucksack off her back, reached her hand inside and pulled out a pen and some paper on which she scribbled something down. She handed the paper to Hubert.

'That's my number at the top, our landline in the middle and Mum's number at the bottom.'

Hubert stared down at the piece of paper in his hand, still quite unable to believe that he was talking to a relative of Joyce's.

'Right, then,' she continued. 'I can see you're busy so I'll get off. But definitely give us a ring, yeah? It'll proper blow Mum's mind when I tell her that I've met you. She'd been on about trying to contact you, but I think she was just a bit too shy to do anything about it.' She slipped her rucksack back on and prepared to leave. 'I just want to say that today has been sick, yeah? Your speech and what that girl said, it proper got me and my friends right in the feels, and we've all been talking about what we can do to help lonely people. Maybe when you come round, I can go through some of the ideas with you?'

'Me would like that,' said Hubert quietly. 'Me would like that very much.'

Taking out her phone, Melody asked Hubert if she could take a selfie with him, and before he could object, she'd positioned herself next to him and, resting her head on his shoulder, she lifted her free hand in a peace sign and took several snaps, changing pose with each one.

She quickly scrolled through the photos with her thumb.

'My mates are going to be proper impressed when I post these.'

Hubert carefully scanned the young girl's face for any resemblance to Joyce and noted that perhaps there were hints in the shape of her face and the slope of her nose.

'Well, it was lovely to meet you, Miss Melody, and me look forward to seeing you again soon.'

Melody ignored Hubert's outstretched hand.

'I'm more of a hugger, yeah?'

She put her arms around him, embraced him tightly, then, giving him a huge grin, turned and walked away.

Ashleigh came over to join him.

'Who was that? Another fan?'

'It's a long story. But a wonderful one, which me have to tell you all about once me speak to Jan. Are she and Layla back yet?'

'I haven't seen them yet . . . actually . . .' She pointed over Hubert's shoulder. 'Here they are now.'

Hubert turned around to see Jan and Layla walking hand in hand across the backstage area towards them. Catching sight of her mother, Layla let go of Jan's hand and rushed screaming excitedly into Ashleigh's open arms. Hubert smiled as Ashleigh showered Layla with kisses, and then, turning his attention to Jan, began walking towards her.

'You were amazing,' said Jan. 'I had a right old sob listening to you. You had the whole crowd in the palm of your hand.'

'Me don't know about that,' said Hubert. 'In fact, me don't know about many things, if the truth be told. But if there's one thing me certain of Jan, it's that me really like you . . . me like you a lot . . . and me know everything me said yesterday about waiting, but the truth is . . . as me stood up there in front of all them people, me kept thinking about how short life is and how precious . . . none of us know how long we've got, none of us know what lies ahead, the only thing any of us truly have is right now. And right now, Dorothy Janet Walsh, what me want is you.'

'But are you sure?' asked Jan. 'I'd hate to think that this was just you feeling guilty.'

In response, and without regard for where they were or who

might be watching, Hubert took Jan in his arms and planted a long and lingering kiss on her lips.

'Well,' said Jan, blushing, 'I suppose that answers that question.'

At Jan's suggestion, they took a walk around the park. The place was still full of people, some chatting around the various stalls representing community groups, some watching the local folk band playing on stage, while others lounged on picnic blankets, making the most of the pleasant weather.

As they picked their way through the crowd, they were stopped every few steps by people who recognised Hubert. Some just wanted to say hello, others to have their photo taken with him, but most heartening of all were those who were simply excited to share what this day had meant to them.

Two elderly ladies told him how they had lived in the same street for thirty years without ever having said hello until today. A group of parents with young children outlined their plan to set up a weekly visit to the local old people's home, and a young man revealed his intention to open up his flat once a week to anybody who wanted to drop by for a cup of tea.

This, thought Hubert, was what the campaign had always been about: getting people to be more outward-looking, to share their stories, to form bonds, and it was happening all around him, it was happening to him. If it hadn't been for the campaign, that young girl Melody would never have found him. He would never have known how much things had changed in Joyce's family. He would never have been able to have enjoyed the peace that he currently felt, knowing that in some small way Joyce had been justified, the sacrifices she'd made for their love had been the right ones, and ultimately the family she'd left behind had become broader, richer and more accepting. A family she would've been proud to be part of, instead of ashamed.

Hubert couldn't wait to meet Melody's parents, to chat to her mother, to try to repair the bonds that had been broken so long ago. It felt like something he could finally do for Joyce even though she wasn't here to see it happen. He could right this wrong, he could bring the family back together, he could honour his wonderful wife's memory in the most fitting way he could imagine.

As he and Jan continued to wend their way through the crowds he felt, for the first time in a very long while, like there might just be some light at the end of the tunnel. He'd been living in the shadows for so long, and holding on so tightly to the past, that he'd let the present pass him by. But that was then, and this was now, and he was finally ready to embrace the future and make the most of every minute he had left. To continue living wasn't a betrayal of Joyce, of Rose, of David, of any of the life that had led him to this moment. In fact, to choose to continue living was to honour the memory of those he had loved and lost, a celebration of the life they had once shared.

Eighteen months later

'Right,' said Ashleigh, retying the bow on Layla's dress as the little girl stamped her feet excitedly, 'has everyone checked in their coat now?'

'Yes,' said Jan, coming to stand next to Ashleigh, 'and I've just had a lovely chat with the girl who took mine. Russian she was, or something like that. Beautiful skin.'

'I'm not leaving my coat with anyone,' said Maude. 'I've got things in here I need.' She pulled up the collar of her dark brown boiled-wool coat and then shoved her hands deep into its pockets. 'Haven't checked my coat in anywhere since 1993 when someone stole my bus pass from the cloakroom at the bingo. Never again.'

'This is hardly the bingo hall, Maude,' said Fiona, gesturing to the ornate chandelier above them. 'No one's going to be stealing your bus pass at the Ritz.'

Emils came and stood next to Ashleigh, and Layla stretched out her hands to him. 'I can't wait to show my mum the photographs we took outside,' he said, sweeping Layla up into his arms. 'She will be very proud.'

'I don't think I've ever been anywhere this posh,' said Randip shyly.

'It's certainly fancy,' said Gus, 'I've just been to the toilet and man, they're out of this world. None of your paper towels and noisy hand-driers here, it's all linen napkins and expensive-looking hand lotion.'

'No doubt all built on the backs of slaves and the working classes,' said Tony bitterly. He pulled uncomfortably at the tie he was wearing under protest. 'I feel all itchy just being here.'

'Thanks for that, Tony,' said Ashleigh. 'But let's just remember why we are here, eh?'.

A waiter appeared and informed them that their table was ready. Gathering themselves together, they followed him up a short flight of marble steps. The table was draped in spotless white linen and set with bone-china tea cups and plates, starched white napkins and silver cutlery so polished that Gus even pretended to check his reflection in a butter knife.

As they sat down, their waiter, a young man smartly dressed in a bow tie, waistcoat and tails, brought over menus, while another filled their glasses with champagne before departing.

Standing up, Ashleigh addressed the table. 'Even after all the practice I've had over the past year and a half, I'm still not great at making speeches, and certainly not the kind of speech I need to make right now.' She paused and Emils, who was sitting next to her, put a reassuring hand on her arm. 'On behalf of Jan and myself, I just want to thank you all for coming today to remember our dear, dear friend, Hubert. It's been just over two months since we lost him, and even now, not a day goes by when I don't walk past his house and look over at it, hoping to see him clipping his front hedge, washing his windows or watering his hanging baskets.' She paused again and glanced over at Jan, who was dabbing at her eyes with a tissue.

'No one's ever ready to let those they love go, but we can take some comfort from the fact that, as Hubert told me himself when he was in hospital, this past year of his life had been one in which he'd found not just happiness and peace but real purpose too. When I think back to his funeral, seeing the church as full as it was, it really gladdens my heart. I lost count of the number of times someone stopped me to say what a difference the campaign had made to them. I remember an old lady telling me how, after years alone, she'd finally had the courage to join one of the social groups that are still going on all these months after the launch week. A single mum who, thanks to the campaign, was able to connect with other mums in the area. A Syrian refugee who joined the Bromley Buddy scheme we set up and told me that because of it, he finally felt like he had somewhere to call home. And I know that every single one of us sitting around this table today has a story to tell about someone they know whose life has been changed for the better by the campaign.'

She looked around the table again and picked up her glass.

'More than that, we've all ourselves been changed for the better by working together and knowing Hubert. And by arranging this lovely treat for us, I know that he wanted to say thank you to all of us for the difference we made to him too. And even though he's not with us, his legacy lives on in the committee and the people we've become as a result of knowing such a kind and wonderful man. So, let's raise our glasses and make a toast to Hubert Bird, our president, our neighbour and our friend!'

Acknowledgements

Huge thanks as always for their time, advice and friendship are due to: everyone at Hodder, everyone at UA, Nick Sayers, Amy Batley, Alice Morley, Jenny Platt, Ariella Feiner, Molly Jamieson, Richard and Judy, The Sunday Night Pub Club, The Board (in all its guises), Neil Price, Jenny Colgan, Jill Mansell, Beth O'Leary, Rosie Walsh, Libby Page, Sophie Kinsella, Lisa Jewell, Julie Cohen, Michelle Collins, Lenny Henry, Clare Mackintosh, Amanda Ross (and all at Cactus), Tracey Rees, Miranda Dickinson, Freya North, Ruth Hogan, all the "Lockdown Reading" regulars (you've made a weird time in history infinitely more bearable) and last but by no means least, my amazing readers for their support, enthusiasm and general loveliness.